O9-ABF-794

By Wendy Corsi Staub

WENDY CORSI STAUB

THE BLACK WIDOW

HARPER

An Imprint of HarperCollinsPublishers

This is a work of fiction. Names, characters, places, and incidents are products of the author's imagination or are used fictitiously and are not to be construed as real. Any resemblance to actual events, locales, organizations, or persons, living or dead, is entirely coincidental.

HARPER

An Imprint of HarperCollins*Publishers*
195 Broadway
New York, New York 10007

Copyright © 2015 by Wendy Corsi Staub
Excerpt from *Mundy's Landing* copyright © 2015
by Wendy Corsi Staub
ISBN 978-0-06-222243-5

First Harper mass market printing: March 2015

HarperCollins® and Harper® are registered trademarks of Harper-Collins Publishers.

Printed in the United States of America

Visit Harper paperbacks on the World Wide Web at
www.harpercollins.com

10 9 8 7 6 5 4 3 2 1

For the girl next door, Shari Lou, with lots of love on her milestone birthday!

And for the big strong guys who always have my back: my father, Reg; my brother, Rick; my husband, Mark; my sons, Morgan and Brody.

Acknowledgments

With gratitude to Mari Corsi, George Catalano, Clay Smith, Mike Shapiro, Dave McEntarfer, Deborah Salanitro, Adriane Avila Vieira, Julianne Goulding Macie, and Tammy Bankoski for their contributions; to my editor, Lucia Macro, and the countless people at HarperCollins who played a role in bringing this book to print; to my literary agent, Laura Blake Peterson, her assistant Mina Feig, and my film agent Holly Frederick at Curtis Brown, Limited; to Carol Fitzgerald and the gang at Bookreporter; to Peter Meluso; to booksellers and librarians everywhere; and above all, to my readers: I'm blessed that I'm able to write because of you, and for you. Thank you for your tremendous support.

THE
BLACK WIDOW

Prologue

"Some things," Carmen used to say, "just don't feel right until the sun goes down."

It was true.

Cocktails . . .

Bedtime stories . . .

Turning on the television . . .

Putting on pajamas . . .

All much better—more natural—after nightfall, regardless of the hour or season.

There are other things, Alex has since discovered, that can only happen under cover of darkness. They're far less appealing than the ones to which Carmen referred, but unfortunately they've become increasingly necessary.

Alex opens the door that leads from the kitchen to the attached garage, aims the key remote at the car, pops the trunk.

It slowly opens wide. The interior bulb throws enough light into the garage so that it's unnecessary to flip a wall switch and illuminate the overhead fixture.

Not that there are any windows that might reveal to the neighbors that someone is up and about at this hour . . .

And not that the crack beneath the closed door is wide enough to emit a telltale shaft of light . . .

And even if it did, it's not likely that elderly Hester Toomey, who lives directly across the street, will be up at this hour, sitting in her usual spot on her porch . . .

But still, it's good to practice discretion. One can't be too careful.

And Mrs. Toomey notices everything.

Alex removes a square-point shovel from a rack on the sidewall. The steel blade has been scrubbed clean with bleach; not a speck of dirt remains from the last wee-hour expedition to the remote stretch of hilly forest seventy miles north of this quiet New York City suburb in Westchester County.

Into the trunk goes the shovel, along with the rake used for clearing the ground of fallen leaves before digging and the headlamp purchased from an online camping supply store.

Now comes the hard part.

Alex returns to the house with a coil of sturdy rope and a lightweight hand truck stolen from a careless deliveryman who foolishly left it unattended behind the supermarket last year. It's come in handy. Alex is strong—but 150 pounds of dead weight is . . .

Well, not dead *yet*.

The figure lying prone on the sofa is out cold, courtesy of the dissolvable pill dropped into booze-laced soda.

Rohypnol—the date rape drug—is no longer prescribed in the United States and thus harder to come by. But Alex wisely stocked up during a trip to Mexico when it became apparent there would be a need for it.

In Mexico nobody asks questions.

When this is all over, and he's back in my arms, maybe that's where we'll go.

But now is not a time to daydream about the future. There's a lot to do before the sun comes up.

Stepping around the usual floor clutter, Alex carries the glass of spiked soda to the kitchen. There's still an inch or two of liquid in the bottom, but the amount that was consumed certainly did the trick. Now, Alex dumps the contents into the sink and washes it down the drain. The glass and the sink are scrubbed with bleach, the glass returned to its place in the cupboard beside a row of colorful plastic sippy cups with tops and baby bottles that are ready and waiting . . .

Just waiting.

Then it's back to the living room. Dozing on his favorite chair, the black cat—a former stray who's been here for a long time now—lazily opens one eye. Alex had named him Señor Don Gato after a childhood song a foster mother sang years ago in a cozy little home that reminded Alex of a gingerbread cottage. The woman loved cats and was always taking in strays. Stray cats, stray kids . . .

Yet for some reason, she didn't want to adopt me.

"It's time for our guest to go now," Alex informs Gato.

In response, not a twitch of movement from either the cat or the guest.

Under Gato's watchful gaze, Alex rolls the hand truck over to the sofa and unfurls a length of rope. The end whips through the air, toppling a framed photo on the end table. It's an old black-and-white baby photo of Carmen, a gift from Alex's mother-in-law the day after their son was born.

"El niño mira justo como mi Carmen," she had said, and then translated in her heavily accented English for Alex's benefit: "He looks just like my Carmen."

On that day, gazing into the newborn's face, all patchy skin and squinty eyes from the drops the nurses had put in, Alex couldn't really see it.

But as the days, then weeks and months, passed, the resemblance became undeniable. Strangers would stop them on the street to exclaim over how much parent and child looked alike.

At first it was sweet. Soon, though, Alex started to feel left out.

"He looks like you, too, sweetie," Carmen, ever the supportive spouse, would claim. But it wasn't true.

"You're just trying to make me feel better."

"No—he has your blue eyes, see?"

"All babies have blue eyes," Alex pointed out, "and he has your *face*. Everything about him is you—even his personality."

The baby had been so easygoing from day one, quick to smile, quick to laugh . . .

As their son grew into a boy, he loved buildings and music, even learned to play the guitar like . . .

Like Carm.

He was nothing like you.

Alex leaves the photo lying facedown on the table.

Carmen—even baby Carmen—doesn't need to witness what's about to happen here.

I know you wouldn't approve, Carm. But too bad. You're not here, and I have no choice. It's the only way.

Five minutes later Alex is in the car heading north on the Taconic Parkway. The cruise control is set at five miles above the posted limit—just fast enough to reach the familiar destination in little over an hour, but not fast enough to be pulled over for speeding.

Even if that were to happen, nothing would appear out of the ordinary to a curious cop peering into the car. Alex would turn over a spotless driver's license and explain that the sleeping person slumped in the passenger's seat simply had too much to drink. No crime in that statement, and quite a measure of truth.

Three hours later the first traces of pink dawn are visible through the open window beyond the empty passenger seat as Alex reenters the southbound lanes on the parkway. All four windows are rolled down and the moon roof is open, too, despite the damp chill in the strong west wind on this first day of March.

Some distance ahead, taillights glow in the dark. Twin red orbs, exactly parallel, that remind Alex of—

No. Stop. Don't think of that.

Alex hits the gas pedal hard and speeds up—a necessary risk in order to pass the other car. But as soon as the disturbing red taillights have given way to a distant glare of headlights in the rearview mirror, Alex slows to a speed that won't attract police radar.

The radio is set, as always, to a classic rock station. *Real* music—that's what Carmen always used to call it.

None of that techno-electro-hip-hop-pop crap for us, babe. Just good old-fashioned rock and roll . . .

Led Zeppelin's "Immigrant Song" opens with a powerful electric guitar; eerie, wailing, lyric-free vocals from Robert Plant.

The fresh air and the music make it better somehow. Easier to forget throwing shovels of dirt over the wooden crate that contains a still unconscious human being lying at the bottom of the pit. Easier not to wonder what it would be like to regain consciousness and find yourself buried alive.

Maybe that won't happen. Maybe it never has, with any of them. Maybe they just drift from sleep to a painless death, never knowing . . .

But that's not very likely, is it?

Chances are it's a frantic, ugly, horrifying death, perhaps clawing helplessly out of the box only to be crushed by the weight of dirt and rocks, struggling for air . . .

Alex reaches over to adjust the volume on the radio, turning it up even higher in an effort to drown out the nagging thoughts.

Sometimes that works.

Other times they persist, refusing to be ignored.

Not tonight, thank goodness.

The voices give way to the music, which shifts from Led Zeppelin to the familiar opening guitar lick of an old Guns N' Roses tune.

Singing along—screaming, shouting—to the lyrics, Alex rejoices. There is no more fitting song to punctuate this moment. It's a sign. It has to be. A sign that everything is going to be okay after all. Someone else will come along. Another chance. Soon enough . . .

"Oh . . . oh-oh-oh . . . sweet child of mine . . ."

Chapter 1

"No, come on. That one wasn't good either. Now you just look annoyed."

"Maybe because I *am* annoyed," Gabriela Duran tells her cousin Jaz, watching her check out the photo she just snapped on her digital camera.

Yes, digital camera.

Gaby had assumed a few cell phone snapshots would suffice, and would make this little photo shoot far less conspicuous. But Jaz, who'd enrolled in a photography class at the New School not long ago, insisted on using a real camera, the kind that has a telephoto lens attached. It's perched atop a tripod, aiming directly at Gaby.

Which might not be a terrible thing if they were in the privacy of her apartment. But in the middle of jam-packed Central Park at high noon on this sunny Sunday before Memorial Day . . .

Yeah. Definitely a terrible thing.

Especially because she's prone to seasonal allergies. This has been the worst spring for mold and pollen in years. Hanging out in the city's greenest pocket has ignited a raging sinus headache.

"Can't you please just smile for two seconds," Jaz begs, "so that I can get a decent shot? Then we can be done."

Gaby sighs and pastes on a grin.

"You just look like you're squinting."

"I *am* squinting." They've been here so long that the sun has changed position, glaring directly into her eyes. Also not helping her headache. "How about if I just turn the other way?" She gestures over her shoulder, preferring to face the clump of trees behind her rather than the parade of New Yorkers jogging, strolling, and rolling past on the adjacent pathway.

"No, I need the light on your face. Here, just take a few steps this way . . . no, not that far, back a little, back . . . back . . . okay, good!"

A group of tourists—identifiable by their pastel windbreakers and purses diagonally strapped across their bodies—stops to gape.

"I think that's Jennifer Lopez," one of them says.

Another calls out, "Is this a movie shoot?"

Jaz laughs and tells them that it isn't, but they don't seem convinced, sticking around to watch the proceedings from a distance, taking pictures with their phones just in case.

Jaz raises the viewfinder again. "Okay, smile . . . *without* clenching your teeth."

"Jaz, I swear—"

"Come on, *mami*," her cousin cuts in, strategically using the Latina term of endearment. "It's for Mr. Perfect."

Gaby already thought she'd found Mr. Perfect, a long time ago. She thought he'd stay with her forever; believed him when he promised he'd never leave, even after—

But he left. Not right away. But one day he walked out the door and he didn't come back, just as she'd expected him to do, almost dared him to do, ever since—

"Mr. Perfect doesn't exist," she snaps at Jaz.

"Not true." Jaz shakes her head, her chestnut ringlets bobbing around her shoulders.

Gaby would have exactly the same hair if she didn't typically pull it back in a ponytail, or blow it out straight, as she did today.

Ben loved her untamed curls . . . back when Ben loved her, and she loved Ben.

But Ben is gone and the curls are gone, and this is how her life is now: posing for her cousin's camera in a public place so she can post her picture online to attract strange men.

"He exists," Jaz goes on, eye to camera, snapping away, "but he doesn't know *you* exist, and he won't unless I get a picture that captures the real you."

The real me . . .

Gaby has no idea who that even is these days. All she knows is that the real Gabriela, who once laughed her way through life and was no pushover when it came to anything, is gone.

She hasn't felt remotely like herself since last fall before the divorce. After five years of marriage—and three years together before that—life without Ben has been unanchored and unfamiliar. Even now, most days she feels as though she's inhabiting a strange body in a strange place, having swapped someone else's life for her own.

In a weak, lonely moment, after too many happy hour cocktails on Cinco de Mayo, the new Gaby allowed Jaz to convince her that online dating was the answer to all her problems.

"Hello, everyone does it," her cousin told her.

"Not everyone."

"I do."

"You're not everyone."

"Everyone else does, too. Trust me . . . Excuse me," Jaz called to a pretty waitress scurrying past their outdoor table with bowls of tortilla chips and guacamole. "Can I ask you a quick question?"

"Sure, what's up?" The waitress paused, looking pleased

at the momentary reprieve from running around in the heat. Hands full, she rested the tray against the top of an empty chair and blew her bangs away from her sweaty forehead.

"Have you ever been on an Internet dating site?"

"It's how I met my husband." Balancing her tray with her right hand, she waved the diamond ring and gold band on her left.

"That's great. Congratulations. That's all I wanted to know. Oh, and we'll take another round when you have a chance."

The waitress walked on, and Jaz looked smugly at Gaby. "See that? You can't argue with a wedding ring."

"Don't bet on that."

She'd been so sure that together, she and Ben could withstand any challenge. For better, for worse . . .

When you're young and in love and standing there in a white dress and veil, you honestly think those wedding day promises mean something. You speak those vows with all your heart, and you keep them . . .

For better, anyway.

When the worst happens . . .

You leave. If you're Ben, you leave.

But Jaz—and the tequila, and the thought of yet another solitary weekend in her tiny studio apartment—had finally worn her down.

She shrugged. "Oh, all right, why not? I'll give it a try."

Naturally, Jaz was thrilled. Even Dr. Milford thought it might be a good idea—another positive step toward getting over Ben, starting a new chapter in her life.

That was three weeks ago.

Gaby talked herself out of the idea in the cold, cruel light of day on May sixth, but her cousin threatened to create a profile for her anyway—and is quite capable of following through.

And so, resigned to the fact that she's going to find herself with an online dating profile one way or another, Gaby manages to muster a halfhearted smile for her cousin's camera.

But the carefree girl she once was had died long ago, along with her fairy-tale marriage and her only child.

Having completely forgotten about the long holiday weekend, Alex is alarmed by the sight of a police roadblock on Main Street in Vanderwaal on Monday morning.

They know. They know, and they're looking for me.

There's nothing to do but stop and dutifully roll down the window as the cop beside the blue barricade comes walking toward the car.

"Good morning, officer."

"Morning. You'll have to turn around and detour back up Bridge Road to get to the other side of town. Memorial Day parade is about to start."

Memorial Day parade!

It's Memorial Day!

Thank God, thank God, it's just a parade, and not . . .

Come on, of course it's not about you. They can't possibly know about you. You've been so careful . . .

"All right, officer. Thanks so much. You have a great day now, okay?"

Was the last part overkill? Alex wonders, carefully making a K-turn and making sure to use directional signals. Is being too polite and friendly a blatant red flag to the cop?

Nah. People always tell each other to have a great day.

Even if Alex were summoned back—and for what?— there's nothing in the car that would alert the cop that anything is amiss. Even if the officer were to examine the contents of the plastic drugstore shopping bag on the passenger's seat, there still wouldn't be any reason for suspicion. Of course not.

And of course it was Alex's imagination—an overactive one, Carmen used to say—that the clerk back at the store had raised her eyebrow when she rang up the purchases: Advil, Band-Aids, *Rolling Stone* magazine, a pack of gum. Decoy items all, meant to distract attention from the main objective: an over-the-counter pregnancy test.

"Find everything?" the clerk had asked—routine question, yet Alex worried for a moment that it was a precursor to something more probing, less discreet.

But of course that was pure paranoia. No clerk would ever question a total stranger about something so personal.

No clerk had any way of knowing that a random customer—paying with cash—had purchased the same test countless times before all over the tristate area.

You have nothing at all to worry about. Just get home and take care of business.

Alex keeps the speedometer precisely at the posted limit all the way up Bridge Road and around to the other side and stops at the intersection, staring unseeingly at the traffic light until it blurs and doubles. Now there are two red lights, glowing elliptical red, a disturbing reminder of—

The light turns green and Alex drives on, past familiar rows of old maples framing well-kept suburban houses that line block after block here in Vanderwaal. Most of them are occupied by young, upper-middle-class families who can afford the astronomical housing costs and property taxes and who take advantage of the high quality public schools. The older people in the neighborhood, who lived here when Carmen was growing up, have either died off or retired someplace where the cost of living is low and the weather is warm.

All is quieter than usual on Cherry Street this morning. It's well within walking distance of Main Street, and the stroller-and-leash brigade has most likely headed out early to claim prime spots along the parade route.

Noticing the flags flying from poles and porches, Alex makes a mental note to put up a flag, too, back home. There's one somewhere in the basement.

The basement.

Back when the Realtor showed them the brick cape at 42 Cherry Street—long before Alex and Carmen were married—there were a couple of major selling points. One was that they'd be able to keep a close eye on Carmen's aging mother, who lived alone in a house right down the street. Another was that it was affordable—smaller than most of the homes in the area, many of which had been renovated and enlarged.

And then there was the basement. The house looked small from the outside, and it *was* small, with only two bedrooms tucked beneath the low, gabled ceilings of the second floor. But the basement was large and finished.

"The family that lived here in the sixties added over five hundred square feet of living space when they turned this into a rec room," the Realtor said, flicking a light switch and leading the way down the flight into a large open area where a familiar scent wafted in the air.

Once, living in a rural foster home—not the gingerbread cottage—Alex had forgotten to roll up a backseat car window. It rained overnight, and the carpet and upholstery got soaked. After that the car's interior was permeated by a strong mildew odor, much to the foster mother's disgust and fury.

The basement smelled the same way. It didn't bring back good memories. But the added space was undeniably attractive.

"This would make a great home gym," Carmen mused, glancing around. "A treadmill, some weight machines . . ."

"Absolutely!" the Realtor agreed, bobbing her blond head enthusiastically. "But let me show you the rest."

She was mostly talking to Alex, which annoyed Carmen. But Alex was the one buying the house, even though they had every intention of getting married at some point. Carmen was essentially broke at the time, facing massive loans for all those years of undergrad and graduate school. Alex had been working at the hospital for a few years by then and was financially solvent.

The Realtor led them across the basement. The walls were paneled in brown wood, the floors covered in green indoor-outdoor carpeting that gave way to linoleum in one corner, where an old olive-green washer and dryer sat alongside a slop sink. Small horizontal rectangular windows were scattered high on three walls. On the fourth there was just a door.

The Realtor opened it, and an even stronger dank smell greeted their nostrils. "Wait until you see this," she trilled, as if she were about to reveal something utterly dazzling: a stocked wine cellar, or fully equipped home theater . . .

"What is it?" Carmen asked, nose wrinkled, peering into the dank—apparently vacant—interior.

"A bomb shelter. The house was built back in the cold war era. People were afraid Russia was going to drop a nuclear bomb."

Alex had seen the black and yellow fallout shelter signs on sturdy public buildings all over the city, but . . .

"A nuclear bomb *here*?"

The Realtor shrugged. "New York is always a major target, and we're right in the suburbs. The assumption was that the radiation contamination would spread up here if the city were hit. People wanted to protect their families. Back in the day, this room was filled with canned goods, bottled water, lamps, cots, a space heater, even a toilet."

"That explains the smell," Carmen murmured. "It's even worse than cat."

The last house they'd looked at had smelled strongly of feline urine, and there was visible fur everywhere, though the pets—and their elderly owner—were long gone. Being severely allergic, Carmen had vetoed it immediately.

"Oh, this is just musty and damp from being closed up

for all these years," the Realtor assured them as they sniffed around the bomb shelter room at 42 Cherry. "A dehumidifier would take care of it. But it's a piece of history. Isn't it fabulous?"

Fabulous wasn't quite the right word. Not back then.

Not now either.

Now . . .

Well, the word *godsend* comes to mind.

Alex never imagined, buying this house, that the underground bunker would ever be used for anything more than extra storage . . . and perhaps a conversation piece.

But then, there were a lot of things Alex never imagined back in those days.

Ordinarily at this hour Gaby would be forty-odd blocks south of here in her office on East 53rd Street, dealing with the usual deluge of Monday morning messages and e-mail.

As a senior editor at Winslow Publishing, she technically works only Monday through Friday, but some of her authors assume she's available 24/7, in keeping with their own unorthodox work schedules. E-mails and voice mails pour in all weekend long, sometimes increasingly frantic ones. Gaby learned early on that there are very few, if any, true editorial emergencies that require weekend attention, though a couple of literary divas might beg to differ.

Today the office is closed for the holiday. Instead of tending to flooded in-boxes, she's home, just pouring her first cup of coffee. According to the microwave clock it's almost ten-thirty, which means she got . . .

Let's see, that would be a whole five hours' sleep—six, counting the first hour.

As always, she'd drifted off soon after climbing into bed at eleven, only to be jerked back to consciousness at midnight.

She wasn't awakened by a thunderstorm, though they were in the forecast last night. Nor was she alerted by the incessant sirens, horns, and car alarms in the street four stories below—she's accustomed to city noise, having been born and raised in Manhattan. And God knows it wasn't Ben's snoring that woke her.

Back when they lived together that never bothered her—a claim that flummoxed both Ben's older brother and his former college roommate, who only half jokingly presented her with noise-canceling headphones at their wedding rehearsal dinner.

Back then she found the rhythmic sound of her husband's snoring as soothing and reassuring as the warmth of his hand resting on her back as she drifted off. It wasn't until later—toward the end of their marriage—that it filled her with rage.

How, she'd wonder, could he be sleeping so soundly, as if nothing had happened? It wasn't fair.

His snoring, which wasn't—and then was—a problem is no longer a problem. Not hers, anyway. Maybe it's somebody else's, in the new apartment he rented in their old neighborhood. Maybe it isn't. Maybe he still sleeps alone, just as she does . . . when she actually manages to sleep.

It's been years since she made it through a night without waking in the wee hours. Two and a half years, to be exact.

November twelfth—that was the day everything changed. The *night* everything changed.

The night Joshua died.

Her baby. Her beautiful baby with a cherubic face and a pile of soft black curls and round dark brown eyes so like her own and Ben's—they looked alike, as so many married couples do, and so their son resembled both of them.

Gaby abruptly lifts the cup she just filled from the carafe. Coffee splashes onto the countertop.

She grabs a sponge to wipe it up right away. If she doesn't, it'll stain the ugly white laminate.

Her old kitchen, the spacious one in the last apartment

where she lived with Ben, had granite counters. The polished stone never stained.

"See that?" Ben said when they first moved in. "This stuff is indestructible."

"Nothing is indestructible."

"Really? Look. You can set down a cookie sheet right out of the oven."

She cringed when he did just that, with a steaming tray of those horrible freezer french fries he loved so much. But soon enough she, too, was putting hot cookware directly on the counter.

Then she moved in here, forgot, and did the same thing. Now there's a faint scorch mark on the laminate that no amount of scrubbing will completely erase. Every time she looks at the scar, she thinks of those granite countertops, of Ben, of Josh . . .

And she remembers that nothing—*nothing*—is indestructible.

She tosses aside the sponge and lifts the coffee cup to her lips, sipping so that the cup won't be so full. The liquid is hot—much too hot—burning the back of her tongue, blistering the roof of her mouth.

Perhaps it will leave another scar. No shortage of those around here.

Gaby carries the coffee away from the tiny kitchen alcove, past her unmade futon. When she moved into the studio six months ago, she promised herself that she'd fold up the pullout every morning and stash the bedding in the closet.

She hasn't done it once. Why bother? No one but Jaz has ever visited her here, and that was only once, when her cousin insisted on coming to see the new place.

"It's nice, *mami*," Jaz said, handing over the potted plant she'd brought as a housewarming gift. "Tiny, but nice. With some curtains, some new furniture, pictures on the wall, it'll be cute and cozy."

Maybe. But there are still no curtains, new furniture, or pictures. There is, however, plenty of evidence of her hobby, her livelihood, her passion—though *passion* is a strong word for anything that pertains to her life these days. But she's an avid reader, and an editor. The shelves in her apartment are lined with books, and there are stacks of them everywhere—towering on the tables, on the floor, and, precariously, atop the cardboard carton shoved into the corner.

Inside that box: a collection of Ben's belongings. She never opened it, but she watched him pack it with his high school yearbook, old family photo albums, a few precious childhood toys, and his baseball card collection. Somehow it got mixed in with her belongings when they separated.

She's always meant to call him and tell him that she has it. But that would mean opening the door that had slammed shut between them, and she hasn't felt ready to do that yet.

The box is too large to tuck away on a closet shelf, and she's not hardhearted enough to throw away his mementos, so there it sits, where she has to look at it every day, taking up four precious square feet of the apartment's measly few hundred.

Gaby sinks into a chair by the open window, clutching her coffee cup with both hands, stifling a yawn. She got more rest last night than she usually does, but it still wasn't enough.

An hour or so after drifting off she was awakened, as always, by a familiar stab of dread: the awareness that something was terribly wrong.

If only it had happened that night, November twelfth.

But back then she fell asleep as soon as her head hit the pillow and stayed that way until something tangible—the baby's cries, the alarm clock, Ben, in the mood for wee-hour romance—woke her.

That night, she slept straight through, opening her eyes to bright light streaming in beneath the drawn blinds. Ben was snoring beside her, still with a half hour to go before the alarm would rouse him for work. Josh was in his crib in the next room.

The doctors, the marriage counselor, and her own therapist all said that even if Josh had been sleeping right beside their bed that night, he still would have died.

But what about the cold he'd had in the days before? The damned cold he'd caught from Ben, who got sick after he insisted on running the New York Marathon as planned, even though he wasn't feeling up to it.

Some studies have linked the common cold with sudden infant death syndrome, others are inconclusive.

But all babies catch cold sooner or later.

Colds aren't deadly.

Intellectually, she gets it: the very nature of sudden infant death syndrome is that it strikes inexplicably and without warning. You lay your baby down to sleep, never imagining that the next time you see him he'll be stiff and cold, the way Joshua was when she wandered into his room to check on him that terrible morning.

Wandered—not rushed—because even when she woke up to find that he'd slept through the night, she wasn't concerned. She took her time in the bathroom and detoured to the kitchen to start coffee before opening the nursery door, never sensing that anything might be wrong.

She thought he was sleeping, picked him up . . .

The horror, the utter shock of that moment, will never lose its grip on her soul. Never again will she wake up in the morning and assume that all is right in the world.

Things are different now, so different . . .

Now that she knows that terrible things happen in the night.

The test was negative.

As in *not pregnant*.

Alex tosses the white plastic indicator stick into the wastebasket, along with the packaging promising that it provides the earliest and most accurate over-the-counter test available, capable of detecting pregnancy hormones in urine several days before a missed period.

Maybe it's just too early.

Maybe, in another day or two, with another test, there will be two lines in the little window just like on that happy day years ago—and the one before that.

The first time, Carmen—ever the pack rat—wanted to save that plastic stick, the one that confirmed they were going to become parents at last, after months of vainly trying to conceive.

"Are you serious? That's disgusting! There's pee on it!"

"I don't care." Of course not. Laid-back Carmen . . .

Alex turns abruptly away from the wastebasket and heads back downstairs and into the kitchen.

Hearing the door to the utility cupboard creak open, the cat materializes instantly, knowing that's where his food is kept.

"What's the matter, Gato? Are you hungry again?" With a sigh, Alex grabs a can of Friskies from the shelf, opens it, dumps it into a bowl, and sets the bowl on the floor. "You'd better eat it this time. Last time, you made a big fuss and then you didn't even touch your food."

Purring loudly, the cat promptly strolls over to the bowl and begins eating.

"How about some milk, too?"

Alex carefully opens and closes the fridge, covered in so many magnet-held crayon drawings that not an inch of door remains visible. "There you go. There's your milk. Good kitty."

It's nice to have a pet in the house. That wasn't possible back when Carmen was here, but now it doesn't matter. Alex doesn't have allergies, thank goodness.

Once Carmen was gone, Gato showed up meowing on

the doorstep, almost as if he'd been waiting until the coast was clear.

"And I adopted you," Alex tells the cat, "because that's what people do when someone needs a home. They take them in and keep them and love them. Right?"

Gato seems to lift his head and nod in agreement.

Satisfied, Alex takes a flashlight from the utility cupboard, closes the creaky door, and descends the basement steps.

Everything—even the mildew smell—is similar to the way it was that first day the Realtor showed them the house. A treadmill and a couple of weight machines take up one half of the room. On the far wall, the one that has no windows, a tall bookshelf seems to have replaced the door that led to the bomb shelter.

But it hasn't. Alex constructed it to conceal the door.

It wasn't easy for someone lacking in carpentry skills, but thanks to the Internet, it was at least in the realm of possibility. All you had to do was Google the phrase, *How do you build a bookcase to hide a door?* and a list of instructional links popped up.

Alex crosses the basement, takes the last book from the row on a middle shelf, and pulls a camouflaged latch. The bookcase swings forward, rolling on castors concealed behind the bottom strip of molding. Alex opens the door to the underground bunker meant to protect a long-gone family from nuclear fallout that never materialized. The flashlight beam reveals the room's lone occupant, huddled beneath a quilt on the cot across the room. The figure stirs, sitting up with a squeaking of bedsprings and a jangling of wrist and ankle shackles, squinting into the bright light.

"Bad news," Alex says. "I thought you'd want to know. It was negative again. We'll do another test in a few more days, but if it's still negative . . . well, you know what that means, don't you?"

No reply.

"All right, then I'll remind you. It's like I said in the beginning. You only get three strikes before you're out. And just in case the next test is negative . . ."

Leaving the rest unsaid, Alex clicks off the flashlight and closes the door, moving the bookcase into place with a heavy sigh.

Back upstairs, Gato has vanished, and the food and milk sits barely touched on the floor where Alex left it.

"Hey! Where did you go?"

The cat is nowhere to be found, and now isn't the time to conduct a thorough search. Not for the cat, anyway. No, it's time to sign into the online dating account again and launch the hunt for a new prospective candidate. Just in case . . .

Chapter 2

On Tuesday morning Gaby arrives at work well before 7:00 A.M. Last night was one of those nights when she couldn't fall back to sleep after waking up, not even after taking an antihistamine for her allergies. She finally decided she might as well get an early start on the day after the long weekend.

The receptionist's desk is deserted as she steps off the elevator on the twenty-sixth floor and unlocks the glass door with her electronic key card. She makes her way through darkened corridors, past rows of bookshelves holding recently published titles, cubicles housing assistants' desks piled high with more books and manuscripts, and her colleagues' closed doors.

She unlocks her own, flips on a light, and drops her tote bag on the lone guest chair. It usually doesn't discourage coworkers from plopping themselves down there to distract her with chitchat once the day gets under way, but it never hurts to try.

She sits down at her desk with a large coffee and bagel she bought from the cart on the corner, same as she used to do way back in her entry-level days as an impoverished editorial assistant. Back then, as a recent City College grad, she was still living with Abuela, her Puerto Rican grandmother, in a tiny walk-up just off the Grand Concourse in the Bronx.

Later, when she was married to Ben, she upgraded to espresso and scones from various coffee chains. He made good money and encouraged her to spend it. Now that he's gone . . .

Well, the comfortable lifestyle is by far the least of what she misses. But it was nice—while it lasted—not to worry about affording the daily basics on her publishing salary.

Their divorce agreement was straightforward, with virtually no shared assets and no custody issues. Her attorney cautioned her not to move out of their apartment and advised her to go after spousal support, among other things, but she just wanted it to be over as quickly as possible.

She doesn't regret that decision. Lingering in dead-marriage limbo would have been even more excruciating than finding herself completely on her own again, seemingly overnight.

She sips her coffee and finds it too weak for her liking. That's ironic. Most days it's too strong.

All right, Goldilocks, time to get down to business.

Reluctantly turning her attention to her computer screen, she signs into her e-mail account.

It takes just over an hour to go through her in-box and address the issues that have arisen since she left the office Friday evening. She checks her voice mail, too, and returns a call to a British author who touched base yesterday wanting to brainstorm titles. It goes straight into voice mail: "I'm busy writing. Leave your number and I'll call when I finish the bloody book!"

Gaby leaves a brief message, then hangs up and checks the clock on the computer screen. It's still too early to return the other calls.

Now, while the office is still quiet, would be a good time to get some manuscript reading done, but first . . .

She logs into her InTune account.

The familiar logo pops up: a pair of musical notes—

beamed notes, the kind connected by a bar across the tops—
that have smiling faces. Jaz told her that the Web site had
originally been created to match couples based on their musical tastes, just as other niche sites match them based on
religion, income level, hobby—any number of societal sub-
categories. InTune has maintained its music-themed name
and logo, but has since morphed into a mainstream dating
site that seems to be favored by the vast majority of New
York singles.

It takes Gaby three tries to remember the password. She'd
changed it last night from the original one she and Jaz had
created, worried that if her well-meaning but meddling
cousin still had access to the account, she might use it to
pose as Gaby, flirting with strangers left and right . . .

Which is the whole point of these sites in the first place,
right?

But her style isn't nearly as brash as Jaz's. Plus, she's
looking for a very specific type of man.

"Oh, really?" Jaz said yesterday afternoon, after upload-
ing the Central Park photos and helping her finish her profile. "What type is that?"

All right, so maybe she doesn't know exactly what she's
looking for. But she definitely knows what she doesn't want:
a fling with a jerk who's trolling around online for easy bait.

"Who wants that?" Jaz asked with an easy shrug. "Listen,
we all want the same thing. Love. So come on . . . are you
ready to let this account go live?"

"Not yet."

"You'll never be ready."

"I will be. Just . . . let me get used to it for a few more days."

"Why wait? The sooner, the better. Don't you want to see
how many guys you attract?"

"What if there are none?"

"With those pictures? Come on, *mami*, you know you're
beautiful."

Beautiful?

There may have been times in her life when Gaby really did feel beautiful. A long, long time ago. Definitely when she was a little girl, and her daddy used to come home on leave to visit her at Abuela's. He always called her "Bonita"—pretty little one.

But he went to Iraq and never came back. Not because something happened to him over there. No, he still sent e-mails from time to time—from Iraq, but later from Las Vegas, from Texas, from California. So far as she knew, he was still alive and well, safely back in the States. He just stopped visiting. Stopped calling her Bonita.

Right around the time she realized he'd left her behind for good, teenage Gaby decided her hair was too wild, her skin too dark, her hips too wide, and her features too exotic to conform to anyone's idea of beauty.

Years later, when she and Ben fell in love, he complimented her all the time. Not just on her looks, of course. But it meant a lot, especially when she was pregnant and ballooning toward two hundred pounds, to see the desire in his eyes and hear him say sweet things without sounding sappy. Somehow, he managed to convince her that she was beautiful—and that he loved her, would always love her, no matter what.

Interesting that the two men in her life who professed their adoration eventually abandoned her.

So. Beautiful? No, she doesn't think of herself that way.

But Jaz, ever her personal cheerleader, promised, "As soon as your dating profile goes live, guys are going to come crawling out of the woodwork."

"Like *cucarachas*. Terrific."

Her cousin rolled her eyes. "Only you would compare guys to cockroaches. What am I going to do with you, Gabriela?"

Leave me alone, Gaby wanted to say.

But of course that's not what she really wants. *Alone* has come to mean lonely.

Anyway, Jaz really does have her best interests at heart. She isn't just a cousin, she's the sister Gaby never had—though sometimes she also likes to act like the mother Gaby never had.

Jaz's own mother, Tia Yolanda, had—along with Abuela—truly been the mother Gaby never had. Not since she was a toddler, anyway. Tia Yolanda and Gaby's mother, Gloria, were sisters. Cruelly, the lupus that killed Gloria when she was just in her twenties also took Tia Yolanda's life a decade later.

After that it was just Abuela looking out for both Jaz and Gaby, who have always, *always*, had each other's backs.

And so, sitting here on a cloudy Tuesday morning, sipping watery coffee from a paper cup, Gaby signs into the dating Web site and finds that her profile has gone live. As Jaz predicted, a number of guys have reached out, interested in connecting. Like her own page, theirs only show first names.

Gaby skims through the messages, ruling them out one by one.

Jack: too pushy . . .

Greg: too boring . . .

Eli: too creepy . . .

And then . . .

All too familiar.

First the name catches her eye, then the postage-stamp-sized photograph attached to the response, which consists of only one line: *Fancy meeting you here.*

Ben.

Online, a person can be anyone he or she wants to be.

That's the beauty of these Internet dating sites. You can call yourself by another name, make up an exciting background and glamorous career, even use a photo-shopped head shot—within reason, of course. You don't go and shave fifty pounds off your body or twenty-five years off your age, and you don't claim to be a celebrity or a billionaire, because those are things you obviously can't pull off once you meet someone in person.

But early on, when you're trying to bait the trap, so to speak, you really have to offer something that will tempt anyone who comes across your profile.

The picture he just uploaded to his latest page on the InTune Web site hasn't been digitally altered, but it is a few years old. In it he's wearing a red sweater. He read someplace that a splash of red attracts the opposite sex when it comes to online photos.

The snapshot was taken a couple of Christmases ago, at his former in-laws' home. He was thinner and more handsome then, still hitting the gym every day and getting a good night's sleep every night, back before all the trouble started. He had more hair and fewer wrinkles—issues that can be easily remedied with the right imaging software.

Expensive software—which he can no longer afford, thanks to *her*.

Thanks to her—his ex-wife, who left him for another man—he has to take a little white pill every morning. It's an antidepressant that causes all kinds of fun side effects, like nausea, dry mouth, and headaches. And, the doctor warned him, even worse ones if he forgets to take it: crying spells, dizziness, even suicidal tendencies. So of course he takes it daily—thanks to her.

And thanks to her, and all the stress and heartache she's wreaked upon his life, he didn't even consider taking new pictures for his new online dating profile. When he looks in the mirror lately, he doesn't like what he sees. When he looks at old pictures, he does. Case closed.

He leans back in his chair and surveys his latest profile.

Any eligible female who stumbles across "Nick's" tall, dark, and handsome picture will most likely click through to read his questionnaire.

First, she'll check out his age, thirty-one; his location, Upper West Side; his occupation, architect.

Already impressed, she'll see that he's never been married and has no children. That will most likely be met with approval because, really, who wants that kind of baggage?

Not me. Not most single people in their right mind.

With Nick Santana—that's the name he'll be using this time—a woman seeking an unencumbered man won't even have to worry about pets. He lied that he's allergic, to keep the crazy cat ladies away.

He couldn't believe how many of those he found when he first entered the realm of online dating. It seemed like such a cliché until he started noticing just how many single women posted photos of themselves cradling kittens, or managed to work feline-centric answers into their questionnaires.

Nick Santana's questionnaire just covers the basic favorites in every category.

Favorite Food: Italian. Who doesn't love Italian food?

Favorite Movie: *The Last of The Mohicans.* An oldie but not ancient; suitably rugged, with both historic and literary appeal, plus a romance.

Favorite Music—

Someone clears her throat behind him and he jumps, startled. Turning around, he sees Ivy Sacks, the project manager, standing in the doorway of his cubicle.

"How's it coming along?"

Ivy is referring to the spreadsheet that has, with a quick click of the mouse, replaced the dating questionnaire on his desktop screen.

"It's . . . you know. Coming along."

"When do you think it'll be finished?"

"Soon. Very soon."

"Good. I need to get it to Bill before he leaves on vacation at the end of the day." She pauses. "How about you? Are you thinking of taking a vacation this summer?"

"Me?"

"You have three weeks coming. You know what they say—use it or lose it."

"I'll see," he mutters. Thanks to his ex and all the money they racked up in legal fees for the divorce attorneys, he won't be able to afford a vacation for a long, long time.

Still, Ivy lingers. "So how are things in the neighborhood? Any more excitement lately?"

"What? Oh—no. Not lately."

He'd made the mistake of telling her about a drive-by shooting last month just a few blocks from his apartment in Howard Beach, and a break-in on a lower floor in his building. He'd figured that if he emphasized what a rough neighborhood he'd been forced to move to after the divorce, she'd take pity on him and maybe raise his salary. All he'd accomplished was to generate more topics for the small talk she likes to force on him.

"Everything's been pretty quiet around the 'hood," he assures her now.

"That's good. Really good."

For a moment she just stands there looking at him. Her expression is impossible to read.

"Anything else?" he asks, hands poised on the keyboard as though eager to get back to work on the spreadsheet.

"I was just wondering . . ."

When she trails off, he doesn't prompt her to continue. He's tempted to, because she might want to talk to him about a raise or promotion. Then again, what if she's on the verge of asking him out?

This wouldn't be the first time, since the divorce, that he's gotten that vibe.

It's bad enough that she sent him a friend request on

Facebook. He ignored it, hoping she wouldn't bring it up. She hasn't. But he still suspects she's interested in more than a professional relationship.

Not cool. Ivy is his supervisor. She's also the only woman at the firm who happens to be roughly his age and single. Her facial features and build are far too angular for his taste, and she's blond—so blond that her hair is almost white, her eyelashes and eyebrows invisible. He likes brunettes. It isn't just Ivy's looks that don't appeal to him, though. He's shallow, but not that shallow. Her retiring, overly earnest personality makes it impossible to imagine her ever kicking back and having the slightest bit of fun.

"Never mind," she says. "Just shoot that spreadsheet over to me when you're done, okay?"

"Sure, no problem."

He waits for her to leave.

The moment she does, he clicks away from the spreadsheet, back to his online profile.

Favorite Music?

Perhaps the easiest question of all.

Smiling to himself, he writes *Classic Rock*.

Chapter 3

Friday evening, Gaby leans into the mirror above the sink in the ladies' room down the hall from her office. This isn't the first time she's applied mascara without a handy place to rest her elbow, but she used to be a lot more proficient at it. Tonight it's smudge city.

Maybe the shaky hand is due to the extra large coffee she bought on the street after lunch, hoping to make up for another sleepless night.

More likely it's caused by nerves.

She's about to go on her first date in . . .

How long has it been?

Years.

Her last first date was with Ben, of course. They'd been friends for a long time before he asked her out, so she wasn't nervous. Well, maybe in a good, butterflies-in-the-stomach way. Not like this.

A nearby stall door opens. Kasey Leibock, a fellow editor, comes out, high-heeled pumps clicking on the tile floor. She's carrying a large tote bag, probably off to catch her commuter train home to the suburbs.

Seeing Gaby, she raises an eyebrow. "Wow! Look at you! Hot date?"

"I don't know about 'hot,' but . . . yeah, I have a date."

"Lucky you. What I wouldn't give." Kasey turns on the water and pumps soap into her hands, not noticing the incredulity on Gaby's face.

Kasey is going home tonight to her husband and three kids, the youngest a toddler born a few months after Josh. Every time Gaby overhears Kasey talking about something her son—his name is Dylan—is doing, she thinks, *Josh would be doing that now. He'd be saying funny things, and going to preschool, and throwing tantrums that we'd laugh about later.*

Kasey was still out on maternity leave when Gaby lost Josh. She brought her own infant son to the wake—because she was nursing, she later told a colleague who scolded her that it had been insensitive.

"I said it would have been better for her not to come at all," the colleague, Anne, later told Gaby. "And she was offended. You know Kasey."

Yes. She knows Kasey. They've worked together for almost a decade—through both their engagements and weddings, pregnancies and childbirths. All milestone events, to be sure—but with Kasey, everything is a big noisy production. She brags, she complains, she shares endless pictures, she solicits advice and freely doles it out . . .

Anne, a quiet fellow senior editor who lives alone with her cats and seems to like it that way, has very little patience for Kasey. "She's missing a sensitivity chip," she's been saying for years—though never as vocally as after the nursing-baby-at-the-wake incident.

On that awful day, standing beside her son's tiny casket with Ben, Gaby was in such a daze that she didn't even realize at first that Kasey was there in the crowd, let alone with Dylan in tow. But then the baby started whimpering, and the sound seemed to pierce the air with all the subtlety of an air horn blasting in a library. Dylan's cries filled Gaby's head, drowning out the hushed voices and muffled sobs. She wasn't hearing Kasey's son, but her own. She heard Josh crying in the night, crying for help, crying for her, crying instead of slipping silently away before she could save his life.

When she finally snapped out of it and caught sight of black-clad blond Kasey holding a white-wrapped, squirming bundle, she was overcome by jealousy so profound that it made her physically ill. It wasn't fair. It wasn't fair that Kasey's son was cuddled in her arms while her own son was all alone in a cold, dark wooden box. Grief had hit her anew; the cruelty of it all was staggering.

Now here's Kasey, heading home to spend the weekend with her husband and children but acting as though she'd like to switch places. It's all Gaby can do not to lash out at her.

"Do you know how long it's been since Adam and I went out to dinner?" Kasey lathers her hands, staring at her own reflection in the mirror. "I can't even remember the last time. It's been forever."

"That's too bad." Gaby tosses her mascara back into her purse. Only one eye is done, but that's enough for now—or maybe for the night. There are worse things than sporting one raccoon eye when meeting a blind date.

"I'm not talking about anything fancy. I'd be thrilled with burgers and beers at the pub down the road if I could get away from the kids for a night."

How do you reply to a statement like that?

You don't. Gaby zips her purse.

"So where are you going tonight?" Kasey asks her, still sounding wistful.

"I'm not sure. Have a good night," she says, and leaves the room.

In truth, Gaby knows exactly where she's going: to a new bistro in Chelsea. What she doesn't know—and isn't about to tell Kasey—is who she's going out with.

Oh, she knows his name, and what he does for a living; knows that he's in his mid-thirties and lives in the city and has no children. A man with children—after what she's been through—would be out of the question right now.

But really, she wonders as she waits for the elevator, what does the profile questionnaire really tell you about a person?

"It tells you everything you need to know," Jaz said on the phone last night, when Gaby reported that one of her InTune connections had asked her out.

"It tells me almost nothing I need to know."

"Does he seem nice?"

"Yes," she admitted. "He seems nice."

Surprisingly nice, and surprisingly normal. He'd struck up a conversation by instant message that first time she signed into her account—right after she saw the message from Ben.

Fancy meeting you here.

There she was, contemplating the fact that Ben had a profile on a dating Web site—that he now also knew *she* had a profile on a dating Web site—when a little box popped up on the corner of her screen, with a tiny rectangle picture and a single word: *hi.*

"I meant to disable the instant message setting," she later told Jaz. "You have to show me how to do that."

"Why?"

"Because I can't have people popping up and wanting to socialize every time I sign into my account."

Jaz just looked at her. "That's the point. Socializing."

"Well, I socialized. So you should be proud of me. I have a date with this guy Friday night."

"I'm proud. I'd be even more proud if I didn't think it had something to do with Ben."

"What do you mean?"

"You saw Ben's profile, and the next thing you know, you're saying yes to a date. If you hadn't seen Ben's profile . . ."

Gaby denied it, of course. To Jaz, anyway.

But the truth is, if she hadn't been faced with blatant

evidence that her ex-husband had moved on, she probably wouldn't have impulsively said yes when a total stranger asked her out.

She never did answer Ben's message.

It didn't really seem to require a response.

Fancy meeting you here.

Maybe she'll write back to him at some point, if only just to remind him that she still has a box of his belongings. It's only fair. He cherishes those things; he probably thinks he lost them, like all his other childhood possessions.

But if she reminds him, he'll have to come get his stuff, and she'll have to see him again. She's not ready for that yet.

Not in person, anyway. She did check out his online profile thoroughly.

The photos all appeared to be recent ones. The last time she saw him, he was gaunt and his olive skin seemed to have taken on a sickly pallor. These snapshots showed—well, not the old Ben, the one she fell in love with. It's true that he's looking like his broad-shouldered, muscular old self, and his complexion has a familiar, healthy-looking glow, as if he just came back from a week at the beach. But the Ben in these recent photos has a sprinkling of salt and pepper at his temples that was never there before, and a faint network of wrinkles around his eyes and mouth. Laugh lines? Has New Ben been laughing again? Maybe even laughing with someone else, the way he used to laugh with her when they were young and unencumbered?

When was the last time she really laughed? How did she become this brittle, sad, too-serious woman?

How?

You know how. It's hard to find joy when you've lost everyone who ever mattered: not just Josh and Ben, but Mama and Daddy and Abuela . . .

Everyone but Jaz.

Despite having been born a mere week earlier than Gaby,

Jaz has always done her best to bulldoze her like a bossy big sister.

"Don't you let her push you around, Gabriela," her grandmother would warn her, and when Ben came along, he said the same thing.

Neither of them seemed to grasp that Gaby only did what Gaby wanted to do. Her relationship with her cousin was complicated, but she'd inherited her share of fiery Latin temper. Hers just tended to simmer long after the rest of the family would have boiled over. But when she did explode— look out.

"Es como un volcan en erupcion!" Abuela would say, colorfully comparing her to an erupting volcano.

Now Abuela is long dead and Ben is long gone. Only Jaz is still there for her.

For all her cousin's faults, Gaby truly loves her and would do anything for her. Including joining the dating Web site that has now brought her ex-husband back again.

She stared at Ben's photos for a long time before allowing herself to click past them and see what he'd written about himself.

There was the usual biographical information—age, location, occupation, marital status . . .

Divorced.

That gave her pause.

Of course it's accurate. Her own profile says the same thing. But it's such an ugly word. She's still not used to it.

The next item on the questionnaire, regarding children, hits her like a sucker punch.

When she answered it on her own profile, she simply wrote *none.* She wasn't ready or willing to explain her wrenching loss to anyone.

But Ben had written *one (deceased).*

How could he put something so tragic, so private, out there on the Internet?

And on a dating Web site? Was he looking for sympathy from women who read his profile?

She felt sick.

To think he'd accused her of dwelling on the tragedy, not being able to pick up the pieces and move on.

Scanning the rest of his profile—the usual questions about hobbies and habits, likes and dislikes—she wondered how many women were doing the same thing; wondered how many were deciding Ben was Mr. Right. How many were feeling sorry for the man who had lost a child? How many were flirting with him in private messages right at that moment?

She had to force herself to read the essay section headed WHAT I'M LOOKING FOR, afraid of what it might say.

Like . . .

I'm looking for someone who's the polar opposite of my ex-wife.

But Ben didn't say that.

His answer was just one word. It wasn't *love*, which Jaz claims everyone on InTune is looking for. Nor was Ben's answer *fun* or *marriage* or *you* or any of the pithy answers she'd seen on other profiles.

No, Ben was simply looking for *happiness*.

Well, who the hell isn't?

We had that once. We were so damned happy, Ben . . .

How dare you look for that again, with someone else? How dare you assume that you can find it, keep it? How dare you tell a stranger—a world full of strangers—about our lost child?

Gaby's elevator arrives, jerking her back to reality, back to the present and the immediate future. She steps on and rides down to the lobby with a couple of silent business-men and a group of young secretaries from an upper floor. They're laughing and chatting, on their way to a party.

For them, the night is full of promise.

For her . . .

Who knows? Maybe this will turn out to be fun, she tells herself as she pushes through the revolving door onto the street. If nothing else, at least it's a step in the right direction.

He'd arranged to meet her in the bar area of Tequila Sam's at seven.

He arrives at seven-eighteen, having spent the past hour nursing a draft beer at a dive around the corner.

He's learned that here in New York no woman bats an eye if you're fifteen or twenty minutes late. Twenty-five minutes, half an hour—then she might get cranky. But losing twenty minutes to mass transit problems is entirely plausible.

Most women arrive early. By the time he gets there, she'll have already bought, consumed, and paid for—because the bar at his favorite Mexican restaurant will be too crowded to run a tab—a drink. Maybe even two drinks. If he doesn't like what he sees, he leaves, goes straight home, and deletes his latest profile. She'll never find him again.

If he does like what he sees, he introduces himself and suggests that they go straight to the table, since the reservation is for seven-thirty.

The benefit to this trick—aside from the obvious, sparing his wallet a pricey bar tab—is that she'll be relieved when he finally shows up, having almost convinced herself he was going to stand her up. She'll also be liquored up enough to be relaxed when they sit down at the table and for obligatory getting-to-know-you BS.

He'll order a bottle of Spanish wine with dinner—not the cheapest one on the menu, but the second cheapest—and he'll sip one glass slowly while she drains hers and the waiter refills it. By the time they've shared dessert, she'll often agree to a nightcap nearby—or even invite him back to her place.

Most women would never agree to come to his. Not on a

first date, not with a stranger. Which is, of course, even more
to his advantage, because the Upper West Side apartment he
mentioned in his profile—the one in a historic prewar building, with a Hudson River view—doesn't exist, any more
than "Nick Santana" exists.

The bar is crowded tonight as he makes his way through,
looking for his date. She said she'd be wearing a red dress,
having read in his profile that it's his favorite color.

It isn't.

His favorite color is black, but when he wrote that in a past
profile, he found it tended to attract artsy, depressing women.

Live and learn, right?

Shouldering through crowds of boisterous white-collar
professionals who linger on, having taken advantage of the
happy hour two-for-one drink specials and free bar food,
he spots her at the far end. She's standing beside a high-top
table not far from the three-deep bar, holding a glass that's
half empty—or half full, depending on how you look at it.

Unlike the other women here who are noticeably alone,
she's not busy with her phone, or looking around wistfully.
She just seems to be waiting; expectant, but comfortable.

She's tall—taller than him, probably. She has long dark
hair and attractive facial features. Attractive features below
the face, too: plenty of curves, shown off by a crimson dress
with a plunging neckline. Just like her profile promised,
which is unusual. Too many times, self-professed "curvy"
women turn out to be downright porcine, having posted old
or doctored photos of themselves.

Skinny women turn him off. He likes curves. The healthy
kind, like this. But you don't dare advertise that it's what
you're looking for, because you'll be inundated with mor-
bidly obese lonely hearts.

Again, live and learn.

Pleased with what he sees from a distance, he hurries
over to her. "Sofia?"

She nods, extends her right hand. "Nick?"

"That's me. Nick Santana." *For tonight, anyway.*

The bar is dimly lit. Up close he can see that she's older than he thought. And her curves appear to be more toned and muscular than soft.

With a strong handshake, she says, "Nice to meet you."

"You, too. I'm so sorry I'm late. I hope you didn't think I was going to stand you up. There was track work on the downtown express." Blame it on the MTA, as always.

She shrugs and says nothing, flicking her gaze over him from head to toe as though sizing him up. She's probably comparing him to his profile photo, the red sweater one from several Christmases ago.

Uncomfortable, he points to his watch, a convincing Gucci knockoff. "We might as well go straight to the table."

"Oh, not yet."

"I have a seven-thirty reservation."

"It's all right. I already spoke to the maitre d'. They'll hold the table so that we can have our drinks first."

Caught off guard, he protests, "That's okay, I don't—"

"I got you a Bourbon and water."

That stops him in his tracks. *She* bought *him* a drink?

She reaches for a glass filled with brownish-gold liquid and slides it along the high-top table toward him. "It's Maker's Mark—you said you like it, right?"

Pleasantly surprised, he nods. He probably did say that. He said a lot of things in the private messages they've been sending back and forth for a few weeks now, ever since she first reached out to him. It's nice to know she was paying such close attention.

"Thank you. What are you drinking?" he asks her, and feels obliged to add, "Can I get you a refill?"

"Vodka tonic. And no, thank you, this is my second."

Vodka tonic. A nice surprise. Most women go for the watered-down margaritas.

She lifts her own glass—half full, he decides—in a toast. "Here's to tonight," she says simply.

He grins and clinks his drink against hers. "To tonight."

Gaby is surprised—not pleasantly—to find that her blind date, Ryan Hunter, is even more handsome than he appeared to be in his profile photograph, and even more nice and normal than he came across in their correspondence.

On the way over to the bistro from the office—including a quick stop in the restroom at Grand Central Terminal, where she'd applied makeup to her other eye—she'd convinced herself that he was going to turn out to be a loser. In that case, she figured she could call it an early night, inform her cousin that this online dating stuff isn't for her, and delete herself from the InTune Web site.

Tried it, hated it, case closed.

That would have been easy.

This—sitting across a small table from a man who's not only handsome, but polite, witty, and utterly appealing—is complicated. Five minutes into the date she's already wondering what she'll do if he wants to see her again.

She should, of course, *want* him to want to see her again.

She should want to see him again.

But somehow Ben has worked his way into the back of her mind and refuses to budge. Probably because seeing Kasey in the ladies' room back at the office reminded her of their loss.

Ben is the only other person in the world who knows what it was like to be Josh's parent—and to lose him. At least when he was in her life, there was someone who shared her grief.

This man, this stranger, Ryan Hunter—he'll never share that. He'll never understand her. So why bother?

"Do you want red wine, or white?" he asks, studying the list the waiter left on the table in a skinny leather binder.

"Either is fine."

"How about white? A sauvignon blanc?"

"Sure," she says, though her favorite is red. Malbec. Ben would have known that without being told. She's too shy to tell Ryan.

He motions the waiter over.

She watches him order the wine, admiring his dark good looks, the expensive cut of his suit, the easygoing banter as he and the waiter discuss his choice. He doesn't pretend to be sophisticated, isn't trying to impress her or the waiter with his knowledge of wine.

He's a good guy. A nice, normal guy. He could have been a jerk, a loser—a serial killer, for that matter. She'd taken the precaution of telling Jaz exactly where she was going tonight, and with whom.

She'd read that advice this afternoon in an article about online dating. Nothing like being reminded, at the eleventh hour, that the Internet is crawling with dangerous predators.

Luckily, Ryan doesn't seem to be one of them.

She feels herself relax, just a little bit, as the waiter leaves, and Ryan smiles at her. He has a nice smile.

"I love this place," he tells her. "Great wine list, great food, great service."

"You've been here before?"

"Many times." He doesn't elaborate, leaving her to wonder if he's come with other women.

Probably.

Should she care?

Is Ben on a date right now with a woman who's wondering or asking about his ex-wife?

"So you're an editor?" Ryan props his elbows on the table, laces his fingers together and rests his chin on them as though he's really interested in her work. "What kind of books? Fiction?"

"Yes."

"Anything I'd enjoy?"

"That depends on what you like to read."

"Novels. No particular genre. I like just about anything as long as the characters are strong and the plot isn't convoluted," he adds.

Well, naturally, she finds herself thinking. Who enjoys weak characters and convoluted plots?

Ryan claimed to be an avid reader in his online profile and listed an eclectic mix of favorite authors, but that doesn't mean he'd actually read them.

For all they had in common, Ben was never much of a reader. Early in their relationship she tried to get him interested in whatever novel she was passionate about at the time. He would gamely read a few pages and then hand it back, saying he couldn't get into it.

He balked when she was pregnant and longing to name the baby after one of her favorite literary characters. She suggested Heathcliff for a boy, or Hermione for a girl.

"Herman?" He lit up.

"Hermione," she repeated. "For a girl."

"What kind of name is that?"

"It's from Harry Potter."

He shook his head. "I like Herman a lot better."

"For a *girl*?"

"If you want."

"I *don't* want! For a girl *or* for a boy."

"It's Babe Ruth's middle name."

"I don't care. There's no way we're naming our son Herman."

"Well, there's no way we're naming our son Heathcliff," he countered. "The kids will tease him."

"They won't tease Herman? Anyway, we can call him Heath, or Cliff—"

"Or a regular name."

"Like?"

"Like—I don't know—Josh or something. Josh is a good name."

It *was* a good name. A great name. Maybe even better than Heathcliff, although Ben almost, *almost* gave in to that during her grueling labor. As a compromise, he agreed to consider a literary name for their next child, and even promised to read Emily Brontë and J.K. Rowling for inspiration. Of course, he never did.

It might be nice, Gaby tells herself now, to be in a relationship with a fellow bibliophile.

Then again, Ryan might just be feigning interest.

Right. The way you did when he was talking about last night's ball game?

It's not that she doesn't like baseball. She grew up watching the Yankees in the Bronx; she's just not a fanatic like Ben.

Ryan roots for the Yankees' archrivals, the Red Sox. He might live in New York, he told her, but he's technically from New England—the Connecticut suburbs.

Greenwich, he mentioned—but only when she asked where. He wasn't trying to brag.

Still, "Greenwich" speaks volumes. Ben's friend Peter had been married to a woman who'd grown up there. Gaby attended her wedding shower at a bridesmaid's stately mansion set behind brick walls, the couple's engagement party at a bigger, better stately mansion set behind brick walls *and* a guard house, and of course the wedding itself at a fancy country club.

To his credit, Ryan doesn't mention whether his family is part of the polo-playing, yachting set, but it's safe to assume they're at least fairly well off. Not that it matters to Gaby.

"What are you working on now?" he asks, and she tells him briefly about the manuscript she's editing, a cold war spy thriller set in the United States.

At least, she intended to be brief. But he has questions. Intelligent ones.

He in turn tells her about the book he just finished read-ing, a historical mystery that's currently sitting atop the vast to-be-read pile on her nightstand.

Convinced he wasn't just showing polite interest in her literary world, she relaxes a little bit more and asks him what else he's read recently.

Talking about books, sipping cold white wine, nibbling a piece of nutty whole grain bread from the basket on the table, Gaby finds herself firmly pushing Ben to the back of her mind every time he tries to intrude.

Tonight is about forgetting, not remembering. It's about the future, not the past.

It's about her, and about Ryan; about giving him a chance; about daring to believe that if she found happiness once, she might actually find it again.

It's no accident that the woman seated across the table from Ben Duran looks nothing like Gabriela.

He'd chosen the petite blonde for that very reason.

When he first joined InTune, he'd found himself gravitat-ing toward tall, shapely brunettes, preferably those who, like him—and like Gabriela—had at least a splash of Hispanic blood running through their veins.

Women like that turned out to be plentiful on the dating Web site. Online, they seemed exactly right for Ben. In person, they were all wrong.

Either they were too outgoing or not outgoing enough, too affectionate or not affectionate enough, too intellectual or not intellectual enough . . .

In short, they weren't Gabriela.

But of course he didn't realize that was the problem until his friend Peter—long-divorced and an online dating veteran—pointed it out to him.

"You're supposed to be trying to meet someone new and move on, son." Peter always called him—called everyone—

son. "You're not supposed to be recapturing what you had with Gaby. That's not possible."

Yeah. No kidding.

He'd tried. He really had. Tried hard to reach her during the last year of their marriage. He was convinced the real Gaby, the woman he loved, was still there, hidden away behind the emotional barrier she'd constructed after they lost their son.

But he couldn't permeate those walls. Finally, he concluded that the only way to lure her out was to leave, hoping she'd be shaken enough to come after him.

She didn't.

Ben wasn't accustomed to failure.

He'd done everything within his power to avoid it. He'd excelled in high school, both in sports—he ran track and was captain of the swim team—and academically. He'd won acceptance, with partial scholarships, to M.I.T. He worked his way through, emerged with an engineering degree, and left Co-op City behind for good, landing a structural engineering job and his own apartment a few miles—and a world—away in Manhattan.

He fell in love with and married the woman of his dreams, moved to a bigger, better home where they could raise a family, had a son . . .

Lost it all. Everything that mattered.

Gradually, he's rebuilt his life. But it hasn't been easy—and he sure as hell doesn't want to spend the duration on a self-imposed exile. Not after watching his widowed father make that mistake, consumed by grief and misery.

Ben found that the dating scene had changed drastically since he was last single in the city. Back then you counted on meeting other eligible singles at parties and in bars. Now everyone seems to be making those connections online, and Peter convinced him to give it a try.

After dating several women whose profiles reminded him

of his ex-wife, Ben took Peter's advice and shifted gears. Essentially, that's meant looking for women who aren't his type.

Women like Camilla, who's sitting across the table from him tonight. She's sipping a cosmopolitan—served, as is tradition, in a martini glass—through a straw.

"I don't like to drink out of a glass when I'm wearing lipstick," she explained to the waiter and to Ben when she asked for the straw.

They both nodded, as if it made sense.

Maybe it did to the waiter.

For his part, Ben decided she was wearing too much of that pink lipstick in the first place. Too much eyeliner, too, and too much perfume . . . too much everything. Except clothing.

She has on a skimpy little black dress that was probably meant to entice him but just shows that much more of her fake tan and skeletal body. The more flattering description she used to describe herself on her Web site was "svelte," but to Ben, she's just plain scrawny. There's nothing wrong with that, per se. Some men probably appreciate a female figure that's not particularly—well, feminine.

Ben has always preferred flesh to bone, curves to angles.

Camilla takes one last sip from the straw, leaving a slick pink smudge at the top, and pushes away her empty glass with a jangling of bracelets. "That was yummy."

"Do you want to order another one?"

He expects her to decline. Their meals are on the way.

"Are you twisting my arm, Ben?"

"Nah, I'd never do that," he assures her. *No, because it would snap like a twig.*

"Well, it *is* the weekend. Why not? TGIF, right?"

"Sure. Right." Ben signals the waiter.

"Another round, sir?"

"No, I'm fine. Just the cosmopolitan."

The waiter walks away, and Ben sips his beer as Camilla goes back to the long, involved story she'd been telling him earlier—one he'd hoped she'd forget she was telling.

Something about her sister—or maybe her roommate?— and a dog—or a cat—named Foo Foo. Every time she says the name, she punctuates it with a tipsy giggle.

As first dates go, this isn't the worst he's had since the divorce, but it's not exactly the best, either.

Sometimes it takes longer for him to figure out that he has no intention of ever seeing the woman again. This time it was almost instantaneous.

Which means that at the end of the night, he'll have to figure out whether to come right out and say that to her, or let her think he'll be in touch.

He's always believed honesty is the best policy. He doesn't necessarily believe that anymore. Not when it comes to dating. Not after having had one woman burst into tears when he told her he didn't think they were compatible, while another lashed out at him in a screeching, angry tirade on the street in front of the restaurant.

Sometimes he wonders why he's even doing this at all. Meeting strangers online, asking them out . . .

"You're a single guy. It's what you do," Peter told him. "Unless you want to be a recluse."

No. He doesn't want that.

That's what happened to his father after his mother died of a fast-growing cancer about ten years ago, not long after their retirement.

Pop used to be a vital, interesting guy. Plenty of friends, and an active social life that revolved around their sizable, vibrant Puerto Rican family . . .

"They're all couples," he said when Ben urged him to accept invitations to dinner and parties. "They don't need me hanging around."

"They care about you, Pop."

"That's fine. They can care. But nobody wants to be a third wheel."

"You're not a—"

"Benito. Stop. Leave it alone."

What Pop meant was *Leave me alone*.

Ben's brother had done just that, and tried to convince him to do the same.

"He's a stubborn old man. He's been a stubborn old man since he was *young*. Why try to change him now?"

"I'm not trying to change him. I'm trying to encourage him to keep things the way they've always been. He's always had people around him."

"Yes, because Mom was a people person. He wasn't. All he ever needed was her."

It was true, Ben realized. He'd never thought about it before. Looking back at the way his parents behaved in social situations, he remembered that his extroverted mother could work a room like nobody's business. Pop mostly stayed by her side, focusing on her while she focused on socializing.

"Now that she's gone, Pop doesn't need anyone," his brother said. "Just let him be."

"Let him be? You want me to wash my hands of him? Is that what you're planning to do?"

"Of course not. We'll both check in on him, visit him— but we can't drag him out and force him to live again. It's never going to happen."

Ben realized his brother was right.

It was Gaby who wouldn't let him give up. She never stopped trying to coax Pop back to the land of the living.

Ironic in so many ways . . .

Years after he stopped living, Pop finally died of a heart attack. He was alone in the apartment, of course. It happened not long before Gaby got pregnant with Josh. She was the one who found him that morning when she stopped by to drop off some homemade meals.

Pop never met his grandson. But Ben's devout Catholic mother had instilled a firm believe in the afterlife, and he found comfort in the fact that his parents were waiting to greet Josh in heaven.

Gaby took no comfort in that; no comfort in anything he or anyone else had to offer. She cried about Josh being alone and afraid in a cold, dark place. She lost her grasp on her own faith and retreated into grim isolation after losing their son, much as Ben's father had after losing his wife.

Well, that's not going to happen to me. I'm not spending the rest of my days alone and miserable.

The waiter arrives at the table with the second cosmopolitan on a tray, trailed by a busboy with their salads.

Camilla puts a straw into the fresh drink and lifts the glass toward him. "Cheers."

"What are we drinking to?"

"To us."

He obliges, echoing her toast though he knows there will never be an *us* that involves the two of them.

But somewhere out there—in this vast city, or in cyberspace—there might be a woman he will eventually love the way he loved his wife. Sooner or later he's hoping to find her. He just has to keep on looking.

"Okay, you have *got* to try this." Ryan holds out a forkful of warm apple tart, topped by a dollop of vanilla bean ice cream. "It's amazing."

Gaby leans over to taste it and nods. "It *is* amazing."

"Here—share the rest with me." Ryan slides the dessert plate toward her, but she shakes her head.

"I'm so full. I can't eat another bite."

"Sure you can."

"Well . . . maybe one more. Or two . . ."

He laughs as she lifts another forkful to her mouth. "I love a woman who loves to eat."

The apple confection turns mealy and sour in her mouth. She forces herself to swallow it, puts her fork down, sips the herbal tea she ordered in lieu of her own dessert.

Ryan is oblivious, dredging another wedge of tart through the rapidly melting ice cream on his dish and telling her about the pies his mom used to bake after they all went apple picking in the fall when he was a kid. He painted such a cozy scene that Gaby was willing to forgive him for consistently referring to Greenwich as if it were some far-flung New England town. It might lie within those geographical boundaries, but really, it's a New York suburb largely populated by wealthy white-collar commuters.

Until now she's been having a great time with him, but . . .

I love a woman who loves to eat.

Ben said those same words—or something very similar—on their first date years ago. They'd gone to a twenty-four-hour diner at four in the morning after a night out on the town. It was Labor Day weekend, early September, but August's swampy heat lingered in the air.

He'd ordered a BLT. She'd ordered half a roast chicken, which came with soup and salad, her choice of two sides—she got the mashed potatoes and string beans—and a Jell-O square for dessert.

"What?" she asked, seeing the look on Ben's face after the waiter who'd taken their order walked away. "Aren't you starving after all that dancing?"

Ben teased her about it for the rest of the night. Well, morning. After the diner, they went to the beach to watch the sunrise. In fact, he teased her about her appetite for years afterward, especially when she was pregnant and insatiable.

I love a woman who loves to eat . . .

"You haven't taken your second bite," Ryan tells Gaby.

"I really am stuffed." She sets down her fork.

"You know what? So am I. How about if we go walk off some of this food? It's a nice night. We could head down toward the Village, see a late movie or stop off someplace for a glass of wine . . ."

She looks at her watch, pretending to calmly contemplate that idea as her mind screams, *No way!*

"It's almost ten. I'd better not," she tells him, hoping she sounds sufficiently reluctant to say no. "I have an early morning tomorrow."

"On a Saturday?"

"I have to work—you know, at home. Still trying to catch up after the long weekend. And being outside wouldn't be good for my allergies, with all the pollen in the air right now. You know . . . the trees are in bloom . . ."

"We don't have to walk. We can take a cab."

"No, really. I should get home."

"You sure?"

"Positive," she says, although suddenly she isn't.

Can she take it back?

Why not walk to the Village on a warm, beautiful night and have a glass of wine?

Ryan is a great guy. She's just spent the last couple of hours laughing and talking with him. She never mentioned her marriage, and he—also divorced—didn't mention his. Naturally, she didn't tell him she'd had—and lost—a child. For a little while she'd actually forgotten that, too.

"Next time, then," Ryan says with a shrug.

"Next time," she agrees.

Maybe it's guilt that makes her stick with the lie about having to work in the morning. Maybe it's fear.

Five minutes later they're out on the street. She's planning to take the subway uptown, but Ryan insists on putting her into a cab. They're plentiful, eliminating the need to prolong the date a moment longer.

"I had a good time," he says, leaning in the open back seat window after handing the driver a twenty. "I hope you did, too."

"I did."

"We'll do it again."

"We will," she agrees.

As the cab races away up Tenth Avenue, she refuses to allow herself to look over her shoulder.

You did it, she tells herself, leaning her head back against the seat and closing her eyes. *You met a stranger, and he turned out to be halfway decent.*

Halfway decent?

Ryan Hunter is exactly the kind of man she should be looking for—and she'd actually found him online.

So she was wrong. Jaz was right.

But I'm not admitting that to her, Gaby thinks, as the cab speeds toward her apartment sixty blocks north. *Not yet, anyway.*

Steering the BMW out of the parking garage conveniently located just across the street from Tequila Sam's, Alex gives a friendly wave to the attendant.

The kid, who has oversized bushy sideburns, perhaps in an unsuccessful effort to mask the acne scars on his cheeks, can't be more than nineteen or twenty. He nods and smiles back, undoubtedly pleased with the extralarge tip he just pocketed for lending a helping hand with the passenger's-side door—not to mention the passenger.

"My date had a little too much to drink, unfortunately," Alex had explained while fishing for the receipt. "Right, sweetie?"

The response was too slurred to make out.

"Yo, want to sit down?" the attendant had asked, and offered a chair before disappearing up the ramp to retrieve the car. By the time he came back, Alex had no choice but to ask for a helping hand.

"Looks like your friend here is down for the count, huh?"

"Looks that way."

"How about you? Are you all right to drive?"

"Me? I'm fine. All I've had is seltzer." Seltzer with a wedge of lime—masquerading as a vodka tonic.

Now, heading north up Tenth Avenue, then making a left toward the West Side Highway, Alex glances over.

Still out cold.

That's fine.

Better than fine.

"You can rest all the way home," Alex says, reaching for the radio knob. "Don't worry. I'll take good care of you."

Electric guitar fills the car. AC/DC's *Back in Black*. Nice.

"How's that? Good? You did write on your profile that you enjoy classic rock," Alex tells her passenger, with a small smile. "We have so much in common, don't we?"

Nick Santana, passed out in the passenger seat courtesy of the Rohypnol she dumped into his Maker's Mark before he got there, doesn't respond.

Chapter 4

June heat shimmers in waves on the pavement this evening as Gabriela steps out of her building's lobby. It's not even summer yet, according to the calendar, but already the city is in the throes of its first official heat wave.

Upstairs in the refrigerated air of her office, she needed a cardigan all day. Now, as the full impact of the sidewalk steam bath hits her, she hastily takes it off and tucks it into her tote bag, wondering if she should run back up and leave it on the back of her door. There's no way she's going to need it at Yankee Stadium tonight.

But, checking her watch, she realizes she doesn't have time to go back up. She's meeting Ryan in ten minutes.

As she heads down the block and turns south on Madison Avenue toward Grand Central Terminal, she finds that she's looking forward to spending this June evening—hot or not—at the ballpark with Ryan.

She really wasn't even sure she'd ever see him again after her skittish exit from their first date. But he texted her to make sure she'd gotten home all right, and called a few days later. He waited just long enough for her to assume she'd heard the last of him; just long enough for her to be too caught off guard to come up with a reason why she couldn't go out with him again.

They've had a couple of dates since. First, he took her out to dinner again; the second time, to a Broadway play. The more time she spent with him, the more she found herself forgetting the past—at least for a few hours. He was fun, and funny—not to mention sweet, and sexy.

Realizing he was about to kiss her good-night after their second date, she forced herself to close her eyes and let it happen.

She'd expected it to feel all wrong: kissing someone other than Ben. But somehow it didn't.

Maybe because it's been so long since she and Ben had actually even kissed in a romantic way.

They'd tried—and failed—to regain their passion after Josh died.

Well, Ben had tried. Semblances of normalcy were important to him. That felt wrong to her, but her therapist told her that everyone's journey through grief and healing is individual. It's not fair to judge. And their marriage counselor had encouraged her to open herself up to her husband not just emotionally, but physically. She found it impossible to do either.

Looking back, Gaby sometimes wonders if she'd made any real effort at all. Maybe not. Numb with grief, she never imagined her heart could be capable of feeling anything ever again—for Ben or anyone else.

But Ryan kissed her and it was okay. More than okay. The second time he leaned in, she didn't hesitate to wrap her arms around him and kiss him back.

Since then, slowly but surely, she's been coming alive again.

Sleeping Beauty stirring back to life. That's the analogy Jaz chose to use.

"You and your fairy tales." Gaby rolled her eyes at her cousin.

"You're the one who got me into them in the first place, when we were little kids, remember?"

She remembers. Jaz was a reluctant reader, Gaby an avid bookworm. She started reading stories aloud to her cousin from a book of fairy tales, drawing her into the story and then leaving off at a pivotal point. Thus, a curious Jaz was forced to keep reading herself if she wanted to find out what happened.

"You're Sleeping Beauty," Jaz insisted, "and Ryan is your handsome prince, and now you're alive again."

When she saw Dr. Milford yesterday, the therapist noticed right away that her mood had brightened.

"I've never seen you this chipper, Gabriela," she said. "What's changed?"

"Not much, really," she said, but as she began to talk about what had gone on since her last appointment, she realized that quite a bit had changed. Good things had been happening for her.

Last week, a debut novel she acquired—against the executive editor's better judgment, albeit with her eventual blessing—hit the *New York Times* best-seller list. Anne and a couple of the other editors—Kasey not included—took her out to dinner to celebrate.

Another day, heading to the subway after work, she spontaneously ducked into Saks Fifth Avenue to get out of a sudden thunderstorm and found the store in the midst of a tremendous clearance sale. She bought three designer dresses she'd never have been able to afford otherwise.

"Amazing what a new outfit can do to improve your outlook," Dr. Milford said with a smile.

Gaby told her that her allergies have improved lately, too, now that spring is finally giving way to summer. No more daily sinus headaches. After two weeks of endless rain that served to wash away all that pollen, the sun has been shining against a brilliant blue sky for the last few days.

And then there was Ryan. When she told Dr. Milford

she'd met someone and gone out on a couple of dates, the woman nodded her approval.

"I'm not jumping into another full-blown relationship or anything, though," Gaby hastened to tell her.

"No, of course you're not. You're just having fun."

"I am," she realized. "I'm having fun."

"It's about time. And you deserve it, Gabriela."

Yes, she does.

And so later last night, when Ryan texted her to ask if she was busy tonight—a weeknight—she almost breezily wrote back *I'm free!*

Great! Just got 2 seats behind home plate—Red Sox/ Yankees.

Maybe she did have an uncomfortable little twinge when she saw that, thinking of Ben. He'd never call it the Red Sox/ Yankees game; it would be the other way around.

Yankees/Red Sox.

How well she remembers his enthusiasm for the century-old archrivalry, remembers how much he loved to hate the Sox.

He'd probably hate Ryan as well.

Too bad. She's happy for a change. Maybe just fleetingly; maybe she doesn't know where they're headed, but she won't let herself worry about that. For the first time in ages, she's living in the present.

Naturally, Jaz has been thrilled with this turn of events. It seems like every other sentence out of her mouth is a variation of "I told you so" or "Does he have a friend for me?"

Never married, with her thirtieth birthday looming in August, Jaz has been even more determined lately to find Mr. Right.

Or maybe *determined* isn't quite the right word. *Desperate* seems more accurate. At her most dramatic, Jaz is convinced she'll wind up a *jamona* like their spinster great-aunt Ula.

Gaby told her she couldn't possibly fix her up with one of Ryan's friends. Not at this stage, anyway.

"Why not?"

"Because . . . it's not like we're a couple."

"Maybe not yet. But you're on your way. And there's nothing wrong with sniffing around to see if maybe he has someone nice for your favorite cousin."

"I thought you were into meeting guys the old-fashioned way—online."

"Hey, I'm open to anything, *mami*. Aren't you glad you were, too?"

Yes. She's glad. Yes, it's nice to be dating someone, but really, it's about having turned a corner at last—a sharp corner—on the road to healing.

Having reached 47th Street, she falls in with the throng of commuters streaming into Grand Central Terminal's northern passage entrance.

There was a time, after Josh was born, when she couldn't imagine herself ever being a part of the professional rat race again. She'd negotiated a part-time work-at-home editorial consulting schedule after her maternity leave ended, and she and Ben had discussed her eventually phasing out her career altogether in favor of full-time motherhood. Instead . . .

Instead.

After the unthinkable happened, she got her job back. Full-time. In the office. Her boss offered her the option of continuing to work at home: *Whatever you need, Gabriela. Whatever makes it easier.*

Being at home didn't make it easier. Nothing made it easier. And she couldn't bear to be in that apartment any longer.

Stop. Don't think about that.

At the bottom of the long escalator, she makes her way quickly through the air-conditioned network of tunnels to the main concourse.

The vast open area is a sea of striding New Yorkers and gawking, photo-snapping tourists who—oblivious to the rhythms of rush-hour Manhattan—wander into the purposeful paths of impatient, exhausted commuters rushing for trains home to their Westchester or Connecticut suburbs. Tonight there are baseball fans in the mix as well, most of them wearing Yankees gear and heading for the Metro North and subway lines that will carry them to the stadium in the Bronx, just a stone's throw from Abuela's apartment where Gaby had grown up.

When Ryan texted Gaby to meet him here "by the clock," she didn't have to ask for clarification. The information booth, topped by an enormous brass clock, is the quintessential meeting place for New Yorkers. She used to meet friends here back in high school and college, and later she'd meet Ben . . .

But it's Ryan, not Ben, who's waiting for her by the clock tonight. Still in his suit and tie, he's intently typing on his phone as she walks toward him, and doesn't see her.

She wonders whether he's catching up on work e-mail or maybe just texting with a friend. She touches his arm and he looks up.

"Hey!" He smiles, quickly tucking his phone away without bothering to finish what he was doing, and gives her a hug. "How are you?"

"I'm great," she says truthfully, and together they head for the train.

"You owe me big for this," Ben's brother, Luis, tells him as they settle into their prime seats—courtesy of Luis's boss—to watch batting practice.

"What? *You* owed *me* big for helping you carry that old TV down three flights of stairs last month."

"No, you did that because I helped you move last fall, remember?"

"*After* I walked Budgie and Paris for a week in September while you and Ada went to Vieques for a second honeymoon." Ben doesn't bother to remind him that Budgie and Paris are the yappiest, crappiest—literally—dogs in New York. Luis knows that better than anyone. The family pets have been a bone of marital contention between him and Ada for years.

Then again, so have their twin daughters—and just about everything else.

His brother's marriage has always been volatile, though things improved after Bettina and Marisol went off to college last August—ironically, right around the time Ben's own marriage was dying a final death.

"It wasn't a second honeymoon," Luis points out. "It was our only honeymoon. We couldn't afford one twenty years ago. We couldn't afford it now, but I always promised Ada we'd do it as soon as the girls left. Too bad she's not a baseball fan. I could have promised her a game in these seats instead."

"They probably cost more than your week in Vieques. Here's to your boss." Ben lifts his plastic cupful of beer in a toast. "Anyway, looks like you and I are even now, so—"

"What? Bro, field level corporate seats behind home plate for the Yankees/Red Sox doesn't make us even. It makes you—" Luis breaks off, staring wide-eyed at something other than the players on the field.

"What?" Ben follows his gaze to the crowd filing into the rows ahead of theirs, down to the right.

"Nothing, I just thought . . ." Luis shakes his head. "Never mind. What was I saying?"

"You were saying we need some better pitching, same thing you say every game, every season."

"Because it's true. It's always true. But I mean after I said that— Oh, yeah. I was saying you owe me, big-time, for inviting you to come tonight."

"Yeah, guess I do. Thanks, Luis." Ben grins, takes a sip of cold beer, and settles back to watch batting practice.

Nick Santana's real name is Carlos Diaz.

Alex discovered that—among other things—when she went through his wallet that first night, while he was still passed out in the front seat of her car.

Carlos—three letters away from Carmen. A very good sign. Maybe an omen.

Carlos Diaz. There must be dozens—maybe hundreds—of other guys with that name in New York alone.

Is that why he decided to change it to Nick Santana? Was he merely trying to be unique? He could have done a better job with that.

Or was it a discretionary move, covering his tracks on the dating site?

Alex wondered at first whether he might be married.

It doesn't really matter in the long run. But things would certainly be easier if he were single. That way, there was less chance anyone would be waiting for him to come home that night.

After going through his wallet, she carefully replaced it in his pocket and turned her attention to the other belongings he was carrying.

There was a small prescription medication vial containing a couple of pills she later identified as SSRNs—antidepressants. She confiscated those. The only medication she wants him taking is what she gives him—with or without his knowledge.

And then there was his cell phone.

A little targeted snooping through his texts, e-mails, and contact lists told her that he was most likely single, as he'd claimed. But you never know.

She also figured out that he's no architect, doesn't live on the Upper West Side, and isn't a mere thirty-one years old—

though he might have been when he posed for that photo he used on his InTune profile, the one where he's standing in front of the Christmas tree wearing a red sweater.

He lied on his profile. Does it matter?

If she were looking for a romantic hero, it might. But the love of her life has already come and gone.

Now she needs a man for only one thing. A man with very specific qualifications.

Nick—Carlos—may not be an architect, as he'd claimed, but he does work for a construction company. She doesn't know exactly what he does there. But when they met that night in the bar, he told her that building is in his blood, and she believed him. She could hear the passion in his voice. That's what counts.

I'll bet you used to love to play with Legos when you were a little boy, she wrote in one of their message exchanges before they met.

How did you know?

Wild guess.

Yet another thing she could check off her list.

She brought up music in another online exchange, and he warmed to that subject, too. He'd been to many of the same classic rock festivals she'd attended; even plays the electric guitar.

Are you good? she asked.

I could have been. Didn't have the money for lessons. But I played in a band for a while. I wasn't bad. Had some groupies, he claimed.

Perfect. He was—*is*—perfect.

As for the details that don't match up, now that she's met him in person . . .

Minor business. Who cares that he really lives in Queens and is much closer to forty years old than he is to thirty?

What counts is that he has the right look, the right interests, the right *blood*.

It's all about the blood.

When she asked about his family background, he wrote that his mother is Costa Rican, his father Dominican.

Where are they now? she asked, hoping they're not too close—or that he doesn't, God forbid, live with them.

Costa Rica, was the reply.

On vacation?

No, they've been living there since they retired.

Good. Realizing he fit the bill, she arranged to meet him for a date.

From there, everything went according to plan.

Before Carlos regained consciousness, Alex used his phone to check out the last few people he'd contacted.

He'd exchanged texts with someone named Roberto—his brother, most likely, because Roberto wrote to say that Carlos should: *give Mom a call or text her—she keeps saying she hasn't heard from u lately.*

Carlos had responded simply: *Ok, I will.*

Then came a text dutifully sent to "Mom" and written in Spanish: *Te extraño. Cómo estás?*

Alex, having picked up enough Spanish over the years, was able to translate: *I miss you. How are you?*

Mom wrote back promptly: *Somos grandes! Tan contento de tener noticias de usted. Cómo es su trabajo?*

Translation: *We are great! So happy to hear from you. How is work?*

Carlos responded: *He estado ocupado. Son los dos que te diviertas en CR?*

Translation: *I've been busy. Are the two of you having fun in CR?*

Based on what he'd told Alex, CR meant Costa Rica. So at least he'd been honest, too, about his family background.

The mother-son text exchange went on with a bit more small talk, Carlos promising to be in touch again soon and telling his mother to *Dale mi amor a P.*

Give my love to P.

P, undoubtedly, was short for Pop or Papi or whatever he called his father.

Now, Alex used Carlos's phone to send a new text to Mom: *Me tengo que ir en un viaje de negocios y estará ausente una semana. Hablaré contigo cuando vuelva!*

She sent the same thing in English to Roberto: *I have to leave on a business trip and will be gone about a week. Talk to you when I get back.*

Alex then sent an e-mail from Carlos's work account to his supervisor, a woman named Ivy Sacks.

According to the brief conversation she'd had with Carlos—as the macho Nick—in the bar that night, before the medication rendered him a slurring bundle of incohérence, his female boss had more than just a professional interest in him.

Maybe that was true. Maybe, like so many other things he told her, it was a lie.

Either way, Alex carefully worded the e-mail telling Carlos's boss that his parents had been in a terrible car accident in Costa Rica. His father had been killed and his mother was in the hospital; he was catching the first flight out and wouldn't be at work next week.

That way, even if Ivy Sacks has a crush on her employee, she won't be sniffing around looking for him right away, trying to pick up his immediate trail while it's still fresh.

Not that it would even be possible, now, for anyone to connect Carlos to Alex. She signed into his InTune account—he'd saved the password for that account, like all the others, on his phone, how convenient!—and deleted "Nick Santana's" entire profile. For good measure she also went into Carlos's Facebook account and disabled that as well. She was pleased to note that Ivy Sacks wasn't listed on his friends' list.

Later, she deleted her own latest profile on InTune. With

the press of a button, "Sofia" evaporated from cyberspace, never to be heard from again.

She kept Carlos's phone and his wallet. If he checked his pockets for them when he woke up, she could always lead him to assume he must have drunkenly dropped them somewhere along the way.

She waited patiently that night in the driver's seat of the BMW until Carlos Diaz—aka Nick Santana—regained consciousness.

When he did, he was understandably bewildered. He didn't bother to check for his phone and wallet, just wanted to know where he was and how he'd gotten here. She explained that he'd suggested they go back to her place, then drunkenly passed out in her car on the way home.

"You mean you don't remember anything?" she asked him incredulously as she led him—on unsteady legs—into the house.

As embarrassed as he was confused, he downplayed the whole thing—especially once they were comfortable on the couch and he sensed what was about to happen.

Seducing him was the easy part.

That first night, anyway.

It always is. After that—after they've settled into her basement guest quarters—it becomes a bit more . . . challenging.

But it must be done.

And she has a foolproof way to get it done.

No reason to get ahead of herself just yet, though.

Now, Alex turns her attention back to the task at hand.

She opens the fast food bag she bought on the way home from her nursing job. She unwraps the double cheeseburger and sets it on a sturdy plastic plate, dumps the french fries beside it, and pours the milk shake into a tall plastic cup.

Then she sets the plate on a tray and adds a vase holding a bouquet of cheerful red flowers.

There. That's a nice, thoughtful little touch. She's not a monster, after all.

She stopped to pick the blooms from the overgrown perennial patch by the back door on her way into the house. The gardens surrounding the house were planted decades ago by former owners, and she doesn't bother to tend them.

Carmen did, when he was here. But as a commercial architect, he traveled often. Once, when Alex was newly pregnant and he was leaving for an entire summer in South America, he said, "All you have to do is pluck the weeds now and then, and water the beds if it doesn't rain for a week."

"Okay. I'll try to remember. But if I forget, don't take it as a sign that I'll be a lousy mother."

"You, *mi amor*, will be a wonderful mother." He'd kissed her on the head, picked up his bag, and headed out the door.

That time, he came back home again.

Alex carries the tray and a flashlight across the kitchen to the basement door, turns on the light and walks down the steps.

She hasn't used the gym equipment in a couple of days. Once she's pregnant, she'll have to stop altogether. It's okay. Strong muscles won't be so important then. She won't need them to carry anything but her precious son.

She walks over to the bookcase, sets the tray on the floor and the flashlight on the tray, removes the books on the far right of the middle shelf, and pulls the latch that allows the bookshelf to swing out toward her.

Then she picks up the tray again, turns on the flashlight, and reaches for the doorknob.

Every evening, the same ritual. It becomes exhausting after a while.

But maybe this will be the last time.

There's another pregnancy test waiting upstairs in the medicine cabinet. The last few were negative, but maybe they were taken too early. This might be the one.

She really hopes so.

Otherwise, she's looking at another month of this. Another month, at least, before it's Carlos Diaz's turn to be lugged into the car trunk, driven upstate, and buried alongside the others.

Halfway through the third inning, Gaby spots him.

Not in person. No, she sees his face on the stadium's enormous Jumbotron as the camera pans the crowd. He's here.

Ben is here.

She forces down the mouthful of Crackerjacks she was crunching when Ryan pointed to the screen and said, "Here comes our section. Look for us."

Ben was only visible for a second or two before the camera swept on past, but it was unmistakably him. Like many other men in the crowd, he was wearing a navy blue cap embroidered with an interlocking white NY logo. He had a pair of sunglasses sitting above the brim the way he often did, and he was sitting with his brother Luis.

His cheeks were stubbly—she's not a fan of stubble—but still, he looked good. Casual and handsome, his skin bronzed as though he's had some beach weekends already this summer.

Ryan literally pales by comparison. He's attractive, too, but not as strikingly handsome as Ben. And he looks a little stiff, still dressed in his work clothes, though he's removed his tie and jacket. He isn't wearing a cap, thank goodness. If he were, it would have a Boston B on it. And if Ben saw that—

"Want some more?" Ryan holds out the bag of Crackerjacks.

"Hmm?"

He shakes the bag. "Crackerjack?"

"Oh. Umm . . . no. No, thanks . . ." Thoughts racing, she fights the urge to turn and scan the crowd sitting behind them, where the camera had focused.

Suddenly, the evening heat feels oppressive. Sweat trickles down the back of her neck and beads her forehead. She clutches the almost empty water bottle in shaky hands, trying to stay focused on the Red Sox batter stepping up to the plate.

Fancy meeting you here . . .

She never did respond to the private message Ben sent her on InTune. Maybe she should take out her phone and type a reply right now using the exact same words.

Fancy meeting you here . . .

Except she doesn't want him to know she's here.

"Swing and a miss," Ryan mutters, reaching into his pocket as a vendor holding a strapped-on box of water bottles ascends the steps toward their section. "I don't know if it's the heat or the Crackerjacks or that big pretzel I ate before the game even started, but I'm dying of thirst. Want another water? Or a beer or something?"

"No, thank you." She, too, is thirsty, but she was already thinking she'd have to visit the ladies' room before the end of the inning. Now that's out of the question.

It's located behind her, and so is Ben's seat. She'll just have to wait until the end of the game. And if that proves impossible . . .

Gaby shifts in her seat as the batter swings and misses again and Ryan opens his fresh water bottle and takes a long drink.

Yes, it's impossible. She suddenly has to go, and badly. But she's trapped.

This is crazy.

What are the odds that this could happen?

Oh, come on . . . the odds are pretty high, actually.

He's a huge fan, goes to plenty of games every season, and this is one of the biggest of the year. Of course he'd want to be here.

"Want some water?" Ryan offers her the bottle.

"No thanks, I . . . I . . ." She's on her feet.

No! Sit down! What are you doing?

Ryan looks up at her, startled. "Are you okay?"

"Yes, I'm going to the ladies' room. I'll be right back."

"Okay." He stands to let her out of the row, as do the other disgruntled fans between her seat and the aisle. She should have waited until the top of the inning gave way to the bottom—or at least until the action was between batters. But it's too late now.

She begins the long climb up the concrete steps, keeping her eyes focused straight ahead.

On the field behind her she hears the crack of a bat hitting a ball, and the crowd erupts. She picks up her pace, scurrying the rest of the way with her head down.

Making it all the way to the ladies' room without running into Ben, she wants to hide there for the rest of the game. The announcers' coverage is piped in. The batter who hit the ball as she left her seat was out on a pop fly; the next struck out. As the top of the inning gives way to the bottom, the ladies' room grows more crowded. Still, she lingers aimlessly at the sink area in front of the mirror, scrubbing her hands, scrubbing again, blotting her sweaty face, blotting again . . . wishing she'd thought to grab her bag so she could at least comb her hair, put on lipstick, find some reason not to make her exit.

Eventually, though, she has to head back out into the stands.

Making her way back out through the throng, she looks for the doorway leading to her section. Seeing a security guard posted there, she remembers that Ryan has her ticket stub; it hadn't occurred to her to grab it. Hopefully the guard won't stop her and ask for proof that she belongs in these premium seats.

He doesn't stop her.

She hurries past him, and then, feeling a hand on her arm, stops short. So he did stop her after all.

No, he didn't.

It's Ben.

"Aren't you going to eat?"

Carlos shakes his head mutely, though his stomach rumbles loudly in protest as he stares at the food on the tray she brought him, illuminated in the flashlight's beam.

Not homemade this time, but fast food. He can tell by the look and smell of it, though she removed it from the wrappers.

"Come on, I know you're hungry."

He is. But that's the least of his worries. Sometimes he does manage to choke down what she brings him, but only when he's utterly weak with hunger or so overcome by thirst that he's willing to take a chance.

So far she hasn't poisoned him.

Not since that first night, anyway.

He should have been suspicious when she handed him that Maker's Mark.

Why, oh why, wasn't he suspicious?

It was because he was so damned appreciative at how the tables had turned, that's why. For a change a woman was buying him a drink! He stupidly guzzled it down without hesitation.

He felt woozy before he'd finished it, but what did he know about good whiskey? He figured it was just the normal effect.

A few more sips, and he decided he'd better stick with the cheap stuff from now on.

That's the last coherent thought he remembers having, along with a vague recollection of stepping outside with her to get some air.

When he came to, it was hours later. Well past midnight. He was in her car, parked in a garage with the door closed.

They were at her place, she said. His idea.

That made sense. That, after all, had been the master plan—to get her wasted and go back to her place. It's always been the plan, with everyone he's dated since the divorce.

Maker's Mark aside, there was no reason for him to be suspicious, or think Sofia—if that's even her real name—was different from any of the others.

She seemed so normal, so appealing. She was such an attractive woman, capable of holding an ordinary conversation just like anyone else. Better, even.

Some women you meet just offer a running monologue about themselves. Not her. In the bar, and then again later in her car that night, both before and after they had sex right there in the backseat, she asked him question after question. She seemed genuinely interested in finding out more about him.

At the time, he thought she was just into him.

It's agonizing to realize that he could have—*should* have—gotten the hell away from her the second she handed him that drink.

He woke up in her bed—with no memory of having gotten there—and stumbled downstairs to find her making him a nice hot breakfast with coffee, black and strong, just the way he likes it. Still . . .

"You have a cat?" he asked her, sickened and irritated by the sight of pet bowls on the floor.

"I do, but I let him out."

"I'm allergic to cats."

"I know you are. I read it in your profile. That's why I let him out."

"What about kids?" he asked, seeing the crayoned art gallery that all but hid the refrigerator.

"No, no kids."

Yeah, he thought. *Sure.*

"Do you take milk in your coffee?"

"No!" he said quickly, though he does. "I don't want coffee."

"Of course you do."

"I have to go." He's not the neatest person in the world, but the thought of eating anything in that house, permeated with the fetid smell of cat food and sour milk, made him sick.

"I know you do. After breakfast. Have a seat."

He tried to beat a hasty retreat—said thanks but no thanks to breakfast and told her he'd find his way to the train station—but then he realized he didn't even have his wallet or phone. She told him he must have lost it at Tequila Sam's.

"They won't be open now, but you should call later and check," she said blandly, cracking eggs into a bowl. "Just relax and get something into your stomach, and after you eat, I'll take you to the train station. I can lend you money for a ticket back to the city."

That seemed reasonable at the time. But as he sat there at her kitchen table sipping the coffee she handed him, watching her fry up an omelet, he began to feel woozy again.

He shouldn't have accepted the coffee. But he was exhausted, needed the caffeine, and it seemed safe enough. Coffee is only hot water strained through ground coffee beans, right? How terrible could it be?

It tasted off to him, but he drank it anyway, telling himself it was simply because it was black. He was used to coffee *con leche.*

But that wasn't it. His head was spinning; the room was spinning. He should have grasped sooner that something was seriously wrong with the coffee. With *her.*

When Carlos came to, he was here, alone in a dark, silent dungeon with shackles around his ankles, chained to the wall.

He has no way of knowing for sure how long he's been

held prisoner here. There are no windows allowing him to keep track of the rhythm of days passing: sunrise, sunset.

There's only pitch-blackness—unless, of course, she's here. She carries a flashlight when she comes, and the bright beam hurts his eyes. It's better to be in the dark; better to be alone.

Then he can lie here and fantasize about the police breaking down the door.

By now someone must have reported him missing.

If only he'd told someone where he was going.

But the divorce hadn't been easy. He had never been so isolated in his life. He hadn't just lost money—not to mention most of his worthwhile possessions, plus his dignity: he'd also lost his closest friends. His social circle in recent years consisted mainly of a group of couples he and his ex had gotten to know while they were married. When she left him, the wives sided with her, and the husbands—*pendejos,* all of them—went along with the wives.

His other closest pals, in recent years, had been his wife's brothers and cousins. Naturally, those ties were also cut when she dumped him.

His father had died years ago and his mother has been living in Costa Rica with her gentleman friend, Pasqual. His only brother, Roberto, is in Florida. They're all used to not hearing from him for weeks or even months at a time, and he'd been in touch just recently.

Still—when he didn't show up at work on Monday, someone there would have known something was wrong. Ivy would have tried to reach him, and when she couldn't get in touch, she'd have been concerned.

Surely she would have called the police. But . . .

How are they going to find me here? How are they going to trace me here, to this crazy person?

Once, early on, he tried to overpower Sofia when she came to bring him a meal.

He lay very still as she came into the room, forcing her to come closer, closer, bending over him, calling his name . . .

Then he lunged at her, got his hands around her neck.

She fought back like a tiger, though. She wasn't just tall, she was strong—freakishly strong.

"Don't you ever try that again," she snarled, having freed herself from his grasp and retreated to the doorway again. "If you do, you'll be sorry. You're chained to the wall, remember? And if you think I carry the keys to those shackles when I come in here, you're wrong. They're tucked away where you'll never get to them. No one knows you're here. If anything happens to me, no one is going to show up looking for me, believe me. And if you scream for help, no one will hear you. You'll lie here wasting away until you die of hunger and thirst. Is that what you want?"

No. Jesus, no. That's not what he wants. None of this is what he wants.

That time, apparently to teach him a lesson, she let days go by before she returned with food and water. He was convinced she'd abandoned him to die.

Maybe he wishes she would have. Just get it over with, instead of keeping him alive . . . for what?

"I thought you'd like to know," she tells him now, "that last night's test was negative."

Test. She's talking about pregnancy tests again. She's been doing that, the last few times he's seen her—telling him that the tests are negative but it might be too soon and she'll try again tomorrow.

"You have one more chance," she tells him now.

One more chance . . .

"I'll take another test tonight."

"You're crazy! You can't—"

"If it goes well," she talks over him, raising her voice, "then you'll be the first to know. And if it doesn't . . ."

She trails off ominously.

He doesn't prompt her to continue. Gut twisting, he forces himself to remain calm and still, trying to figure a way out of here. There must be something, some way to slip out of these chains that don't allow him to venture past the bed, the chair, and the portable toilet . . .

She turns off the flashlight with a click and he hears her moving across the room.

Silhouetted in the doorway, she tells him, "I'll leave the tray. If I were you, I'd eat that. You have to keep up your strength. Just in case the test is negative again."

With that, she's gone.

Locked into the dank black cell once more, Carlos lets out a breath of relief. Anything is better than lying here listening to her talk about what she wants from him; what she *needs* from him.

A baby.

No—not *a* baby.

"My baby," she's told him, over and over. "I just need my baby. I need you to give me my baby."

My baby. It's strange.

She's strange; she's freaking *loco*.

And the thought of a baby—*his* baby—growing inside of her is enough to make him vomit.

But it's possible, he knows. He slept with her willingly that first night; didn't even stop to think to use protection. Who cared? That, he figured, was her problem.

Little did he know that pregnancy wouldn't be a problem for her. On the contrary: it was her goal.

She told him—after she cornered him here—how she'd hand-selected him; how she'd timed their date to coincide with the most fertile day in her—cycle.

"Why couldn't you just let me go after that?" he'd been naive enough to ask.

The answer sent chills down his spine.

"In case it didn't work. We'll need to try again."

"Over my dead body."

"Oh, Carlos, don't talk like that." Her tone had been eerily calm.

"If you think I'm ever going to touch you again, then you're—"

"If I can't have you one way," she cut in, "then trust me, I'll have you another."

"What's that supposed to mean?"

"You'll see. Or maybe you won't. Let's just hope the first time was the charm."

Okay, he thought, *what if it was?*

What would happen to him after she got what she wanted? And . . . what would happen to him if she didn't?

Now, common sense tells him that either way, she's not going to simply unchain him, open the door, and let him walk back out into the world, back to his life.

"Gabriela."

He watches her open her mouth and close again, wide-eyed. Finally, she manages, "Hi, Ben."

"What are you doing here? Wait. I didn't mean that the way it sounded."

"How did it sound?"

"Like . . . I don't know. You know."

She doesn't say anything, just stands there looking as startled to see him as he was to see her—even though he's had a good forty-five minutes to get used to the idea.

It was Luis who first spotted her sitting about twenty rows ahead of them. He grabbed Ben's arm during the second inning and pointed. "Oh my God, look."

Ben looked. Thinking his brother was referring to a belligerent standoff between opposing fans in the aisle below, he shook his head. "That's crazy."

"It is. I mean, I thought I saw her when we first got here and I was going to say something to you then, but I wasn't sure it was her, and I didn't want to ruin your night by bringing her up."

"Who? What are you talking about?"

"Your ex-wife—Gaby."

"What? What about her?"

"She's right there." Luis pointed again, just as Ben saw her for himself.

It was Gaby all right. Her long hair was down and wavy, the way it always looked in sticky summer weather. He used to love to watch her run her fingers through it, twisting it into a bun and holding it there to get it off her neck; loved how it would be even more tousled when she let go and it cascaded down her back again.

She was doing that tonight. He watched her, aching for the old days, aching to be right there with her instead of perched above like a voyeuristic stranger.

But she was with someone else.

Ben had never seen him before. He wore a dress shirt with the sleeves rolled up. Was he someone she met on InTune? If so, it couldn't be a first date. Even from a distance he could tell there was a connection between Gaby and the stranger. They laughed with their heads tilted together, shared a hot pretzel, and his arm rested across the back of her seat for a while, even in this heat.

Ben watched them for the rest of that inning and into the next, so distracted he lost track of the score and wasn't even properly thrilled when he and his brother were shown on the Jumbotron, a longtime ambition.

Luis was proud enough for both of them. "I wonder if we were on TV?"

Who knows? Who cares?

Gaby is here. She's here, with some guy.

"Try to ignore it," Luis advised him, but he found that impossible to do.

It's been so long since he'd seen her.

He couldn't help but fixate on her, remembering old times, wondering how the hell they'd come to this. Wondering how the hell he'd become the stranger, on the outside looking in, as some guy he'd never seen before fed his wife a pretzel.

Ex-wife.

Intellectually, he's well aware of their marital status. It's easy enough to remember with Gaby conspicuously absent from his day-to-day life.

But now, seeing her again, he was suddenly second-guessing everything.

Then Gaby was on her feet, pushing her way determinedly up the aisle. He impulsively leapt out of his seat. So did everyone else, but it was because they were watching the batter hit a pop-up.

Ben tried to chase her, but he lost sight of her in the cheering crowd as an outfielder caught the ball.

He checked the concession lines, hoping to catch a glimpse of her.

Now that they're face-to-face, he still doesn't know what to do. But he has to say something.

"I just . . . I'm surprised to see you at the game . . . I mean, you were never a big Yankees fan, so . . ."

"Yeah? How do you know I haven't gone over to the dark side?"

"What?"

"Red Sox Nation." She manages a weak smile. "It was a joke."

"Oh!" He laughs. Belatedly, but with relief.

It's been so long since he's seen Gaby, he's no longer accustomed to her sharp wit. Or is it that she'd lost her sense of humor long before, when he last saw her?

This person isn't quite the old Gaby he used to know, but she isn't the angry, brittle woman he'd last seen either.

"You look good," she tells him.

"So do you. The same."

The same . . . what does that even mean? The same as what? The same as when?

She doesn't look the same as she did when he left. Nor does she look the same as she did when he fell in love with her.

Back then she was a young woman with a heavy mane of untamed curls, a quick smile, a quicker laugh, and an unlined face that he assumed had never known true heartache.

Pushing the memories away, he asks Gaby, "So how have you been?"

"Fine. You?"

"Fine."

They stare at each other, but not uncomfortably. That surprises him as much as anything else.

After all this time, after all that's happened, you'd think they would be cringing and making excuses to walk off in opposite directions. But he doesn't want to move, even though something is happening down on the field—the crowd is up and cheering, organ music is playing jauntily, and a quick glance reveals that there's a Yankee on base. "Maybe we can talk," he suggests. "You know, not . . ."

"Here?"

"Right. Not here. Someplace . . ."

"Else?" she supplies, dark eyes smiling.

He nods. "Yeah."

This is not the first time she's ever had him tongue-tied.

Years ago, when they first met, he took one look at the raven-haired knockout in a bright orange-red tank suit and was infatuated. They were both in college then, undergoing the city's rigorous lifeguard training program after having passed the initial qualifying test.

All the trainees bonded quickly during their demanding weeks at the practice facility, but there was little time for flirting. Their numbers dwindled as one waterlogged and exhausted candidate after another dropped out. Those who survived—Gaby and Ben among them—were hired. They found themselves working together at Orchard Beach in the Bronx.

The guards were a tight-knit bunch—a summer family that was occasionally dysfunctional, as most families are. They worked together by day, played together by night. Some played harder than others. Ben wasn't that guy. Gabriela wasn't that girl.

"You're not a partier, huh?" she guessed when they found themselves sitting away from a decidedly rowdier bunch at the first get-together of the season.

"I don't even like the word."

"Party?"

"Not as a verb."

The future editor was mildly impressed by his grammatical reference. Later, he teased her that she initially thought he was just a dim-witted beefcake type. She swore it wasn't true.

"I liked you from the moment I first saw you," she said. "I was hoping you'd ask me out."

He did—finally. But his parents had taught him early on that it's a good idea not to jump headlong into any situation.

"No hay nada tan atrevido como la ignorancia," his mother used to caution him.

Translation: Fools rush in where angels fear to tread.

"Just use your head, Benito. Watch your step and don't be a fool."

His college roommate had similar advice when he came to visit one weekend that first summer.

"You'll screw up the friendship if you sleep with her," Peter told him. "Bad idea."

"I said I want to ask her out, not sleep with her."

"Eventually, you'll sleep with her and that will make her your girlfriend because that's the kind of guy you are. And eventually you'll break up with her."

"Because that's the kind of guy I am?"

"Because everyone breaks up eventually, son."

They were in college. That was how it seemed.

"If you want to keep her in your life—don't do it," Peter counseled him.

Maybe he should have taken Peter's advice, ignored his own instincts, and stuck with the friendship. If he had, Gaby might still be in his life. As a very good friend. Like some of the old lifeguard gang he stays in touch with online, touching base every once in a while with cursory updates about their lives now, or to add a nostalgic comment whenever someone posts an old photo on a social networking site . . .

No. That's not how he wants it to be with Gaby. She wasn't his friend. She was his wife.

In an ideal world, she'd still be both.

"How about if I text you?" he asks. "And we can set up a time to talk. Just . . . you know, to catch up. It's been a long time."

"It has." Is it his imagination or does she sound—and look—wistful?

"Okay. So I'll text. Same number?"

"Yes. Wait—no. I switched carriers when I moved, so the number changed. Maybe I gave it to you . . ."

"You didn't." His tone is sharper than he intended. But the fact that she changed her phone number and didn't bother to update him doesn't sit well with him. It means that for all these months apart, he couldn't have even gotten in touch with her if he wanted to.

"Do you have anything to write on?" she asks him. "I left my bag at my seat."

"No. I left mine at the office. I have my phone, though, if you want to just call it now so I'll have the number." He pulls his iPhone out of his pocket, glad he always has it close at hand. Not only is it his communication lifeline, but it's replaced his iPod, camera, date book, watch . . .

"Hey—I have the same phone in the same exact case," Gaby notices. "But it's in my bag back at my seat. Just send me an e-mail at my work address. That hasn't changed."

"Or I can message you through InTune," he says, and wishes that he hadn't.

The light goes out of her eyes. "I don't check that very often."

"Me either. I'll just send an e-mail. Okay?"

"Okay. Oh, and Ben—I still have your box."

"What?"

"From your father's house. Your mementos. From when you were a kid. You know . . ."

He does know. He thought he'd lost the box in the move. "I figured it accidentally got thrown away."

"No, I have it."

"That's great. I thought it was gone forever. A lifetime's worth of memories—just like that. I'll have to come get it. Thank you for . . ." *For not throwing it away.*

"No problem." She shifts her weight. "I have to get back to . . . you know. My seat."

Right. Her seat.

"Good seeing you, Gabriela. I'll be in touch."

"I hope so." With a little wave, she walks away.

Sitting on the closed lid of the toilet, Alex stares at the plastic stick for a long time, willing it to change.

Of course it doesn't.

One stripe. Just one.

The test is negative.

Not pregnant.

With a curse, she tosses the stick blindly toward the wastebasket beside the sink and leans forward, resting her forehead against her knees.

She'd thought for sure it would happen this time. She'd thought he was the one. He looks so much like Carmen, even acts like him—the way he tilts his head, the way he narrows his dark brows when he's angry . . .

And he's so angry. Whenever she's with him, even in the dim light, she can see the fury etched on his features, can feel it crackling in the air.

He hates me.

That's pretty clear.

They all wind up hating her.

But it doesn't matter. They don't have to love her, or even like her. She doesn't need their affection or their sympathy or understanding. She just needs . . .

"My baby," she whispers. "I need my baby. My boy . . ."

Now it will be almost two weeks before she can try again. Even if it works, almost a year before she'll hold her son in her arms again.

She can wait, though. As long as she knows it's going to happen.

"Over my dead body," Carlos Diaz had the nerve to say before, clearly wanting her to know that his desire for her has completely withered away.

Be that as it may . . . he won't have much choice in the matter.

He has two more chances.

Three strikes and you're out.

Carlos will understand that. He wrote in his online profile that he loves baseball. He's a Yankees fan. One more thing he has in common with Carmen.

And with my baby . . .

My boy.

Dante.

It was Carmen who chose the name for their son. In Spanish, he said, it means "enduring."

Alex lifts her head slowly, then gets to her feet and sighs heavily.

She splashes water on her face, standing at the scarred

porcelain sink where she taught her son to brush his teeth and wash his face before bed, standing on a step stool. She was always so worried he was going to burn himself, because Carmen insisted on keeping the old home's ancient hot water heater turned up high.

Memories.

How she hated this small hall bathroom—the only one in the house—when they first moved in! Hated the old-fashioned fixtures, olive-green subway tile, rectangular bathtub with the cheap glass sliding doors framed by too much sloppy, rubbery white caulking.

Carmen was going to redo it—one of the many things on the household to-do list. But he was always busy working, and when he wasn't, he was focused on designing their dream house.

He never got around to doing much of anything to this one before—

Well, now it doesn't matter.

Alex jerks the faucets, dries her hands on a limp towel that's been hanging there for God knows how long, and leaves the bathroom.

Walking down the short hall that connects the two bedrooms, she glimpses a streak of black fur scooting across the threshold into Dante's room. She'd forgotten and left the door ajar.

"No, Gato!" she calls. "Don't you mess things up in there!"

Like the bathroom, like the rest of the house—except the basement—it's been unchanged now for . . . how many years? Five? Seven? Ten?

She can't be sure. Sometimes, it seems like yesterday that she last saw her son here in the house; other times, he's part of a past so distant she can barely recall it.

All she knows for certain is that the room hasn't been changed since the last time Dante left it: Legos on the floor, a bookmarked book on the pillow, crayons and a thick stack of drawing paper on the desk,

Calling, "'Bye, Mom," as he went, he walked out the door and down the stairs.

"Tell Dad to drive carefully," she called after him. "And be sure you buckle your seat belt!"

It was snowing like crazy that February morning. The roads were slick.

She wasn't there to watch as her son—her baby— strapped himself into the passenger's seat beside his father. Carmen was on his way to work; he was going to drop Dante at school. He was in kindergarten then: five years old.

That snowy morning so long ago was the same as every other weekday morning, except . . .

Except it was the last morning. There would never be another morning.

Gato is curled up on Dante's bed when Alex steps into the room. He stares at her with unblinking green eyes, looking a bit smug.

"Good kitty! You didn't mess it up." Alex steps carefully around the Lego construction on the floor: a nearly completed skyscraper rises amid heaps of stray pieces on the braided rug.

"Can you help me finish it, Mom?"

"Sure I can."

"Let's make it skinnier at the top just like the Chrysler Building, okay?"

"Okay, sweetie. Okay . . ."

"I'm going to build the tallest building in New York when I grow up."

When he wasn't building something, or sorting the baseball cards that still sit in binders on the bookshelf, he was playing the electric guitar Carmen had brought back from one of his trips.

"Why electric?" she'd asked Carmen the first time that

discordant music blasted through the house when they were trying to sleep. "Why not acoustic?"

"That's cowboy music. You know we like good old rock and roll," Carmen said with a grin.

She learned to live with it—and it wasn't discordant for long. Her son had talent, real musical talent.

"Mom, I'm writing a song. You've got to hear it! Are you ready?"

"I'm listening . . ."

"I'm going to be a rock star when I grow up, Mom."

"A rock star who plays baseball and builds skyscrapers?"

"Can I be that?"

"You can be anything, Dante. Anything you want to be."

"I want to be everything, Mom!"

"You *are* everything. You're everything to me . . ."

Alex sits down at the desk, careful not to let the chair bump the Lego towers. She takes a fresh sheet of paper from the stack and reaches for the box of crayons. She'll start with the red, as always.

Gaby arrives back at her seat just as another batter comes up to the plate.

"Long line in the ladies' room?" Ryan asks without taking his eyes off the field.

"How'd you guess?" She settles back and feigns interest in the scoreboard. "What'd I miss?"

"Yankees scored a run. Two outs. Two men on."

She pretends to be absorbed in the ball game—cheering when the crowd cheers, groaning when the crowd groans—but her thoughts are on the past.

When she was a little girl, Abuela would warn her not to run around playing stoopball right after dinner because she'd get a cramp. She did it anyway, of course—egged on by Jaz, who never followed the rules—and learned that

Abuela was right. The pain, right below her rib cage, was so sharp she could barely speak, barely breathe.

That was what it was like after Josh died. Only the pain never subsided. She couldn't do anything—couldn't speak, couldn't move, couldn't think—without being aware of that all-consuming pain . . .

"Yes!" Ryan shouts, jarring her.

Realizing that the inning just came to an end with a third out for the Yankees, Gaby wonders whether Ben is shouting "No!" somewhere behind her.

She'll be seeing him again soon. He has to pick up his box of memories, not lost forever, after all.

"Good game." Ryan rests his arm on her shoulders. "Even if we're rooting for opposite teams. Glad you came?"

"Really glad." She smiles at him and tries to ignore a twinge of guilt.

Alone in the dark, Carlos feels around for the tray she left on the foot of his bed.

His fingers find the linear rim of the tray, the curved plastic edge of the plate. The food on it has already grown cold.

His hunger pains have passed. But past experience—and a rustling, scampering noise somewhere in the corner—tells him he'd better eat it now. Before something else does.

He takes a bite of the burger, eats a few mealy fries. The food seems to lodge in his throat. Is it tainted?

He reaches for the glass to wash it down, raises it to his mouth, and something tickles his face. Startled, he throws the glass and hears it break on the floor—

Then realizes it wasn't the glass after all.

It was a vase. He'd glimpsed it on the tray: a vase, holding red flowers that brushed his cheek just now.

She'd called his attention to it as she set the tray down on the bed, as if bestowing some sort of gift.

Chains jangling, he bends over to pick up the broken glass so he doesn't forget and step on it later. As he feels around on the floor, a shard pierces his fingertip. He sticks it into his mouth and tastes blood.

Blood . . .

All this time, Carlos has been trying to think of a way to escape this hellhole . . .

There is a way out, he realizes. Only one way.

But is he man enough—or desperate enough—to take it?

Chapter 5

The next morning dawns bright and sunny. The heat wave broke with a violent overnight thunderstorm. Rain poured in sideways, waking Gaby, and she's been awake ever since she got out of bed to close the window.

Now she opens it again to let in the fresh air, hoping the rain temporarily washed away a good portion of the pollen that aggravates her allergies.

She still has over an hour before she has to leave for the office, and sits down with her coffee and laptop to check her e-mail.

Ben said last night that he'd get in touch. Maybe he already has.

But when she checks her work e-mail address, everything in her in-box is business-related.

She quickly closes out of the account. It can wait until she gets to the office. Instead, she clicks over to the InTune Web site.

Maybe Ben misunderstood her and sent her a message there.

She hasn't bothered to check the account since her date with Ryan last weekend. There are dozens of new messages from men who are interested in connecting. Some of them are intriguing at a quick glance, but that's not why she's here.

Nothing from Ben.

She looks for him, perusing the files, searching eligible Manhattan men . . .

Maybe the InTune search engine is only showing men who are good matches for her, and its algorithms aren't computing that Ben is a good match.

Or is he even on this site anymore? Maybe he took his profile down. Maybe he's happily settled with someone new already—or maybe he's just no longer interested in finding . . .

Happiness.

That was it, right? The one thing he's looking for.

You make me so happy . . .

Those were the words that kicked off his marriage proposal to her years ago.

She responded—before she realized what he was up to, "No, I don't. You've always been happy, Ben."

His sunny disposition had drawn her to him in the first place, before they even met.

"That guy is always smiling," she remembers saying to one of the other girls after her first few days in the training program. "I wonder why?"

"That's just Ben," said the girl, who knew him from the swim team. "He's a happy guy. You'll see."

She did see. They became fast friends during their long hours at the training facility. Ben's smile was infectious, his laugh even more so. He was fun, and funny, and creative. He did his best to raise the group's morale as the program became increasingly demanding.

Gaby wasn't disappointed when they were both hired at Orchard Beach after passing the written, swimming, and skills certification examinations.

During long days on the job, whenever their breaks coincided, they'd sit watching the clouds drift across the summer sky, telling each other what they saw in the formations. It was their little game: coming up with outlandish cloud visions to make each other laugh. Breaks always ended much too soon—as did summer itself.

She was caught off guard when he asked her out on their last day working together. A few years later there he was, sitting across the table from her at a fancy restaurant, claiming that *she* was the one who made *him* happy. As she argued with him that the opposite was true, he dropped to one knee, pulled out a ring box, and proposed.

Of course she said yes. About a thousand times, giddy with excitement, and then—

Ben's profile page pops up, jerking her back to the present reality.

Yep. He's still out there. Still looking for happiness.

If she'd stumbled across his profile and picture without already having married and divorced the man, she'd probably conclude he's a perfect match. Who wouldn't?

He's a handsome structural engineer living on the Upper East Side . . .

Oh, but he's lost a child.

Damn you, Ben, for putting it in your profile.

Last night when she was face-to-face with him, she'd forgotten he'd done that. Now, renewed anger takes over.

Why did he find it necessary to be so brutally honest here, among strangers?

Come on, Gaby. Ben has always believed in honesty. You know that.

Still . . .

There's a part of her that wonders whether he's really just playing the sympathy card, hoping to capture attention from nurturing women.

How well does she really know him now? How well did she know him *ever*?

One thing is certain: when *worse*—the *worst*—came, she's the one who changed.

I don't like myself anymore, she realizes. *I don't like*

being a joyless person who gets up alone every morning and goes through the motions of the day and goes to bed alone at the end of it. I want—

Her phone, sitting beside her on the table, vibrates with an incoming text.

She picks it up, sees that it's from Ryan.

Great time last nite!

For some reason, his abbreviated spelling rubs her the wrong way.

She's tempted to write back: *It's* night*! Not* nite*! Are you too lazy to type one extra letter?*

Maybe it's the editor in her.

Or maybe she's looking for an excuse not to see him again.

Yes, because that's entirely rational. Using jargon and abbreviations while texting is the ultimate character flaw, right?

Nobody's perfect, Gaby, Ben said to her years ago, when she'd apologized to him for one of her rare volcanic temper explosions. *You have your faults; I have mine. People can love each other despite their faults. And sometimes, even because of them.*

She pushes Ben away—again—and quickly types: *It was fun! Thank you!*

His reply bounces in a moment later: *Busy tonite?*

She isn't.

But she tells him that she is.

His response: a sad face icon.

Again, she's unreasonably irritated.

Just yesterday she'd found Ryan utterly charming. So why, today, is he getting on her nerves?

Ben, under her skin again, dammit. She'd been so sure they'd resolved everything in the divorce.

But now that the fog of grief has begun to lift at last, she still seems to need some kind of closure.

Alex has been working at the small private practice in White Plains for a long time now. Five years, at least. Probably ten. Maybe longer. She loses track.

Located in a small brick building on a mainly residential tree-lined street, the office houses a pair of general practitioners—one who's well past retirement age and another who just came on board last year after completing her residency.

When Alex started, there was just one physician, and Dr. Baird did everything the old-school way—from making house calls to keeping handwritten records. His wife was the office manager and hired Alex to replace the practice's eighty-four-year-old nurse with very few questions asked and most likely no reference or license verification check. Mrs. Baird still oversees the administrative duties, but now that Dr. Patel is on board, everything is done electronically—and by the book.

In some ways, that's better for Alex—more efficient for her unique purposes—though she worries about getting caught doing something she shouldn't be doing.

This morning, she clocks in as usual at 7:45 and is ready for the first round of patient appointments at eight. The hours are preferable to her first job out of nursing school, the one at the hospital in the city. There, she frequently had to be on duty overnight, missing weekends and holidays with Carmen and Dante. But it paid the mortgage on the house, and for the dream house Carmen had designed and was planning to have built for them upstate on his family's acreage.

"Someday, you won't have to work at all," Carmen promised. "Someday . . ."

Now there are no night shifts, and Saturday morning hours are reserved for the part-time staff. Yet now that Alex lives alone, weekends and holidays don't matter nearly so much.

But that's going to change again soon. Soon, she'll be

rocking her baby boy to sleep again. Soon, there will be Saturday morning story hours at the library and Sunday afternoon soccer games, and Santa will come on Christmas, the Easter Bunny on Easter . . .

Soon she'll need those weekends and holidays to be a mommy again.

By eight-thirty she's checked the vitals of a half-dozen patients, most of whom are impoverished or lower middle class, elderly, and have come here for as many years as Dr. Baird has been practicing.

"Nurse!" Dr. Patel, who either never bothered to learn Alex's name or simply doesn't care to use it, stops her in the corridor. "Can you submit these prescriptions right away, please? They're for Mr. Griffith." The doctor hands over a list of prescriptions and contact information for a large chain pharmacy, then turns to grab a folder from the plastic chart holder outside the nearest of the two examination rooms.

"Good morning, Mrs. Halpern. What seems to be the problem today?" Dr. Patel's tone instantly goes from curt to compassionate as she steps over the threshold and closes the door behind her.

"Sure," Alex says to the empty hall. "No problem. And you're *welcome*."

She heads straight to her desk in the cubicle at the end of the hall and signs onto the closed computer network used to transmit electronic prescriptions.

The task is complete less than a minute later.

She returns to the corridor, timing it just as Mr. Griffith, an elderly widower, emerges from the other examination room, leaning heavily on his walker.

"I sent your prescriptions, Mr. Griffith. I'll be happy to pick them up for you again today on my lunch hour and drop them at your house."

"You, my dear, are a saint." The old man, incapacitated by diabetic neuropathy, grins at her and takes out his worn wallet and checkbook. "It hasn't been easy lately. My legs are getting worse, and they ache so much at night that I can't sleep."

"The doctor prescribed something to help with that. You'll sleep soundly tonight if you take it, believe me."

"I hope so. I just wish you'd let me pay you for doing this for me. Especially since my own daughters can't bc bothered to help."

"That's not necessary. Like I always tell you, it gives me an excuse to stop by that great deli next door to the pharmacy."

"This time, treat yourself to lunch on me." He holds out a twenty-dollar bill, but she waves it away.

"Absolutely not. It's my pleasure."

"You're too kind. You'll be going straight to heaven."

"Let's hope so."

Chuckling, Mr. Griffith tucks the twenty back into his wallet, then hands her his Medicare card and writes out a check to cover the co-pay, leaving the amount blank for her to fill in.

"I'll see you around one," she promises him, folding the check around the card and slipping it into the pocket of her scrubs.

"I can't sleep at night, but I have a hard time staying awake during the day. If I'm napping and I don't hear the door, the key is—"

"Shh!" She holds a finger to her lips. "I remember where it is, and you don't want to tell the whole world. You never know who might be listening."

Though it's beside the point. Anyone with even a shred of brain cell can find it where he has it "hidden": under the doormat. When he first told her that, she cautioned him that he might want to make it a little harder to find.

Ironic, because she always leaves her own front door unlocked.

But I have my reasons for that.

"My daughter said to pick a new spot, too," Mr. Griffin is saying, "so I hid it someplace else, and I still can't remember where. Got myself locked out on a rainy day and I'll never do that again. Had to make a copy and it's back under the doormat where it belongs. I've had a key stashed there for fifty years and never had a problem, so there it will stay."

What else could you say to that logic?

Now, Mr. Griffith offers her a warm smile as he positions his walker to make his exit. "I'll see you later. Thank you for making my life easier, my dear."

Right back atcha, Mr. G., she thinks, heading back down the hall.

In the midst of a morning editorial meeting, listening to Kasey gush on about the plot of a recent acquisition, Gaby surreptitiously checks her phone under the table.

There are three new e-mails in her work in-box.

When she checked half an hour ago, there were two—both from authors.

Now there are two more from authors, but the third is from Ben.

It was good seeing you last night. Do you want to have dinner tonight?

Her heart skips a beat, and she has to remind herself that this is just her ex-husband, not a hot new romantic prospect.

Kasey is winding down her monologue at last. Gaby knows she'll be up next, discussing her lukewarm reception to a book proposal from a veteran author whose sales have been slipping.

Quickly, she types a response to Ben: *Sure. Name time & place & I'll be there.*

She hesitates on the verge of hitting Send, realizing she might regret that decision when this evening rolls around.

Does she really want to sit across a table from Ben tonight and rehash the past?

Does she really want to do that again—ever?

"Thank you for that, Kasey. I'll check the schedule and we'll aim to get the project into production later today." Ellen, the executive editor, consults her notes. "All right, Gabriela, what do you have for us?"

Gaby abruptly presses Send.

Too late for second thoughts. The e-mail flies out through cyberspace to find Ben as she tucks her phone into her pocket and turns her attention back to the book proposal.

Located in a busy strip mall a few miles from the medical office, the drugstore is bustling as usual when Alex arrives at half past noon.

She makes her way directly to the pharmacy counter at the back corner of the store. Predictably, there's a long line, and several other customers are sitting in chairs along the wall waiting for their orders to be filled.

The tall, gray-haired woman is behind the register. Good. She's always all business, unlike the bubbly blond chatterbox who's sometimes on duty at this time of day.

As Alex waits her turn, she avoids looking at a nearby shelf that holds over-the-counter pregnancy tests. It'll be almost another month before she needs to buy more of those, though it never hurts to stock up in advance. Not that she'll be doing that on Mr. Griffith's dime.

Disappointment over last night's negative test seeps in, but she reminds herself that it'll happen eventually.

Years ago, when she and Carmen were trying to conceive, she—

"Next!" The woman behind the register beckons her forward. "Can I help you?"

"Yes, I'm picking up prescriptions for my father, John Griffith. There should be four that were sent in this morning from Dr. Patel's office, including the insulin. One won't be covered by Medicare so I'll take care of that separately."

The woman nods and turns away to fish through the bin of filled orders. After a few moments, she plucks a white bag from the rest and returns to the register.

Alex holds her breath. This is the part where it might get tricky. So far the process has always worked like clockwork, but you never know.

"Okay, I have one, two, three that are covered, and one that is not."

"Right. I'll write out the check for the co-pays on the first three and pay for the other one in cash."

Moments later she's on her way with the white bag in her hand. Walking right past the deli—the one she pretended to be so eager to visit—she waits until she's safely back in the car before opening the bag.

First, she tucks the register receipt for the three medications inside, along with Mr. Griffith's Medicare card.

Then she takes out the orange bottle of medication that wasn't covered—the one she paid for with cash from her own wallet—and tucks it into the glove compartment.

Poor old Mr. Griffith. For all she knows, he really does suffer from erectile dysfunction. Too bad he has no idea that Viagra has been prescribed for him.

But that's all right, Alex thinks as she tucks the orange bottle into the glove compartment. *I promise I'll put it to good use.*

She weaves her way from the strip mall to the highway on-ramp and drives a couple of miles, exiting into a neighborhood far different from where she works—or, for that matter, lives.

This, too, is residential, and the houses are old as well—but not charming old. These are shabby old, set so close together that they're separated by mere alleyways instead of yards, fronted by more weeds than grass. Shady-looking characters lounge on porches and corners where storefronts are scattered. Some are boarded up and covered with graffiti. Bodegas that are still open advertise the usual beer and cigarettes, lottery tickets and ATMs, along with the fact that they cash checks and accept food stamps.

Hearing an explosive bang as she drives past a group of kids in an empty parking lot, she's relieved to see that they're only setting off fireworks. Dangerous—not to mention illegal here—but less disconcerting than gunfire.

Halfway down a pothole-pocked block, Alex pulls up in front of a house that's covered in faded salmon-colored siding, with a dented white metal awning hanging crookedly above the small concrete porch.

Mr. Griffith told her that it was damaged by a tree branch a few years back during Hurricane Sandy, and he hasn't been able to get anyone to fix it.

"But that's all right. It looks like it's going to fall on someone's head. Maybe it'll keep people away—the wrong kind of people," he added with narrowed eyes.

Carrying the bag from the pharmacy, Alex makes her way up a cracked sidewalk dotted with bird droppings and littered with seed pods that dropped from trees high overhead. She climbs the uneven steps and knocks on the gray aluminum storm door.

There's a large Beware of Dog sign taped to the glass—another measure to scare off unwanted visitors, the old man once told her with a chuckle. "A sign is all you need. It's a lot cheaper than a watch dog—and a whole lot cheaper than one of those burglar alarm systems."

She'd warned him that he might not want to keep a key to the house hidden under the back doormat, but he told her not to worry about that. "I've got a Beware of Dog sign on the back door, too. And if that doesn't keep intruders away, I'll take care of them myself before they get very far."

It takes a full minute, maybe two, before Mr. Griffith appears, just as she's wondering if she's going to have to go find the key and let herself in.

He breaks into a grin when he sees her.

"Well if it isn't my good Samaritan." He opens the door wide. "Come on in. The coffee's hot. I could use some myself. Been snoozing since I got home."

"Oh, thank you, but I can't. I have to get back to work. I just wanted to give you this." She holds out the bag. "Your Medicare card is inside, and so is the receipt for the check amount."

"Thank you, my dear. Are you sure I can't—" He breaks off as a car passes by on the street, hip-hop music blasting through the open windows.

Mr. Griffith scowls. "Thugs. Didn't used to see them around here. When I bought this house, it was all families. Real nice." He shakes his head. "Now . . . well, you know."

Alex shrugs. Her mother-in-law used to complain about the neighborhood changing, too. But it was the opposite there. She'd bemoan the loss of all her down-to-earth old neighbors who'd passed away or moved away, and criticize the families who'd moved in to take their place. She called them, collectively, *el esnobismo*—as if they were filthy rich snobs living in vast mansions instead of ordinary upper-middle-class families who could afford the skyrocketing suburban real estate prices in a town where a high six-figure sale price would buy a modest fixer-upper.

Mr. Griffith goes on venting about how unsafe his own neighborhood has become.

"Maybe you should move," Alex says, barely keeping the snap from her voice. She used to say the same thing to her mother-in-law, praying the woman would take the advice.

Naturally, she never did. She had to be near her precious son and grandson.

"Bah," Mr. Griffith says, with a wave of his gnarled hand. "I'm not going anywhere. This is my home."

"But if it's not safe anymore—"

"Bah. I've been sleeping with a loaded gun in the drawer

of my bedside table ever since the neighborhood color scheme changed from white to brown and black. A legal gun, by the way, registered and official. It's my right to have it, and you can be damned sure I'll use it on these thugs if I need to."

From white to brown and black . . .

Oh, really?

"My husband and son are Hispanic. Or, as you might say, 'brown.'" Alex smiles sweetly. "Don't know if I ever mentioned that."

Gratified by the startled expression on his weathered face, she sees him glance down at her left hand.

"I didn't even know you were married."

"Oh, I am. Have been for years. I just don't wear my rings when I'm working. All those diamonds . . . well, you know. They get in the way." She turns on her heel. "Take care, Mr. Griffith."

"Wait—"

She turns back to see him fumbling with his wallet, holding out a bill. "Here," he calls. "Take this, for your trouble."

"It was no trouble. Just my good deed for the day."

Back in the car, the forced smile gives way to a clenched jaw as she starts the engine.

"Don't worry," she says aloud, to Carmen and Dante. "I'll make sure he pays for that little remark. I've still got your back, even after . . . even now."

At five-thirty, Ben's phone vibrates with an incoming text. He glances at it, closes his office door, and picks up the phone to call Peter. Ordinarily he'd just text back, but right now he needs an ear and some advice from an old friend who knows him well.

They'd met on their first day at M.I.T. and easily bonded, the way college kids do, over the pleasures of Frisbee and beer and the mysteries of the dorm laundry room.

Though they came from different parts of the country—Peter is from a tiny midwestern town and his parents are farmers—they shared quite a few similarities. Peter, too, was the younger of two brothers. He, too, had been on the high school swim team, had also won academic scholarships, and was working his way through school. He, too, was majoring in engineering. He originally planned to move to Chicago and design skyscrapers once he got his degree. But after visiting Ben in New York over their first Christmas break, he changed his mind.

He lives in Manhattan and designs bridges; Ben is the one who designs skyscrapers. Their offices are five blocks apart, their apartments—now that Ben has moved to an Upper East Side high-rise—a mere twelve.

Peter answers his own cell on the second ring. "So are you good to go?"

He's referring, of course, to the invitation he just extended via text: to go for a run in the park, then grab burgers at the Stumble Inn afterward to watch tonight's ball game.

"Can't," Ben tells him. "I already have plans."

"Don't tell me you're going back to the stadium and you're calling to explain why you didn't invite me this time either?"

"Luis is the one who got the tickets last night. There were only two. I couldn't invite you."

"Yeah, yeah, sure, whatever. So either you're going to the game again tonight or you're watching it someplace without me. Which is it, son?"

"None of the above."

"Come on, I know you, Duran. You'd sooner cut off your you-know-what than miss a Yankees/Red Sox game."

Ben winces. "Yeah, well . . . maybe I cut off my—"

"Stop. What the hell, you forgot about the game and made other plans?"

"Yeah. I don't know what got into me."

"It involves a woman."

"Sort of."

"Sort of?" Peter echoes. "What, it involves a transvestite?"

Not in the mood to trade quips, Ben explains how he ran into Gaby last night at the Stadium—with another guy—and somehow convinced himself, and her, that it would be a great idea to get together and talk. Over dinner. Tonight.

"You're nuts."

"I know."

"You'd be better off with a transvestite."

"Peter. Come on."

"Benjy. What the hell are you doing?"

"I don't know. When I saw her, something just . . . clicked. I miss her."

"Yeah. I missed Leslie, too, at first. But you get over that eventually. It just takes time."

"I've had time. I've done—I'm *still* doing—everything I can to move on. But it just—"

"Listen, as long as you're not thinking of getting back together . . . you're not, are you?" Peter asks. "Because that would be a huge mistake."

Ben is silent, toying with a pen.

"I understand what this is about," Peter goes on. "Leslie and I ran into each other at happy hour at Dos Caminos on Third one night. It was a few months after we separated—but before the divorce was official. We were both drinking those Cosmo del Diablos they make . . ."

Ben thinks of his recent date with—what was her name? Camilla. That's right. With the pink lipstick and the pink drink. Plural. *Drinks.*

"You were drinking Cosmos?"

"Del *Diablo*," Peter clarifies.

"Yeah, that makes it manly."

"Hell, yeah, it does. Stop interrupting me. So Leslie and me—we hooked up. You know—for old times' sake."

"You never told me that."

"I never told anyone that. I wanted to forget it and move on. But maybe I shouldn't be saying it was a huge mistake. Maybe it was the best thing that could have happened."

"Why?"

"Because I thought I still wanted her, you know? She looked great, and we had a lot of laughs the way we used to . . . but then the next morning, she was right back to bitching at me about some stupid thing. Nagging, complaining, criticizing . . . and I remembered all the reasons we weren't together anymore."

"Wow. That's . . ."

Depressing, is what it is. Ben doesn't bother to complete the sentence.

Peter goes on, "Maybe we just had to get it out of our systems that one last time. So that we'd know we'd made the right decision. Maybe you and Gaby need to do the same thing."

"That's not why I'm seeing her. We know we made the right decision. And," he adds, before Peter can elaborate, "that's not what's going to happen. We're not going to hook up."

"Yeah, I know. You're just going to talk, right? Okay, Ben. You go have dinner with her and have a nice heart-to-heart and then go your separate ways."

"I plan to."

"Or you go have dinner and a heart-to-heart and then take her home and sleep with her. One for the road."

"It's not like that. It's—"

"Sure it is, and there's nothing wrong with it. You do what you have to do. I've been there, remember? I know what it's like."

He does . . . and he doesn't.

For all their similarities, Peter has never been a one-woman man in all the years Ben has known him. Besides, he and Leslie were mismatched from the start. They fought constantly, like Luis and Ada.

Peter's marriage lasted a little over a year before they mutually called it quits.

Luis has often said that he and Ada probably would have done the same thing if they hadn't had children. "The kids are the glue that's kept us together," he'd say.

Yeah, well . . . Ben can't relate to that.

A lump rises in his throat.

He doesn't usually allow himself to think about his son in the middle of a workday, much less a conversation. If he allows it, the tears come, and tears . . .

Tears are meant to be shed in private.

He quickly shifts gears. "I've got another call," he tells Peter. "Gotta go."

"Okay. Good luck tonight."

"Good luck? With what?"

"The last hurrah. I know it's not easy to say good-bye, Ben. Even the second time."

It's time, Carlos decides, holding the piece of jagged glass in his hand.

He has to do it now, before she comes back.

Three strikes and you're out . . .

God only knows what fresh hell she has in store for him next.

God.

Please forgive me, Jesus, for what I'm about to do.

He's never been a particularly religious man. Raised Catholic, he stopped attending mass as soon as he left his mother's house. But the Catholic doctrine is ingrained: all those years spent in CCD, and reading the Bible with his mother, and sitting in the pew on Sundays listening to Father Joseph's rambling sermons . . .

Carlos knows right from wrong. He knows that taking a life—even your own—is a sin. He believes in heaven and in hell.

But surely when there are extenuating circumstances . . .

Surely, it's better to die a relatively quick and painless death on your own terms than to suffer torturous death on somebody else's.

Surely, it's better to take your own life than somebody else's.

Yes, he did consider the prospect of using the wedge of glass as a weapon against his captor.

But only briefly, before discarding the idea.

After all, he remembers what she said the day he tried to overpower her.

Even if he manages to incapacitate her, or kill her—where would that leave him?

Still chained to the wall, alone in the dark dungeon to either starve to death or die of thirst. She's already given him an agonizing taste of what that would be like.

No, thank you.

He holds the glass in his right hand, allowing the tentative index finger of his left to identify the sharpest edge. He presses it into the padded flesh of his fingertip just to see what it's like.

It doesn't hurt.

He presses harder, then moves his hand, slicing his fingertip with the makeshift blade.

Now there's pain, but nothing unbearable. This bodes well for what's to come. He bears down and can feel blood from the cut, warm and sticky, running into his palm.

Okay. Not so bad. He's ready. He can do this.

He moves the sharp edge to his left wrist and reflexively closes his eyes—not that it matters. There was only darkness before; now there's simply more, the same unrelenting degree of darkness.

It's a wonder he hasn't lost his mind, living a pitch-black existence interrupted only by the nightmarish glare of a flashlight beam when she visits.

Even if she doesn't kill him, she's not going to let him go. He can't bear the thought of another hour, another day, in the dark . . . let alone the remainder of a life that wasn't all that great even before this happened to him.

He presses the sharp edge into his flesh, then hesitates.

Maybe he should pray first, for real this time. Just in case there's hope for his soul. Just in case he'll be borne away from this hell and into heavenly light.

"Forgive me, merciful Father, for I have sinned," he whispers, tears squeezing from his closed eyelids as he digs the blade into his wrist, slicing into the vein.

This time, there is pain. Explosive pain, and blood, so much blood, running over his fingers . . .

He sinks back onto the filthy mattress and waits for the blackness to give way to the light at last.

Gaby was glad Ben suggested a new restaurant for tonight—someplace they'd never been together. Someplace she's never been at all, actually.

The place is tucked away on a cobblestone street downtown in the meatpacking district, just a block from the southern tip of the Highline, a long, narrow park that runs alongside the Hudson River, built on an abandoned elevated rail line.

Back when they were married, she and Ben occasionally strolled down the Highline on a weekend afternoon and wound up having a late brunch—or early dinner—in this rambling neighborhood of cobblestones and converted warehouses; wine bars and construction awnings and camped out paparazzi.

If tonight he'd asked her to meet him at one of those restaurants—*their* restaurants—she'd have had to say no. Too many memories.

But apparently he wants to avoid them as well.

The restaurant occupies the ground floor of one of the industrial buildings that are so plentiful in this part of the city. The enormous open space has the requisite exposed brick, high ceilings, pillars, and windows that extend from the wide-planked floor to the beamed ceiling high overhead.

The hostess is a skinny, anemic-looking young woman with thick eyeliner, a pierced eyebrow, and long, straight hair parted in the middle. She's wearing a pair of short shorts with clunky mid-calf snow boots—obviously, the height of fashion.

"I'm meeting—"

"Name?"

"Gabriela Duran—wait, you mean my name, or his?"

All but sighing, Short-shorts asks, as if addressing a toddler—or an idiot, "Who made the reservation?"

"He did. Ben Duran." Ordinarily, Gaby wouldn't be the least bit intimidated by a hipster hostess with an attitude, but she's feeling vulnerable tonight on every level.

"Not here yet. Do you want to be seated or wait for him?"

"I'll wait." Then, on second thought. "No, I'll sit."

"Are you *sure*, Mrs. Duran?" she asks with exaggerated patience.

"I'm *not* Mrs. Duran. And yes. I'll sit."

The expressionless girl shrugs, grabs a couple of menus, and leads her through the crowded room to a cozy table by the window. She tosses the menus down and leaves without a word.

Gaby settles into one of the empty chairs and self-consciously wishes she'd chosen the other one. That way she'd have her back to the adjacent table for two, where a man is also facing an empty seat.

He gives a little wave. She waves back before realizing that he's actually looking at someone behind her. His date must have arrived, and by the look on his face, he's thrilled to see her.

Wait—not his date. It must be his wife. The woman is tremendously pregnant. He jumps up to greet her with a kiss and pulls out the empty chair for her. Gold wedding bands glint on both their hands. Their happiness radiates.

A lump forms in Gaby's throat. She and Ben were once like that.

Now Ben is looking for happiness with another woman, and . . .

Well, to be fair, she's looking for the same thing with another man, isn't she?

She might even have found it. The potential for it, anyway. Ryan texted her again late this afternoon, wanting to make plans for the weekend. She agreed to see a movie with him on Saturday night. By then she'll have the closure she needs and be back in the right frame of mind, ready again to move on in a new relationship.

"Hey, sorry I'm late."

Ben at last. He's wearing a suit, straight from the office, carrying the black leather bag she gave him that last Christmas . . .

Not their last Christmas together, though. How well she remembers the unbearable holiday season that kicked off just days after Josh's funeral. And then there was another Christmas after that, one more joyless Christmas, before they separated.

But the last Christmas that really *felt* like Christmas was when she was pregnant. She merrily braved the hordes of holiday shoppers, unbothered by her enormous belly and bulky winter coat, searching for just the right bag to replace the worn canvas satchel Ben had been carrying to work.

So he's still using the leather bag. There's a part of her that's surprised to see it.

Then again, why wouldn't he use it? It's not a particularly sentimental gift, hardly on the same level as the ruby earrings he gave her that same Christmas. She wouldn't dream of wearing them now; they're tucked away in her jewelry box along with her wedding and engagement rings. She isn't quite sure what she's supposed to do with them. Keep them? Sell them? Give them away?

"I tried to get a cab," Ben tells her, putting his suit coat over the back of the chair and sitting across from her, "but you know—rush hour. Midtown. So then I took the subway, but . . . of course there was a delay. Stalled train ahead, or something like that. You look good."

He tacks that last part on as if it's part of the metro traffic report, and it takes a moment for her to react.

Glad she happened to wear one of her new dresses to work this morning—and glad she stopped in the ladies' room to put on mascara and lipstick—she says, "Oh—thank you. So do you."

"You're saying that because I shaved. Yet another reason I was late."

"You shaved for me?"

He nods. "In the men's room at the office. I haven't done that since . . . well, it's been a long time."

"You didn't have to do it on my account."

"Don't tell me you've changed your mind about razor stubble?"

She shakes her head, smiling faintly. "Still not a fan."

The waiter appears to pour water into their glasses and asks if they'd like to order wine.

Ben orders a bottle of Argentine red without consulting her, then belatedly, as the waiter leaves again, asks Gaby, "That's okay, right? The Malbec?"

"It's fine. I love Malbec."

"I know. I remember. Hates stubble, loves Malbec."

"That's me." She sips her water and notices that he's not wearing a watch.

He always used to wear the Movado she gave him for his birthday the year they were married. It was a beautiful watch, and expensive. Not Rolex-expensive, but still . . .

Did he lose it? Sell it? Put it away, as she did the jewelry he gave her? Why hasn't he replaced it with a different watch now? She wants to ask him, but of course she doesn't.

She looks away from his wrist and notices that the couple at the next table are sharing a bottle of Pellegrino and appetizers. They're talking, laughing, probably planning for all the things they'll do when the baby comes.

Are they speculating about whether it's a boy or girl, or do they already know the sex?

When Gaby was pregnant, she and Ben had opted to be surprised. He'd guessed boy, she'd guessed girl. She'd secretly thought she might be disappointed if she was wrong, but she wasn't. The moment she held their son in her arms, she felt an overwhelming rush of—

"Gaby?"

"Hmm?"

"You're staring at those people."

"Oh, I—sorry." She shrugs. "I just . . . I thought I knew them, but . . . I don't. So how's work?"

He pauses, but only for a second, then goes with her conversational shifting of gears. He tells her about the building he's designing and an upcoming conference he's attending. Then he asks about her job, and whether she's acquired anything interesting for her list.

"Nothing that you'd—oh, wait, remember that book I took a chance on last year? The one Ellen hated?"

"The one about the silent film star and the nun?"

"That's the one." She hesitates, surprised he remembers. She only told him about it back then to make conversation during a stilted dinner out one night when they were supposed to be working on their marriage.

"Did it get published yet?"

"Not only did it get published, but it hit the *New York Times* list last week."

"That's fantastic!"

The waiter shows up with their wine, and Ben lifts a glass to her. "Here's to you and your best seller."

"And to you and your building."

Clink.

Drink.

Silence.

Ben clears his throat. "I'm really happy things are going well for you. And you're so—I mean, you look amazing."

"Oh, that's just the wine talking," she quips, and he smiles.

Then, serious again, he clears his throat. "I guess you're seeing someone?"

Ryan. Right. She nods.

"Did you meet him online?"

She wishes he hadn't asked that, wishes she didn't have to answer. Then, realizing she's free not to, she asks, "Can we talk about something else?"

"Sure, why not?"

"Are *you* seeing someone?"

"Not that," he says, without missing a beat, and tilts his head at her, wearing a faint smile. "What else can we talk about? We've covered work. And books . . ."

"Not all books."

"Enough books for my taste."

"Sports?"

"No!" He holds up a hand like a traffic cop. "If you know what's happening in the game, don't tell me. I'm recording it at home."

She laughs and shakes her head. "You still do that?"

"Yeah, and sometimes I make it all the way home without someone ruining it for me."

"Trust me, I have no clue what's going on in the game."

"Trust me—I believe you."

"Hey! I follow the Yankees."

"Since when?"

"Since—I always followed them. Just not as rabidly as you."

"How about your new boyfriend? Is he—"

"We're not talking about him."

"Oh, right." Ben sips some wine.

"And he's not my new boyfriend."

"Okay."

"He's"—she holds back the word *just*—"someone I've been seeing. I'm sure you've been seeing people, too."

Ben shrugs.

Does that mean that he is? Or that he isn't?

Of course he is. He's on InTune, remember?

But they're not talking about that, and they're not talking about Ryan. They chat on about other things. She asks about his brother and sister-in-law and nieces; he asks about Jaz and several other cousins. They order food, discuss movies and music, and then the appetizers arrive and the waiter pours more wine, and Gaby forgets that she was ever uncomfortable; somehow forgets that they're not still married, until . . .

The couple at the next table catches her eye again as they stand up to go. The husband is solicitous of his hugely pregnant wife as she uses both hands on the tabletop to hoist herself out of the chair. They laugh together as they walk away, the husband's arm around her.

Ben follows Gaby's gaze, watching them. Then he looks at her, wearing such a wistful expression that she knows what he's thinking: *That was us. We were them.*

She expects him to say something about it, but he doesn't.

He just pours more wine into her glass, and then his own, and they sip in thoughtful silence.

Driving up Cherry Street, Alex is still thinking about Mr. Griffith when it happens.

Again.

As she passes number 58, the Queen Anne Victorian where Carmen grew up, and where his mother had still lived—and died—after they were married, she sees him.

Carmen.

It isn't her imagination, and it isn't the first time she's spotted him standing on that porch lately. The house was empty for years, but it's not anymore. There are lights on now, and cars in the driveway, and . . .

And that's Carmen, standing right there by the front door.

Her breath catches in her throat. She turns to watch him, and the car swerves, nearly hitting the curb. She slams on the brakes, shaken.

But when she glances back again, he's gone.

Maybe it *was* her imagination.

Maybe it was Carmen's ghost.

But it's not Carmen himself. It can't be, because he's been gone for a long time. Years. He's never coming back.

Alex takes a deep breath, blows it out slowly, hands clenched on the wheel as she drives the remaining distance to her own house.

Mrs. Toomey, her across-the-street neighbor, waves from her porch rocker as Alex slows to pull into the driveway. The elderly woman is a fixture there at this time of year, reading the paper, dozing, or just "keeping an eye on things," as she put it a while back, on a day Alex was forced to venture across the street after the mailman delivered an envelope addressed to Hester Toomey, 45 Cherry Street, to her own mailbox.

"Keeping an eye on what?" Alex had asked the woman, wearing the same bright smile she reserves for pain-in-the-ass patients who ask too many questions.

"Oh, you know . . . the birds, the trees, the flowers. Mother Nature in all her glory."

Yeah, right. Alex has always been grateful the nosy old

lady isn't spry enough to go snooping around other people's houses or looking into windows.

Though she does sometimes wonder whether Hester Toomey may have seen Carmen's ghost, too. Sometimes she's tempted to stop and ask, but she never does.

Today, as always, she waves back at the woman and pulls the car into the garage, quickly turning off the engine and pressing the remote that lowers the door behind her.

For a moment she allows herself to sit there with her head tilted back and eyes closed, absorbing the silence. It's been a long day, capped off by waiting until a late afternoon patient suffering from chest pains could be transported to the hospital via ambulance.

Then her eyes snap open and she leans forward to open the glove compartment. Time to get a move on.

She removes the orange prescription bottle and carries it into the house, along with groceries she bought on the way home.

She drops the bags on the kitchen counter, stepping around bowls of cat food and milk she left out earlier for Gato. As usual, he left most of it.

"Hey, Mr. Finicky," she calls. "Where are you?"

No reply from the cat. Probably napping on the sofa. Must be nice, Alex thinks, heading straight upstairs with the bottle of Viagra.

In the master bedroom, with its low ceilings that follow the slope of the roofline, she opens a bureau drawer still filled with Carmen's neatly paired socks. Reaching all the way to the back, she tucks the prescription bottle inside, then closes the drawer.

She won't be needing it for another few weeks or so—not until she's ovulating again.

Even then—maybe she won't need it. Maybe Carlos will change his mind about her.

Over my dead body . . .

Yeah, he probably won't change his mind.

Whatever.

If he still isn't interested when her time comes, she'll slip a couple of pills into his supper. That's sure to take care of any . . . lack of desire on his part. There are certain biological urges even the strongest-willed man cannot deny when enhanced with medication.

The technique worked well enough with the others who were—like Carlos—all too eager to get physical with her on the first night, but reluctant on subsequent occasions.

Jerks. They should have been nicer to her. Then maybe she'd have been nicer to them.

Alex sits on the bed and quickly unlaces her rubber-soled shoes, fighting the urge to sink back against the pillows. If she allows herself to do that, she'll probably fall asleep and snooze right through tomorrow morning.

But that wouldn't be a good idea. It's been almost twenty-four hours since she last visited the basement room to tend to her guest. Carlos needs to keep his strength up.

She strips off her scrubs, throws on a tank top and shorts, and takes the ponytail holder out of her brown hair, shaking it so that it falls past her bare shoulders. Looking into the mirror on the back of the closet door, she likes what she sees.

She's not a conventional beauty. Her nose is a little too wide, her lips a bit too thin, and her eyes, albeit a deep shade of blue, are set too close together. There are wrinkles now, too, new ones every day around her eyes and mouth.

But Carmen always thought she was attractive. So did other men, before and after he came along. She never had any problem getting dates. That's not why she turned to InTune.

Her reasons are purely practical. She needs to find men with specific genetic characteristics. They aren't Carmen, but they're as close as she can get. With their help, she can recapture what she lost.

She's already created a new persona on InTune and gone back to browsing profiles in search of her next candidate, just in case it doesn't work out with Carlos.

On the way back downstairs, she passes the front door and checks, as always, to make sure it's unlocked.

Just in case . . .

Yes. Unlocked. Good.

In the kitchen, she goes through the grocery bags. She quickly makes a turkey sandwich, heats a bowl of canned soup, pours soda into a tall glass with ice. There. He'll like this.

She puts the soda bottle back into the fridge, opening and closing the door a little too carelessly. One of the magnets drops off, releasing a sheaf of crayoned drawings. As Alex picks them all up, the memories seep in as always.

Carmen.

Dante.

She loads the meal onto a tray, grabs a flashlight, and heads down the basement stairs.

Same old routine: set down the tray, move the books, pull the latch that swings the shelf forward to reveal the door, open the door.

Another month of this, at least, lies before her.

But soon—soon!—he'll be gone, and she'll have her baby boy again. Maybe then she'll turn the basement space into a nice playroom.

Or maybe she'll sell the house, move away, get a fresh start somewhere . . .

Down south, or in Mexico, or the Caribbean or South America, even . . .

Carmen had family there, on his late father's side. He used to talk about visiting them one day, maybe even going back for a year or two.

"I want to show my son his roots," he would say. "He should know where he comes from, since—well, since my side of the family is all the roots he has."

He will know, Alex promises Carmen now. *I'll take him there. I'll show him. I'll make sure he knows about his father . . .*

His father.

But his father won't be—

No! Don't think that way. The details don't matter.

Alex pulls the door open, picks up the flashlight and shines the beam into the room.

Carlos is lying on the bed.

"Hey, sleepyhead," Alex calls softly. "Time to wake up. I brought your supper."

Huddled under the blanket, he doesn't move.

"Carlos," she calls.

Nothing.

Maybe he's still pretending to be someone else. Fine. She'll play along.

"Nick! Nick?"

Still, no response. Keeping the flashlight beam trained on the bed, she takes a step into the room, wondering if it's a trick. He pulled this crap once before.

"Nick?"

Nothing.

Is he going to pounce on her when she comes close enough?

She inches toward the bed, keeping a cautious distance. He doesn't move.

"Nick. Last call for supper."

No response.

She shrugs. She's not falling for this again.

"Fine. Go ahead and be that—" She breaks off, seeing the blood.

It's not easy to say good-bye . . . even the second time.

Peter's words resonate in Ben's head as he tucks his credit card into the bill folder and hands it back to the waiter.

"I don't know why you won't let me split it with you," Gaby says, wallet still in hand.

He rolls his eyes and says to the ceiling, *"Como coco."*

"You sound like Abuela. Only she never called *me* coconut-headed. Jaz was the stubborn one. And so was she."

Ben grins, remembering Gaby's tiny—no more than five feet tall—but tough grandmother. She had a soft spot for her motherless granddaughter, but not much of one for anyone else. That included him. Gaby had hoped she'd like him from the start because he was a fellow Puerto Rican, unlike her former boyfriend, to whom Abuela continued to refer as the *Guebon.*

"At least she doesn't have a derogatory name for you," Gaby told Ben when her grandmother failed to warm up to him immediately. "That's a good sign."

She was right. Eventually—before their wedding day— Abuela came around.

At the reception, she came up to Ben and cupped his cheek in her withered hand. He asked her to dance.

She shook her head. "I can't dance anymore. I just want to say something to you."

"What is it?"

She pointed to Gaby, across the room laughing with her cousins. *"Cuidala."*

Take care of her.

"Don't worry, Abuela. I will. I promise . . ."

Ben pulls out his phone to check the time. It's late—but not too late.

"I'll tell you what," he says impulsively. "I'll let you buy us an after-dinner drink. Will that make you feel better?"

She looks taken aback. "Okay. Sure. Where do you want to go?"

"Anywhere." *Just not home, alone, again.* "You can decide."

The waiter reappears with the bill folder. Ben busies himself adding in the tip, slaps the folder closed, and pockets his credit card.

"Ready?" he asks Gaby.

"Ready."

Out on the street, she points. "I know a nice place off Gansevoort."

"Great. Let's go."

As they walk, Ben fights the urge to take her hand. This isn't a date. They're not together like that. They're just . . .

Saying good-bye? Is that really what this is?

Peter is right. It's not easy. The more time he spends with her, the more he wants to suggest that they give it another try.

But that shouldn't come from him. It should come from her. And that's about as likely as—

"Oh, no! It's gone."

"What?"

"The place I was taking you—it's right over there, but . . ." She points at a small building with a metal security gate covering the entrance of the first-floor business. "I guess it's closed."

"We can go someplace else."

"We can."

They look around.

"Or," she says, and then stops, shaking her head.

"Or what?"

"I was going to say we can just get in a cab and you can come up to my apartment . . . you know, to get your box of stuff. But you probably don't want to—"

"No, I do. That's a good idea. We can do that. Let's do that."

He turns and raises his arm to flag a passing cab, smiling to himself.

Damn him.

Damn Carlos Diaz—Nick Santana—whoever the hell he is.

Damn him for slitting his wrists with a shard of broken glass that came from a vase Carmen brought home on their first Valentine's Day after they were married.

On that day, the vase had held a dozen roses. Yellow ones, because pink and red, he said, were too cliché.

Alex was thrilled—until she bragged about it the next morning to one of the nurses at the hospital.

"Yellow roses are bad luck!" the woman exclaimed. "Don't you know that?"

Alex did not. A chill ran through her.

"You have to get rid of them," her coworker urged. "Before something terrible happens."

She'd gone home and plucked one thorny stem after another from the vase, feeding each one head first into the garbage disposal. She cried, listening to the grinding blades turning the velvety golden petals into pulp.

Carmen didn't even notice the roses were gone. He was working late, working all the time back then. Only came home to shower and sleep for a few hours.

She knew he sometimes went to visit his mother, who at first was friendly toward her. But her mother-in-law kept her distance as time marched on. It was hard to believe that she was even the same woman Alex—as a new bride—had believed might become the mother she'd always wanted.

"She hates me," she'd tell Carmen.

"She doesn't hate you. That's crazy. You're just paranoid."

Crazy . . . Paranoid . . . Imagining things . . .

She was so sick of hearing those accusations, had been hearing them all her life from people she believed really cared about her, people she'd even thought might adopt her and become her family.

Now she was hearing those things from her own husband.

Carmen didn't mean it that way, though. He'd never been fully aware of certain things in her past. Her juvenile records had been sealed, and there was no reason for him to know. If she told him, she might lose him, and she had already lost so many people.

"You won't lose me," Carmen promised whenever she grew insecure. "Don't worry. You have me forever. I love you. I'm not going anywhere."

But then . . .

Then something terrible happened.

Damn Carmen for bringing her yellow roses. Getting rid of them hadn't gotten rid of the bad luck after all. Even now, years later, it continues.

She should have seen it coming, though—Carlos's suicide. Should have taken precautions to keep it from happening.

He was on antidepressants when he came here. You don't stop any medication cold turkey—especially not the one Carlos was taking. That particular drug carries an increased risk of suicide if the patient abruptly discontinues it. She should have tapered him off the drug just as she had her own medication years ago. Or at least she should have made sure he didn't have the means to harm himself.

She'd slipped up, and now look.

With a muttered curse, Alex pries the sharp, bloodied piece of the broken vase from Carlos's hand and drops it into a small bag. Then, crawling on the floor with the flashlight, she collects the rest of the shards. She puts them into the bag and carries it out to the garage.

She puts the bag into the trunk of the car, along with the shovel, rake, and headlamp. Then, leaving the trunk open, she rolls the handcart into the house, jaw set grimly.

Lying naked in Ben's arms in her bed, her head against his bare chest, Gaby keeps her eyes closed, though she's not the least bit sleepy.

If she allows herself to open them, she'll have to stop pretending that the past few years never happened.

Right now she can almost convince herself that they're back in their old apartment—not the junior four with the nice countertops, but the smaller place where they lived together when they were young and in love and . . .

Happy.

We were so happy.

If they'd stayed in that cozy apartment, Josh's crib would have been right next to their bed that morning. He'd still be alive.

That was what Gaby told herself—and Ben—for months after the loss.

Right or wrong . . .

In this moment, it doesn't matter.

She's happy right here, right now, for the first time in so long . . .

She doesn't want to think about what led them here, or where they'll go from here . . .

Ben's fingertips play up and down her bare arm. "You okay?" he asks softly—the first words he's spoken since they somehow tumbled into bed together.

"Yes. Are you?"

"Yeah. But—"

"Don't say it, Ben."

"Don't say what?"

"You know. That it was a mistake, that we shouldn't have let it happen, that—"

"I wasn't going to say that."

"You weren't?"

"No. It wasn't a mistake."

She ponders that, listening to the city's night noises through the open window. Hip-hop music from a club a few doors down mixes with traffic and sirens. Departing patrons shout at the bouncer.

Gaby's fantasy is shattered. The old apartment was on the thirtieth floor, with central air-conditioning. They heard very little even when the windows were open—which was rare.

Reluctantly, she allows her eyes to open. Her gaze falls on two almost empty glasses of wine sitting on the table. They were sitting right there, sipping and chatting, when he leaned in suddenly and kissed her.

"Then what were you going to say?" she asks him. "When you said 'but' . . . ?"

"I was going to say that I don't think we should talk about it."

"About . . ."

"*This.* Not tonight, anyway. I don't think we should try to figure out what it means, or what should happen next . . . okay?"

Relieved, she smiles and closes her eyes again. "Okay."

Muttering to herself, Alex shoves the blade of a shovel into the patch of ground she just raked clear of fallen leaves from the dense patch of trees arching overhead.

"Over your dead body is right, you son of a bitch . . ."

She heaves a shovelful of dirt to the side of the hole and stabs the blade again into the deepening pit.

"If I'd known what you were going to do, I'd have done it for you myself . . ."

Thud. The shovel slams into the hole again.

She grunts, lifts. More dirt hails down, hitting her shoes.

"Would have made it a lot less messy, too . . ."

Thud.

Grunt.

Lift.

Toss.

At last, the hole is deep enough.

The beam of her headlamp bobs along the trail as she pulls the handcart up to the shed that contains a few large wooden crates, the kind used to ship construction materials and furniture. Carmen meant to burn them or repurpose them, but never had the chance. Alex carts a large one back down to the freshly dug crater. She pries off the lid and sets it aside, then pushes the crate over the edge. It lands in the bottom of the hole with a thump, open side up. Waiting.

Panting hard, she pulls the handcart back to the car, parked in a small clearing off a lane that runs up to the property from the main road. At this time of year, there's a good amount of vegetation to conceal it even if someone happened to pass by—not that anyone ever does.

Reaching into her back pocket for the keys, she's seized by momentary panic. They aren't there.

Where can they be? Did she drop them in the shed? Into the dirt? Somewhere along the overgrown trail? If so, she'll never find them. Now what?

It's not as if she can call Triple A for help. And she can't abandon the car here with a dead body in the trunk.

She can if she flees the country.

It isn't the first time the thought has entered her mind. She can make a fresh start in Mexico or South America . . .

No. That was Carmen's fantasy, back before they built their dream house here. He was the one who had faraway family. She had no one.

No one but him, and their son . . .

And when they were gone, she was back to having no one.

Oh. Okay, there they are. The keys. Thank goodness. No fleeing the country tonight, at any rate. She'd tucked the key ring into the back left pocket of her jeans, not the back right.

She presses the remote and pops open the trunk.

The interior is lined with a big blue plastic tarp. On top of it lies a bulky black garbage bag—the oversized, extra-thick kind used by contractors.

With a grunt, she wrestles it out and lets it clunk to the ground. Then, positioning it on the handcart, she backs down the trail to the waiting crate inside the hole.

Every trudging footstep is in time to the refrain running through her head.

Two . . . weeks . . . two . . . weeks . . . two . . . weeks . . .

That's all the time she has to find someone new.

Chapter 6

"Me muero de hambre!" Jaz exclaims, picking up the menu.

"What else is new?" Gaby asks, seated across the table from her, busily texting on her phone. "You're always starving."

"I want the challah French toast *and* the goat cheese omelet. I can't decide. They both sound so good."

"Mm-hmm."

"Or maybe I'll have the deep fried goat brains instead. What do you think? Do you want to split that?"

"Sure, okay, whatever . . ." Gaby murmurs while typing: @ *brunch w/ my cousin, how bout you?*

"Ay Dios mio!"

Startled, Gaby lifts her head. "What?"

"You're not even listening to me!"

"I'm listening."

"You're texting. You should have just stayed home alone and had brunch with your phone."

"I'm sorry." Gaby hastily types *gtg*—shorthand for *got to go*—and guiltily tucks the phone into her pocket.

Jaz is right. She probably should have stayed home.

But when her cousin called to invite her to brunch, she had just noticed the beautiful day beyond her measly window and was feeling as though she should get out there and enjoy it. Credit for that instinct went to Abuela, who had worked in a factory most of her life. She always said it was a crime for anyone who didn't have to be inside not to go outdoors when the sun was shining.

"Sal afruera!" she'd command, and Gaby would obediently get outside.

She had automatically said yes to Jaz's invitation before stopping to realize she was about to spend several hours with someone who asks a lot of questions she's not in the mood to answer on an ordinary day—let alone today.

Jaz still lives in the old neighborhood in the Bronx and has a Jeep that she likes to drive into Manhattan on weekends. Gaby met her on their usual corner near the parking garage a few blocks from her apartment. Luckily, Jaz was so full of news about a new guy she'd met that she did almost all the talking as they strolled through the dappled Saturday morning sunshine to this café just off Central Park West.

Gaby found herself watching the fat white clouds sailing high above the skyline, remembering those long ago beach days with Ben.

"That one looks like a wizard riding a tricycle up the side of a sugar cone with two scoops of strawberry ice cream," he'd say, or, "Look! It's a three-headed duck swimming over a waterfall!"

"What? I don't see it!"

"That's because you're not looking at it the right way, Gaby. If you really want to see something, just look for it, and it'll be there . . ."

Right now all she can see is her cousin shaking her head disapprovingly from across the table, her big hoop earrings swaying back and forth.

"What? I put away the phone."

"I feel like you're still thinking about it."

"I'm not." She reaches for her own menu and tries to focus on it. But she's too distracted for that; too distracted even for simple conversation. Electronic conversation—with *him*—would be a different story.

A tone sounds from her phone in her pocket, signaling a return text. She waits until Jaz looks away to reach for it, but her cousin catches her.

"Gaby! Come on! You're going to see him in a few hours anyway, aren't you?"

"See who?"

"Ryan. Isn't that who you're texting?"

"No. But I am seeing him tonight," she adds quickly. "We're going to a movie. Have you seen anything good lately?"

Diversion foiled: "If you weren't texting Ryan," Jaz says, "then who were you texting?"

"Ben," she admits reluctantly, setting the menu aside again. Might as well get it over with.

"Ben? *Ben*, Ben?"

"Yup."

"Why?"

She takes a deep breath. "We got together the other night, and we—"

"No!"

"What?"

"Please tell me that you did not do what I think you did, Gabriela."

"If you think we went out to a nice dinner, *Jacinda*"— she echoes the deliberate emphasis on her cousin's given name—"we did."

"And that's all?"

"Ladies, have you decided?" Summoned to the rescue by Gaby's subconscious mind, the waiter materializes with his pad in hand.

"I'll have the challah French toast," Gaby tells him, and adds, with a gleam in her eye, "She'll have the deep fried goat brains."

"Goat cheese omelet," Jaz amends. "And here I thought you weren't listening."

"Yeah, well . . . I'm a multitasker."

"I guess so. Juggling Ryan and Ben . . ."

Pen poised on his pad, the waiter asks, "White, rye, or whole grain with the omelet?"

"Whole grain, please. No butter." Jaz smiles at him sweetly, then turns back to Gaby. "Does Ben know about Ryan?"

"Hash browns or fresh fruit?" The waiter again.

"Fruit."

"Got it." The waiter departs.

Jaz looks expectantly at Gaby, who sighs.

"Yes," she says, "Ben knows about Ryan, but—"

"Does Ryan know about Ben?"

"Know that I was married and now I'm divorced? Yes, he knows that."

"But does he know that you and your ex-husband are—"

"No, because we're not *anything*. We saw each other. We're in touch again. That's it."

Jaz is silent.

Gaby toys with the cloth napkin in her lap, rolling and unrolling the hem.

"I love you, *mami*," Jaz says at last. "I just don't want you getting hurt. You were so excited about seeing someone new, moving on . . ."

"I'm still excited. I'm still moving on."

"You can't move on if you're with your ex."

"I'm not with him." She picks up her cup, sips her coffee, fights the urge to take out her phone to check the latest text.

"Is it because you saw his profile on InTune? You said you weren't going to get in touch with him."

"I didn't. I ran into him."

"On purpose?"

"No! By accident. We were both at Yankee Stadium the other night."

"When you went with Ryan? You didn't tell me you saw Ben."

"I know."

"But you're still going out with Ryan tonight?"

"Yes. Of course." She tries to sound enthusiastic.

She's been trying to *feel* enthusiastic, but ever since that night with Ben at her apartment, she's found it hard to look forward to seeing Ryan again. She can't remember what she found so appealing about him, or what they talked about, or why she'd reacted so passionately to his kisses.

But Ben—she can remember everything about Ben. Everything they said, and did, and the way it felt to kiss him and fall asleep in his arms . . .

She was half asleep when he left before dawn that morning to go home to shower and get ready for work. He kissed her forehead and told her he'd be in touch.

"Don't you want to take your box with you?" she asked groggily.

"Not now. I'll get it later," he said before slipping out the door.

A few hours later she got an e-mail from him at the office, asking for her new cell phone number. Since then, they've been texting back and forth. Mostly just casual comments and questions, although he did ask to see her tonight. Tempted to cancel her plans with Ryan, she thought better of it and told Ben she's busy.

She didn't elaborate, and he didn't ask her to; just wrote: *How about Sunday then?*

Not busy, she responded.

He invited her to go to the beach with him. She said yes. She didn't ask him where. She knew: Orchard Beach.

Now, she finds herself confessing the plan to Jaz.

"So many memories there for you, Gaby. I don't know if that's a good idea."

"There are memories everywhere, Jaz. We were together so many years."

"I know." Jaz takes a long sip of her coffee, holding the cup in both her hands and staring at Gaby over the rim. When at last she sets it down again, she says, "So you're dating him, basically. That's what you're telling me."

"No! It's a Sunday afternoon. We're just going to the beach. Some of the guards from the old days are still there, so we can visit them, maybe take a swim."

"Still a date." Jaz sighs heavily, then brightens. "Maybe it'll rain and he'll cancel."

"Come on, Jaz."

"What?"

"First, the weather is supposed to be great—"

"That's not what I heard. And maybe you should cancel anyway, because—*hello*—you're divorced! He left you! He broke your heart!"

"Maybe I broke his first."

The words spill out of her unexpectedly, obviously catching Jaz by surprise—but catching Gaby off guard as well. She hadn't even realized she'd been thinking that way, but . . .

Maybe it's true.

After all, he was the one who'd wanted to keep talking, keep trying, go to therapy . . .

And you? You just wanted to be left alone with your sorrow.

Her response to the tremendous surge of grief had been to shut down her emotions altogether, anesthetizing herself against experiencing not just pain, but anything at all—including love. Yes, she'd gone through the motions of working on her marriage—but if you can't feel, how can you heal?

At last the numbness has finally begun to give way to genuine emotion. Not just because of Ben, but because she's finally allowed herself to start living again.

Part of the credit for that goes to Jaz.

Gaby reaches across the table and squeezes her cousin's hand. "You always have my best interests in mind. I love you for that. Thank you for not turning your back on me and letting me wallow."

"You know I'd never do that. You've been through hell, but it's behind you now. That's what I thought, anyway."

"It is."

"When he left you, you told me that you never wanted to see him again."

"I didn't." She takes a deep breath. "I know you're trying to protect me, but trust me—I know what I'm doing."

Before Jaz can respond to Gaby's words—essentially, a lie—their food arrives.

"I should have gotten the French toast," her cousin decides, looking at Gaby's plate. "Want to switch?"

"No! I told you I'm not in the mood for eggs."

"Neither am I. How about if we just share yours?"

"You do this every time we go out to eat."

"So? You love me anyway."

Laughing and shaking her head, Gaby pushes her plate to the center of the table.

Saturday is Alex's day off.

Ordinarily she sleeps in.

But last night, she didn't sleep at all. She tried, but her thoughts wouldn't stop churning and her entire body was tense, still, from her ordeal.

Not just the shock of discovering Carlos's bloody corpse, or the unexpected rigor of transporting it up to the woods and burying it with the others, or even the painstaking clean-up that involved lugging pails of hot water and bleach to the basement room and scrubbing away the bloodstains.

It was the tremendous letdown that put her emotions, and her nerves, over the edge.

Carlos had seemed so right. His name even began with C-A-R . . .

Well, she'd been correct to take that as an omen. Just— she should have realized that it wasn't necessarily a *good* omen.

The first thing she does, after giving up on the hope of sleep and crawling out of bed at last, is open the medicine cabinet and take out the pregnancy test she'd been saving.

Always before, there's been an air of anticipation when she holds the box in her hand. Today, for the first time, that spark is missing.

It makes her sad, in a way. But more than sad, it makes her angry.

He robbed her of the excitement she should be feeling as she opens the box, pees on the stick, and carries it back to her bedroom. There, she sets the egg timer she keeps in a drawer of her bedside table. She could just use her phone's stopwatch, of course, but this is the good luck timer she used when she found out she was expecting Dante years ago.

She paces, usually remembering to bend her head at the farthest points of the room where the sloped ceiling gets too low. Sometimes, though, she forgets and walks right into it. Her head throbs, and her fury grows with every step.

This should be a peaceful, hopeful time, and yet—

He robbed her of the ability to say the familiar prayer that's become a mantra. She does pray, but not for a positive result.

Please . . . please . . . please . . .

Please let it be negative.

As much as Alex longs to find that she's carrying a child again, she doesn't want it to be his. A positive test will mean that the bad luck has taken root inside of her, and she'll have no choice but to destroy it.

Closing her eyes, remembering how she'd slaughtered the yellow roses in the garbage disposal, she knows now that it wasn't enough.

She should have incinerated them instead. She should have—

The egg timer dings, curtailing her raging thoughts.

She takes a deep breath and crosses the room to check the plastic indicator.

Pleasepleasepleasepleaseplease . . .

Negative.

Grateful, she closes her eyes and tilts her face to the ceiling.

Okay.

Okay.

It's over. Thank God it's over.

Now she can make a fresh start. And she will . . .

Today.

Something is not right.

Ivy Sacks is certain of it.

It's been exactly two weeks now since Carlos Diaz e-mailed to tell her that his father had been killed in a car accident in Costa Rica.

Horrified by the news, she wrote back right away, extending her sympathy and telling him to take all the time he needed. She also asked about the funeral arrangements, wanting to send flowers. A few days later he e-mailed again, from Costa Rica, to say that the funeral was on hold because his mother was still in intensive care and that he couldn't leave her.

No, of course not. Ivy felt terrible for him. She wrote back again, asking if there was anything she could do. She worded the message carefully, straddling the fine line between colleague and friend.

His reply was a terse, *No, but thanks.*

That was it.

But it was enough to arouse her suspicions.

She's since written back—twice, in fact—to inquire about his mother's condition. Both queries were met with silence. Maybe he assumed she was nudging him because she wanted to know when he plans on returning to work.

But it isn't that at all. She's just worried. As a boss, and a friend, and . . .

All right, as a woman who's been secretly infatuated with Carlos from the moment he set foot in her office a few years ago. He was married then, and so her feelings were utterly inappropriate . . .

Of course they still are, even now that he's divorced. A boss should not have romantic thoughts about an employee. Or at least, if one can't control one's romantic thoughts, one shouldn't act on them.

Ivy hasn't. That's why she's spent the last two weeks trying to distance herself, emotionally, from Carlos's personal tragedy. But it's taken every bit of restraint, as this second week wore on, not to pick up the phone and try to contact him directly in Costa Rica.

Eventually the restraint wore thin.

Yesterday morning she arrived at work before anyone else and slipped through the dark, deserted halls into his cubicle to check his computer files. Yes, she knew it was wrong—but her intentions were noble. This time, anyway.

She wasn't sure what she was expecting to find—perhaps evidence that he'd been planning a secret vacation with the woman he'd dated that last weekend—but the files yielded nothing out of the ordinary.

Nothing, that is, other than the fact that his social networking accounts appeared to have been canceled. But that's probably not unusual, given the circumstance. In the aftermath of a family calamity, Facebook and InTune undoubtedly feel frivolous at best—and are a blatant invasion of privacy at worst.

Finally, back in her own office with the door closed, Ivy broke down and called Carlos.

She dialed both his apartment and his cell phone, leaving messages on both voice mails. Then, feeling like a seventh grade girl with a crush, she closed her office door and did some lunch hour sleuthing on the Internet, looking for more information about his parents' accident.

She learned that fatal car accidents are by no means a rarity in Costa Rica, which apparently has one of the highest traffic death rates in the world. There had been many over the past few weeks. But none that she could find seemed to fit the circumstances of Carlos's parents' tragedy.

That probably means nothing—but it could mean something.

That Carlos lied? Why would he lie about something so horrible?

Common sense tells her that he wouldn't. That would be a sick thing to do, and Carlos isn't like that. He can't possibly be that twisted.

Yet there's some part of her—some irrational, immature part—that can't stop wondering. Maybe she doesn't know him as well as she'd like to think she does.

What if he's really just off on vacation someplace, with some woman?

For all she knows, he's skipped town and has no intention of ever coming back.

Sheer speculation, of course.

Still, the more she's thought about it over the last twenty-four hours, the more her genuine concern has given way to anger and resentment.

Finally, last night, she decided it would be perfectly appropriate to take matters even another step further. Working late on a balmy Friday night, when it seemed most Manhattanites had escaped their concrete cages well before rush hour and fled the city for woodsy or beachy weekend retreats, she once again found herself virtually alone on her floor, other than the cleaning staff.

It wasn't hard to convince one of the janitors, who spoke very little English, to unlock the door to the human resources office. When at last he complied, she quickly got her hands on Carlos's file, including his emergency contact page, and made a photocopy.

She tucked it into her briefcase, carried it home, and tried to make herself forget about it.

Now, in the bright light of the next day, sitting in the small studio apartment she shares with her cats, she realizes that her colleagues probably wouldn't have batted an eye if she'd gone into human resources at any point this week to request the information. She could have—*should* have— voiced her concerns through the proper channels. No one would have suspected that her feelings for Carlos run deeper than professional concern.

"Too late for that now, though," she tells her fat orange cat, whose name, of course, is Garfield.

Once, when she posted pictures of Garfield on Facebook, one of her friends—who, she has since decided, is not a true friend—made a comment: *Garfield—what an unusual name for a fat orange cat!*

Ivy responded that he'd been named after the cartoon cat.

For some reason, the friend—whom she has also since defriended—thought that was amusing.

Later, Ivy's younger brother Seth had pointed out that the comment was meant to be ironic.

"You know—like a cliché," he said. "Like—what else would you name a fat orange cat? It's irony, Ivy."

Irony. Okay. She got it.

She thought long and hard before she named her next

cat "Snoopy." He was all white—but he's a cat, not a dog. Irony.

Her Facebook friends appreciated that, judging by the number of people who clicked the Like button when she posted Snoopy's picture and name. Ivy was pleased.

Now, her mind on Carlos, she tells Garfield, "I don't think I should wait until Monday morning to do something about this."

The cat purrs agreeably, rubbing his arched back against Ivy's leg as she sits down at the computer with the photocopied file information.

Carlos had listed someone named Roxanna Diaz as his emergency contact, providing both a home number and a cell phone.

Is she his sister? His ex-wife?

Only one way to find out.

Well, two ways—but Ivy would rather do some snooping around online before boldly dialing one of those numbers.

A Google search turns up far more women named Roxanna Diaz than she expected. Even when she narrows it to New York, there are many. It would take her a long time to even rule out all the ones who likely have no connection to Carlos.

Instead, she Googles the name along with first one phone number, then the other. But again, she comes up with nothing relevant.

Even more frustrating: each phone number, checked separately on a reverse lookup site, comes up with: *Not in our data base.*

Meaning . . . what? That they're unlisted? Or that Carlos made them up? Did he make up Roxanna Diaz, too?

"You know what?" Ivy says to Garfield. "I'm just going to call. I mean, why shouldn't I? Anyone would call, right?"

Garfield, snoozing at her feet now, doesn't even stir as she half stands and leans to reach for the phone on the nearby counter.

That's the nice thing about living in a tiny apartment— pretty much everything is in arm's reach.

It's the *only* nice thing—well that, and the fact that she's located in the heart of midtown, in a safe doorman building. That's much better than having a lot more space in a sketchy neighborhood out in the boroughs, like Carlos.

When Ivy bought this place ten years ago, in her late twenties, it was more than she could comfortably afford. But rent was a waste of money, and she figured she'd be making a lot more within a year or two. Anyway, sooner or later— most likely sooner, she thought—she'd meet Mr. Right, marry him, and move to the suburbs. When that happened, she could either sell the studio, keep it and rent it out, or she and her husband could use it as a pied-à-terre . . .

But here she is, pushing forty, perpetually broke and in debt, making less, not more, than she was back then. Not only that, but she's still single, and when she finally met Mr. Right, he was off-limits because he worked for her. To top things off, he's now fallen off the face of the earth.

Irony. Again.

You have to do something. You have to figure out what's going on.

She starts to dial the first phone number on his emergency contact list, listed as the home phone.

If someone answers, you can always just hang up.

Right. Exactly like a seventh grade girl with a crush.

What is wrong with you?

Ivy pauses, closing her eyes, hating herself. Hating that this is her life. She should be out there in the world, doing something interesting, instead of dwelling on Carlos, letting her imagination run away with her . . .

Except what if something is really wrong?

She finishes dialing. If someone answers, she'll explain

that she's trying to track down her employee and this is the number she was given.

The call is answered on the first ring.

Her breath catches in her throat—until she hears a high-pitched tone and a recording: "The number you have reached is not in service at this time . . ."

Okay.

That's fine. No big deal.

She dials the second number, the cell phone.

Once again it's answered on the first ring.

But this time there's no recording.

"Hello?" a female voice says.

"Uh—huh—hello?" Ivy stammers.

"Hello?" the voice repeats. "*You* called *me*."

"I know. Sorry, I—"

"Who is this?"

"I'm looking for Carlos Diaz," she blurts.

Silence.

Then, "Why?"

"Because he works for me, and I'm concerned about him."

"Why?"

"Because—are you Roxanna?"

"Who is this?"

"My name is Ivy Sacks. I'm his supervisor at—"

"Oh, Ivy. I've heard about you."

That gives her pause. Carlos mentioned her? Wondering what he said about her, she asks, "And you're Roxanna?"

"Yes."

"And you're his . . ."

The woman doesn't make it easy by filling in the blank. She just waits for Ivy to complete the sentence.

She tries, " . . . sister?"

"No. No, I'm not his sister." The woman lets out a prickly laugh. "How did you get this number?"

"Carlos listed you as his emergency contact."

"Wow, did he? I guess that was back when we were still married."

So she's his ex-wife. Got it.

"What's going on with him?" Roxanna asks. "Why are you concerned?"

"Because he's had a family crisis. His father was killed in a car accident last week and his mother was badly injured, and he had to fly—"

"Wait a minute—*what*?"

"There was a car accident," she explains, nudging Garfield away so she can stand and pace. "His father was killed and his mother was hurt—"

"That's impossible," Roxanna cuts in—though not in incredulous disbelief, the way someone might respond to an unexpected tragedy; rather, the words are spoken flatly, as if stating a simple fact.

"Why is it impossible?"

"Because Carlos's father died when he was six. He was a cab driver, and he was killed in a robbery. It happened on Christmas Day. His mother lives with her boyfriend in Costa Rica."

"Oh, well—I mean, he *said* it was his father. I guess he was talking about his mother's—"

"Never in a million years. Carlos was named after his father and he worshipped him. He'd never refer to Pasqual as his father. Trust me."

Trust me? Consumed by intense dislike for Roxanna—and not sure whether it's because of her combative, cavalier attitude or because she was married to Carlos—Ivy doesn't want to trust her. And yet—why would she lie?

But why would Carlos lie? Especially about something so terrible?

"He . . . he never mentioned that his father died years ago," Ivy tells Roxanna, unable to keep herself from feeling—and probably sounding—defensive.

"Yeah, well, he never liked to talk about that. When he and I first started dating and I asked him about his family, he just said his parents were retired and living down South. It was easier for him than having to explain about his father to someone he didn't know very well."

Miffed by the implication that he must not know *her* very well, Ivy clears her throat. "Okay, well . . . *someone* was killed in a car accident in Costa Rica, and his mother was injured. What are their names? Do you know?"

"Of course I know their names. I was married to the man for years."

Hating her, Ivy grabs a piece of paper and a pen. "And do you know where in Costa Rica they live? Do you have their contact information?"

"Of course," Roxanna says again, "unless they've moved. Hang on, I'm looking for the address. I know it's here some-place . . ."

"Thank you."

"You're welcome. But . . ."

"But what?"

"I hate to say it—I mean, I have nothing against Carlos anymore, but—it sounds like he lied to you."

"Why would he do that?"

"Who knows? I mean, especially about an accident, and his mother—Carlos loves his mother. Respects her."

"I know."

Ivy doesn't know, really. But she assumes he loves and respects his mother, and she doesn't want his ex-wife to assume she has the upper hand on all this . . . *knowing*.

"Did he sound upset when you talked to him?" Roxanna asks.

"I didn't talk to him. He sent an e-mail. It happened after hours."

"Oh. Okay, well . . . Hang on, I'm still looking . . ."

Ivy hears a man's voice rumbling in the background. Roxanna's replies are muffled, as if she's covering the receiver, but most of what she says is audible: "I don't know . . . Something about my ex . . . No, from his job . . . How should I know? I haven't talked to him in months."

Then she's back on the line: "Okay, I got it. Are you ready to write it down?"

"Ready." Mouth set grimly, Ivy takes down Carlos's mother's and her boyfriend's names, address, and phone number, not certain what—if anything—she should do with them.

Chapter 7

Sitting on a chair outside a vast warren of department store dressing rooms, Gaby thumb-types in response to Ben's latest text: *At Macy's, waiting for Jaz to try something on. How about you?*

Just finished swimming, is the reply.

She smiles, picturing Ben in the water.

That first summer they met, she often sat on the lifeguard tower and watched him doing laps in the sound, admiring his speed and grace as he pulled himself through the sparkling water with powerful strokes. He swam hard, just the way he did everything else, she'd soon come to realize: as if he were trying to reach some long-sought, distant goal. He'd been the strongest candidate in their training class in part because he was ultra-conditioned and in part because he welcomed and thrived on a challenge.

When at last he'd emerge like a glistening god sprung from the sea, she'd try not to stare. The sun had bronzed his skin and he had a lean swimmer's build—broad shoulders, long torso, tight abs, muscular legs . . .

It's been a long time since she looked at him that way; a long time since she felt that forbidden stirring deep inside of her. Forbidden then because she was young and inexperienced, and they were co-trainees and then coworkers, obligated to focus on the task at hand and not each other.

Forbidden now, because their time together has long since come and gone.

Yet twenty-four hours from now they'll be together on the beach again, and who knows . . .

"Gabriela?" Jaz pokes her head out of the dressing room. "Come check out this dress. What do you think?"

Still holding her phone, Gaby goes to look. Her cousin's hourglass figure is spectacular in a turquoise summer dress with a wide red belt.

"You're gorgeous."

"Does it make me look too hippy?"

"No! You need to buy that dress. And I might need to borrow it—not that it'll look like that on me."

"It'll look better on you. You don't need to lose fifteen pounds like I do. In fact, how about you buy it and I'll borrow it?"

"Can't. I just bought three new dresses at Saks and now I'm broke again."

"Saks? Ooh, *sofisticado*!"

"They were on sale."

"On sale at Saks is still expensive. You must be trying to impress someone."

Before Gaby can reply, her phone buzzes in her hand with another incoming text.

"You're *still* going back and forth with Ben?" Jaz shakes her head, adding, *"Es loco,"* as she retreats into the dressing room again.

Gaby looks at the phone. The text isn't from Ben this time. It's from Ryan.

He's looking forward to their date tonight.

She isn't.

She can't help it.

Maybe she's crazy, as Jaz said. Maybe she should pretend—

for Jaz's sake, and for her own—that she hasn't fallen in love with her ex-husband again. But it's not true.

I love him. I love him again, or maybe . . .

I never stopped loving him.

If only she were convinced that reconnecting—perhaps reuniting—with Ben was truly the right thing to do. But is she really capable of letting go of all that anger and hurt?

Not if it means letting go of Josh.

That's the simple answer.

For Gaby, the only way to truly move past the pain would be to allow herself to forget. But forgetting that Josh died—forgetting *how* he died—might mean the rest of it would start to fade, too.

Memories are all that's left of her son, and . . .

How can I let go?

Ivy's nagging feeling that something isn't quite right has grown into full-blown panic that something has gone terribly, perhaps dangerously, wrong.

She's ninety-nine-point-nine-percent certain there was no car accident in Costa Rica. Either Carlos lied, or . . .

Somebody else did. But who? And why?

Hesitant to call the numbers Roxanna had given her, she'd instead searched online for his mother, Maria-Elena Diaz, and her boyfriend, Pasqual Herrera. Neither was listed in any accident report or death notice, but there was plenty of evidence that they're both alive and well and living in Costa Rica at the address Carlos's ex-wife had provided.

Pasqual is active on several social networking sites, and none of his pages are privacy-protected. Nothing he writes is in English, but Ivy absorbed enough high school Spanish to have a general idea what he's talking about.

According to his Twitter feed, he disagrees with a referee's call in last night's well-publicized World Cup soccer match, and he's spending this Saturday morning fishing for wahoo on Drake Bay. And on his Facebook page there are several recent photographs of him with Maria-Elena, many snapped over the last few weeks. He's one of those people who chronicles daily minutia in his status updates, detailing what he's eaten for dinner, friends he's visited, movies he's seen . . .

Pasqual may not be Carlos's father, but he's very much alive.

Maria-Elena is most definitely Carlos's mother—photos show that she looks just like him—but by no means is she lying in a hospital bed.

And Carlos's father might be dead, but he has been for decades. Armed with his name, thanks to Roxanna, and the date he'd been killed in a robbery, Ivy easily confirmed that information.

She paces her apartment, growing more troubled by the minute.

Why the lie?

Had she actually spoken to Carlos, she could assume that he's just a jerk who was trying to get some unscheduled time off. But he's accumulated three weeks of vacation to use this year, so it's not as if he doesn't have the days coming.

Plus, on every other occasion when he unexpectedly needed time off—because he was sick, or had an appointment, usually with his divorce attorney—he followed company protocol and called to let her know directly. If she wasn't there, he always just left her a voice mail.

Why now, even with a family emergency, would he merely e-mail? And why would he then proceed to ignore her subsequent calls and e-mails?

"He wouldn't do that," Ivy informs Snoopy, her white cat, as he hops from the top of the couch to the countertop in the kitchenette. "I know he wouldn't."

Snoopy arches her back and blinks, as uninterested as

Garfield is, still snoozing on the rug beneath the chair Ivy had vacated.

Anyone could have gained access to Carlos's e-mail account by guessing his password—or by getting their hands on his desktop, his laptop, his phone . . .

"This isn't good," Ivy tells Snoopy.

Carlos lives in a crime-ridden neighborhood. There are shootings and break-ins out there all the time. Something could have happened to him. Someone could be trying to cover up a crime.

"I have to do something," she tells Snoopy, who watches her cross over to pick up the phone again.

She hesitates before dialing, but only briefly.

If she's wrong, and Carlos is putting one over on her, then she'll simply look foolish for calling the police. She'll look even more foolish if anyone finds out she snuck into his office and went through his computer files—and not just after she grew suspicious last week.

Foolish? I could lose my job for that.

But if she doesn't call the police simply to preserve her own dignity, and Carlos is in trouble somewhere—or worse—

I'd never forgive myself.

Her mind made up, Ivy swallows hard and dials 911.

Ben.

Alex has always liked the name. It's manly. A real man is exactly what she needs right now, having disposed of the cowardly Carlos.

Ah, Ben. Ben is promising.

Her mouth curves into a smile as she clicks from his online headshot, depicting classic Latin good looks, to his InTune profile.

Specific criteria—searching for a Hispanic New Yorker

in his thirties or forties—led her to his page. Now she scans the information, hoping the other key pieces will fall into place.

She's never going to find an exact replica of Carmen's DNA. She can only hope to find someone who possesses the most prominent traits her husband passed down to their son. Not just physical characteristics and ethnicity, but a passion for buildings and music and baseball . . .

Ben is a structural engineer. Check.

Ben likes classic rock. Check.

Ben likes the New York Yankees. Check.

Ben . . .

Alex's eyes widen as she reads the entry that clinches for her the idea that she might have found not just the latest candidate for unwitting sperm donor, but—perhaps—her soul mate as well.

Ben lost a child.

Back at home, Gaby slumps in the chair by the window, legs propped on a stack of books, laptop open. Her intent was to read an electronic manuscript submission her assistant discovered in the virtual slush pile last week, but she can't seem to get past the first paragraph. A promising paragraph, all things considered, but still . . .

She can't stop thinking about Ryan.

Not the way she thought about him after their first—or second—kiss, which is unfortunate. She'd give anything to recapture that glimmer of excitement for someone new, someone who isn't Ben.

But as the day wears on, the more she thinks ahead to her date with Ryan, the more certain she is that she can't go through with it.

It isn't fair to let Ryan wine and dine her under the assumption that their relationship will continue to progress.

She thought she was ready to move on, but she clearly still has a lot of healing to do.

In the grand scheme of all that is fair and unfair, her worst crime by far was to blame Ben for what had happened to their son. It was cruel and irrational, but she couldn't help herself then. Placing blame was easier, somehow, than accepting the sheer randomness of the incident.

She'd never imagined herself capable of forgiving Ben.

But maybe she's the one who needs to be forgiven.

How could I have pushed him away when he needed me? We needed each other.

I still need him.

I have to tell him—

But first things first. Sitting up straight, she thrusts aside her laptop and reaches for her phone, plugged into its charger on the end table beside the housewarming plant Jaz brought. It still sits in its foil-wrapped plastic pot on the end table, where it receives very little light, and water only when Gaby thinks to dump the last drops from her Poland Spring bottle into the dirt.

Somehow it's managed to survive despite her neglect, while . . .

Oh, Joshua.

For seven months—no, almost sixteen, from the moment she found out she was expecting a baby—she had been consumed by nurturing that fragile new life. In the end that didn't matter. In the end . . .

She reaches past the plant, picks up her phone, goes into her contacts list and clicks on Ryan's phone number. The call connects instantly.

He answers on the first ring. "Hey! How are you?"

"I'm . . ."

. . . coming down with something.

No. Not fair.

"I'm fine," she tells him.

"That's a relief. I was afraid you might be calling to cancel on me." His tone is teasing.

Her heart sinks. "Actually, I do have to cancel."

"Is everything okay?"

"Not really. I'm dealing with some personal stuff right now, and I can't . . . it's just not a good time for me."

After a long pause, he asks, "Is there anything I can do to help you with whatever's going on?"

"No, it's not . . . not like that."

"Oh." Ryan inhales, exhales. "Okay, well . . . how about if you call me when it is a good time?"

"I will," she lies, and hangs up, knowing she's never going to speak with him again—a great guy, a guy who has no baggage, no connection to her tragic past; the kind of guy any single woman in New York would want to meet.

What the hell did she just do?

The right thing. You did the right thing.

You're not ready for a new relationship when you haven't resolved the old one. And you can't will yourself to care about someone any more than you can will yourself to stop.

Sullivan Leary was—quite literally—born to be a New York City detective.

Her father, her uncles, and her grandfather on the Leary side were all NYPD. So were most of the men in her mother's family—going right back to Paddy Sullivan, a beat cop who'd been born in County Cork and was killed in a Prohibition-era bootlegger brawl.

Back in the late sixties, Sullivan's parents—both the products of sprawling Irish-Catholic families—broke with tradition and didn't marry until they were both thirty, then made the progressive decision to have just one child. One, they felt, was all they could afford to raise on a cop's salary.

This detail certainly wasn't something they shared with

their priest, their families, or even Sullivan herself. Not until recently, a few years back.

That day, Sully called her father and said, "I have some news for you. You might want to sit down."

"Good news or bad news?"

"That depends on how you look at it."

"I'm sitting. Are you pregnant?"

She winced. It was no secret that she and her husband had been trying to conceive for a while.

"No, I'm not pregnant. And that's good news, Da, considering that I was calling to tell you that Rick and I are getting divorced."

Which was also good news—not just for her, as it turned out. That day her father admitted that he and Sully's mother—who had died shortly before Sully and Rick were engaged—had never cared for her husband.

He also promised her that he'd manage to survive if no one ever called him Grandpa.

"I thought you always said you wanted grandchildren."

"I said it would be nice. It would be nice to win the lottery, too, but you won't see me crying if I don't. Anyway, you might meet someone new. You could still make me a grandpa someday"

"I'm already in my late thirties."

"So? Your mother had you when she was in her thirties."

"But she couldn't have any more kids after me, so . . ."

"*Didn't*," her father said. "Not *couldn't*."

That gave her pause. She'd always assumed her parents subscribed to the Catholic Church's Natural Family Planning teachings, as her many—*many*—aunts and uncles did, which had resulted in dozens of cousins. If her parents hadn't had five or six or more kids, Sully figured, it was probably because they couldn't. And perhaps, hereditarily, why she herself had so much trouble conceiving.

She was wrong. Her father told her that she was always

meant to be an only child. He also confessed that he'd been hoping for a son, because he wanted someone to follow in his law enforcement tradition.

"This was before all that women's lib stuff happened," he reminded her. "But your mom—she was always ahead of the times. She said you could be whatever you wanted to be."

"Or whatever *you* wanted me to be," Sully said with a grin, remembering all those childhood nights spent up past her bedtime, curled up on his lap watching *Starsky and Hutch, Kojak, Adam-12* . . .

She never wanted to be anything but a cop. She got her bachelor's degree in criminal justice from John Jay, enrolled in the police academy, and worked her way from rookie patrol cop to detective with the Missing Persons Squad in Manhattan.

Now, she's exactly where she always wanted—and planned—to be.

Generally speaking, that is.

In this moment—on her way to inform the mother of a teenage runaway that her daughter's body was just pulled from litter-strewn swampland in Staten Island—she wouldn't mind being someplace else.

"On a tropical beach with a frozen piña colada," she tells her partner, Stockton Barnes. "How about you?"

"Where would I be if I could be someplace else right this second?" He glances over his shoulder to check for traffic as they merge onto the northbound FDR, heading toward Harlem, where the runaway's family lives.

"You can be anyplace at all," Sully tells him. "Anyplace in the world."

"I'd best be on that beach with you, Gingersnap, holding up an umbrella and coating you in sunscreen," he says with a grin. " 'Cause with that lily white skin o' yours, you gonna fry up crisper and redder than bacon."

"Again with the jokes about my pasty complexion?" She

rolls her eyes. "You know, I could have a great fun if I ever had a day off."

"Yeah, and I could turn white as a sheet if I ever ran into a ghost. But none of those things is gonna happen, so . . ."

"So it is what it is."

"It is what it is."

That's their mantra. They say it to each other a lot.

Some days are harder than others. This is one of them.

Though the vast majority of missing persons cases involve juveniles, nearly all are solved sooner or later, and very few end with homicide.

Sully sighs, gazing out the window at the sun-splashed buildings that line the East River, thinking about the mother of the dead girl. What is she doing right now? Is she sipping her coffee and wondering whether today might be the day her daughter comes home to her? Or did she lose hope long ago? Did she wake up wondering whether this will be the day two detectives come to the door with the worst news a parent can hear . . .

"I just hope she's not alone when we get there," Stockton says, and she knows that his thoughts have taken the same path. That happens a lot.

"She's a single mother with three younger kids. It's better if she *is* alone," Sully points out, wanting to spare the dead girl's siblings the ordeal of witnessing a tragic moment that will leave an indelible mark.

You think about that a lot, when you've done this job long enough. You prepare yourself for the role you're required to play in what will undoubtedly become the worst memory in someone's life. Sometimes it's a stranger who answers the door to the bearers of bad news. That's hard enough. But when it's someone you've gotten to know over the past few months, as is the case with this particular mother . . .

That's brutal. As a cop, you learn to compartmentalize,

but you can never fully disconnect yourself from the emotions that go with the territory.

Stockton has fallen silent again, but Sully knows he's still thinking about the mother and the task at hand.

Detectives are naturally intuitive; reading your partner's mind is another thing you learn after enough time on the job. So is finishing each other's sentences—not that Stockton appreciates it when she does that.

Physically, the two of them are polar opposites. He's tall, beefy, and black; she's a slightly built redhead who is, as Stockton likes to say, "whiter than white." But they have far more in common with each other than either ever did with their ex-spouses.

A fellow detective back at the precinct had asked her—when she and Stockton were simultaneously going through their divorces—if they were romantically involved.

Sully found that laughable. So did Stockton, when she told him, though he feigned disappointment.

"What, you're not into me?"

"Are you kidding? I made the mistake of marrying a fellow cop. You think I'm going to date one now?"

"Ditto, Gingersnap," he said, and they slapped palms in agreement.

Stockton is her partner, best friend, big brother, super hero . . . but not her love interest.

Who the hell has time for a love interest with this crazy job?

As if to punctuate the thought, her cell phone rings.

She takes it out, sees that it's the precinct, and answers it the way she always does—precinct or not: "Yeah. Leary."

The voice on the other end—Hakim Aziza, a fellow Missing Persons detective—wastes no time on preamble. "You know the Fuentes and Delgado case?"

"Do I *know* it?"

She's only spent the last few months trying to figure out

whether the disappearances of two local businessmen were random coincidence, or whether they met with foul play—never an easy determination when you have no body and no evidence pointing in that direction.

Most adults who vanish do so deliberately—though the loved ones they leave behind will often insist they'd never voluntarily walk away from their lives. Sully has discovered plenty of grown men and women alive and well, often having run off with another woman or man. And while you'd rather close a case with a live body than a dead one, it's never a pleasure to tell someone their spouse abandoned them by choice. Nor is it easy to stick with protocol and refuse to disclose the person's whereabouts. All you can say is that they've been found alive, and leave the loved ones to draw their own conclusions.

Jake Fuentes was single and lived alone. When he was reported missing back in December, his family—like so many others—was convinced something terrible must have happened to him. His mother sobbed that her son would never miss Christmas at home with the family; his sister insisted that he would never disappoint his nieces.

"Jake had promised to take them ice skating at Rockefeller Center so they could see the tree on Saturday," she said, clutching a soggy Kleenex, "and then he was going to take them shopping at the American Girl Store. He spoiled my girls. He doted on them. He never would have taken off like this."

Her words rang true, but then . . .

They usually do, when families are talking about the missing person who could never, would never . . .

"I just know something terrible happened to Jake," his sister said worriedly.

At the time, Sully doubted it.

But a few months later, when Tomas Delgado disappeared, she started to wonder. He, too, was single and lived alone.

The two men had other things in common, too. Both were handsome Hispanic men in their thirties. One was a residential architect, the other a civil engineer. Both disappeared on Friday nights, exactly three months apart. Both had sent e-mails to their bosses claiming they needed time off for family emergencies that later proved to be lies.

Sitting up straighter in her seat, Sully asks Hakim, "What about Delgado and Fuentes? Did one of them turn up?"

"No. But there's another one."

"Another one missing?"

"Yeah, and he fits the bill. Works for a construction firm, and his supervisor just called to say he fell off the face of the earth two weeks ago—apparently, on a Friday night, exactly three months after Delgado. His name is Carlos Diaz."

That Gaby very likely has a date tonight shouldn't have surprised Ben, much less bothered him.

Or so he's been reminding himself ever since he reached out to see if they could get together and she responded that she's busy.

If it weren't a date, she would have told him about her plans. She's never been one to skimp on details. Back when they were married, they'd had a couple of minor arguments due to her inability to tell someone she couldn't do something without offering at least one solid reason why.

"You don't owe people an explanation," he would tell her, "because then you're giving them an opening to talk you into something you'd rather not do."

Most of the time, "people" referred to Gaby's cousin Jacinda. Ben always liked her well enough, and they got along for the most part—unless she tried to steal the reins from his wife.

In truth, Gaby was more than capable of keeping Jacinda in her place. She'd been doing it her entire life. For her, Jaz was big sister, best friend, and cousin all rolled into one. But sometimes Jaz's pushiness wore thin.

Or maybe Ben was slightly jealous of the bond between the two women.

"You just want me all to yourself," Gaby would say whenever Jaz tried to talk her into changing plans to spend time with her instead of at home with her husband.

"There's nothing wrong with that. You're my wife. And if you tell someone you can't do something, you can't do it. Just say you're busy and leave it at that. End of story."

This morning, when he'd impulsively reached out to see if Gaby wanted to go to the beach and say hello to some of their old lifeguard friends, she told him that she was at brunch with her cousin. But when he asked her to go out tonight instead, she replied only that she was busy.

Not with her cousin. Not with work, or a friend. Just . . .

Busy.

Yeah—she has a date. And why shouldn't she?

For that matter, why shouldn't *he*?

It's been a few days since he signed into his InTune account. But now he grabs his phone, clicks on the app, and goes to the log-in page. Having saved his user name and password, all he has to do is hit Enter to access his page.

Still—something stops him.

Do you really want to date someone else?

The answer: *No.*

Now that he's seen Gaby again, he only wants to reclaim what they once had together. Whether that's even within the realm of possibility is unclear, but he'll know soon enough.

If it is, he'll delete this online dating account and focus every bit of energy on starting over with his ex-wife.

If it isn't . . .

I still don't want to date anyone else.

But then, he doesn't want to spend the rest of his life alone either.

Okay. If it turns out that Gaby isn't interested in a future with him, he'll force himself to keep trying to meet someone who is.

With a satisfied nod, he closes out of InTune and is about to put the phone aside when it vibrates with an incoming text.

Gaby.

It reads simply: *Still free tonight?*

It's been a hell of a day for Sully.

Technically, it began at midnight, when she and Stockton were on a stakeout that lasted into the early morning hours. She then crawled into bed at home just before dawn, only to be awakened by the crash of a cymbal: her upstairs neighbor's son practicing the drums at eight o'clock.

Shortly afterward came the phone call about the teenage runaway's remains turning up in Staten Island. Not fun. She and Stockton had to notify the mother that her daughter had been found, comforting the poor woman when she collapsed in grief, and calming her distraught younger children, who were all at home when they showed up.

As always, they assured the family that they would do everything possible to find the person who'd killed their loved one.

After that ordeal came the usual endless paperwork. Finally, back at the station, they were briefed on the latest missing persons case.

Carlos Diaz had last been seen fifteen days ago, on a Friday night, when he left his office after work. His supervisor at the construction firm reported that he'd sent an e-mail later that night saying there had been a death in his family and he would be out for at least a week.

There hadn't been a death in his family, though. Not recently anyway. His father is long dead and his mother and her boyfriend are alive and well in Central America.

Jake Fuentes and Tomas Delgado had also last been seen on Friday evenings—one in March, the other last December—and had sent similar e-mails. Both were known to use dating Web sites, and Jake had mentioned to a co-worker the night he disappeared that he had a date with a new woman he met online.

"It's not unusual for a single guy in Manhattan to have an online dating profile," Sully reminds Stockton now, as they drive from the precinct toward the midtown apartment of Ivy Sacks, the woman who reported Carlos Diaz missing.

Sully is behind the wheel this time, while Stockton wolfs down the sandwich he'd bought at a deli right before they got into the car. It's his second lunch. He'd somehow consumed the first right after they saw the photographs of the corpse in the Staten Island swamp. The man has an iron stomach.

"*I* don't have an online profile," he points out, wiping crumbs from his mustache with a paper napkin.

"Maybe you should."

"*Pfft.* This brother right here has *no* problem meeting women."

"You're not dating anyone."

"That's beside the point. I meet plenty of women. I just don't want to date them. What about you? I don't see you going online to meet men."

"I don't go anywhere to meet men. I've met enough men to last me a lifetime," Sully tells him. "But we're not talking about me. Or you."

"You're the one who brought it up."

"The point *is* . . ." She looks over at him for emphasis. "Most single people in this city are trying to meet someone. I bet this guy Carlos had an online profile. And I bet we won't find one if we look. Same as with the other two."

That's the most troubling part of the case.

Both Jake Fuentes and Tomas Delgado had talked about using online dating services, and their credit card records showed payments to InTune, one of the more popular sites. But neither had a profile there.

An attempt to subpoena their records from the site led nowhere. InTune reported that both men had deleted their accounts almost precisely at the time they'd vanished, and had done so by logging in from their usual IP addresses. Unfortunately, the stored content hadn't been preserved long enough for law enforcement to investigate their online connections.

With any luck, this time it will be.

Sully is convinced now that the three disappearances are connected, and that the missing men didn't walk away from their lives of their own accord. She only hopes it's not too late for them.

Human remains matching their descriptions have yet to turn up—but what are the odds that all three are being held somewhere alive?

"Not good," Stockton tells her when she poses the question out loud. "But it happens. There was that case in Cleveland . . ."

"I know. I keep thinking of that. Those victims were found alive after a decade. But the motive there was rape, and we're talking about young females abducted and held as sex slaves. These are grown men . . ."

"Who also could have been abducted and raped and held as sex slaves. They might still be alive."

She nods. It's possible, but not probable. Stockton knows as well as she does that when foul play is involved in a missing persons case, every hour that passes decreases the odds that the victim will be found alive.

"I think we may be looking at an online predator," she muses. "One who could have posed as a woman on a dating site and lured these guys into a trap."

"Or it could have been an actual woman."

She shrugs. Again—possible, but not probable.

"Or," Stockton goes on, "it might have nothing to do with

Internet dating sites. Maybe they're connected by occupation. Construction, architecture, design, engineering . . . these guys travel in the same professional circles."

"That's true."

"Maybe they met someone at a conference or something like that . . ."

"Maybe. We need to check into that," Sully murmurs, still musing about the online connection and the fact that the first two victims' profiles have been deleted.

Her gut is telling her they're going to discover that Carlos Diaz also has—rather, *had*—an InTune profile . . . and a hot date the night he disappeared.

The door buzzes just as Gaby finishes brushing her damp hair in front of the mirror in a bathroom still steamy from her second shower of the day. Last time, she hadn't done a great job shaving her legs or under her arms—maybe as added insurance that she wouldn't allow Ryan to get too close for comfort tonight, or because she already knew it wouldn't be an intimate evening. She can't remember, now, what she was thinking this morning. Already the memory has faded—along with Ryan himself—into a pre-Ben past she'd just as soon forget.

Technically, of course, it's all post-Ben. But she's chosen to consider this—today, tonight—the beginning of a new chapter in their relationship. The only way for her to go forward with him is to close the door on everything that came before.

Still wrapped in a towel, she hurries over to press the intercom button. "Ben?"

"Yeah."

"Um—come on up." She releases the electronic lock to let him past the building's vestibule.

Wow. He didn't waste any time getting here after their text exchange. She'd assumed they wouldn't connect until later, but as he put it, *Why wait?*

They didn't even bother to make plans. He just said he'd come over and they could take it from there.

He must have jumped right into a cab, she thinks, as she quickly yanks open a couple of drawers and grabs a T-shirt and pair of shorts. She can always change later, but for now, being fully clothed is definitely a good idea.

A good idea later, too, she reminds herself, with one last glance in the full-length mirror before she hears a familiar staccato knock on the door.

Bump bah-dah bump-bump . . .

An incomplete knock that begs an answering *bump-bump.*

He's always knocked that way whenever he took her out on a date or, later, when he arrived home at the apartments they shared. Almost always, anyway.

Throughout the happy years they were together, she'd offer a resounding *bump-bump* from the inside before opening the door.

Then, for a long time after they lost Josh, he knocked in the regular way—or not at all, slipping into the apartment late at night with his key and stealing past her if she was pretending to be asleep on the couch, or climbing silently into bed beside her.

After they started therapy, he made a couple of attempts at the old jaunty knock.

Bump bah-dah bump-bump . . .

She didn't have the heart to thump her usual reply; barely managed to open the door to him at all.

Now, though, she does her best to swap the grim memory for a happier one.

Bump-bump, she taps on the door before opening it to see Ben standing there, grinning, with a big bouquet wrapped in a paper cone and cellophane.

"Hi," he says, grinning.

"Hi." She can't keep from grinning back, just as broadly.

For a long moment they just stand there like two happy fools—which is, she realizes, probably exactly what they are. Fools.

Only fools rush in . . .

"Is that for me?" she finally asks, indicating the bouquet.

"No," he says, deadpan, and her smile fades.

"Sorry, I . . ."

He laughs and thrusts the bouquet into her hands. "Of course it's for you! Who else would it be for?"

She laughs, too, a little uneasily, not wanting to think about possible answers to that particular question, even if it's meant to be moot.

"I was planning to bring sunflowers," Ben tells her, and she feels better instantly. Sunflowers are her favorite.

He remembered.

"But," he continues, "the Korean market on my corner didn't have any, so I figured it would be better to get what they had than to get sidetracked hunting for them. At least they're the right color. And they smell nice, too. And I know roses don't bother your allergies the way some flowers do."

"They're beautiful. Thank you," she tells him, smiling as she inhales the heady fragrance of a dozen yellow roses.

Sitting across from two NYPD detectives, toying with the half-full plastic water bottle she was drinking when they showed up, Ivy feels as though she's in a scene from one of those crime dramas she loves to watch on television. She wonders, as she nervously waits for them to start asking her questions, whether they have guns, and whether they've ever had to use them. She considers asking but thinks better of it. According to the TV shows—which are very realistic—the cops are the ones who are supposed to be asking questions here.

The oversized man—Detective Barnes—is by far the more physically intimidating of the two. Yet somehow it's the woman, Detective Leary, an elfin redhead, who seems to have the more commanding presence. She wastes no time getting down to business, quickly but thoroughly going over basic details about Carlos's position at the company and Ivy's professional relationship to him.

"How much do you know about his personal life?"

Under the scrutiny of the woman's neon eyes, Ivy does her best not to shift her own gaze—or her weight on the chair—as she replies, "Not very much."

Met with silence and a slight nod urging her to elaborate, she clears her throat and goes on, "I know that he's divorced, and that he lives in Howard Beach. That's about it."

"Was he seeing anyone?"

"Not that I know of."

"Did he use online dating Web sites?"

The uncapped water bottle slips from Ivy's grasp, spilling on the parquet floor at her feet and splashing Snoopy, who protests with a loud meow.

"Sorry about that," she says—mostly to the cat—and jumps up to grab paper towels.

"No problem, take your time," Detective Leary tells her, pen still poised on her notepad, as is Detective Barnes's.

Ivy hopes they can't see her hands shaking as she bends over and sops up the puddle. She tosses the wet paper towels into the garbage but thinks better of throwing away the empty bottle. She needs something to do with her hands so the shaking won't be so obvious.

Back in her chair, she clutches the bottle as Detective Leary repeats the question about whether Carlos used online dating Web sites.

"I really wouldn't know about that."

"Okay."

Something about the way the woman says the word makes Ivy suspect she doesn't believe the answer. Or maybe it's pure paranoia.

But the detectives can't possibly be aware of her snooping around in Carlos's private files . . . can they?

Of course not. It's not as if they've had her under surveillance. They didn't even realize anything was amiss until a few hours ago; had presumably never even heard of her until she reported Carlos missing.

Detective Barnes asks, "Can you access your office e-mail from here?" and the bottle in Ivy's hands nearly goes flying again.

"Yes, I can."

"Okay if we take a look at the e-mails Mr. Diaz sent to you?"

"No problem." Clearing her throat, she leads them over to her open laptop on the counter and clicks on her in-box, glad the password is stored so she won't have to type it in front of them.

Not that they'd be able to find anything incriminating even if they were to memorize the password to sneak access to her account again later . . .

Still, she feels vulnerable as she scrolls through her electronic files to the folder containing Carlos's initials, hoping they won't notice that she's saved all the e-mails she's ever received from him. Or, if they do notice, they may just assume she saves all the e-mails she's ever received from any employee, which is far from the truth.

"This is the e-mail he sent about his parents' accident," she tells them, opening the one that bears the subject line: *Terrible News.*

Silently, they read it.

> *Ivy—I just found out my parents were in a terrible car accident in Costa Rica. My father was killed and my mother is badly injured. I'm catching the first flight out and I won't be at work this week.*

The message bears the signature line that contains just his name and the addendum: *sent from my iPhone.*

"That's all he sent?" Detective Leary asks.

"The first time."

"There's more?"

"Not much more. I wrote him back—you know, just making sure he was okay and asking about the funeral arrangements for his father. I wanted to send flowers—from all of us at the office," she adds hastily.

"Did Carlos reply?"

"Not until a few days later."

Leary rapid-fires the inevitable question: "Got that one?"

She nods, pulling it up and allowing them to read what Carlos wrote about the funeral being on hold with his mother still in intensive care. Pinned to the bottom of his note is the electronic trail that includes her response to his first e-mail. Not all of it is visible on the screen—it was rather long, she realizes in dismay—and they ask her to scroll down so they can read the entire thing.

She holds her breath as they stare in silence at the screen. Barnes makes notes of the dates and times on the messages.

"Okay. Then what?" Leary again, briskly.

Ivy blinks. "Excuse me?"

"What happened after he sent this?"

"I asked him if there was anything I could do, and he wrote back, 'No, but thanks.' That was the last I heard."

Naturally, they want to look at that e-mail, too. Then they ask her to forward the files to an address within their department. She does, reluctantly, and is relieved when they turn their attention away from the computer at last.

"What made you decide to contact us today?" Leary asks.

Ivy hesitates. "I was worried when I didn't hear back from Carlos—after all, it's been two weeks—and I wanted to track him down at his parents' house. You know, to make sure he's okay and see when he expects to be back. Not that

I'm callous   I mean, I thought he was going through a traumatic time with his family, but . . ."

"But you have a business to run," Detective Barnes supplies.

"Exactly."

"So you tried to track him down . . ."

"I called the emergency numbers in his human resources
file." She doesn't specify how she got her hands on those
numbers. "I wound up speaking to his ex-wife, and that's
when I found out that what he'd told me—what someone had
told me—in that e-mail wasn't true."

"You don't think he wrote it, then?" Leary asks sharply.

"I don't know. If he did write it, it was a lie. And if he
didn't . . ."

"Who do you think did?"

Ivy hesitates.

Should she tell them?

No.

Not yet, anyway.

She'll only get herself into trouble. If she loses this job,
she loses . . .

Everything. You lose everything.

She lives paycheck to paycheck. Her credit cards are
maxed out and she's already a month behind on her mortgage. The bank will take her co-op apartment and she'll
have nowhere else to go. Her parents are dead, and her
younger brother is perpetually unemployed and currently
crashing on someone's couch out in Jersey. Seth can't stay
on her couch, because he's sensitive to cat dander and fur.
He actually had the nerve to tell her that she should get rid
of Garfield and Snoopy so he could move in with her for a
while.

"Get rid of them? They're . . ."

"They're not family," her brother said flatly. "I am."

But they were family. And when she tried to explain that,

he told her she was going to become a crazy, lonely old cat lady someday.

"Ms. Sacks?" Detective Leary prompts.

"Yes?"

"The e-mail . . . ?"

"Oh. I'm sorry. I have no idea who might have written it," Ivy says, rolling the empty plastic bottle back and forth, back and forth, between her sweaty, shaky palms.

With Señor Don Gato occasionally getting underfoot, Alex prowls like a caged wildcat from living room to kitchen and back again, phone in hand.

Every time she completes another round trip, she checks her latest InTune account.

Every time she looks, there's still no response from Ben.

It's been hours now since she first stumbled across his profile and realized she'd discovered someone who not only possesses the necessary genetic traits, but who shares the same awful sorrow that's eaten away at her soul like a battery acid drip.

Like her, Ben is desperate to hold his child in his arms again.

No, he didn't write that in his profile.

He didn't have to. She understands him. Just as he understands her—or at least, he will, when they meet.

In all these years she's been trying to reclaim her lost son, she never once considered that she might actually be able to have the whole package again. Not just a child, but a husband. A family.

Ben would complete the image depicted in all the crayon drawings on the fridge: smiling stick figure mother and father, flanking smaller stick figure boy and girl children. They were standing in front of a square house with a pointed roof and two chimneys and distinctive red oval windows on either side of the door. The house was surrounded by trees:

puffs of scribbled green above parallel vertical brown lines. Lots and lots of trees . . .

Because it's in the woods.

It's the perfect place for a dream house, mi amor. *Peace and quiet . . . no one to disturb us for days, weeks on end . . .*

He was right. It was perfect. Perfect, perfect, perfect.

Those stick figure children didn't bounce from one foster home to another, always hoping the next would be populated by a family that would want them to stay forever. The older she grew, the less likely it became that she'd find parents and siblings to call her own. She would have to create a family as an adult. She would have to be the mommy, not the little girl.

Her dream came true—for a while. They had everything, and it would eventually include a house that looked almost exactly like the one in the pictures, in a wooded area far upstate. He'd modified the design many times, adding details, removing details that she didn't want, like the front porch.

"Why not? I love porches."

"I hate them." She shook her head, thinking of the gingerbread foster house of her youth and of his mother's house down the street. Sometimes, in her mind's eye, the two were interchangeable.

He erased the porch from his sketches. He wanted her to be happy.

At last the dream house was built. They didn't live there full-time, but they went as often as they could. Carmen was the daddy, and she was the mommy, and Dante was the little boy, and . . .

And then I had none of it. Not the daddy or the little boy or the house or . . .

But today, in a flash, she saw that she could have everything again.

After finding Ben, she went back into her own account settings and changed her profile from her latest pseudonym to her real name. That's how certain she was that she was about to make a lasting connection.

She then carefully crafted a private message to Ben. After hitting Send, she sat back and waited for him to respond.

And waited.

And waited.

"Where is he?" Alex asks Gato, who slinks off into the shadows in response, as if he doesn't want to be held accountable for Ben's actions—or inaction.

She'd been expecting him to get back to her immediately, perhaps even to text or call. She'd provided her number. Surely he'd recognize their innate connection. He'd probably want to see her right away—tonight, he'd say, if possible.

And of course she'd agree to meet him, even though it's not the right time of the month.

What they have is real. With Ben, there will be no duplicity; no need for the basement dungeon that's been scrubbed clean of blood and already awaits its next occupant.

But the phone has remained silent in her clenched hand, and each time she checks her account in-box, there's no new activity.

She went to the basement and worked out vigorously on her weight machines, building strength, building muscle. Then she tried to rest, thinking it would be a good idea to get some sleep, in case they got together tonight. But now, when she crawls into bed, her body refuses to relax and her thoughts keep going round and round and round . . .

Finally, frustrated, seething, she gets up again to pace the quiet house as the sun sinks lower in the western sky beyond the windows, casting increasingly long shadows on the hardwoods and the Oriental carpet on the living room floor.

It's looking rather threadbare, Alex notices. It was worn even when it graced her mother-in-law's house down the street. But Carmen insisted on moving it here after the old woman died.

"I love it. It reminds me of my mother."

It reminded Alex of his mother, too.

That's why she hated it, and hated the house. Carmen actually suggested that they move in there after his mother died, saying it had more space and more charm. Alex wouldn't hear of it. She wanted him to sell it, but he couldn't let it go and so it sat empty.

She paces back to the kitchen.

Again she checks her phone to see if Ben has sent a message.

No.

Her jaw tightens.

Back to the living room, and Carmen's baby picture.

Remembering the final confrontation with her mother-in-law, she feels her blood beginning to boil as if it happened just yesterday.

She checks her phone.

No message.

A tension headache plays at her temples. She tucks her phone into her pocket for a moment and stands still, squeezing her eyes shut and pressing her fingertips into the throbbing hollows alongside her brows.

If only she could rest. If only she could crawl into bed and forget . . .

When she first met Carmen's mother, she mistakenly believed she'd found someone who would love and nurture her, the way her own mother should have.

Alex never knew anything at all about her biological parents, who had abandoned her as an infant. According to the foster agency's records, she'd been found in a church, wrapped in a pink blanket with a note pinned to it. She still has the blanket and the note.

Every time she allows herself to look at the yellowed paper, the handwritten two-line message chills her to the bone.

It did, however, contain the one thing her parents—most

likely, her mother—had given her: a first name. But not a last. The sympathetic but unimaginative hospital nurses provided her with that: Jones.

She was placed in foster care. You'd think she'd have stood a good chance of being adopted somewhere along the way—a healthy white baby. A few times, she came close, but something always went wrong. The older she got, the more that saddened her, and angered her, too.

"You poor little thing," her mother-in-law said the first time Alex met her and told her life story. The woman wrapped her arms around her just like a real mom would have, right there in the middle of a busy Manhattan restaurant, and Alex felt as though she'd come home at last.

But as time went on, it turned out she was wrong about her mother-in-law. The woman was just like all the others: the foster parents who would take her in for a little while, then harden their hearts against her; the foster siblings who would befriend her at first, only to turn their backs on her, calling her crazy.

Carmen thought she was just imagining that his mother, too, had become the enemy.

"She loves you!" he'd claim, and point out some sickening sweet thing the woman had said to her in his presence.

He refused to believe that his mother was only nice to Alex when he was around, dropping the act whenever he wasn't. She didn't even tell him the whole, horrible truth: that his mother was trying to take Alex's rightful place with both Carmen and Dante—a fact that didn't become apparent even to Alex right away.

Once she figured it out, it all made sense in a sick, twisted way: the fact that her relationship with her mother-in-law was fine until she got pregnant the first time. The fact that her mother-in-law started coming around more and more often after Dante was born, even when Carmen was traveling.

Especially when Carmen was traveling. Then, the woman

would visit at all hours of the day and night, even wanting to sleep over.

"I feel like she's spying on me," she complained to Carmen, who assured her that it, too, was her imagination.

Those words made her heart sink. She'd heard them so often in her childhood.

This wasn't her imagination. It was really happening. And Carmen didn't believe her.

Alex's gaze falls on the framed baby picture of Carmen on the end table, presented to her at the hospital after Dante's birth.

"El niño mira justo como mi Carmen," her mother-in-law had crooned over the baby.

She'd also said—in Spanish, knowing Alex couldn't understand, "You're a real Daddy's boy, aren't you, sweetie pie?" and, "Like father, like son."

Carmen had to translate for her. He did so wearing an uncomfortable expression.

"Carmen's not a Daddy's boy, though," Alex couldn't help telling her mother-in-law, resting a hand—still bruised from the IV needles—on her husband's arm. "He's a *mamalón*," she added darkly.

That she—who spoke very little Spanish and didn't care to learn—had opted to use their own disparaging term for Mama's boy, didn't go over well with her husband or his mother.

Oh, how she came to loathe that woman. If she and Carmen hadn't moved to Cherry Street, everything would have been okay.

Seething, she turns away from the framed photo to pace back to the kitchen.

"You go ahead. Go up to bed. I'll take the baby." She can hear her mother-in-law's accented English, can still see her smug face on that last night, above Dante's fuzzy little head as the woman took him and cradled him to her own breast.

"He's my baby. I'll take care of him."

"No, you should get some rest . . ."

Massaging her forehead, she remembers how she'd crawled into bed and tried to sleep. She couldn't.

How well she recalls the satisfaction that came later, though. After the sun went down and her mother-in-law had gone back home to sleep.

At the mere memory, the vise of pain seems to loosen its grip on her skull.

Only slightly, though. Just enough to remind her that relief is an eventual possibility.

If only she could sleep now.

If only she had something in her medicine cabinet that would knock her out and allow her to escape for a little while.

If she had it, she would take it. It's not as if she's pregnant. It's not as if she can even try to get pregnant just yet. Her fertile time is over a week away. By the time she's ready to conceive, any medication she takes tonight will be out of her system, right?

What if it's not, though? She would never put anything toxic into her body that might harm the baby. That's how this all began, years ago . . .

But she doesn't want to think about that right now.

If only she could unleash all this pent-up frustration and fury on someone who deserves it, like her mother-in-law did. If only . . .

Her eyes snap open.

No. That's a bad idea.

Now isn't the time to take risks. Not when she's so close to reclaiming what should have been hers all along. A family, a *real* family . . .

Contemplating the possibilities, Alex reaches for her phone again. If Ben responded to her message, then she can forget all about this crazy spark of an idea.

But he hasn't.

She can see Don Gato's glowing, disapproving green gaze watching her from the shadows in the corner.

"Don't worry," she tells the cat. "I've got this."

Again, she paces.

But the idea continues to take shape in her head, and like the tension headache, it seems to grow more persistent with every step as the dusky shadows grow longer on the floor and Carmen's own words beat an endless refrain . . .

Some things just don't feel right until the sun goes down.

Chapter 8

Just a few decades ago, freight trains were still running along this elevated stretch on Manhattan's west side. Back then the busy neighborhoods below—Chelsea and the Meatpacking District—were far more seedy than trendy. Now those streets are lined with chic restaurants and boutiques, and the train tracks above have been transformed into the Highline, a garden promenade with breathtaking views of the Hudson River to the west and the skyline to the north, east, and south.

At dusk, strolling hand in hand with Ben, Gaby gazes at the pink-and-orange-streaked sky above a river dotted with white sailboats. The fat setting sun casts a silvery glow over the water and the towering skyline to the east, glinting on sleek glass and steel facades yet to be artificially illuminated at this hour from within.

"Isn't it amazing how when you're up here, you can almost forget where you are?"

Ben nods. "That's what I love about the Highline. The city seems a million miles away right now."

So does the past, Gaby thinks, and their problems.

If only they could stay up here forever. The walkway is lined with tall grasses that sway in the breeze off the water, and vibrant blooms that attract fluttering butterflies and fat bumblebees. Yes, the lush landscape tickles Gaby's nose and makes her sneeze from time to time, but she doesn't care. Not today.

The mad urban cacophony seems to have fallen away; traffic below seems oddly muted, along with the voices of other pedestrians and even their own footsteps along the path.

It reminds Gaby of the beach where they met years ago: another enchanted sanctuary in the midst of a vast, scarred city teeming with humanity and peril. Some might argue that Orchard Beach—the Bronx Riviera, Jaz always called it, with a roll of her dark eyes—is no paradise. But when the city is all you've ever known, and you're young, and in love . . .

As that first summer drew to a close, Gaby accepted that her feelings for Ben were more than platonic. Their first date lasted until well past dawn. She remembers how they snuck back down to the beach—"their beach"—after breakfast at the diner, where he teased her about her appetite. They sat on the sand, legs outstretched, her back against his chest and his arms wrapped around her, and listened to the water lapping at the shore as the first pink light of a new day began to glow in the September night sky.

Today it's the last light.

But summer has just begun.

"Look." Ben points to another couple vacating a pair of wide wooden chairs that are pushed right next to each other. "Want to sit and watch the sun rise?"

"You mean set."

"*Set* and watch the sun rise?"

She laughs. "No! *Sit* and watch the sun *set*. It's not rising."

"Oh—right. Sorry." He smiles and squeezes her hand.

Clearly, his thoughts meandered along the same path hers have taken to the past.

Does he, too, remember the promise of that first sunrise

they watched together? Does he remember how they kissed for hours? Just kissed, and talked, and kissed some more, because they had all the time in the world . . .

Or so they thought.

With no space between the chairs, they have to walk around to opposite sides in order to sit. He gives her hand a final squeeze before letting go.

"This was a good idea," she tells him as she settles into her seat, facing the water.

"Sitting down after all that walking?"

"That, too. But I meant coming up here in the first place."

"Not much of a date so far."

"So this is a date, then?" she asks.

"Did you not think it was?"

"No. I thought it was. I hoped so, anyway."

He smiles. "Good. I was thinking of a movie, or a museum—but the weather is perfect and I know you can never allow yourself to be inside on days like this."

"No, I can't, thanks to Abuela." She pauses. "You know all my little quirks, don't you?"

"You know all of mine, too."

"Pretty much. Unless you've developed some new ones since . . ." She leaves the sentence unfinished. It's much more pleasant, when dating one's ex-husband, not to mention the divorce.

Dating one's ex-husband . . .

What am I doing? she wonders, not for the first time since she canceled her plans with Ryan and Ben showed up on her doorstep with roses.

To his credit, he didn't ask what her original plans had been, or why she was suddenly free. No, he just seemed happy to be with her, no questions asked.

As she put the yellow roses into a vase, he suggested that they go for a walk.

A *long* walk. They covered a good fifty blocks along Manhattan's west side before even reaching the Highline. Short uptown-downtown blocks, but still quite a distance.

She barely noticed, though. As they walked, they talked, poking in and out of a few stores along the way and stopping to buy *palatas* from a bodega: chocolate with banana for him; guava for her.

"The usual," Ben said with a laugh. "I guess some things never change, do they?"

Some things don't.

As for the rest . . .

So far they've managed not to talk about any of it.

Now, though, watching the sun sink lower in the summer sky, she has to bite her tongue to keep from asking what his life has been like without her. Not in terms of his professional and recreational and social life—they've covered all that. Well, everything except the dating.

But she finds herself wanting to know how he's been feeling, what he's been thinking, whether he's had regrets.

"Look at that cloud," he says. "See it?"

She nods. "Looks like it might rain later."

"Gaby!"

"What?"

"You're not looking at it the right way. It doesn't look like rain; it looks like a cowboy hat with feet, and the feet are wearing boots with spurs, see?"

She tilts her head. "I do see."

"Really?"

"Not really."

"Keep trying. Remember, if you really want to see something . . ."

"I remember. Just keep looking, and it'll be there."

"Exactly." Ben reaches over again and finds her hand. His grasp is warm and strong and familiar.

"I shouldn't have let go," he says simply.

She looks at him, and realizes he's not just talking about holding her hand.

"I pretty much forced you to, Ben."

"What do you mean?"

"I was just going through the motions of working on our marriage. If I couldn't be a mother, I didn't want to be a wife. It's ugly and selfish and horrible, but it's true."

"I know that. And I have to be honest—it hurt. It just about killed me."

"I'm so sorry." She pushes the words past a lump in her throat. "It's too late for apologies, and I know it doesn't help, but I am. I was so cruel to you, and you were hurting, too. No one should have to live like that. I don't blame you for leaving."

"That's not why I left."

"Then why?"

"Because I loved you. Not because I'd stopped. It was a last resort. I thought it would jar you into realizing you loved me and needed me and didn't want to live without me. I was so sure you'd come after me after a few days alone, a few weeks, maybe a month. But . . . you never did."

"Thank you for telling me that. I never realized. I just thought you—" She swallows hard and shakes her head, barely able to speak.

"No. I just didn't know what else I could do to get through to you. I kept thinking there had to be something I was missing, but . . ."

There was, she thinks miserably. *I blamed you for Josh's death.*

She opens her mouth to tell him, but can't seem to find the right words.

"What?" Ben asks. "What is it?"

"Nothing." She shrugs. "It doesn't matter anymore."

He squeezes her hand and they fall silent, watching the sky darken as day becomes night.

"Okay, first we should consider the good news," Sully tells Stockton, as they sit gazing at the chart they've compiled on the white board that covers one of the four windowless walls in this room at the precinct.

There are three columns, each topped by a name.

Jake Fuentes.

Tomas Delgado.

Carlos Diaz.

Listed beneath each name is the date on which the man disappeared, his last known whereabouts, and other basic details, with lines criss-crossing the columns wherever similarities can be found.

There are so many criss-crosses that it looks, as Stockton said, like a damned tic-tac-toe grid where everybody wins—and loses.

"There's good news?" he asks now, tilting his chair back and lacing his fingers at the nape of his beefy neck. "Because the way I see it, these three guys aren't coming back alive. You're talkin' seven months since the first one disappeared, going on four months for the second, over two weeks for the third. You know the statistics."

"I do know the statistics. I'm not talking about good news for those three." Leary waves a hand at the white board. "But they disappeared exactly three months apart, right?"

"Twelve weeks apart," Stockton amends. "Not the same thing."

He's right.

Fuentes vanished on Friday, December 13. Three months later would have been March 13, but Delgado went missing on March 7, a Friday. Exactly twelve weeks after that, on Friday, May 30, Diaz fell off the face of the earth.

"Okay, so if you look at the pattern, there shouldn't be another disappearance until . . ." She starts to reach for her phone, with its electronic calendar.

"August twenty-second," Stockton supplies without missing a beat.

"What are you, some kind of . . ."

"Idiot savant?"

"I was going to say mathematician," she says with a shrug, "but if the shoe fits . . ."

"So you're saying the good news is that the Hispanic single men of the city are safe for another ten weeks."

"Nine weeks, six days. Now who's the idiot savant?"

"Well played, Leary. Well played. Now tell me why whoever's abducting these guys—if they are being abducted—is on the twelve-week plan, and we're on our way to solving the case."

"We may have missed something earlier, too. There could have been others who fit the victim profile. Now that we've nailed the pattern, we need to go back twelve weeks from the first disappearance and see if anything fits."

"That would be Friday, September twentieth."

"Show off."

"And twelve weeks before that would be—"

"Yeah, I get it. Your brain is a freaking calculator."

"Credit where credit is due."

Rolling her eyes, she goes on, "We also still need to figure out whether Diaz had an InTune account."

"Right. Too bad it'll take forever to jump through enough hoops to get our hands on those records."

They've already filed the necessary paperwork. Unfortunately, given the fact that with no solid evidence of foul play, and that most adults who disappear *want* to disappear, this isn't necessarily a high-profile, high-priority case. It's not likely that they'll be granted access to Diaz's financial records, much less his Internet files, anytime in the immediate future.

If only there were a way around the red tape . . .

If only Ivy Sacks had been more forthcoming . . .

If only she—or someone else—had reported him missing before a full two weeks had passed . . .

Stockton leans forward, resting the front legs of his chair on the floor again and his elbows on the table, fists beneath his chin. "So what do you think she was hiding?"

Sully doesn't have to ask who he's talking about.

Ivy Sacks. His thoughts, as usual, have taken the same path as her own.

"I don't know," she tells him, "but it was definitely something."

They discussed this earlier—several times, in fact, beginning in the car after leaving Ivy Sacks's apartment. They'd agreed that the woman was exceedingly nervous.

Witnesses—even the innocent ones—often are. But her body language indicated that she was keeping something from them.

After leaving her apartment, they'd looked into her past, trying to uncover a link between her and the other two victims. They'd found nothing.

Nor did they uncover a profile for her on any of the popular dating Web sites, including InTune. She did have a Facebook page—but of course, none of the three missing men showed up on her friends list.

They could have been there at one time, but none of the missing men have active Facebook profiles. Fuentes and Delgado both had accounts that were abruptly deactivated, according to their families. Diaz doesn't show up in the search engine. But that doesn't mean he wasn't there at one time.

They need a search warrant for his computer files—but

again, that takes time. Meanwhile, all they can do is try to interview everyone who knew him well and saw him regularly.

There aren't many—if any—available candidates. Like many single people in this overpopulated city, Carlos Diaz seems to have led a relatively lonely life.

"Maybe he really did just walk away," Stockton muses, rubbing his double chins.

Leary shakes her head, unable to avoid looking at all the lines criss-crossing the columns on the wall. "Maybe," she says, "but I doubt it. I think he crossed paths with the wrong person on May thirtieth. Let's just hope whoever it is doesn't pounce again until August twenty-second. That should give us enough time to figure out who he is."

"Or who *she* is."

"If it's a woman, then what's her motive?"

"Good old-fashioned perv?" Stockton asks, and then, seeing her expression, "No?"

"Maybe, but I'm thinking it might be a hell of a lot more complicated than that."

"Like . . . ?"

"Damned if I know." Leary shakes her head. "I think I'm too exhausted right now to think clearly."

"You need to get some rest."

"I need to get some good strong tea. Rest can wait until we figure this out."

This time, Alex parks several blocks away, rather than in her usual spot at the curb. Better to risk a walk along the seedy neighborhood streets than to take a chance that someone will recognize the black BMW sitting in front of Mr. Griffith's house.

Anyway, no one is going to mess with her. Not dressed like this. It's a warm night, but she's wearing baggy jeans and a dark sweatshirt with the hood pulled up over an old baseball cap of Carmen's. She looks like any other teenage thug who loiters on street corners and stoops around here. Even the other thugs don't give her a second glance as she passes, head bent, shoulders slumped, hands jammed low into her front pockets.

As she walks, she can't help but wonder whether Ben is going to get back to her this evening while she's out . . . taking care of business.

He hadn't yet when she last looked, about half an hour ago. She left her phone back at home, plugged into the charger. She'd run the battery almost all the way down today with her incessant pacing and futile, constant checking for private messages.

She'd thought it would be good to have a distraction from waiting and wondering, but every muscle in her body is painfully contracted with the stress of the day. Not to mention yesterday.

Too bad Carlos took it upon himself to do a job she'd have gladly done for him. You'd think throwing him into a crate in a hole in the woods and covering it with dirt would have been cathartic, but it didn't begin to ease her anger toward him.

Now, that anger has taken a new direction.

I've been sleeping with a gun under my pillow ever since the neighborhood color scheme changed from white to brown and black . . .

My husband and son are Hispanic . . .

Carmen.

Dante.

And Ben . . .

Ben, too.

Picking up her pace, Alex turns onto the block that runs parallel to Mr. Griffith's street.

As she walks, she surreptitiously scopes out the houses on the left-hand side. Most have lights in the windows and cars in the driveways, but midway down the block—in almost exactly the right spot—she finds a stroke of luck: an empty driveway in front of a deserted-looking house with darkened windows.

She walks casually down the driveway as if she belongs there. In the small backyard, she passes a couple of rank-smelling garbage cans and crosses a patch of overgrown grass to an unkempt shrubbery border separating this property from the one behind it. Peering through the bushes, she recognizes the roofline and salmon-colored siding: Mr. Griffin's house.

There are lights in two upstairs windows.

That's okay. She'll wait for them to go out. She's got all night.

But as she stands in the shrub border, staring at those parallel yellow rectangles, they morph into red ovals, filling her with sorrow—and fueling her rage.

Something's bothering Gaby.

Ben is certain of it.

It's nothing specific that she's said or done. But he sensed a subtle shift in her mood when they were up on the Highline, watching the sunset and talking about the past. He felt better having explained why he'd left, and she seemed to feel better hearing it; she even thanked him for telling her. Then she was about to say something else, and she stopped herself and said it wasn't important.

It must have been, though, because after that she seemed to go from laid-back and contented to . . .

Well, not edgy, exactly. But there's a slight undercurrent of apprehension in the air even though she's still talking, still laughing, as they finish their dessert at the same restaurant where they ate the other night.

"Maybe," he'd said as a different hipster hostess settled

them—by his request—at the same windowed table again,
"we should start thinking of this as 'our place' from now on."

"Maybe we should," she agreed, but her smile was like
a lamp on a dimmer switch turned just a notch below full
glow.

Throughout the meal, he was careful to keep the conversation rooted firmly in the here and now. It wasn't difficult.
With Gaby, conversation has always flowed so naturally. He
had never really appreciated that until now that he's dated so
many other women and found himself struggling to engage
some of them, or trying to keep his eyes from glazing over
during endless monologues from others.

"How's the flan?" she asks him as he scrapes a spoon
through the rich white custard disk on his plate. "As good
as Abuela's?"

"No flan will ever be as good as Abuela's."

"Not even mine, when I used her recipe that time she
broke her wrist and couldn't cook for a month. Remember?"
Gaby asks, poised with a forkful of chocolate layer cake in
front of her lips.

"I remember. You thought she deliberately left out one of
the ingredients so that yours wouldn't turn out right and hers
would always be the best."

"You say that like it was a crazy thing to think! Would
you really put it past her?"

"No," he says, laughing. "I wouldn't."

"That's what she did with her roast pork recipe. I never
could get it quite right, remember?"

"I remember. She was a piece of work. But she loved
you."

"She loved you, too."

"Not in the beginning, she didn't."

"Only because she was so protective of me." Gaby shakes
her head and again pokes the fork into the wedge of cake on

her plate. "Do you know how many guys she scared away back when I was younger? If Paulie Nazario hadn't stepped up to take me to my prom I never would have been able to go."

Paulie—now a hairdresser in Palm Beach—had lived in the apartment upstairs. Not only was he accustomed to Abuela's bluster, but he used to give her home perms and gossip with her about her telenovelas—the Spanish soap operas she loved to watch. For a long time, according to an amused Gaby, her grandmother thought she and Paulie were a match made in heaven, even after he came home one Christmas with his roommate—and future husband—Ray, a dancer with the Miami Ballet.

"Abuela scared me, too," Ben points out. "But not enough to keep me away from you."

"Ah, pero es muy valiente!" she says with a laugh, and in response he strikes a mock he-man pose, lifting his fists and flexing his muscles.

They linger over dessert until the waiter drops a leather bill holder.

Reaching for his wallet, Ben takes out his phone, too, to check the time.

Seeing that there's a new text, he sets it aside on the table, pretty sure the text is going to be from Peter. When Gaby said she was busy tonight, Ben had agreed to meet him at the Stumble Inn to watch the game. When his plans changed, he texted Peter to say something had come up. Peter's response to that: *Gaby again?*

When Ben didn't reply, Peter eventually wrote: *No answer is my answer. I'll be @ SI so meet me later.*

Ben ignored that, too. He felt the phone vibrate in his pocket when this latest text came in during dinner but didn't bother to check it then, and he doesn't now, either.

He's with Gaby tonight. The rest of the world is on hold.

"What time is it?" she asks as they wait for the waiter to return.

"Still early. Let's go have a nightcap."

"I know a nice little place off Gansevoort."

"That didn't quite work out last time, did it?"

"Oh, I think it worked out just fine." Gaby grins at him, and he decides he was probably just imagining a slightly lackluster mood on her end.

"Okay, well, if it's open this time, we can stop there for a drink, and if it's not . . . we'll have to find someplace else."

Like her place. Or maybe his this time.

The thought of later is so distracting that it takes him three tries to do the simple math as he adds the tip to the receipt when the waiter returns. Then he drops his napkin as they stand, and fumbles when he tries to pick it up.

"Estar por la luna," she teases him, just like the old days.

"Es todo culpa tuya," he replies with a grin, blaming his distraction on her.

She stops at the ladies' room on their way to the door, telling him she'll meet him outside.

Ben weaves past the crowd of people waiting for tables and steps out onto the sidewalk. The night air is warm, and a bright full moon rides high in a starry sky. It's a perfect evening; everything has been going well so far.

So why can't he shake the unsettled feeling that something is not quite right?

Alex had initially figured it would be a good idea to wait a full half hour after the light in the upstairs bedroom was extinguished. After all, she thought, she had all night.

But she's never been very good with time. It either flies by or it drags on, and she usually has a hard time keeping track either way.

But she did check her watch earlier. She knows that it's only been ten minutes since she got here. Ten minutes. It feels like hours.

She can't possibly stay here, crouched in the bushes, for

another twenty minutes. Maybe she can endure another ten, at most. Or five.

She's much too warm in layers of denim and fleece from head to toe, but the mosquitoes are biting what little bit of skin she's left exposed on her face and hands. Her legs are cramping, her head is throbbing and—worst of all—her phone is back at home.

Surely by now Ben must have replied to her private message. He might be wondering why she isn't writing back promptly. He might even be giving up on her, right this very second, and moving on to some other woman.

No, Ben, you can't do that!

I need you! We need each other! Wait for me! Please wait!

Sweat from her soaked scalp trickles down the nape of her neck. She lowers her hood momentarily to wipe it away. A mosquito buzzes close to her ear, then sinks its stinger into the newly exposed skin of her neck. She slaps away the engorged insect and finds blood smeared on her fingers.

That does it. She can't stick this out for even another minute. Either she goes in now and does what has to be done, or she goes home and forgets this whole thing.

Which will it be?

. . . *color scheme changed from white to brown and black* . . .

Carmen . . . Dante . . . Ben . . .

In, she decides.

With her heart pounding, she puts up her hood again, and pulls the brim of her cap low over her forehead. She takes a pair of surgical gloves from her pocket and puts them on. Then, with her bloodied hand clenched into a hard fist inside its latex covering, Alex emerges from the bushes and strides toward the salmon-colored house.

Chapter 9

In a candlelit cocktail lounge off Gansevoort Street, Gaby sits across a small table from Ben, twirling her wineglass by its stem.

This time, luckily, the place was open, and crowded with couples on this summery Saturday night. The decor reflects the neighborhood's vintage aesthetic, with century-old mosaic tile floor, pressed tin ceiling, dark wood wainscoting, and a white marble-topped bar running the length of the room.

It reminds Gaby of the granite countertops in the apartment she'd shared with Ben. The bigger, better apartment.

Nothing is indestructible . . .

Voices from the past seem to contradict the lyrics of the bar's piped-in background music, straight out of Pottery Barn and/or the Great American Songbook: Nat King Cole crooning "When I Fall in Love."

"It will be forever . . ."

Gaby tries to focus on what Ben is telling her about the new design he's working on, the one he mentioned the other night. The building is destined to be the tallest in its immediate neighborhood, altering the city's skyline. Naturally, the prospect thrills him.

That's Ben. Always striving to make an impact, reaching for that pinnacle of success.

She'd thought it was one of his greatest attributes back in the days when she first became enamored of him, watching him swim laps in the sound as though he were going for the Olympic gold . . .

After Josh died, of course, she'd thought that perseverance was his greatest fault.

Nobody's perfect, Gaby . . . You have your faults, I have mine. We can love each other despite them . . .

But not *this* particular fault. She just couldn't. Not anymore.

If only they hadn't moved from their original one-bedroom apartment into that bigger one: a "junior four," in New York City real estate parlance. The new rental had a kitchen, a living room, a bedroom, plus another room that was too small to be considered a second bedroom, even in New York—but was large enough for a crib and changing table and had a door that could be closed.

It was Ben who suggested moving, right after she got pregnant. She was surprised he wanted to abandon the old place, just a few blocks from his office, to a new one that would mean a crowded rush hour subway commute with a transfer.

But Ben had grown up in a cramped one bedroom, sharing a pull-out couch with his brother. There was barely enough room in the apartment for the kids themselves, let alone their belongings. He and his brother used to joke that if they fell asleep reading a book in bed, their mother snatched it up and gave it away before dawn.

She was notoriously organized—she had to be, having grown up with several siblings in a one-room apartment in San Juan, then raising two sons in an only slightly larger Co-op City condo up in the Bronx. The only childhood possessions that escaped Ben's mother's constant purging of so-called clutter now reside in the stray box in Gaby's studio.

"Our child will have private space," Ben vowed when she was pregnant, "and so will we."

Damn him. Damn him and his space. Damn him and his plan. Always striving, pushing himself toward something—that was Ben.

Running a marathon when he was feeling rundown, catching a cold . . .

She remembers telling him not to cough near the baby even if he covered his mouth; remembers telling him to scrub his hands well with soap and then rub them with antibacterial gel before touching Josh.

"Maybe you should just get him a little Hazmat suit," Ben said dryly at one point. He liked to tease her about being an overprotective mother. Usually, she smiled at his jokes.

She did at that one, though she said, "I just don't want him getting sick."

"He's going to catch a cold eventually, Gab. All kids do. He's not a fragile newborn anymore. He'll be fine."

He caught the cold. He wasn't fine. Does one have anything to do with the other?

If they'd just stayed in that small apartment, where their baby could sleep within arm's reach . . .

If only he hadn't run the marathon . . .

Back then there was a peculiar and yet overwhelming logic to that line of thinking. Time—time that heals all wounds—seems to have obliterated her ability to make sense of it.

You have to tell him.

All evening long, as she and Ben strolled the last length of the Highline in the twilight, then sat across from each other in the restaurant, and now in this cocktail lounge, the refrain has been running through Gaby's head.

She's been arguing the point with her conscience all evening long.

Why do I have to tell him?

To clear the air. It's the only way you'll be able to move on. You have to be completely honest.

It's what Jaz would say.

It's what the marriage counselor used to say, too: that they had to tell each other what was on their minds.

Okay. So maybe she has to try to explain to him what had happened; what she'd thought back then and how she reacted because of it.

Telling him won't right her wrong, but if she can own it—if she can be accountable for her role in destroying their marriage—then maybe he can love her again despite that terrible flaw, just like he said all those years ago.

"Gaby?"

"Yes?" She looks up to see Ben watching her, wearing a tentative expression.

"I think I lost you somewhere in there. I didn't mean to bore you with the architecture stuff."

"You didn't bore me."

"Good. I hope I didn't upset you either, talking about all the old tenements that are going to be demolished to make room for the new office tower. I know that's not exactly your favorite topic."

She shakes her head, remembering the many discussions they'd had about that topic back when they first met. That wasn't long after the Edgar Allan Poe building near Washington Square Park was deemed historically insignificant enough to be demolished to make way for NYU's new law school building.

"Out with the old, in with the new," Ben said about that, with a shrug.

"But Poe lived there!"

"Poe lived everywhere, including the Bronx. You once said yourself that the guy was a Gypsy. See? I appreciate your literary talk after all," he added, having been accused of the opposite in the past.

"Oh, sure, use that against me." She shook her head.

"As much as I appreciate your literary talk—and your preservationist soul—you can't stand in the way of progress, Gab."

"You can when progress means sacrificing history and character and tradition."

"Not every decrepit old building in this city is worth saving," was his usual response back then.

He repeats it now, and she nods absently.

Imagine that it all seemed to matter so much back then. How could she have argued—sometimes to the point of tears—as though it were a matter of life and death? As though they were talking about saving human lives, not piles of bricks and mortar that had seen better days . . .

Life and death. Back then, before Josh, she thought she'd seen the best and worst of both. How little she knew.

She remembers giving birth to her son, holding his squirming body in her arms . . .

Remembers lifting his stiff, cold body on that last horrible morning . . .

It was so different from her experience a few years earlier. She was the one who found her father-in-law dead of a heart attack one morning when she went to visit. He was still living in that same small Co-op City apartment, all alone now.

She had let herself in, same as always, because his feet had been bothering him and he couldn't get to the door. But she had a feeling, even as she opened the door, that something was off that morning. She walked warily through the living room calling his name, knowing, somehow, what she was going to find.

He was in the bedroom, in his bed. Even from a few yards away, she could see that he was dead.

But with Josh, it was different. With Josh . . .

"Okay, what's up, Gaby?"

"What? Nothing. It's fine. I'm fine."

"Are you sure about that?"

She nods and sips her wine.

You have to tell him . . .

Ben shrugs and lifts his own glass: Bourbon and water on the rocks.

"Nothing cures a cold like a shot of Bourbon . . ."

She can still hear him saying that, long ago, when he was nursing his post-marathon cold in the days before Josh died. Both their grandmothers had often said the same thing. Good old-fashioned folk medicine.

"Well, the baby can't have Bourbon if he catches it from you," she'd told Ben as he paused to cough into the crease of his elbow while pouring himself a shot on that long ago November night. "So be careful with your germs."

Be careful.

But even if you're careful . . .

"How's your Merlot?" he asks her.

"It's good."

"But it's not Malbec."

"It's okay. I like it."

There was no Malbec by the glass on the wine list. Ben had said they should just go ahead and get a bottle, but she didn't think they should drink that much.

He'd teased her about being afraid of what might happen if she got tipsy.

She'd laughed, but the truth is, she was afraid. The other night, they'd wound up back at her place.

Is that what she wants tonight?

Is it right to keep careening forward without resolving the past?

I don't know. I don't know what's right. I don't know what I want.

She watches Ben toy with his glass, wishing he'd go on

talking, desperately wanting him to make things go back to normal, somehow, the way they were before, before . . .

November twelfth.

The last night of normal.

They hadn't even spent it together. Ben worked late, as he often did. Had dinner with his boss and a client. She was sleeping soundly when he came home close to eleven, so exhausted after a string of sleepless nights with her teething baby that she never heard him come in.

She knows that he checked on Josh before going to bed, and found him sound asleep.

Just asleep. Still breathing. Still alive.

Life . . .

Ben was certain of that, he'd told her and the paramedics who burst into the apartment the next morning, there to save Josh. But it was too late, too late . . .

Death . . .

There are many things she doesn't remember about those awful hours in the wake of discovering her son's body in his crib. But she does remember trying to hear what Ben was telling the medical team, and that his voice was nearly drowned out by the terrible sound of someone screaming and sobbing hysterically, and she remembers not realizing at first that it was coming from her own throat until Ben wrapped his arms around her, hard, and tried to quiet her.

She pushed him away. It was the first of many times she would do that, literally and figuratively; the dawn of the dreadful new normal.

He'd been the last one to see Josh alive.

Was there any indication that something terrible was about to happen?

She'd asked him that, countless times, and the answer was always the same: "He was sleeping, Gaby. He was fine."

No, he wasn't!

You said he'd be fine if he caught your cold, and he did, and he wasn't fine!

Had Ben been paying close enough attention when he looked in on the baby that last time? Or had he been too worn-out from the long day at work to notice that something was amiss, the slightest little something that could have made the difference between life and death?

You have to tell him.

She lifts her glass to her mouth to keep words from spilling out of it, feeling as though she's going to choke on the wine, on the words, on the congealed lump of grief rising in her throat.

"Tell me what's going on, Gaby."

She shakes her head mutely.

Ben puts his hand over hers. "What's wrong?"

"I don't know if I can get past this. I thought I could, but . . ."

"Past what?"

"Blaming you." There. She said it. It's out there.

Only it came out all wrong.

"Blaming me? For leaving? I told you, it wasn't because I'd stopped loving you. It was because—"

"No, not for that."

"Then what?"

No turning back now. She forges ahead. She has to be honest. It's the only way to heal.

"For . . . Josh."

"What?" The word is an incredulous whisper.

"I know it's wrong, Ben. I know it wasn't your fault. But . . ."

Something has already begun to harden in Ben's eyes. He lifts his hand abruptly, pulling it away from hers.

"You thought it was *my fault*? That our son *died*?"

"I told you I know it's wrong. I know it wasn't your fault."

"You're repeating yourself. And contradicting yourself, for that matter."

"I know. It's because I . . ."

"Right. You know it's wrong. You know it wasn't my fault. You don't have to say it again. I heard you the first two times."

"Will you please let me talk?"

"Go ahead," he says. "I'm listening."

But the bond of trust and love that had begun to grow again between them has been snuffed like tender green shoots in a late killing frost.

Her thoughts are spinning. What the hell was she even trying to say to him? Why did it seem so important to bring this up?

Honesty. Healing. Forgiveness.

"When you got that cold after you ran the marathon," she begins, "and I was worried that—"

"*That's* what this is about?"

"No. It's not. I know it's not. Just let me talk," she tells him when he opens his mouth to cut in. "Let me say this."

He shrugs.

She talks. She started this. She has to finish it.

"Back then, after it happened, I was so devastated that I—losing Josh destroyed me, Ben. It *destroyed me.*"

"It destroyed me, too."

"I know."

"But I'm not the one who let it destroy us."

She tries to swallow back the sob that rises in her throat. He's right.

"Sorry. I was letting you talk. Go on." Ben picks up his glass, takes a drink, swallows it hard.

Gaby's eyes fill with tears.

She lost Josh. She lost Ben.

Now she's losing Ben again.

"It hurts to be without you," she tells him. "But I don't think it hurts as much as it did when I was with you, after it happened. And I'm afraid that if we're back together, it'll go back to hurting that way again. I'm afraid we'll never figure out how to forgive each other."

"I already figured that out, Gabriela. I already forgave you. I gave it everything I had. You're the one who didn't try. You're the one who can't get past it. Not me."

What is there to say to that?

He's right.

She pushes her glass away, slides her chair back. "I have to go home."

"Okay." He pulls out his wallet, looking around for the waitress. "I'll put you in a cab."

"I can put myself in a cab."

"Gaby, wait two seconds while I—"

"No," she tells him, already on her feet. "I'm fine. I do it all the time. I go home by myself. I go to bed by myself. I get up by myself. I take care of myself. And I can, Ben. Did you know that?"

"No one ever said you can't."

"I take care of myself, and I'm used to it. I'm used to being alone. That's the way it is now. That's the way it's always going to be."

She was a fool to think it could be any other way.

She heads for the door.

He's on his feet, too, coming after her. "Gaby—"

"Sir?" Behind him, the waitress materializes.

"I need the check, please. Gaby—"

She keeps walking.

There are no cabs on the quiet side street outside the restaurant, and she doesn't dare stop and wait until one comes along. He'll have caught up to her by then, and she doesn't want to continue this conversation tonight.

She doesn't want to continue it, ever.

It's over.

As she zigzags cross-town and uptown blocks, her phone in her pocket buzzes with an incoming text.

Probably Ben.

She ignores it.

It vibrates again as she reaches the subway station for the west side local. She leaves it in her pocket and takes out a Metrocard instead, casting a glance over her shoulder as she hurries through the turnstile, half expecting to see Ben behind her. The platform below is crowded. Good. It means she didn't just miss a northbound train, and she can lose herself in the crowd, just in case Ben really does show up.

But then, why would he?

This isn't his line. He'd have walked over to Union Square to catch an east side express train.

No, he'd have taken a cab, and would probably have expected her to do the same at this hour.

He always used to worry about her on the subway at night.

But she's not his problem anymore, is she? He should be relieved, and so should she.

The train roars into the station. The doors open, spilling far fewer passengers than are waiting to board. As Gaby wedges herself into a car, she catches a glimpse of Ben at the opposite end.

Her heart skips a beat. So he *did* come looking for her. That means—

It means you're delusional, she realizes, seeing that it's not Ben after all. It doesn't even look that much like him.

But if you really want to see something . . .

She closes her eyes and turns away.

After letting herself into the house with the key hidden under the back doormat—*Fool*! Alex thinks again—she begins to feel her way through the darkened, airless rooms on the first floor. The place smells stale, as if it's been years since the windows were open with a fresh breeze blowing through.

She bumps her hip on the hard edge of a table and winces.

If she had been thinking more clearly when she left the house earlier, she'd have remembered to grab her headlamp before setting out on this evening's mission. Even just a flashlight would have come in handy.

Rubbing her hip, she listens, hoping the slight thump didn't wake Mr. Griffith. But all is silent above. He must be sleeping by now—especially if he took one of those pills the doctor prescribed for him.

The pills were, initially, the reason she'd decided to come here tonight, right? She just needed something that will help her to relax and sleep.

God knows that prescription will do the trick without leaving her groggy tomorrow morning the way some over-the-counter medications do.

Oh, who are you kidding?

This isn't just about stealing a bottle of sleeping pills. It's about alleviating this pent-up anger and frustration the way she did years ago, when she unleashed it on her mother-in-law.

Carmen never suspected the old lady's death hadn't been a tragic accident. No one did. And even if they had, they never in a million years would have connected her to what happened.

No one will connect her to this either.

Slowly, Alex makes her way to the staircase. She's glimpsed it so many times from the front door when she dropped off his medications. She knows that it's steep, and that the steps are carpeted with a worn runner, the better to muffle her footsteps.

She bumps into something parked at the foot of the steps: Mr. Griffith's walker. It hits the wall with a clatter. She freezes, listening, poised to bolt through the door at the slightest hint of movement from above.

All remains still.

After a long wait, just to be sure, she carefully pulls the walker upright again. Then she begins the long ascent, one step at a time, poised on each tread to listen for movement above.

She did this in her mother-in-law's house, too, years ago—how long ago?

Dante was a baby then, so at least, what, ten years? Twelve? No—more. Dante has been gone a long time.

How long?

What does it matter?

As she nears the top of the flight, she can see a night-light plugged into a baseboard socket in the short hallway.

There was one in her mother-in-law's house, too.

It illuminated the human shadow standing at the top of the stairs. The old woman had heard something and was out of bed to investigate.

"Quién es?" she'd called, and Alex knew enough Spanish by then to know that she was asking: *Who's there?*

Alex didn't answer, just kept coming up the stairs, hands clenched into fists, thoughts spinning.

Carmen was away on another endless business trip.

Her mother-in-law had done nothing but intrude.

"You go ahead. Go up to bed. I'll take care of the baby," she'd said earlier, cradling Dante to her breast.

"He's my baby. I'll take care of him."

"You should get some rest . . ."

She had realized, in that moment, with a stab of horror, that her mother-in-law was trying to get her to leave so that she could nurse Dante.

Alex didn't know how it was even possible, but it was happening. She was certain of it. Carmen's mother was sneaking around nursing her baby. Little by little, she was taking her place in her son's life.

She couldn't let that happen.

There was only one way to stop her.

Long after Dante had been safely tucked into his crib and her mother-in-law went home with a promise to return first thing in the morning to "help," Alex found Carmen's key to the house down the street and slipped out into the night.

She had to leave Dante alone while she was gone. It wasn't a good idea, but of course, she wasn't thinking clearly that night. Anyway, it was her only option, and it wouldn't be for very long.

Her plan was to smother the old lady in her bed with a pillow as she slept.

As it turned out, that would have been a bad idea. She hadn't considered the potential consequences, hadn't considered the fact that smothering wouldn't have looked like an accident.

Not like a fall down the stairs.

No one—not even Carmen—ever suspected that the old woman hadn't tripped over the hem of her nightgown that night, or that she hadn't been alone when she drew her last breath at the foot of the stairs. No one ever knew about Alex's bitter confrontation with her mother-in-law at the top of the stairs before she mightily shoved her to her death.

She didn't die right away, though.

Alex descended to find her lying there on her back, bleeding and moaning.

She remembers grabbing fistfuls of the shirred fabric bodice of the old woman's nightgown and lifting her upper body off the floor so she could look closely into her black eyes.

They were open; filled, Alex thought, with hatred and accusation.

"*My* husband. *My* son," Alex had hissed. "*Mine*. Not yours!"

Then she slammed the woman backward with all her might, so that the back of her skull hit the hardwood floor and cracked open.

She left her there. The next afternoon, she called Carmen to say she was worried because she hadn't heard from his mother all day, which was usual, and that she'd tried to call to make sure everything was all right.

"Did you go over there, Alex?" he asked.

"No. I wanted to, but it's storming and I don't want to take the baby out in this weather. I'm worried about her."

"Don't leave the house. Do you hear me?"

"I hear you! Shhh, you're going to scare the baby."

"I'm going to call the police to go check on my mother." Carmen hung up abruptly.

Alex saw a patrol car go down Cherry Street about ten minutes later, heading toward her mother-in-law's.

A few minutes later, as she was changing the baby, she heard sirens.

She was nursing her son a little while after that when a pair of officers came to the door. There had been a terrible accident, they told her. She stood in the doorway feigning shock and sorrow, cradling her swaddled son against her breast—*her* breast.

Now, she pushes the memory aside as she ascends the dark stairway in Mr. Griffith's house.

She can hear a faint, steady snoring sound.

There are three open doors off the hall; the fourth, nearest to the head of the stairs, is closed. The snoring is coming from behind it.

She reaches for the knob, clasps it, turns it. It makes a clicking sound.

The snoring is disrupted.

Frozen in place, she stands with her hand on the knob, listening for creaking bedsprings or footsteps on the other side of the door.

After an agonizing, endless moment, the snoring resumes.

She waits, making sure it's steady, before turning the doorknob again—only a fraction of an inch this time.

She waits.

Listens.

Steady snoring.

She turns the knob another fraction of an inch . . .

And so it goes, until she can open the door with a slight push, still holding the knob as it arcs inward over the carpeted threshold without so much as a creak.

The snoring, uninterrupted, is louder now.

Alex slips into the room and stands just inside the door, waiting for her eyes to grow accustomed to the dark. Moonlight spills through the sheer curtains at the window. Between that and the reflected glow from the tiny bulb in the hall, she can just make out the bed, and a lump beneath the covers.

There's a small table on either side of the bed.

Both have drawers.

In one, she knows, is a loaded gun.

But which one?

If she makes it all the way across the room to one side of the bed and opens a drawer without waking him, and the gun is in the table on the opposite side . . .

Can she close that drawer and make it around the bed to the other table before he stirs?

And what if he wasn't even telling the truth about the gun in the first place? What if he only says it's there to throw people off, like the Beware of Dog sign?

But why would he lie to her?

He told her there's really no dog. Why would he tell her there's a gun if there isn't?

He wouldn't.

There's a gun. She just has to pick a side of the bed and hope it's the correct one.

She tiptoes stealthily to the left, reasoning that it's on the right to someone lying in the bed. She can't remember whether the man is right-handed, but most people are, and would want the gun to be on that side.

Always shoot with the dominant hand. It's what her foster brother said years ago.

She can't remember what his name was. Eddie? Teddy? Something like that.

They crossed paths for a few months in a crummy farmhouse overrun by kids and pets. They were the only two teenagers. Eddie or Teddy used to sneak the old man's revolvers out of the shed where he kept them, and taught her how to shoot in the woods behind the house. They'd take turns aiming at empty beer bottles on tree stumps.

"You're pretty good for a girl," he told her.

One day he tried to kiss her. She resisted, but he forced himself on her, shoving his disgusting wet tongue down her throat. She went along with it because he was bigger and stronger, and decided then to do some strength training and maybe take martial arts, too.

The next time he handed her the revolver for target practice, she aimed it squarely at him.

"Don't ever touch me again," she told him. "Because I'm pretty good for a girl. Got it?"

Yeah. He got it.

Not long afterward, when the farmhouse burned to the ground, she and Eddie—it was Eddie, she remembers now—were moved to new homes. She never saw him again, and good riddance. But if not for him, she wouldn't know how to handle a gun, so . . .

The old man in the bed snores steadily as she reaches the table. She nearly trips over a second walker, positioned beside the bed. He must keep it at the top of the stairs for use here on the second floor.

After stepping around it, she reaches out and tugs the drawer open slowly, slowly . . .

It's too dark to see what's inside. She feels around gingerly, the layer of latex on her fingers making it hard to tell what's what. She finds what she thinks is the curved metal barrel of a pistol, but it's just a flashlight. Then, as her hand closes on the unmistakable handle of a handgun, she realizes the snoring has come to an abrupt halt. Her blood runs cold.

Swiftly, she pulls the gun from the drawer. It's a revolver. Familiar. Good.

He starts to sit up. "What the—"

She gets a firm grip on the handle, holds her arms out straight, locks her elbows, and aims at the shadowy person in the bed. Applying slow, steady pressure to the trigger, just the way Eddie taught her, she shoots.

There's a resounding blast and flash of light in the dark room, a slight bit of recoil, and her target slumps over.

The shot was louder than she'd expected. Her ears ache and she worries for a moment that she might have burst her eardrums or that one of the neighbors might have heard and will come to investigate . . .

But the ringing subsides pretty quickly, thank goodness. And she reminds herself that this isn't the kind of neighborhood where anyone's going to be particularly startled by a loud blast, much less call the cops. Anyone in earshot will probably just assume it's illegal fireworks.

The man lies silent and motionless on the bed.

She steps closer, pulls back the hammer, puts the gun to his head, braces herself for the noise, and fires again, just to be sure he's dead.

There. That oughta do it.

Her ears are ringing and she can't hear her own voice, but she speaks anyway: "Racist bastard."

About to toss the weapon onto the bed beside him, she thinks better of it. No street thug breaking into the house would use a gun and then leave it behind.

Besides, you never know when a gun might come in handy.

She decides to hang onto it. Yeah, it's registered to the

old man, but she'll be careful with it. It's not as if she's going to use it.

She reaches into the open drawer for the flashlight, turns it on and aims the beam at the body on the bed, surveying the blood. It's everywhere—including all over her.

Quickly, she strips off the sweatshirt and baggy jeans. Beneath them she's wearing a pair of shorts and a T-shirt. To complete the disguise, she turns the baseball hat around so the brim faces backward, hipster style. Checking her shadowy reflection in the mirror above the bureau, she nods with satisfaction. She still blends into the streets around here, and she doesn't look at all like her real-life self.

She grabs a pillow from the opposite side of the bed, strips off the case, and shoves her wadded up clothing inside. The gun follows. Then, after shining the flashlight at the cluster of orange prescription bottles on the nightstand, she grabs the one that contains the sleeping pills and puts that into the pillowcase, too. No thief would ever leave that behind.

Anyway, she might need it, if she's desperate for sleep later.

Desperate enough to risk harming the baby, yours and Ben's?

No. No, I would never risk that. Never. Never. That's why . . .

But that was so long ago. And now isn't the time to think about it. Now is the time to stage the scene, just as she did at her mother-in-law's years ago, and then get the hell out of here.

Alex hurriedly but methodically goes through the room, opening drawers, grabbing cash, jewelry, and some mint coins, anything that looks as though it might be of value. Not because she particularly wants or needs any of this crap, but because the police need to think this is a random burglary gone bad.

In the bathroom, she takes a bottle of prescription painkillers from the medicine cabinet. Again, not something your typical thief would leave behind.

The other bedrooms yield nothing of value, but she ransacks them for good measure, and the first floor, too, opening drawers, cabinets, and closets. She finds a white plastic supermarket bag beneath the sink and puts the pillowcase full of loot inside.

As she opens the kitchen door to make her escape, she can hear barking somewhere in the distance.

Beware of Dog?

Hmm. I don't think so.

Slipping out into the night, she pauses to nudge the doormat—with the key still underneath—so that it's noticeably out of alignment on the back step. The cops will find the key there and probably decide the old geezer got what he deserved.

She peels off the bloodied latex gloves and stuffs them into the bag, then makes her way through the backyard to the neighboring block. Heading down the sidewalk toward her car, she casually clutches the shopping bag as if she's just come from the store.

She doesn't meet a single soul all the way to the car.

She turns on the radio, tuned, as always, to the classic rock station.

Bon Jovi's "Livin' on a Prayer" blasts into the car.

Ben likes classic rock.

She sings along at the top of her lungs, thinking about Ben. He's out there somewhere in the night, listening to the same song. She knows it.

And he, too, is singing the lyrics, right along with her. A long-distance duet, she thinks wistfully. But soon enough she'll be in his arms.

Ten minutes later she pulls off in the familiar strip mall parking lot where she fills Mr. Griffith's prescriptions. The parking lot is largely deserted at this hour on a Saturday night; only the pizzeria is still open.

There's a huge Dumpster behind the building. She's used it before. She drives around back and deposits the bloodied clothing inside. Then she opens the prescription bottles, turns them upside down, and a hailstorm of pills patters into the Dumpster. She doesn't want to take any chances that she'll be tempted, later, to poison her body with medication when she's supposed to be keeping it pure for conception.

She keeps the bottles, though, along with the jewelry, coins, money, and a couple of outdated electronics she stole from the house. And of course, the gun.

For now, anyway.

Then, careful not to go more than five miles over the speed limit, she drives the rest of the way home, still singing, eager to check her private messages again.

By the time Ben emerges from the bar onto the street, Gabriela is nowhere in sight. Exasperated, he reaches into his pocket for his phone. He'll call her and—

His phone isn't there.

He checks his other pocket. Nothing.

Did it fall out onto the floor?

He goes back inside to the table they just vacated. Their half-full glasses have already been cleared away; another couple has swooped in to claim their seats.

"Excuse me . . . did you by any chance find a cell phone here when you sat down?"

They didn't. And they don't seem to appreciate it when he crouches to look beneath the table, brushing against their cozily intertwined legs as he feels around on the floor.

No phone. He finds the waitress standing at the far end of the bar loading drinks onto a tray. She looks none too pleased to see him again.

Belatedly, he realizes he probably hadn't left a great tip. In his haste to catch up with Gaby, rather than wait to run the check through on a credit card, he'd paid for their drinks with cash, tossing down a couple of bills that, in retrospect, probably just covered the drinks and tax.

"I'm sorry about earlier," he tells her. "I was trying to catch up with my . . . wife."

"What, did she run away from you?" she asks, wearing a look that suggests she wouldn't blame her.

"More or less. Anyway, I must have left my phone behind. Did you find it?"

She didn't—and she isn't all that thrilled about the prospect of helping him look for it. She's a little more co-operative after he hands her a ten-dollar bill to make up for shortchanging her tip, but the phone is nowhere to be found.

"Here," she says, handing him a pen and a cocktail napkin. "Give me your home number in case it turns up."

He scribbles it down and heads back outside.

The street is empty. No Gaby. No taxi.

He backtracks to the restaurant where they'd eaten dinner. That was the last time he'd seen it, when he checked the time. Maybe he left it there.

A couple of sections are still open and busy with late-night diners, but the corner where they'd eaten is darkened, the tables unoccupied and already set with napkins and silverware for tomorrow. The hostess informs him that no one turned in a lost cell phone, and that the waiter who served their section has already left for the night. She allows him to retrace his steps and search around the table but his phone is not found.

Dejected, Ben again leaves his name and number on a cocktail napkin and heads back out into the night.

This is crazy. It's not like him to just lose things . . .

Dammit. It's because of her. He was so caught up in re-connecting with her that he wasn't thinking clearly.

Yeah, that's right—it's all her fault. Sure it is. Makes perfect sense.

Irrational? Maybe. But it makes him feel better to blame Gabriela for . . . something. Even the wrong thing.

Damn her.

He shoves his hands deep into his pockets, wondering what he's supposed to do now.

He can check every inch of sidewalk between here and the cocktail lounge for the phone, but if he dropped it, chances are that someone already picked it up and either kept it, sold it, or—depending on character—is making like a Good Samaritan and trying to find him.

In any case, by now Gaby must be wondering why he hasn't called or texted her to make sure she's all right.

Good. Let her wonder.

He stands on Eighth Avenue facing oncoming traffic, arm outstretched to hail a cab. Somehow, this night that seemed so promising just a few hours ago has gone right down the toilet, just as he feared it would when he was standing outside the restaurant waiting for Gaby to come out of the ladies' room.

A full five minutes passes before a taxi finally comes along that isn't off-duty or already occupied.

"Where to?" the driver asks as he climbs in.

Good question.

Ben hesitates, thinking through the options.

New York City cabbies aren't exactly known for their patient listening skills.

"C'mon, where to? Do you speak English?"

Irked, Ben snaps, "Yes, I speak English. I'm just trying to—"

"Where are you going?"

Ben spits out an address.

It isn't his own. For some reason, he just gave the driver the cross streets for Gaby's apartment building. The car jerks into drive and they're off.

What are you doing, Ben? Why are you going to her place?

Maybe he wants to resolve things with her. Or maybe he just needs to have the last word. Or is he hoping for a last hurrah, as Peter would say?

Ordinarily it's a stop and go crawl uptown, but tonight the cab careens along, sailing through one green light after another as if the traffic gods have granted special clearance for a man on a mission.

But what, exactly, is that mission?

Damned if he knows.

He beats a fingertip staccato on the door armrest, helpless and cut off without his phone. By now she might have texted or tried to call him with an apology. She'll read his lack of response as antagonism.

A part of him thinks, *Good. Let her. So what if she decides you're angry?*

He *is* angry.

But that doesn't mean he's stopped loving her. Even after all these years, after everything that's happened, everything that's been said and done . . .

I do. I love her. I can't help it.

Ben stares glumly at the passing blur of buildings and people and cars. The city is alive with action tonight beneath a fat full moon and glittering stars.

He should be walking hand in hand with Gaby right now. He should have her in his arms, he should be kissing her . . .

Dammit. This isn't how the evening was supposed to end.

As bewildered as he is frustrated, he replays the conversation they'd had at the cocktail lounge, trying to make sense of what happened.

Gaby blames *him* for their son's death?

How could she have said something so cruel?

The accusation materialized out of thin air: a razor-sharp spear mercilessly hurtled toward its unwitting human bull's-eye. Even now, merely echoing in his head, the words stab his heart. Gradually, as he replays them, forcing himself to hear what she said, the anger that was his initial reaction is back full force, mingling with the pain and confusion.

The cab stops short for a red light at 28th Street and Ben gazes out the window, watching pedestrians in the cross-walk. There are plenty of couples, gay and straight, hand in hand; a group of rowdy frat-boy types, a pair of tattooed kids who can't be more than teenagers pushing a stroller and laughing like they haven't a care in the world.

They shouldn't have a baby out at this hour of the night. Where the heck are they going? Why aren't they home like responsible parents? Don't they know better than to take chances? Don't they realize that things can happen to children, terrible things?

Judgmental, perhaps irrational, resentment of total strangers on the street isn't typically Ben's style. But very little of what's happened tonight is his style.

He goes back to brooding as the cab sails on, past the largely deserted garment district. The inevitable crawl begins at the theater district, with its congested streets and tourist-clogged, neon-bathed sidewalks. It's as though the traffic gods have bestowed a delay in which he's encouraged to reexamine his motives for going to Gaby's apartment.

He suspects nothing good is likely to happen if he goes.

He's pretty damned sure nothing good will happen if he does not.

To go or not to go? He mulls the question all the way on up to the red light at the Columbus Circle intersection.

North of this point, the city is bisected by Central Park.

Gaby lives on the Upper West Side, he lives on the Upper East . . .

And ne'er the twain shall meet.

He shakes his head, debating.

She never came after you, did she? When you left. You walked out the door and she acted as though she didn't give a damn. You gave her a chance to fight for you, for your marriage, and she ignored it.

Then she tells you she blames you *for the loss of a child you loved with every ounce of your being?*

Ben leans forward abruptly and taps on the plastic partition separating the backseat from the driver. "Excuse me? Can you make a right here, please, onto Central Park South?"

"What? That's not the way to—"

"No, I know. I've changed my mind. I'm going to East 77th and Third Avenue instead."

The driver grumbles something and flicks on the turn signal, trying to switch from a middle to a right lane amid honking horns.

Ben leans back again, resting his head against the back of the seat, fed up not just with the driver's cranky disposition but with Gaby—not to mention with himself.

All this time, he'd been moving in the right direction, away from the heartache of the past. Now he almost managed to undo all that progress.

Almost.

Feeling like a would-be suicide who's had a second thought and grabbed a tree branch at the brink of a waterfall, he promises himself that he'll never let himself get swept away again.

It's high school all over again for Ivy, perched on the outskirts of the bar crowd at Tequila Sam's.

High school, only worse.

In high school, she could—and did—hover on the fringes of the social scene and basically be invisible.

Here, she couldn't be more conspicuous. She leans against the end of the bar, trying to stay out of the way, but people keep jostling her, especially the waiters who come to fill their drink trays. "Excuse me!" they bark, or "Coming through!" and when she tries to move out of the way, she bumps into someone else. Meanwhile, the bartenders don't seem thrilled that she's taking up space without ordering anything but iced tap water.

But she doesn't like liquor—she tried whiskey sours a few times at company functions because it seemed sophisticated and everyone said the taste would grow on her. It didn't. And even if the non-alcoholic drinks weren't so expensive here, there's still too much sugar in juice and soda, and too many chemicals in diet soda.

Anyway, she's not here to quench her thirst. She's here to find out what happened to Carlos.

All she knows—courtesy of having snooped through his personal computer files last month—is that he had a blind date set up for that last Friday night. Using the pseudonym Nick Santana, he was meeting a woman named Sofia at Tequila Sam's.

Not only has Carlos's Nick Santana profile vanished from the InTune site, but so has Sofia's. That, Ivy thinks, is suspicious. Too bad she didn't dare tell the police detectives this afternoon.

Telling them what she knows about Carlos's last known activities—and why she knows—would have put her job on the line. She's better off sniffing around on her own. If she finds out something important, she'll get the information to the proper authorities anonymously. Maybe they have a tip line or something.

Unfortunately, the bartender who served her the water said he didn't have time to look at the picture she wanted to show him. She's been trying to catch the attention of the others, but they seem to be ignoring her.

Maybe they'd pay more attention if she were wearing something more provocative than her best gabardine slacks and a blouse. She wishes she'd unbuttoned the top button, but she doesn't want to do it here, in front of everyone.

Finally, a pair of pretty brunettes in short skirts vacate their nearby bar stools. Ivy slips onto one of them, directly in front of an older male bartender filling a glass at the beer tap. They make eye contact.

"Hi," Ivy says.

"What can I get you, sweetheart?"

Sweetheart. Wow, he seems nice. He kind of reminds her of her grandfather, Pop-Pop Al, who died when she was a little girl.

She shouldn't splurge on a cocktail, but maybe the bartender will be willing to talk to her if she orders something other than free water.

"I'll have a margarita," she hears herself say. She's never had one before, but it seems to be the specialty of the house, and as her father used to tell her, you don't go into a Chinese restaurant and order the eggplant parm.

"Frozen, rocks, or up?"

She blinks. "Excuse me?"

"Do you want it frozen or—"

"Yes. Frozen."

"Salt?"

"Salt?"

"Rim. Salt?"

It's as if he's speaking a foreign language. But not Mexican, because she took three years of high school Spanish and she has no idea what the heck he's saying.

She just shakes her head.

"It's okay, I got it," the nice bartender says, and walks away with the full beers.

He's back a few minutes later with a frozen lime-colored cocktail.

"One margarita."

"Thank you." She puts down a twenty-dollar bill. The drink was less, but maybe he'll think she's leaving the entire difference for him. "Can I ask you a question?"

"Shoot."

"A friend of mine went missing a few weeks ago and this is the last place he was seen. Can I show you a picture of him?"

"You can," the bartender says, "but I've only been working here for a few days."

Deflated, she pulls the picture out of her pocket anyway. She printed it out from an online file. It's Carlos's mug shot, as they call it at the office: the photo all new employees have taken on their first day, to live on forever on their ID cards.

"This is him. Do you recognize him?"

"Nope. Is he your boyfriend?"

"My brother," she says impulsively. Something tells her that she'll find more sympathy if she's looking for a missing family member than an AWOL boyfriend. Not that Carlos was her boyfriend.

She just wanted him to be.

And now she's going to do whatever it takes to save him.

Without sticking her neck on the line at work anyway.

"He had a date and he was meeting the woman here. No one has seen him since. It was May—"

"I wasn't working here then. Let me ask the others, though." The bartender takes the printout and walks away with it.

Ivy sips her drink. She wants to like it, but she doesn't.

A few minutes later the bartender is back with the photo. "No one knows him," he says with a shrug. "Sorry."

"It's okay. Thanks for checking." She slides the twenty toward him. "That's for my drink."

"You need change?"

She nods.

When he brings her back a five and a couple of singles, she leaves a dollar on the bar and slides off the stool.

"Thank you," she calls.

He waves at her, already busy filling someone else's drink.

Out on the street, Ivy ponders her next move.

A neon sign catches her eye: PARK.

When she snooped into Carlos's private messages back in May, Sofia—the woman he was meeting at Tequila Sam's—mentioned she'd be driving into the city from the suburbs. She had to park her car somewhere.

Maybe someone at the garage will know something. It's a long shot, but it's all she's got.

The vase of yellow roses greets Gaby like a forgotten house-guest of dubious welcome.

She almost bursts into tears at the sight of them, remembering how promising everything seemed when she opened the door to find Ben standing on her threshold earlier.

She should have known the past would rear its ugly head and ruin everything.

Then again . . . whose fault is that?

She's the one who brought up the past. She's the one who couldn't let it go.

Was it really because she was trying to clear the air so they could build a future together? Or was she subconsciously trying to keep that very thing from happening?

Maybe she was so afraid of the risk—so terrified of letting him in and then losing him again—that she deliberately sabotaged their relationship. Her actions tonight were the equivalent of water dousing a wick, just to be sure the flame was good and extinguished, and now . . .

Now she is, quite literally, alone in the dark.

What have I done?

She has to call him, right now, and . . .

And what?

Apologize?

Ask him for another chance?

Tell him she made it all up; that she really doesn't feel that way and never did?

Too late for that. He'll never believe it, and anyway, shouldn't she own her role in destroying their marriage?

Maybe they can work through it.

Remembering the steely look in his eyes, she pulls her phone from her pocket, knowing she has to reach out now, before she loses her nerve.

She clicks into the home screen and notices that she has a text. That's right—her phone was vibrating when she was about to get on the subway. She'd thought it was him, even thought he might have come after her.

Now she's pretty sure that's just wishful thinking. There's no way, after the things she said to him, that he's going to want to talk to her or see her again tonight.

Opening her text message in-box, she sees that the text isn't from Ben, it's from . . .

Peter?

Ben's friend Peter? How is Peter texting her? He wouldn't have this phone number, and—

Why is Peter texting her?

Did something happen to Ben?

Her heart stops. In the seconds it takes for her to open the message, her mind goes to a terrible, dark place. What if Ben was running after her when she left the bar and he was mowed down in the street? It's a Saturday night. People drive drunk. What if—

How was last hurrah—take 2?

What, Gaby wonders, is he talking about?

Last hurrah—what last hurrah?

There's another text, sent later:

At SI – get your ass down here son.

And then another: *Someone wants to meet u.*

Below that there's a little video clip, obviously taken in a bar, of a blond bombshell type. "Is it on?" she asks, slurring a little. "It is? You're really taping me? Okay—" She smiles and waves at the camera. "Hi, Ben, I'm Laney. Your friend Pete tells me you've been hooking up with the ex-wife. Bad idea! Come on down and hook up with me instead!" She lifts a stemmed glass and toasts, and the scene cuts out on her giggle.

Gaby feels as though she's been slammed by a wrecking ball.

Hi, Ben . . .

This is Ben's phone.

She fumbles in her purse, coming up with her own— same exact phone in an identical case.

Great minds think alike . . .

She realizes now that Ben must have been the one who left his phone behind when they walked out of the restaurant after dinner. She was on her way to the ladies' room when the waiter spotted her and hurried over with it in his hand.

"I'm glad I caught you! You left this on the table."

She thanked him, shoved it into her pocket and forgot about it. It never occurred to her that it might be Ben's phone and not her own.

Now, as she stares at the text Peter sent—with the accompanying video—her confusion quickly gives way to dismay, with fury right on its heels.

Last hurrah—take 2.

The meaning wasn't immediately clear. But now that she's heard the drunk bimbo's reference to "hooking up with the ex-wife . . ."

Is that what Ben calls it? Hooking up? Was the other

night supposed to be a last hurrah? And tonight he was back for more?

She shakes her head in disgust. It's all she can do not to fling the phone against the exposed brick wall across the room.

Instead she shoves the phone into a drawer and slams it shut hard.

Maybe when she calms down, she'll decide to tell Ben that she has it.

Maybe she'll decide to keep that to herself and toss the phone into the trash incinerator in the basement.

Right now, as she recalls *hooking up with the ex-wife*, she's betting on the latter.

Feeling utterly violated, she strips off her clothes, gets into the shower, and lets the hot water wash away the tears.

"Yeah." The kid working at the parking garage nods at the printout photograph of Carlos's mug shot. "I saw that dude."

Ivy's heart skips a beat. "Really?"

"Yeah."

She looks at him, head tilted, wondering if he's telling the truth.

"Was he with someone?" she asks, and at his nod, asks, "Who was it?"

"Some lady."

That sounds right, but . . . could be a lucky guess.

"What did she look like?"

The kid shifts his weight from one overpriced basketball sneaker to the other and uses splayed finger and thumb to thoughtfully rub furry sideburns that remind Ivy of the mutton chops on portraits of mid-nineteenth-century presidents.

"Yo, I should be working," he tells her. "Time is money."

Money. Right.

Feeling like a character on a detective show, Ivy reaches

into her pocket, glad she didn't tip anything more to the bartender, who, though he reminded her of Pop-Pop Al, couldn't tell her anything about Carlos. She might have better luck with this guy.

She pulls out a wad of money. It looks like more than it is. Lots of ones. She peels off a five-dollar bill to hand to the kid.

He looks at it. Hesitates. Shrugs and puts it into his pocket. "She had dark hair."

Ivy waits. "That's it?" She knew that from the profile photo she saw on the InTune page.

"She was tall."

Yes. Five-foot-ten. That, too, was on the profile.

"What else?" Ivy asks.

"She was older."

"Older . . . than me?"

"How old are you?"

"Thirty," Ivy lies.

"Yeah. A lot older than you."

"This isn't really helping me. Look, my brother has been missing since that night. This is life and death."

"Then why aren't the cops involved?"

"They . . . are. But they're—you know how it is. They have other things going on. I'm—this is all I have. He's all I have. Just tell me . . ." She reaches into her pocket again, pulls out the wad of money. "Tell me what you remember about them."

He eyes the cash. Waits.

She puts a few more bills into his hand. Ones.

"He was effed up," the kid says, stuffing them into his pocket. "Drank way too much."

"Uh-huh."

"She was driving. I thought that was a good thing. You know how many times I've had people stagger in here after too much tequila, get behind the wheel, and take off?"

Fighting the impulse to ask him why he doesn't stop them, Ivy reminds herself that this isn't about one's civic duty to keep the roads of New York safe from drunk drivers. It's about finding Carlos.

"What kind of car were they in?"

He shrugs. "I might be able to remember . . . but . . . I'm not sure."

"I don't suppose you got the license plate number?"

Another shrug.

She sighs. If she gives him any more cash, she'll be out of spending money until payday.

"Never mind." She starts to turn away. There's no way he got the license plate number anyway. She might as well—

"Lady?"

She turns back.

"I didn't get the plate, but we got records here."

"What do you mean?"

"I mean you park here, we get your plate. What day did you say it was?"

Ivy hesitates. "I can tell you, but how are you going to know which car was hers?"

"Because we write down the make and model, too. And I remember your brother—and his date. And what she was driving."

"You do?"

Mutton Chops nods. "She was driving a Beemer. At least fifteen, maybe twenty years old, but in good shape."

"You really remember all that?"

"Yeah, I remember, because I helped her load the dude into the car."

Ivy's heart skips a beat. "What do you mean?"

"I told you—he was wasted."

"So wasted that he couldn't get into the car himself?"

He shrugs. "Happens all the time."

"So . . . you can look up the license plate, then?"

"I can . . ."

For a price.

She gets it. She looks at the money she's clutching—all she has to last another week—then hands it over.

Carlos is worth it.

Back home in the climate-controlled hush of his fortieth-floor apartment, Ben decides it's a good thing he lost his phone tonight.

Yes, it's his lifeline. But as such, it's the only place he has Gaby's new contact information. Without it, he won't be able to break down and call her in a weak moment.

Feeling fairly strong—for now, anyway—he pours himself a Bourbon and sits on the couch in the dark. Beyond the plate-glass window, Manhattan's sparkling skyline illuminates the night sky.

One day in the near future, a new building of his own design will rise to tower above many of the others, replacing the crumbling tenements that have occupied that run-down block for more than a hundred years.

Out with the old, in with the new . . .

You can't stand in the way of progress . . .

Ben thoughtfully sips his Bourbon, staring at his laptop, sitting open on the desk across the room. When Gaby texted this afternoon that she was suddenly free, he'd been about to log onto his InTune account again. That was Peter's suggestion.

"You had your last hurrah, son," Peter had said as they got dressed in the locker room at the gym after a swim. "Now get on with your life. Find someone you want to date."

"I did."

"That's great! Who is she?"

"Gaby."

Peter groaned. "Seriously?"

"Seriously."

"Okay, then, if that's the case . . . then why aren't you?"

"What?"

"Dating her."

"I tried. She's busy tonight."

"With someone else, right?"

"She didn't say."

Peter had no reply to that, just shook his head.

Before they parted ways, he asked Ben to meet him at the Stumble Inn later. Ben figured he might as well, even if it meant being lectured again. Anything was better than sitting home alone on a Saturday night. That's what his father used to do, not just Saturday but every single night, all alone and feeling sorry for himself . . .

That's not going to be me.

But does he really want to go out to a bar now? Nothing good is bound to happen there after midnight. Nothing he won't regret later, anyway—though Peter might beg to differ.

Ben reminds himself that his friend has his best interests at heart. And that he may have been right—about a lot of things.

Peter had said that maybe he and Gaby had to be together one more time to get each other out of their systems for good. He'd said it wasn't easy to say good-bye, even the second time.

He'd also said the key to moving on was to date other women, women who have very little in common with Gabriela.

"You have to force yourself to keep looking, Ben. Sooner or later you'll meet someone worthwhile."

Mind made up, Ben tops off the glass of Bourbon, opens his laptop, and logs into his InTune account.

"That's it." Stockton leans back in his chair and yawns, eyes closed. "I don't know about you, but I had five large coffees in the last couple of hours and I'm still wiped *out*."

Sitting at her own desk across from him, Sully glances up from her computer screen. "Really? I could run a marathon."

"Either you're talkin' smack or you're slipping something extra into that tea of yours," Stockton decides.

"Just the usual: milk and sugar."

She must be the only cop in the precinct—or maybe the entire city—who doesn't drink coffee. She's never been the least bit tempted by the murky brew that perpetually fills the filmy carafes on the two-burner Bunn in the kitchenette—one marked green for decaf, but filled with the caffeinated stuff anyway.

Sully keeps a tin of strong Irish breakfast tea, a strainer, and a teapot and mug next to the stack of Styrofoam cups beside the microwave. She'd spent her girlhood summers in Breezy Point with her Nana Leary, who taught her to brew a proper cup of tea in a vintage copper kettle on her prized white porcelain O'Keefe and Merritt gas stove. Nana would roll over in her grave at the idea of microwaved water, but at least Sully uses the loose leaf variety instead of tea bags.

"Listen, I'm tired, too," she admits to Stockton—understatement of the decade. "But I've got a few more files to look at before I call it a night. I'm up to the second week of October."

She's gone over every missing persons case in the tristate area beginning on Friday, September 20, searching for something that might fit the pattern that emerged with the December 13 disappearance of Jake Fuentes. So far, no luck.

A few cases seemed, on the surface, to potentially fit the bill. There were several Hispanic men in the right age group, and one even worked in construction. But when Sully dug into their files, she found out that every single man has since been located, and all of them had skipped out on their loved ones because they wanted to. The circumstances fit the usual missing persons statistics to a T: eventually resolved, and no foul play involved.

Meanwhile, Stockton has been combing the InTune Web site in search of clues to a possible female predator targeting Hispanic males. He also set up a dummy profile—posing as a single Hispanic man with as many of the victims' matching criteria as possible—in an attempt to lure the predator.

Now, he tosses a stack of empty coffee cups into a nearby wastebasket and gets to his feet.

"Sweet dreams," Sully tells him.

"What sweet dreams? You stay, I stay. Think I'll try some of that miracle tea of yours, though. Give it here, Gingersnap."

She pulls the tin of tea leaves and strainer from her drawer and places them into his outstretched hand.

"Thanks. You want some, too?"

"No, thanks." She's already focused on her screen again, clicking to the next file, though a deep yawn overtakes her. Maybe she should have another cup of tea after all.

She will in a minute. After this file. Let's see . . .

Bobby Springer.

Age thirty-seven, lived in Jersey City, reported missing October first, last seen . . .

September twentieth.

The date is like a caffeine jolt to her tired blood, and she sits up straighter in her chair, scanning the file.

Two facts immediately jump out at her.

Bobby Springer worked in Manhattan as a building infrastructure technician.

And he was reported missing by his uncle, José Morales. Morales?

Sully looks more closely at the photograph of the handsome, dark-haired Bobby Springer, then clicks over to check his ethnicity.

Hispanic.

"Hey, Stockton!" she calls. "I think I've found something."

The dried blood on Alex's hand is her own, from when she slapped away the mosquito before she put on the latex gloves and went into Mr. Griffith's house and killed him.

Still, the moment she walks in the door back home, she scrubs away the caked-on smear with bleach. She hums "Livin' on a Prayer" as she scrubs, standing at the kitchen sink, thinking about Ben.

Gato watches her from beneath a kitchen chair beside a bowl of food Alex left out this afternoon—or was it this morning? It smells foul. She should clean it up. But not now.

She washes out the sink with bleach before going up the stairs into the bathroom, careful not to touch or brush up against anything along the way. Most of Mr. Griffith's blood was on the clothes she threw into the Dumpster, but you never know.

In the shower, she sings as she scrubs herself from head to toe and is pleased to see that the water running down the drain is merely sudsy, not tinted reddish brown with blood.

"Oh . . . we're halfway there," she sings, and wonders again if Ben listens to the same classic rock station on the radio. When they're together, she'll tell him that "Livin' on a Prayer" reminds her of him. It will become their song.

She turns off the water, steps out onto the mat, and pulls on the robe hanging on the door hook. Then she takes a spray bottle and paper towels from beneath the sink and methodically wipes down the tub and the faucet handles.

Back downstairs, humming their song, she cleans the doorknobs she touched coming into the house. Out in the garage, she cleans the steering wheel in her car, and then the leather upholstery.

"Take my hand," she sings, "and we'll make it, I swear . . ."

As she works to obliterate the slightest spot of blood— real or imaginary—that might have been left anywhere in the house, she reminds herself that the task is largely unnecessary. No one would ever link her to the murder of an old man who lives in a bad neighborhood nearly twenty miles away; she would have no motive to do such a thing.

Now that it's over, even she can't quite recall why she felt compelled to do it. There was the racist comment Mr. Griffith made, but that was a while ago and she'd thought she was over it.

She remembers feeling stressed and anxious earlier; remembers that she wished she had some sleeping pills; remembers wishing she could find a way to blow off some steam and relax, but . . .

Murdering an old man in his bed was a little extreme, she tells herself. Some might call it overkill.

Overkill. Ha. Her mouth quirks into an appreciative smile at her own wry wit.

Satisfied that her scrubbing has eliminated any stray speck of blood, she puts the paper towels into a garbage bag, ties it, and sets it in the trash can to go out tomorrow night and be collected Monday morning.

At last, her reward for all that hard work: she turns her attention to her InTune account. It was all she could do not to grab her phone to check for messages the moment she walked in the door. But she didn't want to risk tainting it with her bloody hands, and anyway, she almost relished the buildup now that the other tension—the unpleasant kind of tension that makes her head throb and her mind confused—has been relieved.

She unplugs her phone from the wall charger in the kitchen and logs in, her heart beating faster in anticipation.

This time, she just knows Ben will be there waiting for her.

And this time . . . he is.

Chapter 10

Sunday morning, Gabriela sits, as always, in a chair by the open window with her coffee—iced today; it's far too muggy for hot beverages. And instead of reading the usual morning newspaper or a manuscript on her laptop, she's toying with Ben's cell phone.

What she should be doing is figuring out how to let him know she has it, or throwing it away. Those are the two options she gave herself last night, and she figured sleeping on it would yield the right thing to do.

But she hadn't slept at all, and the gray morning light brought with it a third option.

It's definitely not the right thing to do, but . . .

Temptation, along with the residual sting of what she found on the phone last night, seem to have gotten the better of her.

She has to know what Ben has been saying about her to Peter.

She clicks on the green icon that indicates a new message, and sees that Peter texted a final time, early in the morning: *You never showed. Guess things are going well w/ G after all. Just watch your step and remember what I told you.*

What? What did you tell Ben?

She scrolls to earlier messages. Most of the communication between Ben and Peter involves plans to swim or meet after work, along with their usual banter about sports.

How many times, when she and Ben were dating and married, did she hear the two of them go back and forth endlessly analyzing scores or trades or bad calls?

With a pang she remembers how Peter alternately teased her like a kid sister and confided in her like a big sister. After his divorce, he'd come over for dinner and stay at the table pouring out his heart to her while Ben dozed on the couch.

Peter is Ben's best friend, but he was her friend, too. At least, he acted as though he was. And she considered him a friend. Considered him family.

He stood beside Ben at the altar when they were married. He came to the hospital with an oversized teddy bear when their son was born. And on that horrible morning they lost Josh, Peter came running. It was Peter who held the curious neighbors at bay and accepted wrapped trays of food; Peter who made arrangements that were too heartbreaking for them to consider; Peter who held them up when their own legs wouldn't do the job; Peter who—with Ben's brother— carried the tiny casket at the funeral . . .

Luis. There are text messages from him on the phone as well. Most are brief, a couple of words at most. Gaby scans them. None make reference to her.

Maybe she overreacted to what Ben wrote. Maybe it wasn't about her at all. Maybe *last hurrah—take 2* meant something else.

She remembers that horrible blonde Peter had videotaped at the bar, the one who called him "Pete"—which nobody who knows him well would ever do.

So the woman doesn't know him well, and she doesn't know Ben at all, yet she knows things that are none of her damn business?

Clearly, "last hurrah" meant exactly what she thought it

meant in the first place. Ben had told Peter they slept together the other night, had obviously told him that he was . . .

Hooking up with the ex-wife.

A moment ago she had no intention of snooping further into Ben's files.

Now, a renewed feeling of betrayal snaps that resolve like a sapling in an ice storm.

She clicks on the icon for his InTune account. The password, as she'd guessed, is saved on the log-in page. All she has to do is hit Enter . . .

It's blatantly wrong.

She does it anyway.

I'm not perfect. Nobody is. Right, Ben?

Now she can see not just the public profile she was able to view from her own account, but also Ben's private interaction with other members.

She isn't surprised to see he's connected with quite a few women on the matchmaking site. Most don't seem like his type at all; quite a few are overly made-up blondes, like the woman in the bar last night.

Hi, Ben, I'm Laney.

Every time Gaby thinks of it, she feels violated anew, yet her stomach churns with the wrongness of her own actions as she snoops through Ben's InTune account. It's not that she's completely lost touch with her conscience—it's still there, still sending twinges and the occasional crippling stab of guilt, like a nerve that's been injected with almost—but not quite enough—Novocain.

This isn't me. This isn't who I am; it isn't what I do . . .

No? Really? Then who the hell are you? Do you even know anymore?

She scans Ben's private messages. Many of his female admirers' notes are tentative, sweetly appealing. It hurts to see her ex-husband interacting with those women, flirting with some, even. Yet she forces herself to keep looking, no longer certain whether she's punishing Ben or herself.

As excruciating as it is to read about Ben making plans to meet various women, it's oddly satisfying to see him politely extract himself from those who are a little too breezy, or much too brazen. She knows him well enough, even now, to be able to zero in on the female missteps in the course of an electronic flirtation with Ben.

One woman uses "party" as a verb—a longtime pet peeve of his, and one that brings back poignant memories for Gaby.

Several others have the nerve to ask Ben thinly veiled questions about how much money he has and how he spends it. Another mentions the deadbeat dad of her children so many times in a matter of paragraphs that she's clearly fixated.

Then Gaby stumbles across a woman asking direct questions about the child Ben lost: *What happened? Was it a boy or a girl? How old? How long ago?*

Ben hadn't responded, though Gaby is tempted to, seized by an urge to type, *none of your damn business.*

But then, this account is none of her own damn business, is it? She's prying where she doesn't belong. Yet somehow she still hasn't seen enough, compelled to read on even when she comes across another nosy woman asking Ben about Josh.

And then another.

It serves them right that Ben cut off further communication with all them—though it serves him right that they asked in the first place. What did he think was going to happen, putting it out there for everyone to see?

She'd wondered before whether he'd done it to get sympathy. Now, seeing how he sidestepped the women who attempted to pry into the loss, she knows that wasn't the case.

She continues to read through his messages, from oldest

to newest, noticing that positive connections are becoming fewer and farther between as time goes on. A steady stream of women continues to reach out to Ben, but he seems less interested in dating them. He hasn't done much reaching out of his own accord lately either.

Maybe he decided he was finished with online dating. Maybe it was because he truly did want to try to rekindle their marriage.

The spark of hope sputters and dies when she scrolls to the final private message in the folder. It came in just yesterday from a woman named Alex Jones. According to her profile, she's a nurse and lives in Vanderwaal, a small, well-heeled town in Westchester County.

Ben responded to her well after midnight, after they parted ways so abruptly. She scans through a lengthy back and forth exchange, during which Alex expressed her disappointment that he'd taken so long to get back to her.

So long?

Rather than shut her down right there, as Gaby would expect Ben to do, he responded almost apologetically, saying he'd lost his cell phone and usually uses it to check his account.

The woman wanted to know how that had happened, and he said he must have dropped it on the street somewhere while he was out.

Where were you? she asked—a bold question, Gaby thought. That would turn off Ben for sure.

But rather than skittishly back away from the conversation, he gave the woman a vague reply about having had dinner downtown with a friend.

The next question, even bolder: *Was it a date?*

Gaby's gut twists at his one-word reply: *Nope.*

Why, she wonders, is she doing this to herself? Why not shut off the phone and mail it back to him or toss it out the window or whatever? Why keep reading about Ben's private life when it no longer has anything to do with her?

She'd thought she was punishing Ben—violating his privacy because he'd violated hers. But maybe she's punishing herself, forcing herself to feel the pain. Maybe it's like when somebody dies, and—according to Abuela, anyway—your mind refuses to accept it unless you go to the wake and see the dead person lying there.

This, then, is the metaphorical corpse in the casket. The final step toward beginning to heal.

She reads on.

The woman, Alex, suggests that they get together.

Ben agrees.

Great, she writes. *How about tomorrow?*

Pushy, Gaby thinks.

But again Ben agrees. He's the one who suggests where they should meet.

He's with her right now.

At the beach. *Their* beach. His and hers.

Fury floods Gaby's gut like a tide of molten lava.

At last she clicks out of the screen and tosses the phone aside. She's seen enough.

This, Ben decides, was a bad idea.

It may, in fact, be the worst idea he's ever had in his life.

What was he thinking, suggesting to some woman—a total stranger—that they meet here at Orchard Beach, of all places?

He wasn't thinking; he was drinking.

The Bourbon he'd poured last night when he got home from the disastrous date with Gaby had gone straight to his head. So determined was he to forget her and move on that he'd jumped at the chance to connect with someone— anyone at all—on InTune.

When he woke up this morning, it was to a splitting headache and a series of realizations that went off like grenades in his skull.

Bam! You lost your phone!

Bam! You made a date with a total stranger whose name you can't even remember!

Bam! You and Gaby are finished—again. This time, for good—again.

Remembering what she'd said to him at the cocktail lounge, he grew angry at her all over again—and more determined than ever to get on with the day. With his life. He took a shower, swallowed a couple of Advil, drank a cup of strong coffee. It helped. Not enough, though.

He went back into his InTune account to reread the private message exchange he'd had last night with his date, whose name turned out to be Alex. Last name Jones.

Yeah, sure.

Whatever. He won't hold an uninspired pseudonym against her.

She's a statuesque blue-eyed brunette, and her profile picture is attractive enough. There's something about her smile, though, that seems to lack warmth.

Maybe you're just trying to find something wrong with her, he told himself as he closed out of the account and got dressed. *Give her a chance. You have nothing to lose.*

Now, walking on the beach where he'd spent some of the most carefree moments of his life, he's not so sure.

If only he hadn't suggested that they meet here. The idea had been spontaneous, his filter numbed by Bourbon. Once it was out there, she jumped on it, mentioning that she absolutely loves the beach.

Come on, he thought, rereading the exchange this morning. *Who* doesn't *love the beach?*

But at the time, he wrote back to Alex that he feels the

same way, babbling about the surf and sand being good for the soul—a line that makes him cringe, in retrospect.

She met that with an enthusiastic comment about how much they seem to have in common.

Yeah? Based on . . . what?

They do have the same taste in music, according to her profile. And they're about the same age. But that's about it, as far as Ben can see. It's not as though they've shared a barrage of earth-shattering coincidences.

She lives in Westchester, where she owns a house—a cozy brick cape built back in the 1950s. *Have you ever considered moving to the suburbs, Ben?*

When he responded that he hadn't, she shifted gears and told him all the things she loves about the city.

Her overboard enthusiasm may have pierced the fog of inebriation and inspired him to ask her out last night, but it only made him queasy this morning. Or maybe it was old Bourbon percolating in his stomach with black coffee and ibuprofen.

Somehow, he pulled himself together, rode the subway to the end of the line at Pelham Bay Park in the Bronx, boarded the shuttle bus, and came to the beach.

He'll get this date over with and platonically part ways with this person who thinks they have so much in common for reasons that remain unclear. Tomorrow, he'll be back at work, he'll replace his phone on his lunch hour, and things will be back to normal—whatever normal even is now. The new normal he'd adapted in the months following the divorce suddenly seems as elusive as the old, married normal.

The mile-long beach, always crowded when the season is under way, is swarming with people of every age, race, and socioeconomic status. Cops patrol; hawkers hawk; families spread out on blankets shout to each other and their wandering children; old folks snooze; groups of kids blast hip-hop music; tanned girls chatter, lying on their stomachs with bikini top straps undone; the guards sit high above the action, keeping a watchful eye and occasionally blasting their whistles. No clean salt air smell here, or at least not today. The aroma of fried fish and Cuban food from a boardwalk stand mingles with dank marine life and tobacco smoke courtesy of a group of twelve-year-old punks sneaking their first cigarettes.

Hands shoved in the pockets of his khaki shorts, Ben weaves his way among the umbrella-shaded chairs and people and litter—since when is there so much litter in the sand? Or did he just never notice it before?

He looks for familiar faces, painfully aware that he and Gaby were planning to visit their old lifeguard friends. It's a tradition Ben repeats a few times every summer— sometimes with Gaby, back in the early years of their relationship and marriage, but always without her the past few years since Josh died.

He heard through the Internet grapevine that another bunch of the old crew has graduated to full-time real world jobs since last Labor Day and won't be coming back. An all-new group of guards seem to occupy the chairs now, many of them college age, like the kid perched beneath the familiar orange umbrella where Ben himself had spent so many summer days.

Toned and tan, the kid wears the usual orange swim trunks and spins a whistle on a chain. His gaze is fixed intently on the water, apparently heedless of the gorgeous female guard in an orange tank suit who leans against the base of the stand, waiting to swap places with him.

But the kid knows she's there. Ben is aware of his awareness, remembering how he used to sit high on that very tower like a king on a rickety wooden throne, noticing-but-not-noticing Gabriela below.

"Ben?" a female voice calls and his heart sinks. It lifts

again when he turns to see a woman in an orange tank bathing suit—not his date—hurrying toward him.

"Stella. How's it going?" He gives her a hug.

"Oh, you know . . . it's going."

Stella Kaplan is one of the lifeguards who started here the same summer as Ben and Gaby. When he first met her, with her sun-streaked long brown hair and toned, perfectly tanned body, he developed a fast crush on her. So did every other male guard. He and Stella harmlessly flirted all summer, and kissed a few times, but that was as far as it went. Then he connected with Gaby, and never looked back.

"It's been a few years, hasn't it?" she asks. "I wasn't here last summer."

That's right. Remembering that according to the guard grapevine she'd been on leave then, having recently given birth to her first child, Ben asks about her daughter.

He smiles wistfully when Stella tells him she's a handful, having recently started walking and getting into everything. But she abruptly curtails her account of her daughter's harrowing and messy morning adventure involving a stool and a bowl of milk-soaked Cheerios. "I'm so sorry. I didn't mean to go on and on about my kid."

"You aren't going on and on."

"No, but . . . I mean, I know it must be hard. I'm sorry," she says again.

It is hard, always, hearing about other people's kids and imagining what your own child would be like now, had he lived. But it's hard, too, when you find yourself in stilted conversations in which people awkwardly tiptoe around your feelings.

Gaby understood that. They talked about it yesterday, before . . .

Before everything fell apart all over again. Crap.

"So how's Gabriela?" Stella asks, clearly meaning to

change to a more cheerful subject, and Ben nearly emits a bitter laugh at the irony.

"She's fine," is the simplest answer.

No one in the lifeguard network is aware that they're not together anymore. Plus, Stella and Gaby were never really friends. Stella didn't really pal around with any of the female guards. She was one of those girls the other girls didn't seem to like.

Ben asks her about her husband, and is dismayed to hear that they separated right after Christmas.

"It was just too hard to hold it together once the baby came along. We never were a match made in heaven," she tells Ben. "Not like you and Gaby. Or maybe we just aren't as strong as you guys are. A lot of marriages can't survive what you've been through, but look at you two, still together. You're blessed, Ben, and you guys deserve it. You deserve more children, too. I hope it happens for you and Gaby."

What do you say to that? You smile and you nod and you pretend everything is fine, and you're pretty damned convincing, apparently.

"Well, I've got to get back to the chair," Stella tells him. "Junie's due for a break."

"Junie's here today?" Another blast from the past: Junior Cordero was a good friend of Ben's back in the old days.

"A lot of people are here today. Junie, Miggs, Shakey, Bird Ass . . ."

"Yeah?" The well-worn nicknames bring back a barrage of bittersweet memories. "I've been keeping an eye out, but I haven't seen anyone yet."

"Only a couple of us are working, but a bunch of the old-timers are hanging out over by the Grotto. You should go over and say hi."

"I will, in a while . . ."

"Want to walk down with me now and see Junie?"

"I will, later," he lies again, and gives her another quick hug before she strides away.

He reaches into his pocket for his phone to check the time, remembers again that he doesn't have it, and curses to himself.

Fitting that this day that was forecast to be "picture perfect" has turned out to be overcast. The water is an unappealing greenish gray and undoubtedly still chilly, but the air is warm and uncomfortably humid, and people are splashing around. He wishes he could dive in and swim to the distant shore in an effort to purge the malaise.

Watching a teenage couple laughing as they wade, hand in hand, into the chilly water, he thinks again of himself and Gaby, young and unencumbered.

Oh, hell. All he wants is to flee and put it behind him, all of it. But he can't leave. He has a blind date, of all things.

Maybe this will turn out to be his lucky day and the woman won't show up. Maybe he can just—

"Ben?"

Again, a female voice calls his name.

But this time it's not an old friend. It's a tall brunette, wearing sunglasses and a big hat: his date. Ben sighs inwardly.

So this isn't his lucky day. Surprise, surprise.

Gaby isn't sure exactly when—or how—she arrived at the questionable decision to confront Ben at the beach.

One minute she was furiously dumping the remains of her iced coffee down the drain and trying not to look at the vase filled with yellow roses, the next she was tripping over the cardboard box—Ben's lifetime's worth of memories—on her way to the closet.

Now she finds herself on a crosstown bus, the box on her lap and Ben's cell phone in her pocket.

Staring out the window at the leafy landscape as the bus travels Central Park's 79th Street Transverse in its route from Upper West Side to Upper East, she reminds herself that it's time to reclaim that precious floor space now that she and Ben are most likely estranged for good. Not only that, but she has to get rid of the phone as soon as possible. Otherwise, she'll be tempted to look at his texts again.

As the morning wore on into afternoon, she'd fought the urge to see whether anyone else has reached out to him since last night, or if there are any further clues to what he might have been saying about her to his friends and family.

As long as she has his phone in her possession, she's going to be tempted to snoop.

If she were a different person, a vengeful person, she'd just throw it into the incinerator.

But I'm not vengeful . . .

Am I?

She hadn't stopped to contemplate the idea as she was yanking on shorts and a T-shirt, shoving her feet into flip-flops, and pulling her hair back into a ponytail. She shoved Ben's phone into her pocket along with her own, grabbed the box, and stormed out the door.

The bus slows, preparing to stop at Lexington Avenue. If she gets off here, she can walk a few blocks to get on the subway heading to the Bronx, where she'll transfer to the bus that will take her to out to the beach. Or she can ride one block farther to Third Avenue, grab an uptown bus there, and then transfer to yet another bus in the Bronx. Either way, she'll still have to lug this stuff around in the heat.

All of that just to find Ben at the beach, give him back his stuff—and, let's face it, a piece of your mind.

In the heart of the suburbs, Cherry Street is lined with the kinds of houses Ivy used to picture when she imagined marrying Mr. Right and abandoning her urban studio apartment for a bucolic happily ever after.

Most of the homes she passes on her walk from the train station have front porches and shutters, garage basketball hoops and planters spilling over with summer flowers. There are strollers, tricycles, and puppies everywhere she looks. And there's mulch, too—dark, rich bark mulch layering the garden beds and encircling the trunks of enormous trees whose branches cast dappled shade over the rooftops and pavement.

Cargo-short-wearing dads sponge suds over sports cars in driveways or ride atop fancy mowers more suited to meadows than meager patches of suburban lawn; super-trim or adorably pregnant moms in yoga pants and bouncy ponytails chat, holding paper cup lattes, while their children hit Wiffle balls or jump rope or create driveway chalk murals. Every so often they look up at the overcast sky—all of them, though not all at once—as though searching for storm clouds that might roll in and drown their perfect suburban weekend, washing away chalk masterpieces, rendering ponytails limp, spattering newly washed cars.

Ivy can't help but think that it seems odd that Carlos's date, Sofia, lives in this family-oriented neighborhood. Or does she?

She lied about her name; maybe she lied on her car registration, too.

But this is where the BMW's license plate is registered, according to Ivy's online search—a paid search she charged to her American Express card, along with this morning's train ticket. That's the only card she has that isn't maxed out, because there's no monthly limit. You just have to pay it off in full every month.

Which she won't be able to do.

But at least she has over a month to worry about it.

Right now all she has to worry about is finding Carlos.

Still . . . *here*?

It doesn't seem likely.

Maybe Mutton Chops back at the parking garage got the car wrong—by accident, or deliberately. The BMW in question wasn't registered to a woman named Sofia; its owner was listed as a Carmen Rodriguez in Vanderwaal, up in Westchester County.

Assuming that was Sofia's real name, Ivy had immediately looked for Carmen Rodriguez online, using Google and the InTune Web site. But the name is far too common—with wide variations in spelling—to have yielded anything useful, even when she added the Cherry Street address that accompanied the license plate registration.

According to real estate records, the house is owned by someone named Alex Jones and has been for many years. But that doesn't mean Carmen isn't a tenant there.

There was nothing to do, Ivy realized, but visit in person and hope that Carmen herself answers the door, and that she'll turn out to be the brunette who called herself Sofia on InTune.

What if she does?

What if she doesn't?

Ivy hasn't managed to think that far ahead, though she's had plenty of time during the long walk from the commuter train station. She's spent most of it trying to piece together scenarios for what might have happened to Carlos that Friday night.

If Mutton Chops was telling the truth about Carlos being inebriated when he and his date drove away, any number of disasters could have unfolded.

What if he died of alcohol poisoning, or choked on his own vomit, and the woman got scared and covered it up?

Or what if it was drugs, and not alcohol—the kind of drugs the health teacher used to warn kids about when she was in school, where you could become dangerously addicted by just trying it one time? Maybe that's what happened, and now he's living on the streets, in search of a fix . . .

Or maybe he spent the night with his date, fell in love with her, and they ran off together—a possibility that had entered Ivy's mind long before the police officers paid her a visit, and seems only slightly less tragic, all things considered, than the one where Carlos is a street junkie.

He was supposed to be her own Mr. Right. Maybe he still can be. Maybe, if she can just find him, he'll realize she loved him enough to come looking for him. Maybe the two of them can move to a neighborhood just like this one. Maybe it's not too late for her fairy-tale ending after all.

Checking the addresses—49 . . . 47 . . . 45—she realizes that she's almost reached Carmen Rodriguez's house. It's an even number, 42, which means it's on the opposite side of the street. As she crosses, she notices a woman watching from the porch of number 45.

That's reassuring. If Carmen Rodriguez turns out to be some kind of crazed psycho serial killer, she's not going to try anything at her own front door in broad daylight under the neighbor's watchful gaze. And Ivy doesn't intend to cross the threshold into the house. If, after talking to the woman, she believes she knows something about what happened to Carlos, then she'll have to go to the police.

Even if it means risking your job?

She thinks of her overdue mortgage, and the maxed-out credit cards, and the latest Amex charges she can't afford.

Nothing has changed. She can't lose her job. Maybe there's some other way . . .

"Peter, it's Gabriela—on Ben's phone, obviously. Somehow I wound up with it last night and . . . and I want to get it back to him, but I don't know where to find him. I thought I could maybe leave it with you or with his doorman if you tell me where his building is, but . . . you're not picking up. Okay, never mind."

Standing on the corner of Third Avenue and 79th Street with the box on the sidewalk between her feet, Gaby disconnects the call and toys with Ben's phone.

She'd jumped off the crosstown bus and called Peter on a whim. As much as she dreaded the thought of talking to him, had he answered the phone, her dilemma would have been solved.

Now her only option is to continue the journey to Orchard Beach.

Not your only option. You can always lug all this stuff back home. Or throw it into that garbage can.

She eyes the one on the corner, close enough to touch.

No. She might be furious . . . but she's not cruel.

Hearing the unmistakable whoosh from a bus's air brakes, she turns to see the Bronx-bound BxM7 coming up the avenue.

It's now or . . . well, not never. But now or later, and later isn't an option on this sticky afternoon. At least the bus will be air-conditioned.

When it stops, Gaby gets on. It's standing room only. She jostles her way to the middle, wedges the box onto the floor amid the other passengers' legs, and grabs an overhead bar.

Ten blocks pass. Twenty.

She fights to keep her balance with every lurching stop as the box threatens to slide away like a hockey puck.

Es loco, as Jaz would say.

Maybe she'll get off at the next stop.

But when they reach it, a couple gets up from a pair of seats closest to Gaby and makes their way to the door. She hesitates only briefly before sliding into the vacated row, box on her lap. Leaning her cheek against the glass window, she watches the familiar Bronx scenery flash past as the bus continues its uptown run toward Orchard Beach and Ben.

Ben is everything Alex imagined. Everything and more. Carmen was never quite this handsome.

Well, maybe when he was younger. But it's hard for her to even remember that Carmen, the man she married. Whenever Alex thinks of him, she pictures him weathered and worried, overworked and overtired and . . . unhappy. Always so unhappy.

Not always, to be fair. He seemed happy with her at first. But as their years together went by, he started to complain. To her. And then about her. Nothing she did seemed to satisfy him. Eventually he began to sound just like his nitpicky mother. It was disturbing, and upsetting, and infuriating, but . . .

But she knew she couldn't do to him what she'd done to her mother-in-law. Of course not. And she didn't want to. Most of the time, anyway.

Just, once in awhile, she'd glimpse something ugly in his face, or in his tone, and . . .

Well, her own reaction to that, to the man she loved, scared her. It really did.

Thank goodness things are different with Ben. Maybe because this is only the beginning of their relationship, but still . . .

Everything about him is perfect.

Plus . . .

They share something huge, something very few people could possibly understand. Ben knows what it's like to hold your child in your arms one moment and have him ripped away the next. Ben is longing to make his world whole again, just as she is.

He didn't say it. He didn't have to. She just knows.

She hasn't asked him about his loss, of course. Not yet. Remembering how she would recoil whenever someone asked her about Dante back in the beginning, she would be the last person on earth to ever put Ben in that position.

No, they just walk on the beach, meandering their way around umbrellas and blankets, lifeguard stands and garbage cans, Frisbee games and people, people everywhere, getting in their way.

If only they were alone. If only they were holding hands—which they're not, to her regret. If only they could talk about their future together.

Instead they talk about other things.

Music, mostly.

She can scarcely hold back her enthusiasm when she hears him mention that he likes Bon Jovi. In fact, she asks him, just to be sure that she heard right: "Did you say Bon Jovi?"

She asks because sometimes Carmen would tell her she was reading into things that never happened, or hearing things that nobody ever said.

"Yes, Bon Jovi," Ben confirms, wearing a strange look that strikes a chord of fear in her heart.

Carmen sometimes wore that look, too, back in the beginning.

"I thought you said something else," she quickly tells Ben. "It's hard to hear well with all this noise."

"It is," he agrees, to her relief.

No one would disagree that the din on the beach is distracting. Even the music blasting from portable speakers is unpleasant—most of it hip-hop, with some salsa thrown in here and there.

She loathes hip-hop. And Latin music reminds her of Carmen.

Deciding to drop the subject of Bon Jovi—for now—she asks Ben, "Have you ever been to Mexico?"

"No." He sips from the bottle of iced tea she so thoughtfully brought for him on this hot day. One for him, and one for her—carefully marked, of course, so that she'd know which one was which.

"It's a beautiful place. You should go sometime." She just catches herself before saying, *We should go sometime*.

Maybe it's too soon for that. She doesn't want to scare him off, and something tells her it might have.

In the half hour or so since they met in person, she's glimpsed a fleeting, skittish expression in his eyes. Better not to come on too strong. Maybe he's shy. Or maybe the setting just isn't romantic enough.

If only they were strolling hand in hand on a serene honeymoon beach south of the border instead, where the only sound would be swaying palm fronds and clear aquamarine water lapping at white sand . . .

She's about to tell Ben more about Mexico when a toddler in a diaper darts in front of them, making a beeline for the water.

The child is trailed by a too-large woman in a too-small bikini. "Get your butt back here!" she screeches. "Josh! Josh!"

Noticing the pained expression that crosses Ben's face, Alex is almost certain he's thinking of his lost child.

Maybe, she thinks, it was a drowning. Or maybe that toddler looks like his dead son or daughter.

Which was it? A boy or a girl? How old? How did it happen?

There are so many questions she wants to ask, but again she holds her tongue, asking only, "Are you all right?"

Ben abruptly tosses the iced tea bottle—empty, she realizes—into a garbage can.

"I'm not feeling very well. I'm sorry—I think I've got to go home."

No. He can't leave her. He *can't*.

"You look like you might be a little dehydrated, Ben. I'm a nurse," she adds hastily.

"I'll grab a bottle of water before I get on the bus."

"Bus?"

"Shuttle bus. To the subway."

"You can't wait around for a bus feeling sick. I've got my car. Come on, I'll drive you home."

"I can't let you do that. You live in the opposite direction."

"It's really not a problem."

"It's way out of your way. Thank you anyway," he adds politely—but firmly.

Afraid to push the point and scare him off, she shrugs as if it doesn't matter. "Then I'll just drive you to the subway. Pelham Bay Park, right? That's on my way."

"You don't have to—"

"Don't be silly. But first I'm going to go get you something more to drink. You'll feel better if you sip something cold."

Well over a million people live in the Bronx. Gabriela is pretty sure that most of them are on Orchard Beach today.

But then, she wonders as she trudges up the wide steps leading to the paved veranda above the beach, is it ever *not* busy here?

A memory barges into her mind: sitting with her back to Ben's chest, head against his shoulder, bare legs intertwined on sand that still holds the heat of the day. The only sound is their quiet breathing and the water lapping at the shore and the laughter from distant swimmers . . .

A hard lump of despair forms in her throat at the recollection of that summer night, and hundreds of other nights like it.

Yeah. Okay. So there are times—at least, there *were* times—when the beach felt like a secluded slice of heaven.

What a far cry that was from this garish nightmare of noise and strangers.

She heads toward the sand. Reaching the edge of the boardwalk, she stops to set down Ben's box and wipe sweat from her brow, surveying the scene before her.

Ben is there someplace . . . with someone else.

What if she finds him—them?

What does she say? What does she do?

Oh, come on, who are you kidding? Finding him here would be a miracle.

Deep down, she knew that all along, yet she was swept into this riptide of an odyssey nonetheless.

That's what you do when you get caught in a rip, right? It's one of the first lessons you learn as a lifeguard. You let the current take you away. You go with it rather than struggle against it. Sooner or later it's going to break, so you can swim out of it, back to shore; back where you belong.

But when it grabs you, there's nothing to do but keep moving with it. And so she does, doggedly making her way toward the crowded crescent of sand, keeping an eye out for Ben . . .

Forgetting all about the box she left sitting at the edge of the boardwalk.

Chapter 11

It's Sully's day off, one she was supposed to spend with her father and various Leary family members celebrating the christening of her cousin Paddy's infant son, Patrick III. Or maybe Patrick IV. There are at least half a dozen Patricks in various generations of the Leary family; how is anyone supposed to keep track?

But rather than gathering with the family on this gray summer Sunday for mass in Bay Ridge, followed by food platters from the local pub, Sully is back at work after a long night and a few hours' sleep.

But it's just as well. Eating hot food in an un-air-conditioned apartment packed with hordes of relatives and at least one colicky baby lacks a certain appeal. Anything is better. Even this.

Perspiration beads around her hairline and tickles the sides of her nose as she and Stockton climb a third dimly lit flight of stairs in an un-air-conditioned Harlem apartment building.

The air is heavy with humidity, the unappetizingly mingled scents of curry and basil, and an argument in an unrecognizable guttural-sound-laden language courtesy of the tenants in 2A. From a television or radio somewhere above, a baseball announcer is shouting about a player rounding second, and then third . . .

"Someone just hit a home run," Stockton observes. "Too bad it's the Mets."

He hates the Mets.

"Yeah, well, maybe it's a good omen."

"For who?"

"For us."

"Met home run's never a good omen for anyone."

"It is when you're on a roll with a case that you can't afford to fumble."

"Wrong sport, Gingersnap."

"Okay," she swipes a sticky palm across her stickier forehead, "then we can't afford to strike out. Better?"

"It would be if we already had two strikes. You need three to—"

"I know that, Stockton. I just—"

"Then why—"

"Never mind," they say in unison, before trudging up the final flight in silence. It's too oppressive to bicker, although the people in 2A missed the memo.

José Morales, the man whose nephew, Bobby Springer, apparently went missing exactly three months before Jake Fuentes did, lives on the fourth floor. They'd spoken to him by phone this morning, and he promptly buzzed them into the building when they rang the bell in the vestibule below.

Sully is convinced Springer's disappearance is linked to the others. Her initial search indicated that he maintained an active social networking presence and has profiles on several online dating sites that aren't nearly as popular with local singles as InTune is. Her hunch is that he might have had one on InTune as well—and that someone, perhaps not Bobby himself, deleted it after he vanished.

He'd been planning to leave for a week-long vacation on

Sunday, September 22—flying out to the West Coast to visit his friend Danny, who'd recently gotten married and moved to L.A.. Bobby had e-mailed Danny from his cell phone early on the morning of Saturday the twenty-first to say that he couldn't get away after all; something had come up at work.

That was a lie, according to colleagues who were interviewed last fall by the detectives on the case. There had been no last-minute upheaval at the office. As far as Springer's coworkers knew, he'd gone away on vacation as planned.

Thus, more than a week went by before anyone realized anything was amiss. When he didn't show up back at the office on Monday, September 30, his supervisor assumed he might have missed his flight home and left him a couple of messages. Tuesday, after again trying unsuccessfully to contact him, the supervisor notified Human Resources, and they got in touch with José Morales. He'd gone over to his nephew's apartment, found his packed suitcase and unused plane ticket to California, and called the police.

This morning, Sully and Stockton had met with Detectives Lonnie McClure and Mike Needham, who were handling the case in Jersey, where Springer had lived. Both felt that he might have staged his disappearance. He had an on-and-off drinking problem and a boatload of credit card debt, and was a month behind on his rent.

"What did the uncle think about that?" Sully asked them.

"What do they all think?" McClure shrugged. "He swore up and down that the kid would never walk away."

Yeah. That's what they all think. Most of the time, they're wrong.

Sully blots sweat from her forehead with her sleeve as she and Stockton arrive at the fourth-floor hallway. There are three doors. The middle one is ajar, the baseball game blasting from within.

After checking the number on the door—4B—Sully knocks on it. "Mr. Morales?"

"Yeah, it's open," a male voice calls.

She looks at Stockton.

"Ladies first," he tells her with an exaggerated sweeping gesture, and she rolls her eyes.

"You didn't say that this morning when we made our pit stop at that gas station in Jersey."

There had only been one rest room. Stockton beat her to it.

"After three cups of coffee? Uh-uh." Having given her Irish tea a try last night, he'd declared it ineffective in combating exhaustion. This morning he was right back to the burnt-smelling brew from the Bunn in the office kitchenette.

With Stockton on her heels, Sully crosses the threshold into the apartment's entryway. The room isn't exactly spacious, but they both would have fit comfortably inside were it not for copious clutter. A top-heavy coat tree is layered with so many garments that it's tipped over and precariously balanced against the wall. An oversized bureau sits beside the door, and a chair in front of it blocks the drawers. Magazines and unopened mail are scattered in piles on top of the bureau. On the chair is a plastic crate filled with men's sneakers and shoes, with more crates and boxes stacked on the floor beside it.

Hoarder in residence. You don't have to be much of a detective to reach that conclusion.

Then Sully spots the label on an envelope sitting atop the bureau. It's addressed to Robert Springer, forwarded to José Morales.

Okay. Maybe not a hoarder after all. At least some of this stuff obviously belongs to the missing nephew.

"In here," the voice calls from the next room.

Through the doorway, Sully can see a large flat-screen television where a sports announcer finishes recapping the home run and updating the score as the inning ends and the game goes to a commercial.

She and Stockton step over the threshold to find a man

heaving himself out of an easy chair facing the television, directly in the path of the large white plastic turbo fan humming in the room's lone window.

Here, too, there's more furniture than there should be: two couches, two coffee tables, and two televisions: the flat screen on the wall, plus a big, boxy older television, unplugged and sitting on the floor in a corner.

Sully's father has one of those ancient TVs on the floor in his living room, too. He keeps trying to give it away, but it's too unwieldy for anyone to move. Even charitable organizations aren't interested.

"I bought it for two grand when the Yankees got into the '96 World Series so that your mother and I could watch it on the big screen," he told Sully—the big screen, at the time, encompassing thirty-five inches. "Took me five years to pay it off, with interest. Now I can't even give the damn thing away."

"You'll have to pay someone to haul it to a Dumpster, Da," she told him. But the last time she visited, the TV was still sitting there like Sully's hefty, aged Aunt Eileen, who always overstays her holiday welcome, in part because no one is quite up to transporting her back home to the suburbs.

Sully and Stockton flash their badges at José Morales, introduce themselves, shake his hand. Unshaven and potbellied, the man wears a white sleeveless undershirt, basketball shorts, a backward Mets cap, and a sad, tired expression. He clears a heap of clothing and a thick Sunday newspaper off the nearest couch. In Spanish-accented English he offers them a cold beverage—which they politely decline—and a seat on the couch, which they accept.

Morales sinks heavily back into the chair he'd just vacated. The newspaper, now sitting on an end table, flaps around in front of the fan, with its breeze that doesn't quite reach the spot where Sully and Stockton are sitting.

Again she wipes a trickle of sweat from her forehead.

"Do you mind if we . . ." Stockton gestures at the blasting television.

"Sorry." Morales aims the remote at the TV and presses a button to freeze the action on a beer commercial. "Tie game," he explains.

Sully is about to tell him to turn it off altogether. But then he says heavily, "I know why you're here," and she sees dread mingling with the sorrow and weariness that have already etched deep lines on his face. He buries his forehead in his hands. "You found Bobby. He's dead, isn't he?"

"No, we didn't find him," she tells him. "That's not why we're here."

The man looks up, wide-eyed. "But . . . I thought you said when you called . . . Isn't this about my nephew?"

"It is," Stockton assures him. "But he's not . . . that is, he's still missing, as far as we know."

"Gracias a Dios!" Morales crosses himself and slumps back in his chair. "That's good. I mean—not good, but better than . . ."

Right. Better than hearing that his nephew—whom he'd raised as a son after his sister took off when the kid was ten—has turned up somewhere as a corpse.

"We just want to ask you a few questions about him." Sully takes a pen and pad from her pocket. She flips through, looking for the notes she made this morning in New Jersey. The pages are limp. Freaking humidity.

"I'll tell you anything you want to know," Morales is saying. "I don't have any kids of my own. Bobby is a son to me. He isn't perfect. He used to be a drinker, but he's straightened out, been in AA for a few years now. He doesn't want to end up like my sister."

"And she's his mother?"

"Was." Morales sighs. "She was an alcoholic. She walked out on my nephew. No note, no nothing. One day she was there, the next she was gone."

"Where did she go?"

"Who knows? She was in Florida when she drank herself to death a few years later. But Bobby, he's different. He has a good heart. I miss him."

Sully notes that he speaks of his missing loved one in present tense. They always do—with a few notable exceptions.

Years ago, Sully's first missing person case that ended in homicide involved a missing woman whose husband—a fine, upstanding citizen—referred to her in past tense, but kept correcting himself. As it turned out, he'd bludgeoned her to death on their yacht and tossed her overboard.

She takes notes as Stockton asks him to go over the details leading up to reporting his nephew's disappearance. He recounts the situation pretty much exactly as it was outlined in the case file.

He and his nephew weren't in daily contact, but saw each other once or twice a month. Bobby lived alone now, having moved last summer from the Brooklyn apartment where he'd lived with his girlfriend to a studio in Jersey City.

"Do you know why they broke up?" Sully asks.

"She said she didn't want to get serious."

"And your nephew did?"

"*Sí.* Bobby has old-fashioned values. He wants to get married. Like I said, he has a good heart and he's been sober for a few years now. So he moved out and moved on."

"He was dating other women, then?"

"Sure."

"Do you know who they were? Or how he met them?"

"No."

"Did you know that he had online dating profiles?"

"No."

"Have you met any of his friends?"

"Not lately. Just Danny, and I haven't seen him in a few years now."

McClure and Needham had interviewed Danny, along

with Bobby's ex-girlfriend, colleagues, and a few casual acquaintances, none of whom could shed any light on the disappearance. Reading between the lines, Sully could see the general consensus was that Bobby had simply walked away from his life, just as his mother had years before. Maybe he was upset about the recent breakup; maybe he'd fallen off the wagon; maybe he was trying to escape his financial obligations, feeling underpaid and overworked like the rest of the world.

No one—other than a frustrated José Morales—seemed to think it might be foul play.

"I wish I could believe he just left," the man tells Sully and Stockton now. "But he didn't. I guarantee you that."

"How are you so sure?"

"Because—here, I'll show you." He gets up and weaves his way across the room, stepping around tables and chairs to get to a desk.

"This is Bobby's. A lot of this stuff is his. I couldn't pay his rent, so I had to move it out of his apartment. Do you know how hard it was to carry it up all these flights? Mostly by myself. Threw my back out of whack for a month. It still bothers me. But I'm keeping everything until Bobby comes back. And when he does, I'm going to treat him to a new TV because I like this one. It's a lot better than mine. Does all kinds of fancy stuff."

Mr. Morales opens a desk drawer, rummages through it, closes it, opens another one.

Sully wipes more sweat from her forehead and watches the newspaper fluttering in the breeze from the fan, wishing she'd accepted the offer of a cold drink after all.

The exhausting weekend is beginning to catch up to her. There's a burning ache between her shoulder blades, and her eyeballs feel as though they've been sandblasted. When the alarm went off this morning just a few hours after she'd set it, it was all she could do not to roll over and go back to sleep. Only the thought of the missing men—four of them, at least—got her up and moving.

Now she's even more determined to see this through. José Morales needs closure. All the families do.

"Here it is. See?" He pulls something out of a drawer and carries it back over to the couch.

It's a framed photograph of a grinning, heavyset woman with an arm casually resting on the shoulders of a slender, dark-haired boy. The kid wears a tentative half smile and has both his arms wrapped around her ample middle like he's trying to hold on for dear life.

"That's Bobby with my sister, not long before she left. This is the last picture he ever took with her. Maybe it's the only one he even had. He kept it by his bed here after she took off, and everyplace he ever lived after that. I found it on his nightstand in Jersey City when I went over to his place the day his boss called me. If he was going away for good, this is the one thing he would have taken with him."

How many times has Sully heard a bewildered, abandoned loved one say something like that?

He/She would never have left without . . .

His car.

Her kids.

Me.

How many times has that turned out to be a mistaken assumption?

Every day, without warning or explanation, people willingly leave behind cherished belongings—and cherished people.

Sully would have assumed Bobby Springer is one of them, but there are simply too many coincidences.

Foul play might be rare, but it happens. And Sully is almost positive it happened here.

Making her way across the beach, Gaby takes it all in: the

sea of people, the greenish-gray water beneath a gray sky, the pervasive odor of cooking grease and sweat and garbage baking in the heat, the cacophony of voices and music, screeching whistles and screeching gulls . . .

It's been a few years since she last visited, but she doesn't remember it being like this. Chaos reigns in every direction, and there's no sign of Ben anywhere.

She should never have come.

She should have kept the damned phone and the damned box until—

The box!

She stops short, realizing she's not carrying it.

Someone slams into her from behind.

"What the hell—watch where you're going, lady!"

Gaby spins around, eyes blazing. "You watch where you're going!"

The kid behind her—some bare-chested, tattooed punk—gets right into her face, wearing a menacing expression. "What did you say?"

"I said *you* watch it! You're the one who walked into me!" The old Gaby—streetwise, fiery Latin temper—is, apparently, back in business. Abuela would be proud.

The kid curses at her and walks away.

Feeling sick inside, Gaby hurriedly turns and begins retracing her steps, looking for Ben's box of memories. It's not where she left it by the boardwalk. Nor is it in any nearby trash can.

It's gone.

Number 42 Cherry Street is a brick cape with an attached garage, one of the smallest houses on the block. Ivy notices a few straggly flowers in the overgrown garden beds along the foundation, but here there's no trace of mulch, and there are no cheerful planters. The grass needs to be mowed, the white trim could stand a paint job, and the shades are drawn.

Ivy rings the bell and hears it echoing faintly inside the house. Somehow, she senses that it won't be answered even before she waits . . . knocks on the door . . . waits again in silence marred only by birds chirping, lawn mowers buzzing, sprinklers spritzing, and the distant happy shouts of kids down the block.

Carmen Rodriguez isn't home—or if she is, she's not interested in visitors.

Frustrated, Ivy turns away, descends the steps, and notices that the neighbor is still sitting on the porch, watching her. She hesitates on the sidewalk. She's still carrying the photo of Carlos. Maybe she should show it to the woman across the street just in case she's seen him coming and going.

"Can I talk to you for a second?" Ivy calls.

"Are you selling something? Because if you are—" She gives a pleasant laugh. "—I'm flat broke."

"No, I just wanted to ask a quick question, if that's okay?"

"Sure."

The house is, like the others on the block—with the exception of number 42—well-kept, as evidenced by the splashy planters and mulched beds. If Ivy's cozy suburban happily-ever-after dream ever comes true, she'll have to remember that: flowers + mulch = curb appeal.

Now that the woman on the porch has stood up, Ivy can see that she's pregnant. Not enormously so, just a slight swelling that protrudes from the ubiquitous stretchy yoga pants and top. She's sporting a bouncy blond ponytail as well, and there's a paper latte cup on the glass-topped table beside the porch swing. It's marked in black Sharpie: DC/S. Ivy is well-versed enough in coffee bar lingo to know that stands for Decaf Soy.

"What's up?" she asks Ivy, looking a little cautious, as though she expects Ivy to pull out a suitcase full of cosmetic samples or, at the very least, a political petition on a clipboard.

"You live here, right?" Silly question, but the woman smiles and nods.

"Finally, yes. I inherited the house a couple of years ago after my great-aunt died, but it was tied up in probate forever."

"You *inherited* it?" Some people, Ivy can't help but think, have all the luck. She inherited nothing when her parents died but a bunch of useless tchotchkes and plenty of headaches from a ne'er-do-well kid brother.

"My aunt didn't have kids, so she left the house to me. I thought that was a good thing before I had to deal with all the red tape. It's still a good thing, I guess. That's what my boyfriend says, anyway. We were both living in tiny apartments but now we get to live together—here."

So she's not married to her baby daddy. Ivy wonders how that goes over here in the land of happily ever after. Maybe it explains why this mom-to-be is sitting alone on her porch and not mingling with her fellow Cherry Street breeders.

There's a moment of silence—awkward, Ivy realizes, until the other woman fills it. "I'm Heather Toomey."

"I'm Ivy Sacks. I just took a train up from the city."

As if that explains anything at all.

"Okay, so you're Ivy and I'm Heather. I guess our moms both liked to garden, huh?"

"What?"

"Ivy—Heather—both plants."

"Oh. Um, I don't think my mom was into gardening." Ivy's mother lived most of her life in a twenty-fourth-floor rental. No terrace. Not even any potted plants.

"Oh. Well, maybe you were named after someone in the family. I was named after my aunt—sort of. You know, just the first two letters. Thank goodness they didn't call me Hester. But I was still her favorite. I was the only one of the cousins she invited to come up here and spend summers away from the city—although maybe she felt sorry for me because I'm an only child and my parents went through the world's worst and most dragged-out divorce."

Ivy doesn't know what to say to all that. Heather is the kind of person who talks a lot but doesn't ask many questions, which doesn't leave you with a lot to say when she pauses to let you get a word in.

Now, though, when Ivy fails to speak up, Heather does ask a question: "Are you looking for my neighbor?"

"You mean Carmen? Actually, I'm looking for my brother. He's dating her."

"Dating who?"

"Dating Carmen."

Something flickers in Heather's gray eyes, and is gone. "Are you sure about that?"

So much for not asking questions.

"Am I sure about *what*?"

"That your brother is dating Carmen? I mean, is that what he told you?"

Ivy isn't sure about anything. Anything at all.

Her expression must give that away, because Heather reaches out and touches her arm.

"The thing is," she says gently, "Carmen wasn't a woman. I don't know how you feel about that . . ."

Her words twirl crazily in Ivy's brain.

Carmen wasn't a woman.

Carmen wasn't . . .

Wasn't?

Who the hell is—*was*—Carmen?

"Maybe your brother didn't want you to know he was dating a man," Heather goes on, "because some people aren't cool with that, and—"

"No, it's not like that. Not at all. It's—is Carmen . . . *around*?"

"Nope. His wife is still living in the house, though."

"Is her first name Sofia?"

Heather shakes her head. "I'm not sure what it is. Alison, Alexis—something like that. Definitely not Sofia. I've only actually met her a few times."

"Does she drive a black BMW?"

"Yes."

"An older model?"

Again: "Yes."

Ivy reaches into her pocket, pulling out the picture of Carlos and thrusting it at Heather Toomey. "This is my brother. His name is Carlos Diaz."

Heather glances at the photo and gives her a dubious look. "Wow, you guys . . . you look absolutely nothing alike."

"He's my stepbrother," Ivy amends quickly. "Have you seen him around across the street?"

The woman studies the photograph more carefully, shakes her head, hands it back. "No. Sorry."

"It would only have been recently—in the past week or two."

"No."

"Are you sure?"

"Well, I'm a teacher at a private school so I've been off since the beginning of June, mostly hanging out right here. And actually, I've never seen anyone over there. She's kind of . . ."

When she trails off, Ivy holds her breath, waiting for the rest.

It doesn't come.

"She's kind of what?"

"I don't know. Just—I guess 'not all there' is a nice way to put it. But I barely know her. I just see her over there sometimes. Like I said, I've been sitting out here a lot because my boyfriend redid the hardwoods when we moved in last winter and I can still smell the varnish. I worry about it—you know, about the fumes. With the baby."

Ivy nods as if she cares. "So you've been living here a few months, at least?"

"Right. But Aunt Hester was here forever. She bought this house way back in the 1930s. She's the one who said . . ."

"Said what?" Ivy prompts when Heather trails off.

"You know. That the woman across the street was strange."

"Strange how?" Ivy doesn't wait for that question to be answered, adding another: "What does she look like?"

"Tall. Long dark hair. Really, really toned body. Like, a lot of women around here work out, but she's more . . . muscular. And attractive, I guess, for an older woman."

"How old?"

Heather shrugs. "I have no idea. Probably in her fifties, at least."

"Did you know her husband, too?"

"No, but Aunt Hester knew him his whole life. He grew up down the street, and then he moved back to the block with his wife as an adult."

"Carmen? We're talking about Carmen, right?"

"Right. I was just a little girl then. I can barely remember him. But anyway, his mother used to live over there—" Heather points at a house on the other side of the street "—at number fifty-eight. See it? The Victorian?"

Victorian—yes. Ivy is no old house buff, but she recognizes the distinctive architectural style that sets it apart from the other homes across the street: fish-scale shingled gables, bay windows, and a wraparound gingerbread porch.

"The place was empty for years. A caretaker kept it up. But a family lives there now. They moved in just before we did. They have a bunch of kids, all under five years old. I always see the mom in the yard with them. She looks frazzled."

"So she moved away?"

"Who?"

"The mother!"

"No, but I wouldn't blame her if she took off someday. Like I said, she has all those kids—"

"No, not *her*. I mean Carmen's mother, the one who used to live there." Between the extraneous details and the stifling heat, Ivy has lost all patience.

"Carmen's mother died years ago, probably before I was born. She had a bad fall. You know, with old people . . . that happens. That's why we were always worried about Aunt Hester. She was—"

Ivy quickly steers her back on track. "What else do you remember about Carmen?"

"He used to travel a lot on business. One summer, when I came back to stay, Aunt Hester mentioned that he'd left over the winter and he didn't come back. Aunt Hester was predicting that was going to happen for years before it finally did. She liked to keep an eye on things."

"Did something happen to him?"

"Yeah. I'm guessing he finally got sick of his crazy wife."

"So she's crazy." Unsettling, to say the least.

Heather shakes her head. "I probably shouldn't say that."

"Dangerously crazy?" Ivy's thoughts are whirling.

"No! Definitely not dangerous. Not like—you know. That's not what I meant. She was always really nice to me when I first met her, when I was a little kid. After that, I never saw her. So it's not like I know her very well—at all, really. But there were stories . . ."

"Your aunt told you stories?"

"The kids in the neighborhood did. Aunt Hester told me to mind my own business, which was pretty ironic, you know, because she never did. But anyway, my parents would send me up here to stay with her every June when school got out, and I had summer friends . . ."

"The local kids."

"Yes, and they would talk, you know, the way kids do . . ."

"What did they say?"

"Okay, this is kind of creepy, but since you asked—" Heather breaks off at the sound of a cell phone ring tone. She pulls it out of her pocket and looks at it. "This is my boyfriend. He's at work. He's a cop, and it's hard for me to get ahold of him, so when he calls me to check in, I . . . you know, I have to get it. He worries."

"That's fine. I'll wait."

Heather steps inside with the phone, leaving Ivy alone on the porch to glance uneasily from the Queen Anne Victorian to the brick cape across the street.

The Lost and Found is Gaby's last resort.

Doubtful that anyone would have carried the missing box all the way up here from the boardwalk, she's convinced it's gone forever. Someone probably grabbed it, opened it, kept whatever had any value—old baseball cards, maybe?—and ditched the rest. Although not in any garbage can in the vicinity, because she's searched them all. Not fun in this heat.

A lobster-burnt guy is manning the Lost and Found.

"'Sup?" he greets her, pushing aside a wisp of damp gray hair poking out from beneath his bandana doo-rag in OB orange and green.

"Hi. I'm looking for something I lost out on the boardwalk."

"You and everyone else," he replies, and she instantly recognizes the distinct grind of a voice from the past.

"Shakey?"

She doesn't know his real name, or where he got his nickname, though there are various theories among the guards. Some said Shakey was short for Shakespeare—bestowed not because he was particularly eloquent, but because he was not. Others said it was because he dabbled in his share of drugs back in the day, and Shakey referred to the DTs—delirium tremens. All anyone knows for sure is that the aging Dead Head has been a beloved fixture here at the beach for many decades.

He narrows his eyes at her, then widens them. "Gabriela! That's you! Hey, I heard you people were back here today! Gimme a hug."

She does, but his comment gives her pause. "You people?" she asks, pulling back again.

Shakey groans. "After all these years, you gonna get on me for the way I tawk?"

"No, I just meant . . . 'you people' as in who?"

"You and Bennie. How you been?"

"We're . . . fine," she tells Shakey. If he hasn't heard otherwise, she's not going to be the one to break the divorce news. "How about you?"

"Same. Some things never change, you know? So . . . how'd you manage to lose Ben?"

"What?"

"You know . . . Lost 'n' Found. Thought maybe you lost—" Seeing her expression, he stops grinning. "Hey, everything okay?"

"Sure."

"Yeah?"

"Yeah."

"Hey, where's Ben?"

"Oh, he's out there somewhere. Listen, what I'm actually looking for is a brown cardboard box about this big." She gestures with her hands.

"What's it look like?"

Oh, Shakey. Lifeguard lore always did proclaim that his brain was usually as fried as his fair-skinned face.

She repeats, "Brown. Cardboard. This big."

He gives a cursory glance at the array of swim goggles, clothing, towels, and various beach gear that line the shelf behind him. "Not here. What's in the box?"

"Just . . ." *A lifetime's worth of memories.* "Just a bunch of . . . old . . . stuff."

"Why you lugging a box of old stuff around at the beach?"

Good question. "Never mind. It's—It doesn't matter. I guess it's gone."

"So where's Ben?" Shakey asks again.

"I don't know, exactly. We kind of . . . lost each other."

"Did you try calling his cell?"

"He doesn't have it on him."

"Oh. Well, Stella saw him down by the chairs a little while ago. She said he'd be up here to see me."

Before Gaby can respond, a disgruntled-looking woman and a whiny adolescent girl come up behind her, arguing.

"I told you not to leave it on the blanket when you went in the water."

"I was only gone for like two minutes."

"Well if it's not in the Lost and Found, then that means someone stole it. And I'm not buying you another one."

Gaby steps aside.

"Hey, don't go nowhere," Shakey tells her. "I'm not done catching up with you."

"Don't worry," she says, leaning against a low brick wall to keep an eye out for Ben. "I'll hang around for a while."

"So your nephew wanted to settle down, then?" Stockton is asking José Morales, in the thick of questioning him as Sully continues to take notes. "Trying to meet someone new?"

"Definitely."

"What kind of women did he want to meet?"

"*Nice* women."

"Yeah, well, not a whole lotta men out there who are looking for mean bitches," Stockton says with a grin, adding, "but some of us manage to find 'em anyway."

Sully shoots him a pointed look.

He shoots one back, and she can read his mind: *Just trying to keep it light here.*

"Did Bobby talk about the qualities he wanted in a woman?" she asks Morales. "Besides nice, I mean?"

"Sure. Someone with old-fashioned values."

"Old fashioned—how?"

"You know—someone who wants to get married and have a family. Bobby loves kids. That's the most important thing. He never had a dad—other than me, anyway—and he wants to be a good one. Like me, he always says." José Morales chokes up and turns away to compose himself again.

Stockton quickly wraps up the questioning, telling him they'll be in touch if they find anything, and asks if Morales has any questions.

"*Sí.* What happened to the other detectives who were on the case?"

"McClure and Needham?"

"Did they get fired for not trying hard enough?"

"Fired? No, they're still on it."

"They're trying, Mr. Morales," Sully puts in. "They really are."

"But why did they bring in you two?"

Neither she nor Stockton answers immediately.

Morales looks from one to the other. "I've been here all my life. I know the NYPD detectives don't sit around twiddling their thumbs because there's nothing to do. I been trying to get the other detectives to work harder to find Bobby, but half the time they're too busy to even take my calls. Same thing with the press. I try to get them to, you know, pay attention to what happened to Bobby, but they're not putting him on the front page the way they would if he were some young rich white girl who disappeared. You know what I mean?"

They know. They nod.

"So why," he repeats, "are you two working on my nephew's case now, too? What happened?"

"There have been a couple of similar disappearances since Bobby went missing," Sully admits. "We're not sure they're related."

"You mean they just vanished, like my nephew?"

"Pretty much."

"Why do you think they're connected?"

"They had a lot in common with your nephew."

"Like what?"

"They were all Hispanic men, mid-thirties, using online dating Web sites," Stockton tells him. "That's why we were asking you about Bobby's Internet habits."

Sully shoots him a warning look. Better not to say too much at this stage.

"So you're talking about . . . what? Some kind of serial . . ."

Morales can't bring himself to say the word *killer*. Nor is it accurate. Not yet, anyway.

"We're looking at a number of different scenarios, Mr. Morales," Sully tells him.

"And . . . you haven't found them, have you? These other guys? Alive, or . . ."

"No," Stockton says. "We haven't found them."

"Good. I mean, not good, but . . . you know."

They nod. They know.

"Anything you can do to find Bobby, I want you to do," Morales tells them as they edge their way past the furniture crowding the entryway to open the door. "That kid is my world, you know?"

Yet again they nod. Yet again they know.

They start down the hall to the stairs.

"Hey wait a second—Detectives?"

They turn back to see José Morales beckoning from the doorway. "As a token of my appreciation, I'll be happy to give you my TV."

"Somehow, I don't think he's talking about the flat screen," Stockton mutters. Aloud, he tells the man, "You don't have to do that. This is our job."

"I know, but it's the least I can do."

"That'd be great. I can use a new TV," Sully tells him. "Come on, Stockton—you're a big, strapping guy. This will be a cakewalk for you."

Five minutes later, stopping for a rest on the third-floor landing, sweat streaming into his eyes after lugging the heavy television down the first flight, Stockton glares at her, panting.

"Why are we doing this?"

"Because he wanted to give it to me."

"You just bought yourself a flat-screen plasma TV," he hisses.

"Yeah, and that man has a kid he's most likely never going to see again. You know it and I know it. The least we can do is move this thing out of there so he doesn't have to pay someone to do it for him."

Stockton tilts his head, and a smile slowly replaces his frown. "You've got a good heart. You know that, Gingersnap?"

"So did Bobby Springer."

It isn't until they're moving down the next flight that she realizes she used past tense.

Any second now Ben knows he's going to pass out, or vomit. That he might do both, maybe even simultaneously, is not out of the realm of possibility.

All he wants right now is to go home, crawl into bed, and stay there until tomorrow. If only he could snap his fingers and beam himself there, instead of dealing with this woman. Alex.

It may be because he's battling the mother of all hangovers, but there's something a little . . . *off* about her. She seems a little too into him. Not in an insecure, desperate way, like some women he's met. More in a proprietary way, almost as if they've been seeing each other for a while.

Maybe it's not entirely her fault, given his drunken over-enthusiasm when they were messaging back and forth last night.

That's what you get for being irresponsible, he tells himself now as they rinse the sand off their feet on the boardwalk beneath a cement-colored sky. *That's what you get for letting yourself fall in love with Gaby all over again.*

If he hadn't originally been planning to come here today with her, would he be having a better time now?

Probably not. Even if he didn't feel like crap from all the Bourbon, and even if the weather were picture-perfect, he still wouldn't be interested in this woman.

"Ready?" Alex is barefoot, sandals dangling from her hand, along with a set of car keys. She's still wearing her hat and sunglasses, so he hasn't gotten a good look at the rest of her face, but the network of fine wrinkles around her mouth tells him that she might be at least a decade older than she claimed to be, possibly in her forties. Late forties. Plus— well, her biceps are bigger than his. He's not crazy about women who are all skin and bones, but he prefers curves to muscle.

It doesn't matter that she's not his type, though. He's never going to see her again. She's just another in a long line of dates that didn't work out.

Feeling more light-headed by the second, Ben shoves his wet feet into his flip-flops and reaches for his phone to check the time, but—*dammit, dammit.* That's right. He lost the phone.

"What's wrong?" She's watching him.

"Nothing, I just—I'm going to go wait for the shuttle bus, so I was wondering what time it—"

"Don't be silly. I'll drive you. Not all the way home—just

to the subway," she adds when he opens his mouth to protest. "Remember? Just like we said."

Just like *she* said. He never agreed to that, did he?

"You really do look like you're not feeling well," she tells him before he can argue. "Sit there and I'll go get you a bottle of water."

She points to a nearby bench, then is gone before he can protest.

Ben sits.

Water would also be a good idea. He's definitely dehydrated, thanks to the oppressive weather and his hangover.

But he doesn't want to ride with her, even just to the subway station. That might send the wrong message. He'll take the bus.

A group of teenage girls are talking shrilly nearby, making his head pound. He put a couple of Advil into his pocket before he left home earlier. When Alex brings water, he'll swallow them, even at the risk of feeling more nauseated than he does now.

Why is she taking so long?

Nearby, the girls' conversation—about boys, of course— grows louder and more animated, liberally sprinkled with curse words and slang Ben doesn't even understand. He rubs his temples, wishing they'd go away.

Or maybe he should go away. He can just get up and leave. When Alex comes back, she'll see that he's gone, and yes, she'll be upset and angry, but she'll get over it. They'll never see each other again, so who cares?

Besides, he wouldn't be the first guy to take off on a woman before their date has drawn to a formal close.

He starts to get up. His legs wobble beneath him.

He sits again.

Deciding she's lingered long enough at the Lost and Found, Gaby bids farewell to Shakey at last. She leaves her cell phone number with him, though, telling him to call her if someone drops off the box.

"What about Ben?"

"What about him?"

"You want I should call you if he shows up, too?"

"No, I'll find him sooner or later."

"Don't be so sure about that. It's crazy out there today."

"It's crazy out there every day, isn't it?"

"This time of year? Hell, yeah. But I love it."

She used to love it, too. But she's had enough.

She heads back out into the dreary afternoon. It's time to go back to her life. Tomorrow, she can track down Ben at work and arrange to messenger his phone over to him.

"Gabriela?"

Turning, she recognizes Stella Kaplan, one of the lifeguards she and Ben used to know. She was never Gaby's favorite person. Mainly because she was always flirting with Ben. To be fair, Stella flirted with all the male guards and was aloof to the female ones. But Gaby knew Ben and Stella had a brief fling before she and Ben ever started dating—good reason to be even less fond of her.

"How are you?" Stella hugs her. "Wow, it's been a few years, hasn't it?"

It has, and they've certainly been kind ones to Stella. Gaby thought she'd heard that Stella had gotten married and had a baby, but she's not wearing a wedding ring and her figure is as taut as ever.

"It's been a while," Gaby agrees.

"Well, you look as great as Ben does."

"Oh . . . thanks. So do you."

"You don't have to say that. I'm a single mom with a one-year-old. I look like a raccoon."

"You and me both." Gaby decides she likes Stella after all.

"Listen, I haven't had a chance to talk to you since . . .

well, since your loss. I heard about it too late to come to the service. I wanted to say how sorry I am. Now that I'm a mom, especially, I just can't even . . . I'm so sorry."

Caught off guard, Gaby murmurs something appropriate.

"But I'm really glad you and Ben have stuck together through all of this," Stella adds. "A lot of couples can't stay married even without dealing with something so traumatic. Like I told Ben, you two deserve your happily ever after and I hope you'll be blessed with more children."

"Thank you," Gaby manages to say. "Do you know where he is, by any chance? We . . . lost each other."

"No, he said he'd come by the chair but he never did. I didn't realize you were here, too. What a madhouse, huh? Well, I've got to get back. It was good seeing you."

"You, too."

"I hope you and Ben find each other again."

Gaby hurries away with Stella's last words resonating in her head.

"Ben!"

For a moment, hearing a female voice calling his name, he somehow believes it's Gaby. He looks up, expecting to see her . . .

But it's Alex striding toward him, carrying a couple of plastic bottles.

"Sorry that took so long," she says. "There was a long line at the stand. Here you go."

She hands him one of the bottles, filled with neon green liquid that isn't water.

"Gatorade. It'll help restore your electrolytes. Better than water. I'm a nurse," she adds once again, irritating him.

He's too thirsty not to drink the Gatorade. He opens it, takes a swig, and then, remembering the Advil, reaches into his pocket.

"What are you doing?" Alex almost sounds alarmed.

"Taking these. I have a headache." He holds out the brown pills in his hand to show her. "Why?"

"I don't know. I thought . . . I don't know." She shrugs. "Come on. We can start walking to my car while you drink that. I'm parked kind of far away."

"I'm going to take the bus."

He expects her to protest, but she doesn't.

"Okay," she says. "It's in the same direction. We can walk together. Just drink up. It'll make you feel better."

He sips as they walk. But after a few minutes, instead of feeling better, he feels worse.

He no longer wants to take the bus. Or, for that matter, the subway.

He tries to tell her but he can't seem to form words.

He'll probably feel better if he can just get out of this crushing heat.

"It's okay," she says. "Almost there. Come on."

The sunlight glares unbearably, blurring his vision, and although she keeps talking to him, her voice seems far away.

"It's okay, Ben. Here's the car. Get in." She opens the front passenger door for him. He fumbles, nearly falls.

"You're okay. Sit down. You look terrible."

I feel terrible, he tries to say, but his mouth refuses to form the words.

He hears someone calling his name: "Ben! Ben!"

He tries to focus, but everything is fuzzy.

He can hear Alex talking, far away. Another voice rumbling. She's talking to someone.

Then the car door slams. Slams again. He feels her hand against his forehead. "Heat stroke. I'll turn on the air-conditioning. We'll be home in half an hour. Just lean back and close your eyes . . ."

Gaby is ten minutes into the long walk back down Park Drive toward the shuttle stop when her cell phone rings.

Probably Jaz. She called this morning, wanting to talk about Gaby's upcoming date to the beach with Ben. She didn't know, of course, that it had all fallen apart last night.

Gaby didn't pick up the call. Nor did she answer the text Jaz sent a little later.

Now she pulls her phone from her pocket, checks the number, and sees that it isn't her cousin after all. The number is Unknown.

"Hello?"

There's a pause. Then: "Gabriela?"

"Yes?"

"Yeah, it's Shakey. Are you still here?"

She stops walking. "Why?"

"I know you said not to bother callin' if Ben turned up, but—"

"He's there?"

"Nah, not here. And I wouldn'ta called you except—"

"What's going on, Shakey?"

"Maybe nothing. But . . . something don't seem right. You might want to come back up here."

Chapter 12

Back on Cherry Street, Alex takes the garage door remote from the console. As she slows the car, preparing to pull into the driveway, she notices Mrs. Toomey on the porch across the street, as usual. This time she has a visitor.

Hoping the nosy old biddy won't be able to tell she isn't alone in the car, Alex pulls into the driveway as the garage door slowly rises. Once inside, she closes the garage and turns off the car engine.

"Home, sweet home," she announces.

No response.

She reaches over, worried, and feels for a pulse on the side of his neck, in the hollow between his ear and jawbone. It's there, thank goodness.

"I can't lose you again," she whispers to him, and allows her fingertips to stroke his cheek, relishing the texture of dark stubbly beard growth. "I've been waiting so long . . ."

He doesn't flinch. Ah, but that's good. She wasn't sure the sedative would be strong enough in a nonalcoholic drink, so she'd spiked the Gatorade with twice the usual dose. That did the trick, and then some.

He was out cold, slumped over in the seat, before she even pulled out of the parking lot, and never stirred as she drove north instead of south, all the way here.

She feels inside the pockets of his shorts, looking for his wallet and phone.

The wallet is there. Not the phone.

She'd thought he might have been lying about losing it, but maybe he wasn't. That's good.

Now all she has to do is wait for him to wake up. The basement room is already prepared for a new occupant, but she won't have to resort to that this time. Not with her soul mate. He won't try to get away . . .

Or will he?

Remembering his skittishness back on the beach, she tells herself he was just out of sorts because of the heat, and too little sleep last night, and the trauma of having lost his phone . . .

His phone.

Her initial reaction, when he mentioned that he'd lost it, had been dismay. She's always used her visitors' phones to cancel their InTune Accounts and send e-mails on their behalf, to ensure that no one would notice they were missing. That's not going to be possible this time.

But then this time it won't be necessary.

As soon as he understands just how much they have in common and realizes that together they can reclaim everything they've lost, he'll forget his old life and everything and everyone in it.

She only hopes he'll grasp the truth right away. Any delay could be . . . uncomfortable, to say the least.

She climbs out of the car, closes the door, locks the car, and pockets the garage remote along with his wallet. She long ago disabled the emergency release lever designed to open the wide door from the inside in case of a lost keypad or power failure.

Inside the house, she closes the door leading to the garage and slides the bolt she installed last year. Now if her guest happens to wake up anytime soon—which isn't likely—he'll be locked in the windowless garage.

Humming their song, "Livin' on a Prayer," she steps into the kitchen and stops short. Something smells terrible. What the . . . ?

Oh. The cat food and milk. It must have spoiled in the heat.

"Gato! You naughty boy. You didn't finish your breakfast!" she calls, opening the creaky utility cupboard to take out a fresh can of food.

Poised, she listens for the cat to come running. But apparently it's too muggy for him to move. With a sigh, Alex opens the can, dumps the contents into a bowl, and puts the bowl on the floor.

She opens the fridge, takes out the milk, closes it again a bit too carelessly, causing a sheaf of crayon drawings and magnets to drop to the floor. She picks them up, taking the time to glance through the stick figure drawings again, thinking of Dante, of Carmen, of their dream house . . .

Abruptly replacing the pictures on the fridge door, she walks through the first floor straightening knickknacks, adjusting throw pillows, aligning scatter rugs. She wants everything to look just perfect now that he's home at last.

Home . . .

At last . . .

Wait a minute.

"Gato!" she calls abruptly, remembering. "Gato, come here! Come here, kitty-kitty-kitty!"

Now she hears a distant meow, coming from upstairs.

Okay. That's good. He's already up there. It'll be easier that way.

"Where are you, kitty?" she calls as she stealthily climbs the steps. "Hmm? Where are you hiding?"

He's in Dante's room, as usual. She forgot and left the door open again.

"At least you didn't knock over his beautiful buildings, did you, kitty-kitty?" she croons, sidestepping the cobweb-shrouded Lego construction and scooping the cat off the bed, cradling him against her pounding heart.

Carmen's voice echoes in her head.

Some things just don't feel right until . . .

"That might be true," Alex says aloud. "But this can't wait till sundown. I'm doing it for your sake."

She carries the cat into the bathroom, puts him into the linen closet, and quickly closes the door.

Angry meows come from inside.

"I'm sorry, kitty. Really, I am."

She briskly sets the rubber plug into the tub drain, turns on the tap and starts to fill it with water. Only the hot—which is turned up nice and extra hot, courtesy of the ancient plumbing. It'll be faster that way. Scalding versus drowning: more painful, perhaps, but probably over more quickly.

Standing in front of the mirror, humming the song her foster mother had taught her years ago in a gingerbread cottage—the song about the doomed Señor Don Gato—she methodically rolls up her sleeves, anticipating a struggle. He's not a large cat, but he's strong. And terribly fearful of water.

Most cats are, Alex recalls the foster mother telling her long ago. Funny—she can no longer even remember the woman's name, and she was so sure she'd wind up becoming her mother.

"Why are they afraid, ma'am?" Alex asked the woman, trying to be helpful and polite, still hoping she'd be adopted.

"Because they sense that water is dangerous to them."

"Why is it dangerous?"

"Because they aren't good swimmers."

"So they'll drown if someone puts them into the water, then?"

"Why would you ask such a thing?"

Sleeves in place, Alex turns away from the mirror. The tub is full enough, but not too full. Good. She doesn't want water sloshing everywhere, making a mess. She turns off the tap, still humming.

In the song, Señor Don Gato falls off a roof and breaks—well, just about everything there is to break. His knee, his ribs, his whiskers, and even . . .

"What's a solar plexus, ma'am?" Alex asked her foster mom as she sat stroking one of the woman's many kittens on her lap.

"It's in the stomach."

"And if a cat breaks it, he'll die? Like Don Gato?"

"Why are you asking me these terrible questions?"

"No reason." Alex thoughtfully rubbed the kitten's belly, wondering where, exactly, the solar plexus was.

"Be gentle with the kitty," her foster mother cautioned her.

"I am," Alex said, and she was—that time. While the woman was watching.

It wasn't until later—after she'd learned that she wouldn't be adopted, and would be moving back to a group home—that she found out exactly what would happen to a kitten with a broken solar plexus. A broken everything.

Without the roar of running water, her humming sounds a little hollow in the bathroom.

Maybe she's just sad about what she has to do. But it's the only way. He's allergic to cats.

She stops humming.

"It's him or you, Don Gato."

She reaches for the linen closet doorknob.

She listens for an answering meow but instead hears something else.

The doorbell?

Frowning, she walks to the head of the stairs. Below, she can see the silhouette of a visitor standing on the other side of the frosted window in the unlocked front door.

In the small room adjacent to the Lost and Found, Gaby finds Shakey and Junie Cordero, another old lifeguard friend she hasn't seen in a few years.

"Gaby! I'd know you anywhere. You look exactly like you did when we first met!"

She says the same thing to him, but it isn't true. In the old days, Junie was the self-proclaimed "short, dark, and handsome" ladies' man. Now he has a bit of a paunch protruding through his orange T-shirt, and every last strand of his wavy dark hair has disappeared. He tells her that he'd decided last winter that he might as well shave what little hadn't fallen out.

"I'm getting old, Gaby." He shakes his bald head.

"We all are, Junie."

From Shakey: a choice hand gesture accompanied by a grumpy, "Hey! Speak for yourselves."

Having concluded the niceties—and not-so-niceties—portion of the conversation, Gaby asks them what's going on.

"It pro'ly nothin'," Shakey tells her. "But it's weird."

"It's about Ben?"

"Yeah. Did you talk to him?"

"When?"

"Before he left."

"Why?"

"Go on. You tell her," Shakey says to Junie.

"I was planning on it, Shake."

"Well, you weren't saying nothing."

"Because you were."

"Well now I'm not. So start talkin'."

Junie turns to Gaby. "Okay. So I don't want to upset you, but—"

"Come on. What's going on?"

"I was getting ready to leave, you know, cutting across public parking, heading out toward the guards' lot, and I caught sight of Ben. I haven't seen him since last summer, but I recognized him right away. Ben, he always looks the same. Like you."

She nods, tense.

"Plus, I knew he was around today because Stella Kaplan mentioned it and I was expecting to see him. But I didn't. Until I got to the parking lot. And there he was. I don't know how to say this, Gaby . . . I mean, Stella told me you guys are still together, doing great and all that, so it's not like I thought he was up to something . . ."

Gaby swallows, realizing where this is headed. "You saw him with someone else," she says. "Another woman. Is that it?"

Junie and Shakey look at each other.

"That's not really 'it,'" Shakey tells her.

"I mean, that's not why I was concerned," Junie says, and adds, "Should I be?"

"The thing is . . ." Should she tell them she and Ben are divorced?

Not yet. If seeing Ben with another woman isn't the reason they called her back here, then what is?

"Why did you think there was a problem, Junie, when you saw Ben?"

"Because he looked like he was about to keel over. I mean, I probably wouldn't have batted an eye if he were a real party guy like—" He breaks off to shoot an accusatory look at Shakey.

"Me? What'd I do?"

"What *didn't* you do?" Junie shoots back.

"I done a whole lot of nothing exciting since I had that heart—"

"Anyway," Junie cuts him off, "I never seen Ben like that. And it's the middle of the afternoon on a Sunday, you know what I mean? I thought maybe he was having a freak heart attack or something."

"Like me," Shakey puts in. "I had a—"

"Yeah, only yours wasn't a freak heart attack. Ben is young and healthy."

"What, I'm old and unhealthy?"

"Pretty much. But we're not talking about you, remember?"

Gaby's own heart is racing. Whatever she was expecting . . . it wasn't this.

Again, Junie gets back to his account: "So I went running over there, you know, as Ben and this lady were getting into this car—a black BMW. He was so out of it he didn't even hear me or see me. He was in the passenger's seat, and so I asked this woman what was going on—I told her I was a friend of his. And she tried to tell me he was fine. Said he'd just had too much sun or some bullshit like that."

"No sun today," Shakey contributes, shaking his do-ragged head.

"I asked her who she was and where they were going, and she told me that it was none of my business. And then she slammed the car door in my face and drove off so fast I couldn't even get the plate," Junie adds indignantly. "Believe me, I tried. Maybe I overstepped my bounds, but Bennie's a friend of mine and I didn't like what I saw. I came back here and mentioned it to Shakey, and he said you were looking for him, and we figured we'd better let you know."

"I'm glad you did."

"So then . . . did you know what was going on?" Shakey asks. "With Ben and that bitch?"

Gaby shakes her head uneasily. "No."

"Who was she?"

"I think I know." She reaches into her pocket and pulls out Ben's phone, noticing that the battery is running low. Clicking on the link for the InTune site, she opens his profile and clicks on the photo of the woman he was meeting.

She holds out the phone, showing the headshot to Junie. "Is this her?"

"Oh, yeah. That's her. So you know her, then? Listen, I'm sorry I called her a bitch. I just didn't like—"

"I don't know her," Gaby cuts in.

"Then who is she?"

Time to cut to the chase. "She's Ben's date."

When no one answers the bell on the second ring, Ivy reaches out to knock on the door.

This is ridiculous.

She knows Mrs. Rodriguez is home. She and Heather Toomey watched her pull the BMW into the garage not ten minutes ago, as they sat on the porch sipping the lemonade Heather offered after she hung up the phone with her boyfriend.

Her boyfriend, the cop.

If he weren't a cop, Heather probably would have picked up her story where she'd left off before the call was interrupted.

"You were telling me that the local kids told stories about how strangely Carmen's wife behaved after he left," she prodded Heather when she returned.

"I know, but . . . I shouldn't have been talking about her," Heather said, much to Ivy's frustration. "They were just rumors. Silly things kids say. You know how it is."

"I know, but . . . can't you tell me?"

Heather shook her head. "I can't."

"Did your boyfriend tell you not to?"

"Pretty much. He reminded me that we have to live here, and it's probably not a good idea to go around talking about the neighbors to strangers. Not that you're a stranger."

Oh, but Ivy was, and still is, despite the lemonade and shared conversation—most of it one-sided.

When the black BMW appeared in the street, her heart

skipped a beat. She barely glimpsed the woman inside before she pulled into the garage.

"That's her?" she asked Heather.

"That's her. But I don't want to—"

"No, I know. You don't want to talk about her. That's okay. I get it." Ivy wasn't going to press her now that she had the opportunity to find out for herself.

She lingered after the garage door closed, not wanting Heather to watch her cross the street and knock on her neighbor's door. But luckily, Heather soon announced that she had to go inside to use the restroom after all that lemonade.

"It comes with the territory when you're pregnant," she said wryly, standing up.

Not sure what to say to that, Ivy pretended to check her watch. "I have to catch my train back to the city anyway, so . . . it was nice meeting you. Good luck with . . . um, the baby."

"Good luck finding your brother, too. When was the last time you talked to him?"

"Over two weeks ago."

"Two *weeks*?" Heather echoed, her face etched with concern. "I didn't realize it's been that long. I figured it was just—I mean, maybe you should contact the police."

"I already did. They're looking for him, too."

"Well . . . that's good. I'm sure they'll find him." Poised with her hand on the doorknob, Heather looked uncertain. "If you want me to ask Jimmy—that's my boyfriend—if he can do anything to help—"

"No, that's okay," Ivy said quickly. When she mentioned the police, she'd forgotten all about Heather's boyfriend being a cop.

"If you change your mind . . ." Heather said.

"Thanks. I'll let you know."

"Okay. Good luck."

Ivy thanked her and forced herself to take her time descending the front steps as Heather retreated into the house. The moment the door closed, she made a beeline across the street and rang the bell.

Which is being ignored by the woman inside.

All she wants to do is ask a few questions about Carlos. If the garage attendant was telling the truth, Carlos rode off in this woman's car shortly before he disappeared. And if he wasn't, then this is a dead end.

Just as she starts to turn away, the door jerks open.

The woman standing across the threshold has long dark hair and an attractive face, easily recognizable from the picture she'd posted online when she was calling herself "Sofia." Older, with more wrinkles around her wide mouth and eyes than she'd had in the photo. But it's the same woman.

"Are you Mrs. Rodriguez?"

The woman doesn't nod, but she doesn't shake her head either. She just looks at Ivy.

Presuming she's wary of strange people showing up at her door—and who wouldn't be?— Ivy goes on, "My name is Ivy Sacks. I'm looking for Carlos Diaz. You know him?"

Ivy swears she sees a flicker of recognition in those blue eyes, but it's quickly replaced—if it was there at all—with a slight frown. "Carlos? I don't know anyone named—"

"You met him on InTune, and you went out with him a few weeks ago, on a Friday night."

Now the eyes widen. "*Carlos?* He told me his name was Nick!"

And you told him your name was Sofia, Ivy wants to say, but she forces herself to keep silent. She had good practice for that on Heather's porch.

Unfortunately, this woman isn't nearly as conversational as her neighbor. She just waits, regarding Ivy with a veiled expression.

"I've been really worried about him, trying to find him," Ivy tells her.

"Then how did you?"

"Pardon?"

The woman rephrases: "How did you wind up here?"

"I went to the parking garage across the street from Te-quila Sam's and I talked to the attendant." Ivy doesn't bother to keep the pride from her tone and is gratified with a raised eyebrow telling her she's not the only one impressed with her detective work.

"How did you know about Tequila Sam's?"

Ivy merely shrugs. No need to spill every last detail about the extent of her resourcefulness.

"Then . . . are you a friend?"

"I'm . . ." *His boss? His sister?* "His girlfriend," Ivy hears herself say, discarding both the truth and the earlier lie in favor of this wishful one.

"He didn't tell me he had a girlfriend."

"It sounds like he didn't tell you a lot of things."

"No . . ." The woman shakes her head. "But I thought that was just because of . . . his condition."

"What condition?"

She bites her lip, as if trying to decide how to say some-thing. "Um . . . the night we met, he drank too much."

"I know." Ivy nods. That's in keeping with what Mutton Chops told her.

"You *know*? How do you know?"

"The guy in the parking garage told me." Ivy is starting to feel as though she has the upper hand here.

"Oh! Right. Well . . . Nick—*Carlos*—he passed out—fell and hit his head. When he came to, he was so confused . . . he didn't even know his real name, or where he lived. He'd lost his wallet somewhere along the way, and . . . I didn't know what to do. It was some kind of amnesia."

Ivy nods, her heart pounding. She saw that once on TV—a guy who hit his head and forgot everything about his life. She can't remember if it was one of those news shows, like *Dateline* or *60 Minutes,* or an episode of one of those crime dramas she loves to watch. Either way, she knows it happens. The dramas are very realistic.

"Where did he go when you left him that night, then?" she asks, picturing poor Carlos wandering the streets with no clue where he belonged.

"I didn't leave him."

"What?"

"How could I leave him? He was helpless."

"Then . . . where is he?"

"He's here, of course."

The words leave Ivy breathless with relief. Thank God. Thank God he's here; he's alive . . .

"I'm so glad you came," the woman tells her. "I didn't know what to do."

"Why didn't you just call the police?"

"You're kidding, right?"

She wasn't—but who is she to judge? She might have called the police to report Carlos missing, but she sure didn't tell them everything she could have.

"First of all, I figured he was probably married." At Ivy's wide-eyed look, she elaborates, "It happens. A lot. I mean, it's not like he told me his real name, or that he had a girlfriend—even *before* he drank too much and hit his head."

Okay. So the woman didn't call the police because she was trying to protect Carlos in case he was cheating on a spouse? How is that any more despicable than Ivy not disclosing the full truth to the detectives because she was trying to protect herself?

It isn't. In fact, it's slightly more noble.

She's a more selfless woman than I am. Ivy pushes the thought away quickly, along with her own guilt. No one's giving out medals for altruistic behavior here.

"So . . ." She clears her throat. "Are you saying Carlos is right here in this house?"

"Yes."

"He's been here all this time?"

"Yes."

"And you weren't going to . . . tell anyone?"

"Like who?"

Ivy shrugs.

"I figured sooner or later his memory would come back. Either that, or sooner or later he'd turn up in a missing persons bulletin. I keep checking, but so far he hasn't. So you didn't mention to anyone he's gone missing?"

Ivy shakes her head. She didn't—unless you count the police—and something tells her she might not want to mention that yet. Or at all.

"How about that you were coming up here looking for him? Did you tell anyone that?"

"No, I didn't." For a change, that's the truth. "I don't have many people in my life to talk to . . . other than Carlos. Can I see him?"

The woman opens the door wider. "Believe me, he's all yours. Come on in."

For Gaby, the miserable afternoon's lone saving grace is that Junie drives her home, sparing her subways and buses.

He was heading as far as Morningside Heights, where he lives now, but as he put it, "What's another forty or fifty blocks among friends?"

As they drive, he tells her about his life now—he's a teacher and coach at a public school in Harlem during the school year, has a longtime live-in girlfriend who's pressuring him to marry her. Gaby makes all the right comments, but she isn't really listening.

She can't stop thinking about Ben.

After she told Junie and Shakey that they're divorced now, their concern over what Junie had seen in the parking lot seemed to subside, following their initial shocked reaction.

"Maybe he had too many beers," Junie concluded, pronouncing it *bee-yahs,* just like in the good old days.

"There's no sun," Shakey added, "but it's pretty damned hot out there."

The guys figured Ben had been living it up with his date, overdid it, and was probably sleeping off a buzz somewhere.

Gaby would have been inclined to draw the same conclusion, except . . .

As they'd pointed out earlier, Ben isn't much of a party guy. Not only that, but he never, ever had a drink at the beach, even when they were young and off-duty. He always said that open water and alcohol don't mix. And forget about drugs: not his style at all.

Shakey and Junie both knew that, but they tried to make her aware—in their own awkward way—that her ex-husband might have changed since the divorce.

A week or two ago she might have believed them. But having spent time with Ben now, she realizes she knows him just as well as she ever did. He hasn't changed. That's part of the problem.

She's in love with him all over again; rather, she never stopped loving him.

You just stopped liking yourself.

You're the one who changed.

But it's too late to tell Ben any of that. She tried last night, clumsily, and look where that got her.

Now he's with some woman who . . .

Who . . . what?

Was rude to Junie? Drove away with Ben in her car?

Why is that so surprising? They were on a date.

Yes, but . . .

The scenario Junie painted just doesn't sit right with Gaby. She's worried about Ben. She can't help it.

"Which one is it?" Junie has slowed the car as they head down Columbus Avenue.

"My building? Sorry—it's right there." She points; he brakes hard.

"Oops. Almost missed it."

"My fault. I was spacing out."

"It's probably the heat. Sorry about the air-conditioning." It's broken, as Junie pointed out apologetically when they first got into the car.

"Are you kidding? You just saved me three different buses—or two buses and a subway. Thank you for the ride."

"No problem. Come back and see us at the beach, Gaby. We all miss you."

"I miss you guys, too. I will," she promises. "Take care."

As she walks across the sidewalk toward her building, she pushes sweat-dampened hair back from her face and notes the lazy hush hovering in the sultry air. It's as if the city is holding its breath, waiting for the inevitable storm that will break the heat.

Sure enough, just as she steps into the vestibule, she hears a rumble of thunder in the distance.

Here it comes.

The putrid aroma hits Ivy as soon as Mrs. Rodriguez closes the front door behind her. It's all she can do not to gag.

The house smells like . . . old food. Old, rotten, fishy food.

And no wonder. There are plastic bowls of cat food and milk everywhere—on the floor, on the furniture, even on the steps that lead up to the second floor, right inside the door.

This must be what the neighborhood kids were talking about when they told Heather Toomey that Mrs. Rodriguez is crazy. Eccentric is probably a better word. But harmless.

With her own brother's prediction in mind—*You're going to be a crazy, lonely old cat lady someday*—Ivy finds herself feeling sorry for this woman.

"Carlos is upstairs," Mrs. Rodriguez tells her. "Come on."

Ivy hangs back a little, put off by the smell. "Maybe you should just go get him. Tell him to come down."

"I can try . . . but I don't think he will."

"Why not?"

"Because—what am I supposed to tell him? That his girlfriend is here? He doesn't even know he *has* a girlfriend. He doesn't know his own name. Maybe when he sees you, he'll recognize you. It might trigger his memory to come back."

That makes sense.

Still . . .

Ivy eyes the nearest saucer of milk. She can see that it's curdled, even from here. Beside it sits a bowl of cat food. Is it her imagination or are the contents . . . *moving*?

Following her gaze, Mrs. Rodriguez explains, "That's for my cat. His name is Señor Don Gato. After the song."

"That's nice," she tells the woman, who apparently doesn't grasp the idea of ironic pet names.

"Do you like cats?"

"I love them," Ivy tells her, thinking wistfully of Garfield and Snoopy back home. "I have two."

"Are they afraid of water, do you know?"

"Are they . . ." Trying to wrap her mind around the strange question, Ivy falters. "I guess. I mean, aren't all cats afraid of water?"

"That's what my mother told me when I was little. Well, I shouldn't call her my mother. I thought of her as a mother, but it turned out she hated me. So what else is new?"

Ivy doesn't know what to say to that, but the woman doesn't wait for a reply.

"Come on," she says abruptly. "Let's go find your boyfriend."

As they climb the stairs to the second floor, Ivy mulls her options.

Depending on whether Carlos's memory comes back when he sees her, she may bring him back to her place. It would be good to spend some time alone with him before real life resumes. Anyway, she needs some time to figure out what to tell the police about how she found him.

Upstairs, the ceiling is much lower. There's a short dark hallway with closed doors on either end and another door—ajar with the light on—in between.

The woman pushes it open. "Nick? Someone's here to see you." Over her shoulder, she whispers to Ivy, "He's taking a bath. He does that a lot. It soothes him."

She beckons Ivy to cross the threshold, but Ivy hangs back, gripped by growing uncertainty.

"I don't think he'd want me to—"

"Don't be ridiculous. He's your boyfriend, isn't he? I mean, that's what you *said*."

"He is."

But the woman doesn't believe her. She can tell.

"What are you waiting for? Go ahead." Her voice hardening with every word, she holds the door open wider and takes Ivy's arm, all but pushing her into the bathroom.

Ivy loses her footing and falls against the murky green-tiled wall, hitting her head. Momentarily disoriented, she rubs her forehead, then catches sight of Mrs. Rodriguez watching her from the doorway, her large frame filling it, blocking it.

Maybe she really is crazy, Ivy realizes, seeing the gleam in her eyes. *And . . . not so harmless after all.*

She turns away, seeking the reassurance of Carlos's presence. The tub is filled with water, and a tattered green bath mat is placed on the tile floor in front of it as if someone was about to take a bath, but . . . the tub is empty.

"Where is he?"

"I bet the cat scared him away with all that meowing. He's allergic, you know. So I put him into the linen closet." She points at it. "The cat, I mean. He's in the closet. He's afraid of water, like you said."

"I didn't—"

The woman shakes her head and presses her hands briefly to her ears, shouting "Stop!" as if the room is filled with noise. "I have to do what I have to do! You know that!"

She yanks the narrow door open, exposing shelves full of towels and sheets. Ivy instinctively takes a step back, expecting an angry feline to burst from its depths.

Seeing her movement, the woman whirls and reaches for her. "Where are you going?"

"I'm not . . . I—"

"This is your fault. You should never have come here." Her hands clamp down hard on Ivy's fleshy upper arms.

Propelled backward by her surprising strength, Ivy loses her footing and again falls onto the wall. But this time she can't regain her footing; Mrs. Rodriguez is pushing her down . . . down . . . down . . .

She hits the water face first.

The intense heat instantly blisters her skin. Gripped by agonizing pain, she gasps, sucking the searing water into her lungs. She attempts to lift her head, but the strong hands hold her captive underwater.

She struggles, skin burning, waterlogged lungs on fire. She feels herself being pushed and lifted until her entire body is immersed in the scalding tub, arms flailing, legs kicking in a desperate, futile effort to escape.

At last she does, slipping away into the blackness where nothing can hurt her again.

Back upstairs in her apartment, Gaby is again confronted by the vase of yellow roses Ben brought her—and by the temptation of his cell phone still in her pocket.

Had she not ridden home from the Bronx with Junie, she most certainly would have snooped into Ben's private files again before now.

This time, though, for his own good.

She can't shake the nagging image of Ben, out of it—for whatever reason—driving away with a virtual stranger.

I have to see what I can find out about this woman.

She kicks off her flip-flops, scattering specks of sand on the parquet floors, and sinks into her usual chair by the rain-spattered window.

The phone's warning message indicates that the battery is dangerously low. That's okay. This won't take long. All she wants to do is check out the woman's profile one more time. Just to see whether there are any red flags that might indicate she's into . . .

Drugs? Is that it?

What if she talked Ben into trying something that hadn't agreed with him, and—

And . . . so what? He's a big boy. He'll survive and learn his lesson, just like anyone else.

The thing is, though . . .

This is *Ben.* He isn't so straitlaced that he never had a beer before he turned twenty-one, but he definitely doesn't dabble in illegal substances.

Not by choice anyway.

As the rain pours down outside and the ominous possibilities take hold, Gaby wonders if she should run this by someone else. Someone who not only knows Ben, but knows her. And knows what's been going on—more or less.

She swaps Ben's phone for her own and quickly dials Jaz's number.

Her cousin answers on the first ring. "What happened? Your beach date got rained out?"

She quickly brings her cousin up to speed, and is forced to listen to a couple of well-meaning "I told you so's."

Then her cousin interrupts the story to ask, "Junie Cordero? He's still single? How does he look?"

"He's got a girlfriend, Jaz. And he's about a foot shorter than you are. And bald. So—"

"Okay, okay, never mind. Sorry. Go on."

Gaby finishes the story. Jaz is silent.

"Are you there?"

"I'm here. I'm just trying to— So Ben was really out of it and this woman he was with acted like a bitch to Junie? Is that it?"

"That's it."

"And . . . ?"

"And I'm worried."

"Why? He's not your concern anymore, Gaby. Why were you even there, at the beach?"

Can she possibly explain? She tries. "Remember when Abuela forced us both to go to my mother's wake, even though we were scared and so little? And then the same thing when it came to your mother's wake?"

"We weren't so little then."

"No. But it was so hard anyway. And then there was . . ."

Josh's wake. She can't even say it.

"I know," Jaz says quietly. "You've been through a lot, Gabriela."

"Abuela always said that when you lose someone, it's important to acknowledge the loss."

"See the corpse in the casket."

"Right. Closure. So maybe for me, seeing Ben with another woman was supposed to be—"

"What about Ryan?"

"*Ryan?* What about him?"

"You should reach out to him now that you have your closure. You liked him before this started up again with Ben."

That's true. But the last thing she feels like doing is reconnecting with Ryan. And, as she points out to Jaz, she's pretty sure Ryan isn't sitting around waiting to hear from her.

"If you want my advice," Jaz says, "you should put Ben out of your head and move on. But that's always been my advice. And every time I think you're taking it, you back-pedal."

"I know." Gaby stares out the window at the rain.

"Gaby. I get why this is so hard."

"Do you really? I'm not even sure if I get it. Why can't I get past this? Why do I feel like the rest of my life is going to be about what ifs?"

"Because it will be, unless you make a conscious decision to move on."

"I was trying. I was moving on. I was."

"I know. Listen, how about . . . I can drive down and meet you for dinner if you want." Good old Jaz. She doesn't sound the least bit enthusiastic, but her cousin is there for her. She always has been.

"That's sweet, but . . . I think I'd rather stay in tonight. I have to work tomorrow, and the weather's lousy."

"Tell me about it. I was all set to watch the *Real House-wives* marathon but the storm knocked out almost every station on my cable. All I can get is the local news. And if I see the meteorologist one more time, all breathless and excited when he talks about the storm . . . He was practically fondling the Doppler radar map."

Gaby lets out a much-needed laugh—maybe for the first time all day. "Jaz!"

"What? I swear he's getting off on this weather, Gaby . . ."

They chat good-naturedly for a few more minutes before hanging up, making plans to meet after work tomorrow night for drinks and dinner.

Her smile fading, Gaby reaches again for Ben's cell phone. But when she presses the button, nothing happens.

Okay. So the battery is dead.

It's just as well.

She leans back and closes her eyes, listening to the rain patter on the windowpane as she dozes off.

Alex leaves the dead woman sprawled facedown in the bathtub. For now anyway.

She pulls the vinyl shower curtain across it to hide the corpse, eager to get back out to the garage. Any second now the drug is going to start wearing off. She doesn't want him to wake up and find himself locked in.

"That might give him the wrong idea," she tells Gato, who sits by, unblinking red eyes boring into her as she uses a couple of bath towels to sop up the water that sloshed onto the floor. She throws the towels into the hamper and tells the cat, "There. Done. For now. But don't you get the wrong idea. Your time is coming."

She's surprised he doesn't squirm away when she reaches down to pick him up and put him back into the linen closet. This time, as if resigned to his fate, he doesn't even emit a meow of protest, just stares at her.

She slams the closet door shut and takes one last look around the bathroom. She reaches to adjust the shower curtain a bit.

Then, satisfied everything is in order, Alex hurries back down the stairs, stepping around the obstacle course of bowls and saucers, still unnerved by the thought of those glowing crimson ovals staring from the depths of the linen closet.

Chapter 13

The voice reaches Ben from across a great distance.

At first it seemed to be speaking gibberish, but gradually it's beginning to make sense.

"Wake up . . . come on, sweetie, wake up . . ."

It takes several tries for him to open his eyes. When he does, he can't see anything at all. He closes them again, confused. His head is pounding.

"No! Stay with me, Carm!"

Carm . . .

The words still seem garbled. *Carm* . . .

What does *Carm* mean?

Ben forces his eyes open again. This time he's blinded by a bright beam of light.

"Oh, sorry . . . that's my headlamp. I put it on so that I can help you into the house. It's kind of dark and I don't want to turn on the lights just yet and I don't think you're steady enough to walk on your own . . ."

It's a female voice. Unfamiliar.

Ben tries hard to remember who she might be, and where he might be . . .

"Come on . . . sit up . . ."

He allows himself to be tugged into a sitting position and realizes he's in a car. A car . . .

"Here . . . you can lean on me. That's it . . ."

He's up on rubbery legs, and whoever she is, she's strong. Strong . . .

He remembers.

The woman on the beach.

His date.

"Where . . . ?"

"Shh, it's okay, Carm."

Carm?

What the hell does *Carm* mean?

He struggles to make sense of her words; struggles to voice his own.

A door creaks in front of them.

His foot bumps something.

"Careful," she says. "There's a step. Up . . . that's right. Good."

An unpleasant smell assaults his nostrils.

"Where . . . ?" he manages again.

This time she answers. "You're home."

Sprawled on the couch in front of the window fan, Heather Toomey hears her boyfriend coming in the back door.

"Daddy's home," she whispers, giving her stomach a pat. "Don't you stop kicking like you did the last time, okay? You keep making a liar out of me."

"Heather?" Jimmy Pontillo calls from the kitchen.

"In here."

He appears in the archway, handsome as always in his NYPD uniform. His stubbly short sandy hair is damp and there are dark spots on the shoulders of his blue shirt.

"Is it raining out?" she asks, surprised.

"Yeah. I figured that was why you weren't out on the porch in your usual spot when I drove up."

"It's too steamy out there tonight. Come feel my stomach, babe. The little guy's kicking up a storm."

Jimmy sits beside her on the couch and presses a hand against her belly.

"Feel it?"

"Nope."

"Wait . . . it'll happen again. I ate two chocolate bars after dinner. I think it made him dance. There! Feel that?"

"Nope."

She sighs and shakes her head. Ever since she started feeling the baby's movement, she's been trying to share it with Jimmy. But either he's not around when it happens or he can't feel the fluttery lurches from the outside the way she can from the inside.

Sometimes he acts as though she's making it up. It bothers her when he does things like that, calling her a ditzy blonde.

But if she tries to make him see how offensive that is, he tells her he means it affectionately and that she's being too sensitive. Especially now that she's pregnant.

"Your emotions are in overdrive," he told her just yesterday. "And your brain is preoccupied. It makes you spacier than usual."

The comment made her cry. Which allowed him to prove his point.

Sometimes she wonders if they'd still be living together if she hadn't accidentally gotten pregnant.

"Just keep your hand there," she tells him. "He'll kick again."

"We don't know that he's a he," Jimmy reminds her.

"*I* know he's a he."

"And here we go again with the woman's intuition."

"Hey—I was right when I thought I was pregnant before I even missed my period, remember?"

"Well if you're right again and this kid is a boy, then he kicks like a girl. I'll have to do something about that before he gets to the soccer field."

"If you're insinuating that girls can't be great soccer players—"

"Yeah, I know, you were an amazing soccer player. But that's because you don't kick like a girl." Jimmy leans against her bare legs and the back of the couch, looking exhausted.

She decides to let his chauvinistic remarks pass for once. She doesn't feel like launching into an argument; they've had far too many in the scant year they've been together. Which is why, when he said he wanted to marry her and "make it right"—the baby, that is—she told him they shouldn't jump into anything. It didn't stop him from continuing to ask. Maybe one of these days she'll say yes. Single motherhood is almost as scary a prospect as turbulent marriage.

"How was your day?" she asks.

"Crazy as usual. How was yours?"

"Not crazy as usual."

"Yeah? What about that woman who popped up looking for her brother? That sounds pretty crazy."

"Oh, right." Heather had almost forgotten about that.

Jimmy, who—by nature and by profession, trusts no one—definitely wasn't thrilled to hear about her visitor when he called this afternoon. In fact, he told her to get rid of her.

And what did you do? You gave her lemonade.

Maybe she was just lonely for company. Or maybe it was to spite him. She does get tired of him telling her what to do.

But at least she didn't share the local gossip about their across-the-street neighbor—which he also warned her not to do.

"You don't want to go around spreading rumors about the neighbors, Heather, when we're new on the block," Jimmy said, and he was right.

It really was all just hearsay. Heather never personally witnessed Mrs. Rodriguez's bizarre behavior.

The other kids did, though. They said it was really creepy.

They said, too, that it was why her husband had left her.

Remembering the stories, Heather instinctively wraps her arms protectively around her midsection. She herself might go off the deep end, too, if—

"Heather?"

"Hmm?"

"You okay? You're not having stomach pain or anything, are you?"

"Oh, no. Nothing like that. I was just remembering something about Mrs. Rodriguez."

"What about her?" Jimmy asks, eyes closed, leaning back against the couch cushions again, worn out from his day.

Heather hesitates, remembering something else. It had troubled her earlier, but then she took a long nap and forgot about it.

Maybe sometimes you really are a ditz, she scolds herself.

"The woman who was here—her name was Ivy," she tells Jimmy. "When she said she was looking for her brother, I wasn't thinking it was some kind of missing persons thing. But it turned out that it was. She said the police are involved."

Jimmy's eyes snap open. "What does that have to do with you—or with the house across the street?"

"Well at first, she said her brother was dating Carmen Rodriguez."

"Who?"

"Our neighbor's husband. He lived there with her years ago, when I was a kid. But I don't think Ivy knew he's a man, and when I assumed the brother might have been trying to cover up that he was gay or something, it turned out she might have been talking about the wife instead . . ."

"You're not making sense."

"It wasn't very clear. She seemed kind of confused."

"Well, so do you. Maybe there is no brother. Maybe she made it up."

"Maybe she did. I can check." Heather pulls her iPhone out of her pocket. "She told me his name. Carlos Diaz. He's her stepbrother, actually—or so she said."

"What do you mean?"

"I almost felt like I caught her in a lie. When she said her brother's name, I was surprised that it was Hispanic because she didn't look like she is. She showed me his picture, and they didn't look like they can possibly be related . . ."

"Okay," he says, wearing that overly patient expression he gets when he thinks she's being flighty, "but that doesn't mean they aren't related. Plenty of people who—"

"No, I know that, but when she changed brother to stepbrother as soon as she realized I was curious about it—it was kind of like she was trying to cover up a slip or something."

From Jimmy, ever the devil's advocate: "I call my stepbrothers my brothers all the time."

"I know. It's just the way she said it . . ." She quickly types *Carlos Diaz* into the search engine, along with the word *missing,* and hits Enter.

The search results are instantaneous.

"So if she made it up," Jimmy is saying, "then why—"

"She didn't make it up," Heather cuts him off. She clicks on a link and gets a close-up look at an official flyer bearing the familiar department logo and the very same photo Ivy showed her this afternoon. "He really is a missing person."

"Here, let me see."

She hands Jimmy the phone and watches him examine the listing, fiddling with the screen to enlarge it. "I'm going to call Leary."

"Who's Leary?"

"The detective in charge of this case, see?" Jimmy shows her the name and phone number at the bottom of the online flyer.

"You know him?"

"There are 35,000 cops in New York, Heather. We don't all know each other. We don't sit around drinking coffee and shooting the breeze like you do in the teachers' lounge."

"Why do you have to be so sarcastic?"

"Why do you have to be so sensitive?"

She swallows back her irritation. "What are you going to say when you call?"

"That someone was here asking about this guy and claiming to be his sister."

"She might really have been his sister."

"Or maybe not. Sometimes you have to go with your gut. And your gut told you she wasn't, right? Or should I say your 'woman's intuition'?"

Naturally, the second Jimmy stands up and walks away to place the call, the baby kicks. Hard. As if to say, *Don't worry, Mom, everything's going to be okay. Sometimes he's a jerk, but he doesn't mean to be.*

She smiles and pats her stomach. *Hey, thanks, little guy.*

Another kick.

Amazing, she thinks, the way she's bonded with this baby already and he won't even be born for another five months.

She thinks again of the stories about Mrs. Rodriguez. Now that she's expecting a baby herself . . .

Well, there's nothing funny about a woman whose baby died—a woman who had lost everything—holding a blanket-wrapped doll, talking to an imaginary toddler, pushing an empty swing in the backyard . . .

Nothing funny at all.

Gaby is awakened by a ringing telephone.

Disoriented, she realizes she's still in the chair where she sat down when she got home from the beach. Twilight has fallen and the room is cast in shadows. It takes a moment of fumbling to figure out which phone is ringing. There are three: her cell phone, the landline—and Ben's.

This afternoon's drama rushes back at her as she answers the landline. "Hello?"

"Gaby? Are you still home?"

"Jaz?"

"Are you home?" her cousin repeats urgently.

"Yes."

"Turn on the TV. *Now.*"

"What—"

"Just turn it on! Channel 4! They're about to come back from the commercial. Hurry!"

Gaby lurches into motion, grabbing the remote, aiming it at the television, tuning it to Channel 4.

She finds herself looking at a middle-aged man in a backward Mets cap, sitting on a couch in the glare of bright television lights, talking to a female reporter well-known for her *Crimestoppers* segments.

"What is this?" Gaby asks Jaz.

"Shh! Listen!"

" . . . and they told me, my nephew, he isn't the first one this has happened to. They think there's a serial killer out there."

"A serial killer, Mr. Morales?" the reporter asks. "That's what they said?"

"Well no, not exactly. No one was killed . . ." The man stops to cross himself. "But they said that a couple of other guys have disappeared. Latino guys, just like Bobby. And they think it might have something to do with those dating Web sites Bobby was using. Like maybe he met a woman online who was, you know, up to no good. Maybe they all did."

Gaby's heart stops.

The scene cuts back to the news desk, and the anchor is talking, but fear roars through Gaby's head, drowning out every word.

Still wearing her headlamp, Alex leads Carmen through the dark house without turning on the lights. It's more romantic that way, and besides . . .

Well, the house isn't quite as clean as he likes it. She hadn't realized that until she caught sight of her earlier visitor glancing in distaste at the bowl of cat food and milk by the stairs. That was when she realized that the milk had soured and the food in the bowl was wriggling, alive.

It would serve Gato—Mr. Finicky—right if she decides to force-feed it to him before she drowns him in the tub alongside the unfortunate woman who'd shown up telling lies about . . .

Wait, why was she here again?

Alex can no longer remember. It's so hard to keep track of details.

All she knows for certain is that Carmen is back at last. After all these years of leaving the front door unlocked just in case he or Dante found their way home again . . . it's actually happened.

He's home. He's home. He's home!

The refrain in her head matches the beat of the rain pattering on the roof. She likes the sound of rain again now, and the earthy smell of it, and even the rumble of thunder. Storms sometimes scared her after he left. But that doesn't matter anymore.

Stomach filled with giddy butterflies, she tells him, "You probably think I'm completely surprised that you're here, but I'm not."

"What?"

"I saw you before. Down the street. I knew that was you. I knew it!"

"What?" He still sounds confused . . . but a little less groggy now.

"On the porch at your mother's house."

"What are you talking about?"

She feels him falter and sway beneath her grasp. "Careful. You're still weak. It's the heat. I'll get you a cold drink. Sit down . . . here's the couch."

He stiffens. "You put something in my drink."

"I did," she agrees. "To help you relax. I was afraid you wouldn't come with me."

"*You put something in my drink?*" he repeats. "Why—"

"I just told you that, darling. Now sit down."

He pushes her away.

What the . . . ?

She puts her hands on his arms again. "Carmen—"

"I don't know who you think I am or what you think you're doing, lady," he says, "but get your hands off me."

Lady?

He called her *Lady*?

As if she's a total stranger?

It's the medication, she reminds herself. *He's still confused. It'll wear off, and then he'll realize . . .*

Again he pushes her away, starting to walk in the opposite direction.

"Stop!" she calls. "Stop right now!"

He keeps going, feet unsteady but carrying him right toward the front door. Bowls of food clatter as his feet encounter them.

"You're making a bigger mess, Carm!" she shrieks. "Stop it!"

"I'm not Carm! I don't know who that is, but . . . You're crazy."

Crazy.

The word hits her like a bullet. The butterflies are gone, replaced by a sickening ache and the realization that she'd tucked Mr. Griffith's gun into her pocket before answering the door earlier.

She had decided not to use it on her visitor, though. It would have been so bloody, and so loud, and the hot tub was already waiting . . .

Now, though, she aims the gun at the back of the man she loves. She never imagined it would come to this.

Yes, you did. Of course you did.

Back when he was still here, but not the same. Nothing was the same after . . .

The gun in her hand trembles.

After . . .

Afterward. He grew more and more distant. Just when she needed him most. And then one day he was gone, and so was Dante, and she was all alone here.

"Don't you dare walk out that door. Don't you dare leave me again."

He keeps walking.

"Stop," she says calmly, and cocks the gun, "or I swear I'll shoot."

That stops him in his tracks.

Sully and Stockton are back at the white-board diagram.

Bobby Springer's name has been added, in chronological order of disappearance. He apparently went missing on September 20. Exactly twelve weeks later to the day, Jake Fuentes vanished on December 13. Another twelve weeks and Tomas Delgado went missing on March 7. Twelve more weeks and Carlos Diaz fell off the face of the earth on May 30. All happened on Fridays. All were single Hispanic men who used Internet dating services. All were employed in the same general industry.

If Sully and Stockton had any doubt before that the cases were related, the pattern has become unmistakable with the addition of a fourth name.

"I said it before and I'll say it again . . ." Stockton pauses to carefully tear a sip hole into the white plastic lid of his take-out coffee cup. "At least we got a few months before we have to worry about anyone else going missing."

"Yes, but why? Why twelve weeks? Think about things that are cyclical. What happens every twelve weeks?"

"I keep going back to seasons."

"And I keep telling you they're not perfectly spaced! We're looking at something that's perfectly rhythmic. What is it?"

"Nothing that makes sense. Because we're dealing with some kind of crazy psycho mutha—"

"And possibly a female."

"You said it, not me."

Sully rolls her eyes. "What I mean is, females are driven by a monthly cycle."

"Right."

"And some women's cycles are like clockwork, every twenty-eight days or whatever. I was like that. Every four weeks—boom."

"Boom?" Stockton gulps some coffee. "You just crossed into TMI territory, Gingersnap."

"What I mean is, when Rick and I were trying to get pregnant, I knew exactly when I was ovulating every month to the day. We called it date night. You could be exhausted, or in a crappy mood, or sick with the flu, but if date night rolled around, you just had to suck it up and do it."

"Romantic. If you two lovebirds couldn't pull off happily ever after, then I don't know who can."

Ignoring the snark, Sully goes on, "I know it doesn't have to be related to anything like that, but when I Googled trying to find things that are cyclical, no matter what combination of key words I used . . . I always found my way back to female reproductive links."

"But those cycles are every four weeks, give or take,"

Stockton points out when she trails off. "Not every twelve weeks."

"Right. So what if we overlooked more connected cases? What if there have been disappearances every four weeks and we're just missing them?"

"We're not. We been over every missing persons case going back to last summer, and there is no way we're missing half a dozen files that fit."

"You're right."

"And you'd be assuming . . . what? That some woman out there is kidnapping these guys because she needs to get laid on a certain day because she's ovulating?"

"It makes a certain kind of sense."

"Not to me."

"The victims all have certain things in common."

"They're all Hispanic."

"Which is a genetic factor. They have similar occupations . . ."

"Which isn't."

"Or is it? I'm a cop, my father was a cop, my ancestors were cops going back over a hundred years. Your father was a cop, and your brother is, too."

"Yeah . . ."

"I've done some research. Some studies link career choice to genetics. Identical twins who are separated at birth are sometimes drawn to the same kinds of jobs."

"And sometimes they're not."

Sully shakes her head wearily and rubs her eyes. "I know. I know I'm on the wrong track, trying to make something fit. I need to move past it. So let's see . . . what else happens without fail every twelve weeks on the dot? Because something is triggering this cycle, and if we just can figure out what it is, then we'll be—"

She breaks off as the door opens. A rookie cop pokes his

head into the room to announce, "Looks like you got a leak on your hands."

"A leak?"

The one-word reply makes Sully's heart plummet: "Press."

Ben is frozen, staring straight ahead at the front door of this stench-filled hell house.

Behind him, the woman speaks again. "Turn around. Slowly. Don't try anything. Got it?"

Yeah. He's got it. Even if he weren't convinced she has a gun—and he is, having heard the unmistakable click of a weapon poised to shoot—he doesn't trust his own legs to carry him to salvation. Whatever she'd put into his drink at the beach—both drinks, he realizes, remembering that she'd brought him that bottle of iced tea when they first met—was powerful stuff.

"Turn around!" she barks.

He does. Slowly. Sees the gun, and the unmistakable glint of madness in her blue eyes.

"I thought things were going to be different this time, Carmen."

Carmen.

She's delusional, convinced he's someone else.

He has to bring her back to reality. "I'm not—"

He breaks off, seeing her dart a glance at the stairway behind him.

"What are you doing here?" she calls.

He turns his head far enough to see that the stairway is empty.

"How did you get out of the closet? He's allergic to you, remember? Stay away from him." Her gaze shifts again, as if she's staring at something right at Ben's feet.

There's nothing there but a bowl of cat food. Looking

down at it, he sees that the gelatinous goo is infested with a mass of fat white maggots.

Is he hallucinating? From the drug?

He squeezes his eyes shut, opens them again. The maggots are still there.

Sheer disgust mingles with cold terror in his brain, helping to keep the fog at bay. He's not hallucinating. She is.

"Okay, go ahead, you stupid cat. Rub that fur all over his legs. It will serve him right if he breaks out in hives."

Swallowing a mouthful of bile, Ben slowly raises his head. Clearly she sees a cat that isn't there, so what—or who—does she see when she looks at him?

Trying not to let his voice waver, he says, "I'm not Carmen. I'm not. I'm Ben, remember?"

"Ben?" Recognition seems to flicker.

"We met at the beach. Well, we met online. On the InTune Web site. Remember?"

That triggers it. "InTune."

"Yes."

"You lost your baby."

"What?"

"You wrote that on your profile. It's true, isn't it?"

He can't find his voice.

"Isn't it?" she demands. "Or was it a lie?"

"No," he says hoarsely. "It wasn't a lie. I lost my son."

She nods. "So did I. His name was Dante. What was your son's name?" .

"Josh." Saying it here, now, to her— it's torture. Yet it's keeping her focus on something other than shooting him. The gun is still in her hand, but no longer aiming directly at him.

"Josh," she repeats. "Yes. I guessed that. That woman we saw at the beach, the one who ran in front of us, chasing her little boy into the water . . . she was calling that name. It made you sad, didn't it?"

"Yes."

"I know how you feel. I lost my son, too. And my daughter. She was just a baby. She was in her crib and . . . she died. And he blamed me. Do you know how that made me feel?"

Yes.

I know it's wrong, Ben. I know it wasn't your fault . . .

He can't speak. She doesn't wait for him to.

"He said . . . he said I smothered her with a pillow."

Swallowing a surge of raw emotion, he asks, "Who said that? Carmen?"

"Yes. Carmen blamed me. I told him that I loved her. And Dante—I loved Dante. More than anything in the world. But he said he was worried I was going to hurt him, too. Why would I do something like that?"

"You wouldn't." Ben shakes his head. "You wouldn't hurt your own child. Ever."

"No. But he thought I did."

Ben has no idea whether the memory is real, but the pain is: her voice is constricted and her face contorted with the agony of loss.

"I'm so sorry, Alex—is that your real name? Alex?"

She blinks. Nods. "My mother named me Alex."

"It's nice."

"It's my real name. My mother gave it to me," she repeats. "And then she left me."

"I'm sorry."

Keep her talking. Keep her calm.

"It's hard," he says, "when people leave. I know how hard it must have been for you."

"Yes. You know. That's why we belong together, Ben."

Ben. Not Carmen.

Okay. Good.

"Yes," he agrees. "You're right. We do."

She smiles. "I wasn't sure if you realized it."

"Of course I do. Let's talk about it. But first—why don't you hand me the gun, Alex?"

Wrong thing to say.

"You tried to leave, too," she accuses, and the gun is on him once again. "If I didn't have this, you would have walked out that door."

"No, I—"

"Don't lie to me!" Her voice is colder than the fear in his gut.

He remains silent.

Still aiming the gun with her right hand, she reaches into her pocket with her left and pulls out a cell phone. Clumsily working the buttons with one thumb, she mutters, "I should never have done that."

"Done what?"

"My real name. Alex Jones. It's on my profile. Well, it was. I just deleted it. Your turn. Time to delete your account."

"Why?" he asks uneasily.

"Why do you think?"

"I'm . . . not sure." Wisps of murkiness still linger in his brain, but an idea is taking shape. "Here, give me the phone and I'll delete it, if that's what you want me to do."

"Give you the phone? Do you think I'm crazy?"

Yes. I sure as hell do.

"You said you wanted me to—"

"Shut up. What's your user name?"

"What?"

"For InTune." The gun points straight at him. "What's your user name?"

"Benito Duran. All lowercase. No spaces."

"Your name is Benito?"

"No one ever calls me that. Except my wife, sometimes."

When she's teasing him, or pretending to be angry . . .

Benito . . .

Gaby's voice sweeps into his head on a gust of home-sickness.

"I thought you were divorced."

"We are."

"You called her your wife. Not your ex-wife."

"I meant my ex-wife."

She regards him shrewdly. "What's her name?"

"Why do you want to know?"

She glares for a moment, then thumb-types on her phone. "Okay. Password?"

He hesitates.

"I will kill you," she says calmly, "if you don't tell me. And if you don't believe me—"

He believes her. He reluctantly tells her the password.

She types it in. Waits. Nods. Presses a few more buttons.

"There. No sign that you ever even existed on InTune. Let's go."

"What? Where?"

"Home."

"But—" Cold dread snakes into his brain. "I thought you said we were home."

"This was never your home. Only mine. Remember?"

"No. I don't remember . . ."

"You designed your dream house, and then you had it built—for us, you said. But you were lying. It was always only for you. You wanted to live there yourself, with Dante—without me."

Something has snapped once again. She's back to thinking he's Carmen. Her ex—or is it late?—husband.

"I saw those e-mails you were sending to the lawyer. I knew what you were planning to do. That's why I destroyed it. You didn't know I could do that, did you? It never dawned on you, because my records were sealed. You never knew about the fires, or what happened to the stupid kittens they adopted when they wouldn't even adopt *me*."

The sinister words and the look on her face leave no doubt in Ben's mind what happened to those kittens.

She steps closer to him. "Come on."

"Alex—"

"I'm through talking." She rests the tip of the gun barrel against his shirt. "It's time to go."

It takes Gaby three tries, with trembling hands, to insert her own phone charger into Ben's phone, and another couple of tries to plug the charger into the wall. It'll be at least a few minutes before it generates enough power to boot up the phone again. But she's not going to sit around and wait for that, or for Jaz, who's on her way over.

"Don't go anywhere until I get there," she said.

"I won't."

"Just call the police."

"I will."

She did. She called Detective McClure, whose name was listed at the bottom of the notice the television news put on the screen for Bobby Springer, the missing New Jersey man. But the line was tied up and bounced into voice mail. She left a harried message.

Now, leaving Ben's phone to charge, she presses Redial on her own.

Voice mail again.

"Hello, my name is Gabriela Duran and my husband is with a woman he met online—my ex-husband—he's Hispanic—and my friend saw them and thought something might be wrong, and I saw on TV that . . ."

This message is more jumbled than the previous one. She curtails it, leaving her phone number, then hangs up and dials 911.

"What is your emergency?"

"My husband is in trouble."

"Is he there with you?" the operator asks.

"No."

"What kind of trouble is he in?"

"I'm not sure. He . . . someone might have drugged him."

"Where is he?"

"I don't know. With a woman. He met her online."

"What—"

Hearing a buzzing noise across the room, Gabriela realizes it came from Ben's phone. She quickly disconnects the call: 911 won't be able to help her if she doesn't know where Ben is.

But maybe she can find out.

She hurriedly picks up his phone, clicks on the InTune log-in screen, and hits Enter.

An error code pops up: *e-mail/username or password is incorrect. Try again.*

She does.

Same error.

Again.

And then again.

Frustrated, she turns to her laptop. After swiftly signing into her own account, she looks for Ben's profile. She's had enough practice at that to know how to bring it up immediately. Only . . .

It isn't there.

According to the Web site, there's no such person registered on InTune.

And the only Alex Jones on the site, when she looks for her, turns out to be an older African-American gentleman who lives in SoHo.

The truth is apparent—and ominous: both accounts have been deleted without a trace.

Sully gulps the tea she just poured into her cup, then curses as boiling water scorches her throat.

"You okay?" Stockton asks.

"Not really. I'm delirious and supremely pissed off."

"You can't blame Morales. He's trying to call attention to his nephew's case."

She nods grimly. She understands that José Morales is desperate to find Bobby, frustrated by the many months that have gone by and the lack of media attention. But a good many people in the tristate area have now seen the frenzied reports of a potential serial killer.

"The last thing we need is for whoever took Bobby Springer and the others to see the news, panic, and harm them."

"If they're still alive."

"A big if," Sully contends. "But possible. Dammit." She shakes her head and blows on the mug of tea clasped in both her hands. "I wanted to control what was released to the press, and when."

"I'm thinking someone might come forward with information about one of the other cases."

"Maybe. Along with all the stark raving lunatics we're going to have to weed out."

"Goes with the territory. You know that. Easy there, Gingersnap."

She blows on her tea again and sets down the mug to rub her aching back.

The other three missing men's names haven't been released in the press—yet. But it's only a matter of time before someone figures out who they are. Their families will need to be warned, and—

"Detectives?" The rookie again, poking his head in the door.

Sully and Stockton look up expectantly.

"There's a phone call. About Carlos Diaz."

"That was fast." She looks at Stockton. "You want to take it, or should I?"

"Depends. Is it a stark raving lunatic?"

"I hope not. It's a cop. NYPD," the rookie adds. "Said he might have a lead for you."

Gaby is waiting on the curb in the rain without an umbrella when Jaz pulls up in front of her building. She jumps into the passenger's seat. "Go around the block," she says, "and head north."

"Where are we going?"

"Vanderwaal. It's up in Westchester."

"What? Why?"

"Please, let's just get going. I'll program the address into your GPS in a second."

Jaz starts driving. "Why are we going to Westchester?"

"Because that's where she lives."

"The woman Ben is with? How do you know?"

"She wrote it in her profile. I saw it before she deleted it. She said she's a nurse and she owns a house in Vanderwaal and her name is Alex Jones."

"That sounds fake."

"It might be, but when I Googled, I found an address—the house is owned by an Alex Jones. It's a brick cape built in the fifties. That's exactly what she described to Ben."

"Did you tell the police all this?"

"I keep trying. I left a few messages with the detective in New Jersey, and then I called 911, but when I heard myself trying to describe what had happened, I sounded crazy. Please tell me I'm not crazy, Jaz."

"You're not crazy. I can't believe I'm saying that, but . . ."

Gaby flashes a brief smile. "I just called my local precinct, and they gave me a number for Missing Persons."

"Did you call it?"

"I'm calling it now." She takes out her cell phone and the

scrap of paper where she'd scribbled the number. "Just keep heading north."

"What are we going to do when we get there? Knock on her door and ask where Ben is? Because if he really is in danger—"

"We have to help him."

"How? I'm pretty sure you're not a superhero, Gaby. And I *know* I'm not. We have to let the police handle it."

"We will, as soon as we can get the right person to listen to what's going on. But I'm not going to sit at home waiting for that to happen. I love him, Jaz."

"Obviously. And I'll keep driving you up there on one condition."

"What is it?"

"That when this is over and everything is fine and Ben is back where he belongs . . . you'll stop pretending."

"Pretending what?"

"Pretending that you're moving on, pretending you're over your marriage, pretending you're thinking about a future with someone new. 'Cause none of that is happening. You're wasting your time and my time, acting like it is. If you want Ben, then go back to Ben."

"You make it seem so easy."

"You make it seem impossible."

"Maybe it is."

"No room for maybes anymore, Gaby. This wishy-washy stuff . . . it isn't you."

"People change. Things change them."

"Good. Then let this change you back to the way you used to be. If you're brave enough to go barreling up to Westchester to save Ben, then you're brave enough to either give your marriage a second chance or cut him loose forever. Period. That's what I think."

"Yeah, well . . ." Gabriela turns her attention back to the scrap of paper. "Just drive."

"I will. And just you remember our deal."

Ivy Sacks isn't answering her home phone or her cell phone. That isn't surprising. Sully left messages on both voice mails asking her to call immediately.

"You really think she's gonna call you back?" Stockton asks from the passenger seat as they barrel up the Henry Hudson Parkway through the rainy dusk, heading toward the northern suburbs.

"Do you?"

"Depends on what she wasn't telling us."

Sully nods, hands clenched on the wheel, trying to picture the benign Ivy Sacks as some kind of black widow serial killer. It isn't particularly hard to do. She's met her share of unlikely psychopaths.

Still . . .

"If she was responsible for his disappearance," she asks Stockton, "then why go looking for him? And why claim he's her brother?"

"Good question. Maybe she—" Breaking off as his cell phone rings, he answers it immediately. "Barnes here . . . Yeah, we are . . . Yeah . . . Yeah . . ."

Impatiently listening to his end of the conversation, Sully can tell by his tone that something's up. He pulls out a notebook and scribbles, asking questions like, "When was this?" and "Where is it?"

At last he hangs up.

"What?" Sully asks.

"I know you were on a roll with your three-month-cycle theory, but . . . we got another one."

"Another disappearance? When?"

"Today. Hispanic male. Benito Duran. Thirties. Structural engineer. Went to meet a woman he met online and no one knows where he is now, but someone saw them together and he was acting like he might have been drugged."

She shakes her head. "Doesn't fit the pattern. It's too soon."

"The timing doesn't fit. The rest does. He had an InTune account that was deleted sometime today, and so was the profile of the woman he was meeting."

"How do we know this?"

"His ex-wife. Gabriela Duran. She's the one who called the police. She admitted that she was looking through his files. She saw the private messages between Duran and this woman. She got a name and everything."

"Way to go Gabriela Duran! What did she say the woman's name is?"

"Alex Jones. They're running it now. The other thing is . . . you ready for this? She drives a black BMW."

Sully's eyes widen. Jimmy Pontillo, the cop who lives in Vanderwaal, had also mentioned a black BMW, saying that Ivy Sacks claimed Carlos had been a passenger in one the night he disappeared.

Ivy hadn't mentioned that to her and Stockton when they interviewed her yesterday. Either she hadn't been aware of it then or she didn't want them to know about it. If the latter—why not? And if the prior . . . then the latter is also the case, because she didn't share the information with them as soon as she got it.

Thoughts spinning, Sully presses down a little harder on the gas pedal. The sooner they get up to Vanderwaal, the better.

Five minutes later Stockton's phone rings again. This time the call is brief.

He hangs up and looks at Sully.

"We got the name for Pontillo's neighbor. The house is owned by an Alex Jones."

Chapter 14

Still holding the gun, Alex takes a shovel from the garage wall, keeping an eye on the passenger's seat. She doesn't have to guess what's running through his mind when he sees her drop the shovel into the trunk.

He's afraid. She can feel it.

She slams the trunk closed. All set. Again.

But this is the last time she's going to make this trip. It isn't working out. All she wanted was to get her son back in her arms—Dante. Her beautiful boy. All she wanted was another chance.

She'd been so certain it was going to happen now that Carmen is back, but—

Climbing into the driver's seat, she gasps.

It's not Carmen waiting for her. It's . . . Ben.

That's right. You knew that. Remember?

She frowns, troubled by her own confusion.

Ben . . .

Carmen . . .

They're so much alike. So are all the others who have come and gone. They had all the right qualities to recreate the son who had been stolen away from her.

Maybe she should have given Ben a chance to try, too.

But her fertile time is still weeks away.

If only it had worked before now, with one of the others. If only her son was in her womb again. If only . . .

She'd been so excited that day in the obstetrician's office last summer, before the doctor uttered those terrible words: "You're not pregnant, Alex."

"But . . . but I have to be. I've missed my period for months now. My husband and I have been trying, and now I'm late."

"Your husband?"

"Yes, Carmen is away on business, and—"

"You seem a little confused," the doctor cut in gently. "Your husband isn't—"

Alex talked on in a rush, not wanting to hear the doctor's words, not wanting to see the look of concern—or was it alarm?—in her eyes.

"Before Carmen left, we were trying for a baby, and we did just what you told us to do, Doctor. We used the calendar to mark my cycle, and I took my temperature, and—"

"Alex, that was twenty-five years ago. It was—"

"—and it worked, and now my period is late. I've been keeping track. It's been months. I can show you the calendar!"

"I believe you. But you're not pregnant. You're fifty-five years old, and you're in menopause, and your husband isn't away on business, he's—"

"No!" she shouts now, pushing away the memory of that awful February day.

The man in the passenger's seat flinches violently.

Again she's startled to see Ben, and not Carmen, sitting there.

It's unnerving, the way she keeps forgetting and mixing them up.

"We're going now," she tells him, pressing the garage remote and then shifting into reverse, all with her left hand. The gun is still clutched tightly in her right.

The garage door whirs into motion, slowly rising behind the car. The night beyond is dark and rainy.

"If you try anything stupid—like opening the car door and jumping out—I will shoot you. Get it?"

"Yes."

But he might be willing to take that chance, she realizes. He's probably weighing the odds that she'll be able to spontaneously take aim and shoot accurately from behind the wheel of a moving car.

She backs out into the rain and flips on the windshield wipers with her left hand. "Ben? Remember when I asked your ex-wife's name?"

She can feel him stiffen. "Yes."

"I will find her. And I will kill her."

"But . . . why?"

She shrugs, not interested in explaining that she's betting he still cares about his ex; that if they hadn't lost their child, they would still be together.

"I will kill her," she repeats. "Do you understand?"

"Yes."

"Good."

She shifts the car into Drive and heads down the street, beginning the familiar route upstate to the property where Carmen built his dream house before she burned it down.

Stockton hangs up yet another phone call. "Gotta love suspicious wives. Ex-wives, anyway."

"Yeah? What have you got?" Sully brakes for a car that's creeping along in the left lane on the parkway, blocking traffic.

For the past ten minutes Stockton's been talking to Ben Duran's ex-wife, Gabriela, and taking notes like crazy.

"I've got a lot. I'll fill you in. She's on her way up there."

"Up where?"

"Same place we're going."

"Cherry Street? She's meeting us there?"

"Yeah, sounds like she's maybe five, ten minutes behind us." Stockton refers to his notes and begins running through them, going over everything Gabriela Duran said during their conversation. He's thorough, as always.

When he finishes, he says, "So that's where we're at. Got any questions?"

"Just one. Is she coming up there to kick her ex-husband's ass or to save it?"

In the passenger's seat of the BMW, Ben stares bleakly out the windshield, wondering where the hell she's taking him.

He's familiar enough with the area to know they're heading north, away from the city and the suburbs. When he was a kid, his parents sent him and Luis to camp up here the one summer they managed to afford it. He remembers very little about it other than being homesick and feeling as though he were in the middle of nowhere. Less than two hours from the city, yet nothing but woods and mountains all around. He hated it.

His father thought he was ungrateful when Ben said that later, after he was home again. But his mother understood. *"Eres un nino cuidad,"* she said. *He's a city boy.*

They never sent him away to camp again.

Now, staring at the forested black landscape rising around the car, he feels more isolated than he ever has in his life.

In the city there are millions of people around to notice you, to hear you, to help you. Up here there's no one.

If he tries to jump out of the car at this speed, he might be killed.

If he waits till she slows the car and gets off the road—sooner or later she'll have to—he can jump more safely, but he might be shot.

And even if he isn't . . .

I will find her. And I will kill her.

The ominous words ring in his ears.

Ben can't take a chance that this lunatic will go after Gaby. He just can't put her at risk. No matter what.

Cuidala, Abuela had said to him on his wedding day, and he in turn had assured her that he would take care of Gaby. Despite all that's unfolded in the years since, he intends to keep that promise.

Arriving at 45 Cherry Street, Sully and Stockton note that the house across the street—number 42—is dark.

"How come no one in my family ever dies and leaves me Westchester real estate?" he grumbles to Sully as they walk up the driveway of the house Jimmy Pontillo's girlfriend inherited from a great-aunt.

"You're wishing your loved ones dead so that you can inherit real estate?"

"They're dying off anyway, Gingersnap, and they're not leaving me anything but piles of crap nobody wants. You think your father's big-ass television set's a problem? You should see what my mama had piling up in her place for sixty years."

Stockton is all business once they're inside the home's foyer with Jimmy, who informs them that he watched his neighbor through the window as she drove away ten minutes ago.

"It caught me off guard that she left. But I did get the plate." He hands over a scrap of paper.

"I'll have them run this," Stockton says, stepping aside with his cell phone.

"Was she alone in the car?" Sully asks Jimmy.

"No, there was someone with her."

"Man? Woman?"

"Too dark to tell. What the hell is going on over there?"

"We're not sure. What else do you know about your neighbor?"

"My girlfriend knows a lot more than I do. Hey, Heather!" he calls, and an attractive young blonde materializes instantly in the curved archway leading to the next room.

She was listening, Sully realizes. But keeping her distance, letting Pontillo call the shots. Is it because he's the cop—or the man?

"They'll run the plate," Stockton announces, rejoining them.

Jimmy makes introductions and Heather invites them into the living room, offering lemonade.

They turn it down politely but hurriedly. Ben Duran's life is hanging in the balance.

"Like I told Ivy when she was here this afternoon," Heather says, "I really don't think my neighbor is dangerous. She's just crazy. I might be, too, if I lost a child."

Sully opens her notebook, grabs a pen. "What happened? What child?"

"It was years ago. I was a kid myself. I spent summers here. She had a son, Dante, who was about my age."

"Dante," Sully echoes, writing it down. "As in . . ."

"Bichette." That comes from Jimmy.

"What?"

"Dante Bichette. The baseball player." Jimmy's tone implies Heather should know that.

Stockton shrugs. "I was gonna say *Inferno*."

"Tell us about Dante, Heather."

"I didn't really know him," she tells Sully. "He never got to play outside with the other kids. She was really overprotective of him even before . . ."

"Before what?"

Heather shifts her weight on the couch. "Dante's sister died. I wasn't around then. I remember his mother being pregnant during the summer . . ."

"Which summer?"

"I think I was five or six, maybe. Almost twenty years ago?"

"Be more specific," Jimmy tells her.

"But I'm not sure."

"It's fine," Sully assures her. "For now, let's call it twenty years. What else do you remember? Did the woman have any friends, do you know? Any at all?"

Heather shakes her head. "Her mother-in-law used to live on the block, too. Just a few doors down. She was a friend of my aunt's. But she died, too. Before I was born, maybe."

"Which house?"

"It's across the street. I can point it out to you. A new family lives there now." Heather leads the way to the porch and points. "It's right there. See? Where the car is just pulling into the driveway?"

"That the new owners?" Stockton asks.

"I guess so."

"Do they know your across-the-street friend, too?"

"I'm not sure. Probably not. She keeps to herself."

"I'm going to go over there," Stockton tells Sully, "and see if I can find out anything. You good with that?"

She nods, fine with that, and even better— "Maybe you can go with him?" she suggests to Jimmy Pontillo, anxious for Heather to relax a bit.

The two men head across the street.

"Do you want to sit out here?" Heather asks, pointing at the comfortable-looking wicker porch furniture. "It's cooler than in the house."

"Sure." Sully sits in a wicker rocker. "Let's get back to the baby. What do you remember about her?"

"She was born during the winter. I never saw her, though, before she died."

"How?"

"Crib death or something, I think. She was only a few days old. I didn't hear about it until I came back up the following summer. By then the husband—his name was

Carmen—had picked up and left. He took Dante with him."

"How do you know that?"

Heather shrugs. "It was just what everyone said. They left, and the mom was there all alone, and she went off the deep end. I used to see her out there on the porch with a bundle I would have thought was a baby, except . . ."

"The baby had died."

"Right. It was just a doll she was holding. She would act like it was a baby, though, and she would talk to Dante, too, like he was still there. It was creepy."

"Yeah, I'll bet." Unsettled, Sully looks back at her notes. "Let's get back to this afternoon. How would you describe Ivy Sacks's mood when she got here?"

"She was kind of agitated. She seemed really worried about her brother. Except—Jimmy says it's not really her brother, right?"

"It doesn't look that way," Sully tells them. "So when she—"

"Sully!"

She breaks off, startled to hear Stockton calling her from across the street.

"Get over here! Sully!"

Frowning, she gets to her feet.

"What's going on?" Heather asks.

"Good question. I'll go find out."

"Dig!"

"I'm digging!"

"Dig faster!" Alex commands, watching him slowly tilt the shovel to deposit another heap of dirt on the wet ground beside the hole. "You're taking your time."

He glares at her. "It's heavy. It's mud."

"Too bad. Dig."

She waves the gun to remind him and then falls back to silently appreciating the rhythm of the falling rain and his labored breathing and the grunt that coincides with every dull thud of the shovel slicing into the ground.

Does he realize why he's digging that hole?

He must. He's no idiot.

In fact, he's a genius. That was one of the main reasons she was so attracted to him when they first met, years ago. He had it all: brains, looks, personality—

Everything but money.

His family wasn't impoverished, but their assets weren't liquid. They had the house in Vanderwaal and this upstate acreage where his parents planned to build a retirement home. His father cashed in a life insurance policy to purchase it—and was killed in a car accident during a snowstorm just a few months later.

Carmen's grieving mother wanted no part of the land where her husband intended them to live out their golden years, but her son loved it up here. Carmen designed their porchless dream house, his and Alex's. It used to sit on a wooded knoll overlooking a sweeping valley, a short distance from where she stands now, in the rain, watching him dig his own grave.

He worked on those plans for years, not only ridding them of architectural detail she vetoed but incorporating personalized touches: exposed beams cut from ancient trees felled to make room for the structure, hearths made of rare tiles they'd bought on their Mexican honeymoon, windows using red oval stained-glass panes that had once adorned a Tuscan chapel . . .

For Alex, it was as cathartic to stand there on a frigid February night watching that house go up in flames as it had been years earlier to destroy the gingerbread house.

She even stayed for a few minutes to toast her icy hands in the warmth of the blaze before she hurried back out to the car and drove back home where Carmen and Dante lay sleeping. The prized Tuscan stained-glass windows glared after her in the rearview mirror like a pair of fiery eyes.

By the time Carmen got word of the fire, the house had been reduced to wet, smoking cinders. The investigators told him it was most likely started by local kids partying in the vacant house.

Still, Alex fully expected him to accuse her.

He didn't. He didn't say much of anything at all, just watched her closely, suspiciously, just as he had ever since their daughter had died a month earlier.

"Did it bother you for all those years you were gone?" she asks now, watching him pause to lean on the shovel and wipe sweat or rain from his forehead. "That you never knew for sure, I mean."

"Never knew what?"

"Exactly what happened. The night of the fire. Or the night the baby died."

He stiffens. "What do you mean?"

"I can tell you if you want to know. Do you want to know?"

"Yes."

"Are you sure?"

"Tell me."

She shrugs and leans closer to him, whispering, "It was *her.*"

"What?"

"She was back. I could see it in her eyes, every time she looked up at me. The eyes don't lie. You were the one who said that."

"Who was back?"

"Your mother! Don't act like you don't know what I'm talking about. She came back masquerading as that innocent little baby, thinking I wouldn't realize it was her. Every time I picked her up and she looked at me, I saw her mocking me.

I'd already gotten rid of her once before. I wasn't going to let her—"

"You're insane."

"Shut up!"

"You are. You're insane, and—"

"Stop saying that! You don't know—you don't know anything! The records are sealed!"

"I know that you killed your own baby."

"No! It wasn't my baby! It was your mother! You knew it, too!" She aims the gun at him, holding her arms straight out in front of her, trembling. "You knew it and you pretended I was wrong. You told me that I was . . . *crazy*." She whispers the final word, the one that had haunted her all these years, the one that had kept her from being adopted, and loved . . .

He shakes his head, as if in disgust.

Turns away. Picks up the shovel again.

Then, in one swift movement, he picks it up and swings it toward her.

She pulls the trigger.

A shot rings out and he falls to the ground.

Street lamps are reflected in the rain-slicked pavement of Cherry Street as Sully hurries across, heading in the direction of Stockton's voice. Grabbing her flashlight from her belt, she turns it on and sees her partner silhouetted on the driveway, along with a much smaller man—the current homeowner?

Striding closer, Sully can see that he's slightly built, with dark hair. He's wearing a suit and has a leather satchel over his shoulder, looking like he just stepped off the commuter train that stops less than a mile away.

He looks uncomfortable standing there with Stockton—and even more uncomfortable when he spots Sully coming toward them.

"What's going on?" she asks Stockton.

"This is Detective Sullivan Leary. Detective Leary, this gentleman moved into that house about six months ago, with his wife and their children. He inherited it from his father," Stockton informs her, wearing a meaningful expression that irks her.

What does he want her to do? Congratulate the guy? Commiserate with poor Stockton who never inherits anything but a bunch of crap from his own dead relatives?

But Stockton goes on, "I'm sure my partner will be interested to hear your name, sir. Can you tell her, please?"

"My name?"

"Yes."

Still looking uncertain, the man turns to Sully. "It's Dante. Dante Rodriguez."

Pain explodes in Ben's shoulder.

He drops to the ground, hit by a bullet.

He'd been close, so close, to catching her off guard, knowing he only had one chance. Timing was everything. He was waiting for just the right moment to attack her with the shovel, but . . .

He chose the wrong one.

Now he's going to pay with his life.

The woman stands over him, still holding the gun, an unmistakable firestorm of madness flashing in her eyes.

"You lied to me! You said you would always be there for me. But you left, and you took him away! My son . . ."

"I'm not Carmen!" Ben shouts at her, writhing in agony.

"Shut up!" she screams, taking aim again.

He closes his eyes.

This is it.

He's going to die, lying in the mud in this godforsaken spot.

"No!"

At her shriek, he opens his eyes and sees her striding toward him. She reaches down . . . but her hands are no longer holding the gun. Instead, they close around the handle of the shovel.

"This is going to go my way! Mine! Not yours!"

She thrusts the blade into the ground, ferociously deepening the hole he'd been slowly digging to her specifications: long and narrow and deep.

Wet dirt flies over her shoulder, pelting Ben with chunks and pebbles as he drifts away to a place that's mercifully free of pain.

"You're Dante Rodriguez?"

"Sí," the man tells Sully. "You know my name?"

"Yes. We're investigating your mother."

"What about her?"

"She may be involved in a case we're working on."

"There seems to be some mistake," he says in a distinctive Spanish accent. "My mother died twenty years ago."

"Excuse me?"

"She died when I was a boy. Five years old."

"I'm so sorry." Sully masks her confusion.

"What happened to her?" Stockton asks.

"She got sick. My father and I, we went to South America to stay with family because she wasn't doing so well, and she died not long after that."

"How do you know that?"

"My father told me."

"And how did you come to be here," Sully asks, "in Vanderwaal? In this house?"

"When my father passed away last year, I inherited it. He grew up here. All these years, he was paying someone to take care of it."

"Was he planning on coming back, then?"

"No! Never. He never wanted to come back to the United States. He never wanted me to come either. But not long after he died, a job opportunity came up in New York, and my wife and I thought it would be good if I took it."

"But you haven't seen your mother . . ."

Dante Rodriguez looks frustrated. "I told you. She died when I was a kid."

"And you're sure about that?"

"*Sí.*" He looks from Sully to Stockton. "Shouldn't I be?"

Before they can react to the question, the glare of head-lights arcs over the street. A Jeep turns onto the block and goes tearing past, braking to an abrupt stop at the curb in front of the brick cape. Sully and Stockton glance at the Jeep and then at each other.

"Gabriela Duran," Sully realizes. She heads in that direction, calling over her shoulder to Stockton, "Don't let him disappear!"

With one shovelful at a time, her headlamp illuminating the gaping hole at her feet, Alex peels away the black earth as if she's laying bare a long-forgotten trove of secrets that were supposed to stay buried forever.

"Your records are sealed," the caseworker told her on that long ago day. "No one will ever know. Not unless you choose to tell."

Choose to tell? She would never tell a soul about any of it: not about the kittens or the fire; certainly not about having been diagnosed, as a teenager, with some bizarre mental illness she'd never even heard of.

The psychiatrist tried to explain it to her. "Delusional disorder involves psychosis. Do you know what psychosis is?"

She shook her head numbly.

"It's when you can't tell what is real from what is imagined. Do you understand that, Alex?"

"Are you saying I don't know what's real and what isn't?"

"This disorder can make it very difficult to tell them apart."

"But I'm not crazy. I've seen crazy people. They rant and rave and—"

"People who are afflicted with this particular mental illness can interact very well with others and behave just like anyone else, apart from their particular delusional subject. It only disrupts their lives when they become fixated on their skewed perceptions of reality."

He went on talking, explaining, but Alex stopped listening, deciding he was the one who was imagining things. She was just fine. Yes, she'd had some problems—some issues with anger—but who wouldn't, after what she'd been through?

Afterward, as she waited in the next room wondering what was going to happen to her now, she heard him ask her caseworker, "Is there a family history?"

She heard only one word of the caseworker's response—*abandoned*—before she stopped trying to eavesdrop. It was a pointless conversation. You can't have a family history if you don't have a family. And if people find out that there's something seriously wrong with you—something called delusional disorder—then you never will.

But the doctor prescribed antipsychotic medication and the caseworker and her next foster parents forced her to take it. The pills made the troubling thoughts and urges go away at last. They made her more comfortable in her own skin, allowed her to live a normal life, go to nursing school, get a job, fall in love, get married . . .

It was real, the doctor reassured her, time and again. All of those wonderful things were really happening to her. She wasn't hallucinating anymore.

But once Carmen was in her life and she'd settled into her job at the hospital, she stopped seeing the doctor. She had no choice because once, when she'd snuck away for an appointment, Carmen caught her in a lie and thought she was up to something.

"Where were you?"

"Shopping."

"You weren't shopping. Don't lie to me. I can see it in your eyes. The eyes don't lie. Who were you with?"

"I was alone!"

"You were with another man. Why else would you lie?"

"I would never cheat on you!" she protested, and she meant it.

She realized then that she couldn't risk going back to the doctor, ever again.

But that was okay. Psychotherapy was a waste of time now. All she really needed was the medication the doctor prescribed. In her profession, there were other ways to get her hands on it. As long as she kept taking it, everything would be fine.

But then it was time to start a family, and she knew she had to go off the medication for her baby's sake. She was going to be a good mother, the mother she'd never had and always wanted. Good mothers didn't ingest chemicals.

She slowly tapered off the drug, knowing it could be dangerous to go cold turkey. She didn't even tell her obstetrician she'd been on anything, because then it would be in her record and Carmen might find out.

She figured she'd simply go back on it after she'd had the baby. Surely it couldn't hurt to take a break.

She was right about that. Everything seemed fine after the medication left her system. Apparently, she didn't need it after all.

All she needed was Dante.

For a while she had him, and Carmen, too.

He traveled a lot, though. Too much. His mother kept coming around, poking her nose where it didn't belong.

"He was *my* son," Alex tells Carmen, lying unconscious on the ground beside the hole that yawns wide and deep enough at last. "Not hers! Mine! And you were mine! But she tried to take you both away, and I made her stop . . . but then she came back . . ."

She closes her eyes, remembering the terrible night she looked into her newborn daughter's eyes; eyes that weren't blue, like hers and Dante's, or even a warm brown like Carmen's. They were pitch-black like his mother's, contaminated with familiar accusation.

It was a cold January night, snowing. Carmen was working late in the city. He'd stopped traveling in the month before the baby was born and wasn't scheduled for another trip until February.

February . . .

But this was still January: he came into the nursery that night when he got home and found her standing by the crib with the pillow in her hands.

"What are you doing?" he asked frantically. "The baby's blue! She's not breathing! What did you do?"

So much of what happened after that is a blur . . .

Carmen told her what to say, what to do . . . It was a long time before it sunk in that he had protected her. The death certificate said the baby had died of natural causes. Crib death.

Privately, Carmen kept telling her she was sick. That she had to get help.

She didn't need help. She just needed her boy.

But one cold February morning, a few days before he was scheduled to leave on his trip, Carmen drove away with Dante in the backseat. He said he was dropping him at school, but . . . they never came back.

They just vanished into thin air.

She knew they had died, just like Carmen's father had, on an icy winter road. No one came and told her the news. She figured it out when their ghosts came back to haunt her.

The man on the ground isn't Carmen's ghost, though.

This is Carmen himself. He's come back from the dead in someone else's body, just like his mother did.

"And now I'm going to bury you. Forever."

She makes her way up to the shed that still stands just a stone's throw from the ruins of their dream house.

Inside, she rummages until she finds the perfect wooden crate—the one in which his precious stained-glass windows had been shipped from Tuscany.

She drags it back out to the hole, pulling off the top and setting it aside.

The rain has stopped now. The night is glistening, dripping, poised, waiting . . .

Night.

Down, down into the hole goes the wooden crate, open side up, waiting to receive its cargo.

She turns toward Carmen, lying on the ground.

"It's time," she says simply.

She drags him to the hole and kicks him until he topples limply into the box. She bends over and arranges his body so that his arms, one of them still bleeding from the bullet wound, are folded across his chest, hands clasped peacefully as if in prayer.

He looks dead but he isn't. Not yet. She can feel his heart still beating.

She remembers the night she pressed the pillow over the baby's face with one hand and pressed the other against her spindly little neck until her pulse ceased.

Satisfied, she turns to grab the lid and reaches toward the hole.

But now, illuminated in the beam of her headlamp, she sees Carmen's eyes snap open abruptly.

For a split second they're bewildered. Then they flicker with the horror of what's about to happen.

Alex brings down the lid with a resounding thud.

"Wait, where are you going?" Jaz asks as Gaby jumps out of the Jeep. "It doesn't even look like she's home."

"It's not like she's going to leave on the welcome light for us."

"No, but you can't just go barging up to the door."

"Why not?"

"Esto esta loco!"

"I don't—"

"It's dangerous. Where are the cops?"

"I don't know, but we're here, and—" Gaby hesitates at the foot of the steps, looking up at the house. "What if Ben is in there?"

"He's not," a voice says behind her, and she turns to see a woman moving purposefully up the walk toward her. "Are you Gabriela Duran?"

"Yes."

"Detective Sullivan Leary, NYPD." She flashes a badge. Gaby barely glances at it.

Jaz is out of the Jeep now, swiftly coming to stand beside Gaby, resting a protective hand on her shoulder as she introduces herself to the detective.

Gaby interrupts. "How do you know he's not in there?" Fearfully, hopefully—but mostly fearfully—she adds, "Did you find him?"

"No. But the woman who lives here drove away a little while ago with someone in the car."

"Was it Ben?" Jaz asks, tightening her grip on Gaby's shoulder.

"We don't know. We didn't see them leave."

"Who did?"

"Neighbors across the street."

Gaby finds her voice at last. "So this is just based on what they said?"

"If you're insinuating that—"

"I'm not insinuating anything. But did you make sure no one else is here?"

"Not yet. Wait, where are you going?"

"To see if anyone is home." Gaby takes the front steps two at a time and rings the doorbell.

"Mrs. Duran, you can't—"

She's not Mrs. Duran anymore. But she's not inclined to correct the detective as she reaches for the doorknob.

Ben. That's all that matters. Getting to Ben.

"What are you doing?"

Ignoring the question posed in unison by the detective and Jaz, she turns the knob and gives it a push. To her shock, the door swings open.

"Gaby!" Jaz is beside her again, grabbing her arm.

"We need to look for Ben." She turns a pleading gaze on the detective.

"We can't go in."

"You're the one who said no one is here, Detective. And the door is unlocked."

"That doesn't matter. We don't have a warrant."

"*You* don't. But I don't need one," Gaby shoots back, and boldly plucks the flashlight from the detective's hand before darting over the threshold.

Ben had known, when she commanded him to dig the hole, that it would serve a sinister purpose. But staring down the barrel of that gun, he'd assumed he would meet his fate long before his body was tossed into that crude grave. By then, he assumed, his soul would be well on its way to being reunited with Josh.

Now, lying on his back in pitch-black, he flinches at an explosive thud that comes not from a gun going off, but from the unmistakable weight of several pounds of dirt being deposited just inches from his face. Only a panel of wood separates him from immediate suffocation.

Another blast of noise.

More dirt.

She's burying him alive—but he won't be for long, unless he does something.

Ignoring the sting where the bullet hit his shoulder, he impulsively starts to sit up. His head immediately encounters the lid of his makeshift coffin.

He raises his knees; they, too, hit the lid of the box.

And when he moves the only arm he can move, the one that hasn't been shot, his bent elbow hits the side of the box.

It's no use. He's trapped. Helpless. There's no way out.

The chilling words of his captor ring in Ben's ears with every thump of dirt hitting the box overhead.

I will kill her . . .

There's a part of Sullivan Leary that's deeply infuriated with Gabriela Duran's brazen move.

There's also a part of her that can't help but admire it.

She tries to quell the admiring part as the infuriated part informs the cousin, Jacinda, "She can't do that."

"She just did."

"What the hell is going on?" Stockton has arrived on the scene, with Dante beside him.

"Call the local police. She's inside the house."

"Who's inside the house?"

"My cousin." Jacinda raises her voice, shouting, "Gaby! Are you okay?"

No answer.

"Gaby!"

They wait uneasily. Then . . .

"Come in here, Jaz!" Gaby shouts. "You too, Detective!"

It takes Alex a long time to shovel the heap of dirt back into the hole. At last the wooden crate is buried with Carmen inside it. No one will ever know unless she chooses to tell.

She never will. She's about to make sure of that.

Spent, she walks a short distance away and sits on the ground in a small clearing surrounded by shrubs.

It's peaceful here. That's why Carmen's father liked it. He wanted to spend the rest of his days here. When he died, his wife and son scattered his ashes in this very spot.

"This is where I want to be, too," Carmen told her the first time he brought her up here when they were young and in love and the future was full of promise. "For the rest of our lives. And when I die, I want to be buried here."

"You got your wish," she whispers into the emptiness.

And so it's over.

Really, it's been over for a while now, ever since that day in the obstetrician's office last summer when she received the devastating news that she wasn't pregnant—nor could she ever be pregnant again. Something had snapped inside her that day. She had been so sure the doctor was wrong, so desperate to hold her son in her arms again, so convinced that it could happen . . .

Is it possible she only saw what she wanted to see?

Reaching into her pocket, she pulls out a frayed scrap of pink fabric and a yellowed piece of paper scrawled with words she memorized years ago, when she first learned to read.

Her name is Alex. Please keep her. I'm afraid I might hurt her.

"Is there a family history?" the doctor had asked Alex's caseworker.

Alex never heard the reply. She didn't have to.

She reaches into her pocket again for the gun, puts it to her temple.

Carmen's voice floats back to her: *Some things just don't feel right until the sun goes down.*

You were right, she thinks. *About everything.*

The last thing she sees before she pulls the trigger is the starless night sky.

In the kitchen of the deserted house, Gaby stands in a sea of rotten cat food and spoiled milk, her flashlight beam trained on a refrigerator covered in crayoned drawings.

Not just a few, or even a dozen, but dozens—hundreds of drawings, stacks of them, precariously clinging to the refrigerator beneath magnets.

At a glance, they're typical kid art: stick figures, a rudimentary house and trees.

Beyond a glance, though, it gets disturbing.

For one thing, every picture is identical. Four figures—large and small pairs, male and female in each—are posed before a house depicted in the usual triangle-atop-a-rectangle way. But instead of one chimney, there are two—depicted in red crayon as rectangles encompassing tic-tack-toe grid lines. The obligatory windows on either side of the rectangle front door are ovals, filled in with the red crayon. And there aren't just one or two trees beside the house; there are countless trees, meant to depict a forest.

The quirks would seem to indicate a creative kid-artist—but it goes beyond that.

In every picture, the house is encompassed by orange and yellow plumes clearly meant to depict fire. And in every picture, the large male figure and small male and female figures are crossed out, each covered by a bold black X.

There are footsteps in the next room, voices, Jaz exclaiming over the stench.

Then they're in the kitchen: Jaz and Detective Leary, accompanied by two men. Covering their mouths and noses, they pause to take in the scene.

Then, gaping at the drawings on the refrigerator, the

smaller of the two men utters a few incredulous words: *"Es la casa de mi padre."*

Gaby doesn't know whether the detectives can translate, but she sure as hell understood what he just said.

That's my father's house.

Overwhelmed by the irrational urge to bend his arms and his legs and sit up, Ben forces himself to lie still and flat. The pain in his shoulder is agonizing. He can feel that the wound is soaked in blood, can smell it filling the close, stale air.

He tries to breathe slowly, deeply. The more he panics, the more oxygen he'll waste.

Does it matter?

When death is inevitable, why prolong it?

He isn't afraid.

His son is waiting. His son, and his parents, and yes even Abuela.

Cuidala . . .

I meant it when I made that promise, he tells the old woman. *I took care of her the best I could, for as long as she'd let me. I'm still trying. I hope you know I tried to the end. I hope Gaby knows that.*

But of course, she won't. She'll never know what became of him. No one is going to find his body buried up here in the middle of nowhere.

He only prays that this lunatic—who so chillingly described the murder of her own daughter—will stop here, with him.

If he only could be sure that she'll leave Gaby alone—that Gaby will go on to live a full life, the life she deserves, even if it's without him . . .

She will. He has to believe that. It's the only thing that will make this okay: believing that Gaby will be happy again. That she'll find someone else, marry again, have another child . . .

She was such a devoted mother. When Josh died, a part of her died as well.

How do you heal from something like that?

You don't.

Or do you?

He'd glimpsed her again the last few days—the old Gaby. He'd found hope that she might somehow come back to him, battered and bruised, but having survived her worst nightmare . . .

He remembers how she used to cry in the night, inconsolable at the thought of Josh being alone and afraid without them . . .

It's okay, he tells her now, as his eyelids close. *I've got this. I'll be with him.*

"Who lives here?" Dante Rodriguez asks, and something in his voice tells Sully that he already knows the answer. "Who drew those pictures of my father's house?"

"Mr. Rodriguez—"

"Please, tell me . . ."

Sully turns from the drawings on the refrigerator to Dante Rodriguez. The man's blue eyes beseech her to voice the truth he already knows.

"The house is owned by a woman named Alex Jones."

"My mother. She died—"

"She didn't. She's alive. She lives here. I'm . . . I'm sorry."

Dante seems to crumple. "I lived here, too. I knew when I walked in—it seemed so familiar. But I forgot. My father—he wanted me to forget this. Forget her. She was too sick to take care of me, he said. I thought it was cancer, something . . . Why would he tell me she died?"

"Maybe it was easier that way."

"Not for me."

"For him, but maybe for you, too."

He seems to consider that before nodding. "We had a

good life, the two of us. But I always remembered her. She'd crawl around on the floor with me, playing, and we'd draw pictures, and I wondered . . . I wondered . . . if she died alone. Once, I asked my father. He said he was here with her when it happened. I thought that was a lie, but I didn't question him. It was easier . . ."

He sighs, shakes his head, looks around the kitchen, then again at the drawings.

Sully follows his gaze. "Where is that house? The one she drew?"

"About an hour from here. I inherited the property when my father died, but the house burned down years ago. He used to talk about it—"

"But do you know where it is, exactly?"

Dante nods. "I told you, I own it. I'm going to build a house there again someday—"

Gabriela Duran cuts him off. "That's where she is. That's where she took Ben."

The ride up to the country in the backseat of Detective Leary's car is endless.

Sitting beside Dante Rodriguez, Gabriela stares silently out at the black night sky, thinking about Ben, remembering a long-ago sunrise when the world was full of promise.

In the front seat, Detective Barnes's cell phone rings abruptly.

He'd called the local police up in the country. By now they must be on the property. Gaby keeps thinking they're going to call and say they've found Ben alive.

"Yeah?" Barnes says into his phone. "Yeah? Okay, good. Good. No? Keep looking. We're almost there."

He hangs up the phone.

Gaby sees Leary shoot him a questioning look.

"They found the car. Black BMW."

"Where?"

"There," is all he says. "Where we thought."

Gaby's heart pounds.

The headlights illuminate a green sign.

"That's the exit," Dante says, and Leary flicks on the turn signal.

Gaby thinks about Ben as they follow the curved ramp off the exit and begin a slow climb up into the foothills of the Catskill Mountains. He'd want her to be strong.

Jaz, too—

"Be strong," she had said when they parted ways back on Cherry Street, forced to stay behind as they drove off into the night.

"I'm strong," Gaby assured her.

"I know you are. You really are."

They make a turn, another turn, following winding roads beneath an inky sky. She can't remember a night this dark.

Yes, she can.

November twelfth, three years ago. There was no visible moon that night; there were no stars. She remembers. She looked.

But the sun will rise again. It did even then. It always does.

In the front seat, Barnes's phone rings.

"Yeah. What? Where?" Long pause. "And what about— No. No. Got it. Okay. Almost there."

He hangs up.

"News?" Leary asks.

He nods.

"They found something?"

Barnes glances over his shoulder into the backseat. "They found . . . her. That's all."

"Is she . . . ?"

Barnes nods again, says nothing.

Leary asks no further questions.

Gaby doesn't know how much Dante Rodriguez has

heard, or whether the language barrier allows him to understand the nuances of the conversation in the front seat.

But she understands. They've found Alex Jones, and it sounds like she's . . .

Dead.

"And what about—" Barnes had started to ask, and then, "No."

He'd been asking about Ben.

Did the no mean they'd found him, too?

Is he also dead?

Gaby's mind races through the possibilities as they speed on through the night.

"Slow down," Dante Rodriguez eventually says, and then, "Almost . . . right there."

The car makes a final turn, crawling past a sign marked NO TRESPASSING.

There are lights up ahead. Flashing red and blue lights, and big yellow spotlights illuminating cops on foot, dogs on leashes. Misty vapor floats in the beam of the headlights as the car stops before a clearing filled with activity.

"Wait right here," Leary commands as she and Barnes climb out of the front seat.

Gaby ignores her.

After a moment, so does Dante. The two of them climb out and trail the detectives toward the clearing.

There's a figure lying on the ground. Blood. There's so much blood, around the head, and it's impossible to tell from here . . .

Gaby stops walking, frozen in place, terrified that it's Ben.

Then she hears a strangled sob from the throat of the man beside her and she realizes: it's not Ben.

It's the woman.

Dante's mother.

It doesn't seem to make sense, though, that the person

responsible is somehow also a mother. A mother Dante himself had affectionately described as a good mother . . .

What happened along the way to turn her into a monster? What does it take to change a person so drastically?

Dogs are barking in the distance, among the trees.

"I found a shovel!" a voice calls, and then . . .

"Holy crap! There! There! Get more lights! We need another shovel! Get shovels! Get more guys over here! Hurry!"

Gaby arrives in the clearing in time to see them start frantically digging at a patch of bare dirt, and she knows . . .

Ben.

She sinks to the ground and looks up at the sky, searching for stars. Stars would be a good sign. Even one star. Just a tiny glimmer of light . . .

There are none.

But for a long time, she looks.

For a long time, they dig.

Then she hears shouts. Several men descend upon the hole and pull something out of it: a flat piece of wood.

"He's here!" someone shouts.

Somehow, Gaby is on her feet again. She watches as a lifeless-looking body is pulled from the hole and laid upon the ground.

Ben.

No.

Noooooooooo.

She pushes her way forward. "Let me through! I'm his wife! I'm his wife!"

"Stay back!"

Gaby sinks to her knees beside Ben. He's covered in dirt, and . . .

Blood.

His eyes are closed.

"Ben," she says, "please, Ben . . . please be all right . . . I need you . . ."

She reaches for his hand, steeling herself for what she found once before when she reached for someone she loved: cold flesh, hardened in death.

But not this time.

Not this time.

"It's me," she whispers, close to his ear. "I'm here."

His warm hand squeezes hers, and when she looks away, up at the night sky to blink away her tears, she sees it: a single star twinkling in the heavens.

Epilogue

The sun is shining.

"That's the most important thing," Gabriela reminds Ben as he adjusts his black bow tie, sweat glistening in his dark hair and on his forehead.

"If the sun wasn't out," he tells her, "it wouldn't be this hot."

"It can be really hot without the sun, Ben."

"No kidding," he says grimly, and she knows he's thinking of that June day three years ago, right here at Orchard Beach: the gray, oppressive day when she came here looking for him, carrying his phone and his box of memories from the past.

That she lost the box somewhere along the way doesn't matter now. It didn't matter even when she told him about it, as he was propped in a hospital bed with a bandaged shoulder.

The bullet had ripped through his rotator cuff and shattered the bones. It was too early then to tell whether he would be able to swim again, but he'd taken that news in stride—as he did her confession about the lost box.

"It was just stuff, Gaby."

"It was a lifetime worth of memories. That's what you told me."

"Turns out I was wrong. The memories are still here." He'd tapped his head. "Impossible to lose."

"You're just trying to make me feel better. I'm so sorry, Ben."

"Gaby—I forgive you." With his good arm, he pulled her close, held her fast against his beating heart. "Things happen. People make mistakes. But if there's anyone I'd trust to safeguard my most precious memories, or even my most precious . . . *stuff*—it's you."

In that moment of forgiveness, she'd grasped that it was time for her, too, to let go—and to hang on tight.

At last, she'd found her closure. At last, the healing could begin.

It was a long time before they discussed the past again, or even what they wanted out of the future. They gave themselves permission to simply live in the present, spending that summer together without analyzing or second-guessing anything.

When autumn came, they found that they were ready to embrace a new season. Ben was swimming again. And Gaby was pregnant.

Now, she turns to look at the sleeping child in a stroller parked in the corner, a miniature bow tie tucked beneath his drool-soaked chin.

Ben follows her gaze. "Poor kid. It's so hot. And it's nap time."

"I know. How are we going to wake him up, let alone get him to walk down the aisle?"

"It's not really an aisle—just sand. We can carry him down."

"I know, but . . ."

"Everyone will understand. It's just friends and family, and he's just a baby."

"Not really. He's two."

Two. Growing up fast, with parents who are becoming

quite proficient at balancing the hanging on with the letting go . . .

Shakey sticks his do-ragged head through the doorway of the small room ordinarily used to store beach equipment. Today it's a dressing room for the wedding party, and they're the last to leave.

"Are you guys ready?" he asks. "Everyone's already out there on the beach waiting for you."

"We're ready."

"Then get a move on. The bride is getting restless."

"You think she's still worried the groom is going to run away?" Ben asks Gaby as Shakey disappears.

"If I know Jaz, she won't relax until she has a ring on her finger."

"Well if I know Junie, that'll be in about five minutes. He swore that if he was going to do this, he didn't want anything dragged out."

"Dragged out? She's been looking forward to this day her whole life."

"Then let's not keep her waiting another minute," Ben says, consulting the watch Gaby gave him as a gift on their own wedding day—the second one, here at the beach. That was in the autumn, under a hurricane warning. He reminds her of that now.

"But the storm didn't hit until the next day. It was perfect. And I still love summer weddings."

"You love all weddings."

"Believing in happily ever after," she reminds him, "is not a bad thing."

"Nobody's arguing with that. What do you say, ring bearer? Are you ready?" He leans toward the stroller, then grins up at Gaby. "He's ready. Are you?"

"Always," she tells him.

Ben picks up their drowsy son and together they head out into the bright summer sunshine.

Don't miss the next thrilling novel from

New York Times **best-selling author**

WENDY CORSI STAUB

BLOOD RED

Mundy's Landing: Book One

Coming Fall 2015!

Nestled in New York's Hudson Valley, Mundy's Landing is famous for its picturesque setting, historic architecture . . . and violent past. Founded by colonists whose unspeakable crime casts a shadow even centuries later, the town was revisited by murder one hundred years ago. That notorious case remains unsolved, but every summer, crime buffs from around the world gather in an attempt to solve it. Now, a new predator has set Mundy's Landing in the crosshairs, and bloodshed isn't just the village's past—it's in the immediate future as well.

Chapter 1

Six minutes.

That's exactly how long it takes to drive between the elementary school where Rowan Mundy teaches and the riverside home where she lives with her family.

The route meanders along the brick-paved streets of the village: past the Dutch Colonial where she grew up, the little white clapboard church where she was baptized and married, and Holy Angels cemetery where her parents and father-in-law are buried alongside generations of local citizens and the trio of young girls whose deaths put Mundy's Landing on the map a century ago.

Most days, she drives on past those landmarks without taking note, her mind on whatever happened during the past few hours or on whatever needs to get done in the next few.

Once in awhile, though, she allows herself to get caught up in nostalgia for long gone loved ones and places that will never be the same.

Today is one of those days. Christmas music plays on the car stereo courtesy of her iPod, and the business district is decked out in wreaths and garlands that seem to have materialized overnight. She wistfully remembers cozy holidays when her parents were alive and her brothers and sister weren't scattered from east coast to west.

Now Rowan's two oldest children are gone as well. Braden is a junior at Dartmouth; Katie a freshman at Cornell. Both were here for the long Thanksgiving weekend that just passed, but it was all too fleeting. They headed back yesterday in opposite directions.

"I hate this letting go thing," she told Jake, wiping tears as they stood on the front porch watching taillights disappear.

"They'll be home on break for a whole month before you know it, and you'll be counting down the days until they go back to school in January."

"No I won't."

"Oh, right. I'm the one who does that." Jake flashed his good-natured grin and went back to eating a leftover turkey drumstick and watching the Giants win in overtime.

Passing the Mundy's Landing Historical Society, which occupies a grand turreted mansion facing the village square, Rowan is reminded of an unpleasant phone call she received this morning from the mother of one of her fourth-grade students.

Bari Hicks moved to town from New York City over the summer, and has proven to be one of those people who always manages to find something to complain about. This week, she was calling to express her displeasure with the upcoming class field trip to see the Colonial Christmas exhibit.

The annual excursion has been a well-loved school tradition since Rowan herself was in fourth grade, back when this turreted mansion was still a private residence and the historical society was housed in the basement of the local library.

"I just don't think a trip like this sounds appropriate for children this age," Bari insisted. *Appropriate* seems to be her favorite word. Rather, *inappropriate*.

Rowan reminded her that the fourth grade social studies

curriculum encompasses New York State history and some of the most colorful chapters unfolded right here in Mundy's Landing. She treaded carefully in her response though, assuming the woman's gripe must have something to do with religious beliefs and Christmas. She was wrong.

"My Amanda still isn't used to her new bedroom and she has enough problems falling asleep at night without being dragged through a gory chamber of horrors that's going to give her nightmares for years."

Although Rowan immediately grasped what she was referring to, she couldn't resist feigning ignorance.

"Oh, you must have this mixed up with the high school's haunted hallway fund-raiser, Mrs. Hicks. That was back in October on Halloween, and I wouldn't dream of exposing my class to— "

"No, I'm talking about the historical society. The *murders*."

"Which murders?" That time, Rowan wasn't playing dumb. Mundy's Landing is famous for not one, but two notorious murder cases.

The first unfolded in the mid-seventeenth century, when James and Elizabeth Mundy were executed on the gallows for butchering and cannibalizing their fellow colonists. Jake is directly descended from the couple's only son Jeremiah Mundy, who, along with his offspring and subsequent generations, lived such exemplary lives that the town was later named in their honor.

Mundy's Landing itself wasn't quite so fortunate in terms of redemption and reputation. Precisely two and a half centuries after the hangings, a serial killer committed the so-called Sleeping Beauty murders. That bloody summer in Mundy's Landing marked one of the most notorious unsolved crime sprees in American history. The young female victims, whose identities were never known, were lain to rest beneath white granite markers simply etched with the year 1916 and the word *Angel*.

Bari Hicks was referring to the Sleeping Beauty murders. "I heard the museum has bloody clothing on display, and the murder weapon, and a disembodied skull. Do you really think it's necessary to—"

"There's no skull," Rowan quickly assured her, though she'd heard that rumor all her life, "and it isn't the actual murder weapon, it's just an antique razor blade someone's grandfather donated as an example, and the bloody clothing is only exhibited in the summer during . . ."

She couldn't quite bring herself to call the event Mundy-palooza, the flippant popular term for the annual historical society-sponsored gathering that draws crime buffs, reporters, tourists, and plain old fruitcakes from all over the globe.

" . . . the convention," she chose to say instead, and hastily added, "We're only visiting the Colonial Christmas exhibit on our field trip. I promise Amanda will love it. All the kids do."

Naturally, Bari Hicks still had reservations. Rowan wound up inviting her to come along as a chaperone so that she can see for herself. She regrets that already, but at the time, it seemed like the easiest way to avoid additional Monday morning stress.

Now, winding up Riverview Drive toward home, she blinks against the glare of sinking autumn sun at every west-bound hairpin curve. Lowering the visor doesn't help at all.

She worries about Mick.

In about ten minutes, her youngest son will be getting off the late bus after varsity basketball practice. Even if he's not plugged into his iPod—despite her warnings about the dangers of walking or jogging along the road wearing headphones—he'll have his head in the clouds as usual.

At this time of year, the angle of the late day sun is blinding. What if a car comes careening up the hill and doesn't see him until it's too late?

Long gone are Rowan's days of waiting in the minivan at the bus stop on Highland Road, a busy north-south thoroughfare. Even on stormy afternoons—there are plenty of those in Mundy's Landing—Mick insists on walking home up Riverview Drive, just as his older siblings did when they were in high school.

I'll walk Doofus, she decides as she brakes at the curbside mailbox in front of their rambling Victorian house perched on the bluff above the Hudson.

Doofus the aging basset hound was originally named Rufus, but earned his current name when it became evident that he wasn't exactly the smartest canine in the world.

Rowan ordinarily lets him out into the yard when she gets home after a long day, but Doofus—although increasingly lazy—might welcome some exercise, and she can use it herself.

She bought a tasteless but slimming couscous salad for lunch today, courtesy of Wholesome & Hearty, the school district's new lunch program. But then someone left a plate of cookies in the teachers' break room after lunch and one of her students brought in birthday cupcakes. Plus there's still half an apple pie in the fridge at home, leftover from Thanksgiving dinner.

There was a time when Rowan could gobble anything she felt like eating and never gain an ounce. Those days, too, are long gone. According to her doctor, she needs to exercise nearly an hour a day at her age just to keep her weight the same. And the hair colorist who's been hiding her gray for a few years now recently told her that her natural red shade was making her "mature" skin look sallow, and that the long hair she'd had all her life was too "weighty."

"I think you should try a short, youthful cut and go a few shades lighter, maybe a biscuit blond with honey highlights and caramel lowlights. What do you think?"

"I think biscuits and honey and caramel sound like something I'd want to eat right now if I didn't have to run ten miles to work off the extra calories," Rowan said with a sigh of resignation.

She finally agreed to the new hairstyle right before Thanksgiving. It got mixed reviews at home. Jake and Katie liked it; Braden, who resents change of any sort, did not; Mick was indifferent. Back at work today, her colleagues complimented her, her students questioned her, and the janitor told her she looks hot—which might be inappropriate, but as the forty-seven-year-old mother of three nearly grown kids, she'll take it.

She gets out of the car, goes around to grab the mail out of the box, and finds that it's full of catalogues. No surprise on this first Monday of the official holiday shopping season. Given the stack of bills that are also in the box, plus the two college tuition payments coming due for next semester, the catalogues will go straight into the recycling bin.

Money has been tight lately, and Jake is worried about his job as a regional sales manager amid rumors that his company might be bought out.

Lead us not into temptation, she thinks, tossing the heap of mail—which also includes a red envelope addressed to the family in her older sister Noreen's perfect handwriting, and a small package addressed to her—onto the passenger's seat.

As she pulls into the driveway, she wonders how the heck Noreen, a busy Long Island attorney, manages to get Christmas cards out at all, let alone ahead of the masses. Somehow, she even hand-addresses the envelopes, rather than use those typed labels you can so easily print out year after year.

Rowan knows without opening the card that it'll have a photo of the svelte and lovely Noreen, her handsome trauma surgeon husband, and their four gorgeous kids, all color-coordinated in khaki and red or navy and white. Inside, there will be a handwritten note and the signature of each member of the family scrawled in red or green Sharpie.

Noreen has always managed to do so much and make it look so easy . . .

Which drives someone like me absolutely crazy. Which is

why, when I was a kid, I didn't even bother to try to follow in her footsteps.

Rowan is so caught up in the familiar combination of envy and longing for her sister that she doesn't think twice about the package that came in the mail. She tosses it aside and takes her medication—the first thing she does every morning, and again every afternoon when she walks in the door.

It wasn't until Mick was diagnosed with ADHD back in elementary school that Rowan learned that it was hereditary.

"With this disability, the apple doesn't fall far from the tree," the doctor told her, leading her to recognize similar symptoms in herself.

It was as if a puzzle piece she hadn't even realized was missing had suddenly dropped into place to complete a long-frustrating jigsaw.

If only someone—her parents, her teachers, her doctors—had figured it out when she was Mick's age. Now she understands why she spent so much of her childhood in trouble—academically, behaviorally—and why she so often felt restlessly uncomfortable in her own skin, even as an adult.

Things aren't perfect now—far from it—but at least she's more in control of her life, with better focus and the ability to quell her impulsive tendencies. Most of the time, anyway.

After swallowing the pill, she walks the dog down to the bus stop and returned with a grumbling Mick.

"Where's all the turkey?" he asks, poking his stubbly auburn head— exactly the same shade as her own—into the fridge.

"I tossed it last night."

"What? Why?"

"Because it was old, Mick. You can't eat leftovers after a few days."

"You didn't toss the pie." He pulls out the dish.

"Pie isn't poultry. That's still good."

She watches her son put the whole thing into the microwave and punches the quick start button, then open the freezer.

So much for Rowan's dessert plans. Oh, well. She can't afford to indulge, and Mick can. Half a pie smothered in Vanilla Bean Häagen-Dazs is nothing more than a light afternoon snack for a famished, lanky sixteen-year-old athlete who begins every morning with a three-mile run.

The stack of mail still sits on the granite counter along with her tote bag and the usual household clutter plus additional clutter accumulated over Thanksgiving: clean platters that need to go back to the dining room, a bread basket filled with cloth napkins that still have to be washed, bottles of open and unopened Beaujolais . . .

She needs to get busy cleaning it up. She needs to do a lot of things. As always, now that the medication has begun to take hold again, it all seems more manageable.

"What time do you have to be at work?" she asks Mick. Three nights a week, he's a busboy at Marrana's Trattoria in town.

"Five-thirty."

"I need you to do me a favor while you're there. Can you please get me a gift certificate for twenty-five dollars?" She pulls the cash from her wallet and hands it to him.

"Who's it for?"

"Marlena, the library aide. I pulled her name for the Secret Santa."

He looks at her as if she's speaking a foreign language. "I don't even know what that means."

"You know . . . or maybe you don't know. Secret Santa is something we do every year at work—we pick names and then we have to anonymously surprise the person with a little treat every day next week—"

"I don't really think a gift certificate counts as a treat, Mom. How about cookies or something?"

"No, the gift certificate is for the big gift on Friday."

"Big? You'd better do fifty bucks, then. Twenty-five seems cheap."

"The limit is twenty-five, Big Spender." She grins, shaking her head. "So, how much homework do you have?"

"Not a lot."

Same question every night; same answer. The truth is, he usually has a lot of homework, and it doesn't always get done.

"Look on the bright side," Jake says, whenever she frets that even with an early diagnosis, academic accommodations, and medication, Mick has shortchanged himself. "We won't be paying Ivy League tuition when it's his turn."

"No, we'll just be supporting him for the rest of his life."

"It might be the other way around. He's an enterprising kid. Maybe he'll invent a billion-dollar video game."

Maybe. Or maybe he'll turn himself around academically, find his way into a decent college, make something of himself . . .

You did, she reminds herself. *And if Mom and Dad were still alive, they'd still be reminding you they weren't so sure that was ever going to happen.*

"Did you get your grade back yet on the English test?"

"Which test?"

As if he doesn't know. She'd spent two hours helping him study for it last Monday night. "The one on literary devices."

"Oh. That test. Nope."

"Are you sure?"

"Yep. So stop looking at me like a detective who thinks the witness is lying." He flashes her a grin. "See? I know what a metaphor is. I bet I got an A plus on that test."

"I hate to break it to you, kiddo, but that's not a metaphor. It's a simile."

"That's what I meant." Mick pushes aside some clutter and settles on a stool with the pile of mail, looking for something to leaf through while he eats, which will take all of two minutes.

"What's this?" He holds up the brown parcel addressed to Rowan.

"Probably something I ordered for you for Christmas. Don't open it."

"Is it the keys to my new car? Because don't forget, I'm taking my road test in less than a month."

"It is not—" she plucks the package from his hand—"the keys to your new car because there will *be* no new car."

"Then what am I going to drive?"

"You can share the minivan with me. And you already have the keys to that, so you're all set. Here—" she gives him the red envelope—"you can open Aunt Noreen's Christmas card."

"Bet you anything they made Goliath wear those stupid reindeer antlers again." Goliath is a German Shepherd whose dignity is compromised, as far as Rowan's kids are concerned, by a costume every Christmas and Halloween.

"Don't worry, Doofus," Mick says, patting the dog, who lies on the hardwood floor at the base of his stool, hoping to catch a stray crumb with little effort. "We'd never do anything like that to you if *we* had a Christmas card picture."

"He wouldn't know he had a costume on if we zipped him into a horse suit and hitched him to a buggy," Rowan points out. "Plus, we do have a Christmas card picture. I mean, we *have* had one."

"When?"

"Back in the old days."

"When?" Classic Mick, persisting to demonstrate that he, as the youngest kid in the family, has suffered some slight, real or imagined.

It rarely works on Rowan, who as the lastborn of Kate and Jonathan Carmichael's four children is all too familiar with that technique.

"Back when we lived in Westchester," she tells Mick. She distinctly remembers having to cancel a family portrait shoot repeatedly to accommodate Jake's schedule. He was working in the city then, never home.

"Before I was born doesn't count, Mom."

"We had a few after you were born."

"We did not."

"Sure we did." *Did we?*

It's a wonder they even found time to conceive Mick back then, let alone take a family photo.

"I don't think so."

"Maybe not," she concedes. "After we moved here, I probably didn't get my act together to send cards. But God knows we have plenty of family pictures. They're just not portraits." Her favorites—and there are many—are framed, cluttered on tabletops and hanging along the foyer stairs in a hodgepodge gallery.

"That's not the same thing."

"You poor, poor neglected little working mom's son."

"Stop." He squirms away from her exaggerated sympathetic hug.

"But I feel so sorry for you!"

"Yeah, right."

She shrugs. Her mother never wasted much time feeling guilty for being a working mom, and she tries not to, either.

She used to be a stay at home mom. Giving it up hasn't always been easy, but she's never questioned that it was the right decision for her family, or her marriage.

Mick was three when she resumed the teaching career she'd launched back when she and Jake were newlyweds. She could have waited to go back until the kids were older if they'd stayed in the New York City suburbs and Jake had stuck with the higher-paying advertising sales job that kept him away for weeks at a time. But that would have been tempting fate, because . . .

She doesn't like to think back to those days. Things were so different then. She and Jake were different people then: different from each other; different from the way they are now.

He quit his job and they sold the house and moved back

to their hometown. The cost of living is much lower in Mundy's Landing than had been in Westchester County, allowing Jake to take a lower-paying, less glamorous job as a sales rep in Albany. They still couldn't make ends meet on one salary, though, even after he was promoted within the first year. She had to work, too.

"Oh, geez! Poor Goliath!" Mick waves the Christmas card at her.

"Antlers?" she guesses.

"Worse. An elf hat. A whole elf costume. Look at this!"

Rowan takes in the sight of a humiliated-looking German Shepherd decked out in green felt and red pompons alongside her sister's picture-perfect family. "Poor Goliath," she agrees. "But everyone else looks great. I miss them. Maybe we should try to get together for Christmas."

"Mom—you said never again, remember?"

"That wasn't me, that was Dad."

"That was all of us, including you. It took us a whole day to get home in traffic last time we went to see Aunt Noreen for Christmas."

"That was a freak blizzard. It doesn't usually snow on Long Island over the holidays."

"Well, it always snows *here*."

Mick is right. In Mundy's Landing, Currier and Ives Christmases are the norm. On the banks of the Hudson River, cradled by the Catskill mountains just to the south and the Adirondacks to the north, the village sees more than its share of treacherous weather from October through May although, as the hardy locals like to say, "We know how to handle it." Plows and salt trucks rumble into motion, shovels and windshield scrapers are kept close at hand, and it's business as usual.

She opens three drawers before she finds a pair of scissors to slit open the packing tape on the box addressed to her.

It's not from Amazon or Zappo's or any number of places

where she does most of her online shopping. There's no return address, just her own, computer-printed on a plain white label—yes, the kind over-achievers like Noreen refuse to use for their Christmas cards.

Inside is a layer of crumpled newspaper.

Slightly yellowed newspaper, which strikes her as strange even before she sees what's beneath it.

"What is it?" Mick asks, looking up from his pie.

"I . . . I have no idea." She pulls out a flat black disk, turning it over in her hands.

"Who sent it?"

She shakes her head, clueless.

"I bet it's from your Secret Santa." Mick is beside her, rummaging through the box.

"That doesn't start until next week, and we leave the gifts for each other at school. We don't mail them."

"There's a bunch of those things in here," he notes, counting.

Yes . . . a bunch of what? Charcoal? There's a charred smell to the disks, whatever they are.

"There are twelve," Mick tells her. "Thirteen altogether, with the one you're holding. Unlucky number. Hey, this newspaper is pretty old. Cool, check it out. It's the *New York Times* from fourteen years ago. I was only two."

Fourteen years ago . . .

A memory slams into her.

It can't be. Nobody knows about that. Nobody other than—

"What's the date?" she asks Mick abruptly. "On the newspaper?"

"Whoa—it's November 30th, same as today! Think that's a coincidence?"

No. It's not a coincidence.

Nor is the fact that there are thirteen blackened disks in the box.

A voice—*his* voice—floats back over the years; fourteen years: "A baker's dozen . . ."

It happened fourteen years ago today. A Friday, not a Monday. In Westchester. It was snowing.

"Hey, I think these are cookies," Mick says. "Looks like your Secret Santa burnt your treat."

Cookies . . .

Rowan's fingers let go and the charred object drops back into the box.

Either *he* tracked her down and sent this package as some kind of reminder, or a sick, twisted joke, or . . .

Someone else did.

Someone who knows her secret.

Driving along the New York State Thruway, northbound from New York City toward Mundy's Landing, Casey has had the same tune looping on the car's speakers for almost two hours now.

The songs are important. You can't just play any random tune when you're driving. That's one of the rules. You have to play a specific song, over and over, until you get to where you're going.

Sometimes it's country: Glen Campbell's "Wichita Lineman" or Willie Nelson's "On the Road Again."

Sometimes it's rock and roll: Journey's "Lights" or The Doors' "Riders on the Storm."

Today's song has great significance, a strong reminder of why this has to happen.

Every time it begins anew, Casey's fingers thrum the military drumbeat on the steering wheel until it's time to howl the chorus again: *"Sunday, bloody Sunday . . ."*

By now, Rowan must have gotten the package that had been mailed on Friday from the city.

If her weekday unfolded the way it usually does, she was the one who reached into the mailbox this afternoon and found it.

Throughout the fall, Casey seized every opportunity to

watch her, documenting her daily routine. Sometimes, that could even be accomplished from inside the school where she teaches. Security at Mundy's Landing Elementary is a joke. There are plenty of news articles online that would seem to indicate otherwise, dating back to the most recent school shooting and meant to reassure jittery parents that their precious children were well-protected under the new security measures.

It's true that all visitors have to be buzzed past the locked front door, but there are plenty of other ways into the building. It's surrounded by woods on three sides, so you can easily hide there watching for some delivery man to leave a door propped open, or try tugging doors and windows until you find one that's unlocked.

Once, feeling especially bold, Casey even showed up at the front door wearing a uniform and got buzzed in by the secretary. She didn't even bother to request credentials or double-check the made-up story about a faulty meter in the basement.

That was in the early morning, before the students arrived. Casey wandered the halls searching the teachers' names, written in black Sharpie on cardboard cutouts shaped like bright yellow pencils and taped beside every classroom. Rowan's was evident even before Casey spotted the pencil marked *Ms. Mundy*: she was in there talking to another teacher, and her voice echoed down the halls.

Some might find her chattiness endearing.

I used to.

Now it grates.

Four days a week, Casey knows, Rowan leaves school not long after the bell, just after three-thirty. But she always stays at least an hour later on Mondays. That's when she supervises the tutoring organization that matches volunteers from a nearby community college with local elementary school students.

Perched with binoculars high in a tree across the road from the house—a vantage that never failed to inspire a unique exhilaration in and of itself—Casey loved to watch her pull up in front of the mailbox at the foot of the driveway. She'd usually rifle through the stack of letters and catalogues quickly, toss them onto the seat, and drive on up to the house. But once in awhile, something seemed to catch her eye and she'd open an envelope or package right there at the curb.

Sometimes, Casey seized the opportunity to stick around watching the house long after she'd disappeared inside, occasionally daring to scale a tree right on the property. Daring not because of the height—Casey has always been exhilarated by great heights—but because of the proximity to the house.

All any of them ever had to do was take a good, hard look, and they'd have seen me. But they never did.

Casey would sometimes stay late into the night until the last light was extinguished. Oblivious to a voyeur in their midst, the Mundy family went about their lives behind the sturdy plaster walls of the home that had been built well over a century ago—one hundred and twenty-seven years ago, to be exact.

Casey had left no stone unturned when it came to investigating Rowan's charmed life. One never knows when a seemingly irrelevant detail might come in handy.

An entire year of preparation has finally paid off.

November 30th has finally arrived.

The endgame has begun.

SPINE-TINGLING SUSPENSE FROM
NEW YORK TIMES BESTSELLING AUTHOR

WENDY CORSI STAUB

LIVE TO TELL
978-0-06-189506-7

All Lauren Walsh wants to do is protect her children from the pain of a messy divorce. But when their father goes missing, a case of mistaken identity puts all their lives in danger, and a stealthy predator lurks in the shadows, watching and waiting.

SCARED TO DEATH
978-0-06-189507-4

Perfect strangers whose once-perfect lives were cruelly shattered, Elsa Cavalon and Marin Quinn are bound together by a long-lost child, a fragile strand of new maternal hope, and mutual loneliness. Yet Elsa and Marin are never truly alone. Someone is always nearby, watching them and their children . . .

HELL TO PAY
978-0-06-189508-1

Survivors of a serial killer who invaded their childhood, Lucy Walsh and Jeremy Cavalon are happily married now. But a shadowy predator wants to complete a deadly mission that was interrupted so long ago.

SPINE-TINGLING SUSPENSE FROM
NEW YORK TIMES BESTSELLING AUTHOR

WENDY CORSI STAUB

NIGHTWATCHER
978-0-06-207028-9

Allison Taylor adores her adopted city, New York. But on a bright and clear September morning in 2001, the familiar landscape around her is savagely altered—and in the midst of widespread chaos and fear, a woman living upstairs from her is found, brutally slaughtered and mutilated. Now a different kind of terror has entered Allison's life . . . and it's coming to claim her as its next victim.

SLEEPWALKER
978-0-06-207030-2

The nightmare of 9/11 is a distant but still painful memory for Allison Taylor MacKenna—now married and living in a quiet Westchester suburb. She has moved on with her life ten years after barely escaping death at the hands of New York's Nightwatcher serial killer. But now here, north of the city, more women are being savagely murdered, their bodies bearing the Nightwatcher's unmistakable signature.

SHADOWKILLER
978-0-06-207032-6

Nestled in the warm, domestic cocoon of loving husband and family, Allison finally feels safe—unaware that a stranger's brutal murder on a Caribbean island is the first step in an intricate plan to destroy everything in her life.

Visit www.AuthorTracker.com for exclusive
information on your favorite HarperCollins authors.

Available wherever books are sold or please call 1-800-331-3761 to order.

WCS1 1112